Tales from the Stellar Realms 01

Time

BY VICTORIA WARFIELD

DORRANCE
PUBLISHING CO
EST. 1920
PITTSBURGH, PENNSYLVANIA 15238

This is a work of fiction. Names, characters, places, and incidents are either the product of the author's imagination or are used fictitiously, and any resemblance to actual persons, living or dead; events; or locales is entirely coincidental.

Dorrance Publishing Co
585 Alpha Drive
Pittsburgh, PA 15238
Visit our website at *www.dorrancebookstore.com*

ISBN: 979-8-88925-148-4
eISBN: 979-8-88925-648-9

Tales from the Stellar Realms 01

Time

Prologue

The crash of thunder filled the summer's dry night air. Dark, thick storm clouds covered the sky, blocking out any starlight that tried to creep through. Standing atop the Arch Mountain was a cloaked figure; his silver eyes glistening as he watched the storm rage. "How are we to combat them? A fallen god?" he murmured as his claws tightened on a gold-colored leather tome.

A crash of lightning struck near his feet, shaking the very foundation of the mountain. The ground shook as it began splitting apart. As though responding to his question, the tome leapt free from the creature's grip. Landing roughly upon the ground, the book fluttered as it flipped open to a specific spell. Warp. The cloaked figure looked at the spell and nodded softly. "Yes… That could work," he spoke, his voice barely above a whisper, as he picked up the book in his claws once again. His left claw began sparking with magic as he read over the spell. "Come from afar, heroes. Warriors from the Outrealms, come and take up arms. Come and save not only your worlds but save all worlds," he said as the ball of magic exploded into the sky.

There was an evil cackle from behind the tome user. He hesitated slightly but turned to face the newcomer. Standing before him was an eight-foot-tall creature shrouded in darkness. "Do you honestly believe some *warriors* from the *Outrealms* can stop what's already begun?" The newcomer cackled, their teeth clicking and their emphasis on warriors and Outrealms sticking out. Their tone upon saying those two words was one of disgust.

"Time Eater…" the tome user began as he clutched the book tighter in his claws.

Time Eater smirked, their blood-stained fangs shimmering under the veil of darkness that surrounded them. "I will purge this world and all others into a new era! One where my power is unquestioned!" they roared as their tail slammed against the ground. Their smirk grew twisted and gnarled as they eyed their foe. "I will destroy any who oppose me, starting with your precious warriors of the Outrealms." They sneered as they drew their demonic claymore and held it high.

"Is power all you desire? I know the true you. You once said *having power did not make one strong*," the tome user responded as he took a step back.

"To have power is to be strong! You should know that better than any, Arcanist! For it was your kin who granted me such limitless power." Time Eater snarled.

Another crackle of lightning filled the sky as a distortion formed in the sky. Arcanist merely nodded to himself. "'Tis done. Warriors, the best from each realm, are being summoned. Their might combined, they will stop you," he said as he watched the distortion.

Time Eater was unamused as their forked tongue flicked out of the veil of darkness. "I will consume their flesh as I've done before." They cackled as they sheathed their claymore. "A single year, Arcanist. A single year of time is what stands between me and my goal. Though even if your so-called warriors had a thousand years, they would still be nowhere near my power." They laughed as their large wings shot out from the veil of darkness surrounding them. Their powerful wings tore across the night as they flew off to their domain.

Arcanist sighed regretting to himself as he looked to the tome in his claws. "If they fail, it won't only be their individual worlds purged, it will be all of time and space," he murmured as he looked to the distortion in the sky. His silver eyes focusing as he saw four beacons light up. A frown hung on his face. "I had hoped for more. Four…" he paused as he watched the rifts, "Four is less than last time. And the nine last time failed. Heroes, we're counting on you. I'm counting on you. May your courage and skill save us all in these dark times."

Azura sat alone in her chambers. She stared longingly out the window, recounting her adventures that led her to this point. Absent-mindedly she toyed with her light blue hair, her lilac eyes shimmering in the light of the setting sun. Her thoughts drifted to the simpler times before everything. Never in her wildest dreams did Azura think she would be the one to take up the throne of Kardax. She always believed it would be her older brother, Henry, but he was gone.

She turned her gaze to the longsword and longbow in the corner of her room. A deep empty sigh escaped her as she recounted the two who had given their lives for her. Her elder brother, Henry, a paladin of the god of healing and mercy, Patrokolos. Henry was once the wielder of the longsword, Starfang, as he called it. He had been killed by a fiendish undead blue dragon, along with its master. Azura recalled how her brother had thrown himself in front of the monster's claws to shield her from the assault. His final words still ringing in her mind. *Live for me in the world you shape.*

Henry had always believed she would make the better ruler. For it was Azura who believed in others, believed in the goodness within people. He was stronger and more disciplined, but she was the one with words. Azura wiped tears from her eyes trying to regain her composure. Every time she thought of how she was to rule, she would remember her brother and how he would encourage her.

Her gaze shifted to the longbow, Astra, the name given to it by its wielder. It was a simply crafted yew bow, but the carvings along the back of it made it look more elegant. Astra had belonged to a lavender-haired woman, Camilla Windstride; she was Azura's retainer and best friend. Any retainer to those of noble birth would talk of willingly giving their life for their liege, though many never had to. Camilla however was different. Azura recalled how Camilla never spoke of such willingness, but when the time came, the bow user had done such. Azura gripped her spell book tightly as her eyes remained fixed on the longbow. It was the dark wizard, Narcian, that murdered Camilla. He had aimed a dark beam at the young sorceress, but the lavender haired ranger took the hit. She had tackled Azura out of the blast and taken such upon herself.

Azura was brought back to the present by a knock at her door. "Milady, everyone has gathered for your coronation," came the maid's voice.

She nodded, drying her tears as best she could. "Yes, of course. Thank you, Hannah," Azura replied, standing. Her coronation had finally come, and though it was meant to be a day of celebration, she felt empty. But she had to be strong, she had to appear as regal as her older brother had when he rallied the outer provinces. Walking to the door, Azura felt everything grow cold. Her vision became fuzzy, and before long she saw only darkness. A rift appeared before her, the young future queen walking through without even realizing what she was doing or where she was going.

Chuck hefted his greataxe high into the air as he let out a victorious roar. He had conquered another clan master, taking the women and children as his own. Murdering clan leaders, all the men from the clan and taking his prize, this was what the mighty half dwarf, half orc lived for. His clan consisted of nothing but women, children and himself. All the women and children from other clans that he had ruthlessly murdered.

He would not have it any other way. He was enthralled with the power and dominance. "Chuck, claim another prize for clan Bloodscourge!" Chuck roared as he inspected the new members being added to his clan. If any looked weak or sickly, he would dispose of them.

As he went down the line-up, he noticed a single child that caught his eye. "You!" Chuck began as he pointed at the young boy. "How fight you with axe?" he questioned as he approached.

The young orc stepped forward, his hands shaking as he gripped his hand axe. He took a swing at the half-orc that towered over him. Chuck scoffed as the axe splintered against his sturdy frame. The sounds of gasping and gurgling filled the air as Chuck hefted the boy into the air. "Chuck, see you as waste. You moxie, but to strike Chuck?" Chuck growled as he choked the young orc. The women gasped as they watched the large half-orc kill the boy. "Let be example!" he roared.

Night soon fell upon the bloodied fields and the clan pitched their camp for the night. Chuck stalked through the camp, as was usual for him after acquiring new additions to his clan. As he reached his tent, he heard a distant roar of combat. Hefting his axe in one hand, Chuck charged towards the sounds. Not even looking, the half-orc entered an unusual ripple in the scenery.

Warren sat upon his lofty throne. Before him, the people had laid out a fine feast, for he reminded them every day that it was he who slayed the monstrous blue dragon. The elf smirked as he stood and walked over to one of his men. "Tell me, guard." He paused.

"Yes, sir!" the guard responded as he stood straighter.

"What is your purpose in Frothcrest?" Warren asked as he watched the nervous man.

"M-m-m-my purpo-s-s-se? Well… uh… My purpose is to serve you, King Couseland," he replied, trying to hide his fear.

"Very good. So, if I were to ask you to demonstrate your loyalty to me?" Warren began his question, watching the guard.

"Anything you ask, milord!" the guard sharply replied with no hesitation.

Warren smirked; he loved it, when his men were so quick to respond. "Very good. I grow bored with the court jesters and their antics for amusement. I've decided on a new show for my amusement. Go to the arena and await further instructions," he ordered.

"Yes, sir!" the guard stated, then bowed to the elf. He took his leave, leaving the elf to the vast feast laid out.

Warren felt himself become very excited with the show soon to begin. He sat upon his throne once more, overlooking the arena. He snapped his fingers drawing the attention of the gatekeepers. "Let the games begin." He chuckled as the three men moved forward. As the first two gates opened, the guard from earlier stepped forward from one side. And from the other side was a young man, black hair, green eyes. From the third gate, an executioner emerged dragging a young woman; she appeared to be in her early teens, black hair and green eyes much like the young man.

"Father!" both the children responded, seeing the guard.

"Carver? Leandra?" the guard exclaimed in confusion.

The elf felt it, the thrilling rush of absolute power. Warren smirked as he watched the confused family. "Thomas Hemmington, Carver Hemmington, you're both excellent fighters. So, I'll cut to the chase." He snapped his fingers, pausing as he did so. The executioner brandished his axe, letting it hover over the girl's neck. "You two will fight to the death for my amusement. If either of you refuses, Leandra here is the one who will suffer."

Both men hesitated for a moment before drawing their weapons. Leandra had tears in her eyes as she yelled for them to stop. The men rushed one another. Sounds of metal clanging as Thomas's greatsword clashed against Carver's longsword. Warren leaned forward in his seat watching the fight ongoing. He devoured the feast as he watched the men fight in the arena. Blood stained the ground indicating one or both of them wounded. From the distance he was, Warren could not tell nor did he care which of them was wounded. He giggled excitedly as he watched the son best the father in the fight. "Kill him, Carver," he ordered.

"No," Carver responded as he dug his longsword into the ground.

"Then that's it. Your sister dies instead." Warren laughed. Thomas got to his feet, his greatsword in hand. He looked from the elf to his children. The father swung his blade around, decapitating his son; the squelching of blood filling the room. There was no remorse in the father's eyes as his son's lifeless body fell to the ground and head rolled to a stop. "My, my, Thomas, that truly was impressive. Such loyalty. Good man. Executioner, release the girl," he added as he stood from his throne and turned away. He could hear the agonizing screams of the man as the axe came down severing the girl's head from the body. How he enjoyed the screams, the anguish of others. Warren smiled as he walked out of the room.

He found himself in the royal gardens and frowned. "This world bores me. I need new subjects to amuse myself," he said as he looked at the sky. As though responding to his very commands, a rift appeared before him. A smirk formed upon Warren's face as he eyed the rift. He held out his hands to either side of his form. Armor soon covered his figure and a morning star and tower shield flew to his hands. "Let the carnage begin." He chuckled as he walked through the rift.

Camilla took a deep breath before plunging into the drainage system. She had heard the sounds of the armored men pursuing her and knew this was her only option. Her only regret was not having a way to cover her ears for this escape. She felt the rushing water in them and mentally groaned knowing how putrid the drainage of the town was. As the ranger was dumped outside the city's limits, she tumbled to her feet. "Not the most pleasant side of things," she muttered as she stepped out of the mess of sewage. The squelching and squishing sounds filled the dull night's air as Camilla got clear of the drainage. She shook off, trying to clear the guck from her hair and figure.

The ranger walked a small distance before coming upon a steady stream. She sighed as she cupped her hands in the stream using the water to clean herself off. It took some time, but she soon had herself cleaned up enough that she felt comfortable. She shook off, sending the water everywhere as she straightened out. Camilla sighed to herself again before walking into the tree line, looking for a place to set up camp. She tied a line five feet from her camp all the way around it. Hanging from the line were a series of bells and other small objects that could make sound. Once the perimeter was set up, Camilla sat by the small campfire skinning a rabbit she had trapped. While there was not much meat, it was still in her eyes enough. She roasted the rabbit before tossing the meat into the small stewing pot hanging above the flame. "Why?" she muttered to herself as she watched the flame. Her yellow eyes gleaming in the darkness. "Why did I trust them?" she murmured as she recalled the events with the supposed Guardians of Kardax. Camilla closed her eyes, shaking her head. Her thoughts drifted to the events leading to this point.

The arrows rained down. Everything went so fast. Roy and Kanna fighting the bandits. While she provided cover fire to allow Lun and Thrall to advance up and help in the fight. Gemma had gone invisible at the start of the fight. Before long, they were dead, all twelve bandits. Then came the night spent in Roy's cave; the lizardman pulled the ranger aside to talk to her. "You can't just rain arrows down on random people!" Roy growled.

"They were breaking into your home," Camilla responded.

"They're still people!" Roy snarled as he slammed his tail against the ground.

Camilla shook her head slowly opening her eyes as she recalled the event. She groaned as she slumped back against some of the rocks in her campsite. She took a deep breath before exhaling slowly. "Stupid. Stupid. Stupid. You let people in, and they eventually exile you. Just like before, how stupid are you!" she yelled at herself. Camilla shook the thoughts from her mind as she served herself a bowl of stew. After the meal, she laid back on her bedroll and fell asleep.

The next night Camilla walked through the town, the hood of her cloak draped over her head, covering her from view. She remembered the intel she got from the guild; the town duke was the target. She watched him and moved silently. Camilla had seen him dozens of times, and each time was committing an act against various townsfolk. Whether it was the man trafficking children or raping young women. The thoughts of his acts sickened Camilla. She climbed the side of a nearby shop and perched upon the roof, watching the target. She let out a low steady breath as she nocked an arrow on her bow. Even now, he was up to no good. He dragged five children, all chained at the hands and chained together, forced to walk. Positioned not too far was the next man in the trafficking line. He had a wagon and looked ready to run.

Camilla watched for a moment, lining up her shot. She had to make multiple shots in rapid succession. One for each set on manacles, five. One for the target. Six. And one for the other man, but not a killing shot. Seven. She took a deep breath, nocking two additional arrows on her bow, three arrows on the string. Camilla pulled back the string, her body steadying itself as she released and quickly nocked two more arrows and fired. The five arrows hit their marks breaking the manacles. Before the duke or the other man could react, the sixth arrow flew forward, splintering the duke's skull. Arrow seven left the string soon after and pierced the other man's calf muscle. The children fled each one running a different direction. Camilla heard the man cursing under his breath as he reached for the arrow in his leg. She leapt down from the rooftop, drawing her short sword as she did so.

"I wouldn't touch that if I were you," Camilla stated as she landed nimbly on her feet. She smirked slightly as the slavery drew his hand axe and glared at her. "I missed any vital areas intentionally. I want intel," she said calmly.

"Bitch cost me my slaves. I was going to make big money for each of those brats. You know how much they worth?" He paused as he tried to look intimidating but failed. He winced as he lost the ability to put pressure on his right leg. The man grunted in man as he slumped against a wall and collapsed to the ground.

"Where was Duke Kilan getting the children?" Camilla asked as she watched the slavery closely.

"Orphanages. There's dozens of children trickling in every day, none getting adopted. No one would notice if they just started disappearing." He growled as he tugged at the arrow.

"Why?" Camilla continued as she listened intently.

"Huh? Why? We sold children? It paid well. Each of those brats was worth five hundred gold, six hundred if they were healthy." The man grunted as he fumbled with the arrow. He looked up when he noticed the shadow looming over him. "You're going to help me, right? This arrow is yours after all." He growled.

Camilla was silent as she stared into the man's eyes. Her yellow eyes giving him a cold stare and causing him to swallow nervously. She drew forth her short sword, swinging it with all her strength and severing the man's head from his body. The ranger stood, cleaning the blade off on the man's attire. There was no remorse in her eyes as she sheathed her blade on her belt. "They got what they deserved," she muttered as she pulled her hood up and disappeared down the alley.

It was not long before the guards caught wind of what was done and were investigating the deaths. Camilla left town, hearing the commotion of the townsfolk as she crossed the drawbridge out of town. She inhaled deeply as she set off into the wilds to the north of Kaylyntowne. Her feet quickening their pace when she heard the movement of the guards nearing the drawbridge. The wilds were her home; she spent much of her life in such and could easily lose her pursuers. Her yellow eyes beading everything she needed to know about the area as all light vanished from the density of the forest.

Night had fallen, and even the moon's graceful light could not penetrate the forest overgrowth. Camilla frowned as she looked at the locket she carried. "Where are you, Lady Azura?" she questioned aloud before looking over her map. She tucked the locket back into her cloak pocket before drawing out her route. In the distance, Camilla heard a sound that drew her attention. It sounded like singing. She nocked an arrow on her bow and carefully approached. No one. There was no one in the area, but the ranger knew she heard singing. Her heartbeat slowed as her yellow eyes scanned the area, taking everything in in the low light conditions. Before her was a watery looking rift. The singing was coming from the rift itself, or from the other side. Behind her, Camilla her the sounds of guards rushing in her direction. She cursed under her breath. Her choices were limited. The rift or be captured. She silently nodded before diving into the rift. The guards came to stop upon the area but found nothing. There was no way their suspect could have disappeared. They split up searching the area but still found nothing. Nothing but the map with a drawn-out route upon it. They run off in pursuit of the route noted.

Chapter 1 – Chance Meetings

Chuck looked around as he found himself in an alleyway of a large city. He was not used to such; the barbarian was normally in the vast open lands of his wilds. He shouldered his great axe as he began walking around and looked for answers. “Hey, big guy, aren’t you out of place?” came a voice, causing the half orc to look over. Standing before him was an elf clad in full plate armor, brandishing an impressive looking morning star and tower shield. Chuck sized him up before drawing his greataxe and letting out a loud war cry. The elf smirked as he steeled himself. “Looks like I get a fight right out the get go. Alright, come on.”

“Hey! Don’t fight!” came another voice. A young girl with pale blue hair called as she rushed over to the two men. She was breathing heavily, clearly not used to running. Her lavender eyes glancing between the two men.

“Stay out of this, girl. This is a fight between men!” the elf stated as he rushed the barbarian. The two men exchanged strikes, both going for crippling wounds. Several guards began rushing toward the sound of combat; they shouted to the men to end their fight. It was not suited for city streets. There was a smirk from the elf as he swung out his morningstar crushing the skulls of three of the guards. “I’d like to see you try to stop me,” he stated.

Chuck roared, his greataxe cleaving through four guards as he rushed the elf again. The girl flinched back as she saw the bloodshed. “Please, stop this, both of you,” she began, her body trembling as she spoke.

Two arrows shot past, one striking the half orc-half dwarf's bicep. The second arrow found its mark hitting a small chink in the elf's armor and pierced his armpit. Both men staggered briefly before looking for the new attacker. "Lower your weapons. You've already caused a scene. More guards coming this way," a lavender-haired ranger stated as she nocked another arrow. Her yellow eyes gleaming as she watched the three. "Besides, the young lass did ask you nicely."

"You always so cowardly you ambush your foes?" the elf questioned as he removed the arrow and healed his wound.

"Chuck fight ranger!" Chuck roared as he lunged for the ranger.

She was fast and easily dodged the bullrush from the barbarian. A subtle smirk lit up her face as she fired an arrow at him. It did no damage but did explode creating a smokescreen. Chuck coughed a few times as he tried to wave off the smoke. As he moved, he felt something sharp against his throat. "Move and I slit you right here," the ranger whispered as she held a short sword to his throat.

"All three of you, stop this!" the blue-haired woman cried as she watched the three others.

Before long, more guards were upon them. The ranger shook her head as she sheathed her short sword. "Let's be away, shall we?" she said before taking off in a sprint. The others soon followed as she seemed to know where she was going. Guards could be heard from all over the city, pursuing them. As the four reached the outskirts, they came upon a vast cavern. With brief exchange of looks, they set forth into the darkness of the cavern.

The elf easily took the lead being able to see in the dark with his dark-vision ability. Not far behind him was the half orc-half dwarf. And behind him was the blue-haired girl. Stumbling at the back of the party was the ranger. "What's the matter, Hood? Can't see in the darkness?" the elf taunted.

There was a chuckle from the ranger as she fumbled with something. "You'd like to think that, wouldn't ya? Nah, I'm just clumsy outside of combat," she jested as she finished putting something over her eyes. The blue-haired girl glanced back, her eyes widening slightly when she saw the impressive pair of goggles the ranger had donned. "What? Something wrong?" the ranger asked looking over the blue-haired girl.

"No. No. Nothing like that! I uh… you just look like someone I once knew," she stammered. After several hours of walking, they reached a more open room. The four paused before deciding to stop and catch their breaths. The blue-haired girl looked at the center of the room and cast a small fireball. Flames ignited the ground, illuminating the room and allowing the group to better view their surroundings and each other. "I guess introductions are in order. I'm Azura Vaughan," she began.

"Warren Couseland of Frothcrest," the elf proudly introduced.

"Chuck," the half orc bellowed as he pounded a fist against his chest.

There was a chuckle from the ranger as she removed her goggles, allowing them to hang around her neck. "Name's Camilla." She was the last to introduce herself. Silence. Each stared at one another, trying to assess how to proceed. Camilla stretched her arms over her head, giving the three a mildly amused look. "Well, like it or not, seems like we're stuck together."

"How do you figure, outlaw?" Warren quickly shot back as he watched Camilla closely.

"Outlaw? You figure that by my weapon choice? Or my fighting style?" Camilla teased before letting her arms fall to her sides. She was clad in a forest green tunic; under such was a dark gray long sleeve shirt. Brown knee high boots covered her feet, and small pieces of leather covered her shoulders. Hanging from her shoulder armor was a black cloak with a hood. Brown faux leather gloves covered her hands. The fingers for her ring and pinky fingers were torn off, a single ring rested upon her left ring finger. Her lavender hair covered her left eye, giving her a faint aura of mystery. But the most concerning thing to the elf were her yellow eyes. "Or perhaps how I dress?" Camilla added with a slight click in her speech. Hanging from her belt were two short-swords, her quiver and a small bag. Over her shoulder was her longbow.

Warren narrowed his gaze. "I've seen many of your kind. Steal from the rich, give to the poor. Kill those in power and create chaos." He spat. Warren was an elf, yet his armor would make many give him a second glance. Clad in full plate armor, he looked very intimidating. His blonde hair was pulled back in a single ponytail. His dark blue eyes sizing up the ranger. In his left hand was a massive tower shield that in a pinch could easily protect his entire figure. In his right hand was a massive morningstar that more closely resembled a mace.

Camilla rolled her eyes as she sat back upon a rock and watched Warren. "And I suppose you think you know all about a *common thief* like me?" she said with sarcasm in her voice.

"Hey, break it up!" Azura chimed in as she watched the pair. Azura was half elf-half human and had features from both. Her complexion was pale like an elf, and she had the slightly pointed ears of one. Her hair was long and pale blue in color; her lilac eyes glanced between the others. She was garbed in a very simple attire, a pale blue dress with black leggings underneath. White gloves covered her hands; small lumps at her ring fingers made it easy to tell she wore two rings. Around her neck was a simple amulet with her house crest engraved in it. She wore a pair of light brown ankle high boots to cover her feet. But the most stand-out feature to the young sorceress was how large her breasts were.

Chuck merely sat to the side, watching with a bit of confusion as the scene unfolded. He had black hair, his dark brown eyes glancing back and forth. The massive half orc was clad in nothing more than a loincloth and even that seemed to be not covering anything. His muscles were toned and very well defined, rippling with every moment. "Chuck wonder what we do now?" he finally spoke up.

"We? What do you mean we?" Warren responded as he looked to the half orc.

"Well, we all did flee the scene of crime. Involved or not, we're all seen in the same light by the guards. Outlaws. Criminals. Murderers," Camilla noted as she began setting up a wire around where the group was sitting.

"And what are you doing, thief?" the elf demanded. He watched as the human ignored him and continued. She was hanging bells, small trinkets, coins and other metallic objects from the wire before finally sitting by the small flame. "Excuse me, I asked you a question."

"Correction, you demanded an answer. And I don't take orders from you," Camilla replied as she opened her pack and began looking through it. She mumbled a bit to herself before pulling out a bedroll and bag of dried meat. "Looks like as good a spot as any to set camp," she added as she laid out her bedroll.

Azura nodded. "Why don't we all get some sleep and we can continue this discussion another time? All of us are riled up with emotions right now and aren't thinking clearly," she suggested as she withdrew her bedroll from the small bag tucked under her skirt.

Chuck yawned loudly as he pounded his fist against his firm chest. "Chuck agree. Chuck think we talk more after rest."

Warren hesitated but finally gave a nod. While he was an elf and did not require much sleep, he still required rest. He sat to the side, watching the others get comfortable on their bedrolls and soon doze off. With a faint grunt, Warren began undoing his armor, setting the full plate to the side. Once each piece of armor was off, he flicked his wrist, and the armor was called back into the bracelet he wore on his right wrist. "*What am I doing here?*" he wondered as he watched the other three.

The group rested for a few hours, nowhere near enough to be considered adequate sleep. Each gathered their few belongings back to their bags and readied to continue. Azura looked everyone over and smiled slightly. "Ok, now that we're all rested and calmed down a bit, why don't we discuss our next course of action?"

"Alright, I'm all ears," Camilla replied as she collected her wire and metallic objects.

"What happened to those guards, it affected all of us. So, like it or not, I'd say that means we're in this together," Azura duly noted. She paused as she watched the other three. "So why don't we at the least get through this cavern together then maybe, just maybe see from there?"

"Chuck like plan." Chuck grunted as he stood.

"Yeah, alright, sounds like as good a plan as any," Camilla said as she drew her longbow.

Warren sighed then nodded. "Alright, but once we're out of this place, I'll likely bid you three a farewell."

The four began their descent into the depths of the cavern. Chuck had taken the lead, Warren behind him. Azura walked behind Warren, and behind her was Camilla, the human made certain to pull her goggles over her eyes before they continued. As they reached a series of tunnels, they found that there were many offshoots and branch points. Each studied the tunnels trying to decide which way to go. Camila walked along the tunnel mouths, throwing small pieces of chalk down each tunnel. "What're you doing?" Warren asked, curious this time.

"Checking for traps. If there's traps, those chalk pieces are enchanted to create a small flash followed by a loud bang," she explained as she tossed a piece of chalk down the last tunnel. Most of the chalk pieces emitted a flash before loud bangs were heard. "Hmm… Five trap tunnels, and three safe ones.

What do you guys think?" she asked as she nocked an arrow, listening for movement.

Azura threw a small fireball down each safe tunnel, illuminating them further than the group could initially see. "Ah shi—" Warren began as dozens of goblins rushed from the shadows of the *safe tunnels*. He flicked his wrist, his armor forming around him as he drew his morningstar and tower shield.

Chuck let out a war cry as he drew his greataxe and rushed forward. Camilla smirked as she nocked three arrows. "Let the good times roll," she jested before saying something in a different language, a more reptilian sounding language. As she finished, her arrows began glowing different colors. One red, one blue and one yellow. She fired her arrows, each one splitting into more arrows of the same color as the original as they flew down the tunnels.

Azura began making very specific hand gestures conjuring various spells in her palms. In her right hand was a fireball, and in her left a blue orb that dissipated and flew into each of the other three. She flung the fireball forward, taking out six goblins. Chuck mercilessly cleaved his way through the horde, taking the heads off any who opposed him. Warren stayed toward the center of the group, using his shield to block incoming attacks. Camilla nocked three more arrows and spoke in the reptilian language again before letting the arrows fly. This time one was white, one was green and the last gray. The white arrow exploded upon impact with a goblin. The green one sent poison everywhere. And the gray arrow ignited the areas with the poison.

"Nice trick, Hood," Warren jested as his morningstar crushed a goblin's skull. He stepped forward, his tower shield bashing two goblins and forcing them to stagger.

"Azura, Chuck, get down!" Camilla called as she nocked an arrow. The shot was perfect. Both obeyed and ducked as the arrow whizzed pass. One. Two. Three. The arrow continued. Four. Five. Six. Six clean through and through targets off a single arrow. The seventh goblin hissed as the arrow became lodged in his chest. Before he could attempt to remove it, the arrow exploded within his chest.

The four exchanged glances as they realized they had dispatched the goblin horde. Not as individuals but as a team. All turned quickly to state which tunnel they should try, only to realize they had all turned to the same tunnel. Once again, Chuck took the lead, Warren behind him. Azura walked behind the cleric, and Camilla was behind her. Every so often the group would hear movement that was not their own.

Once the tunnel opened up again, they were met with a sudden drop and free fall. Azura and Warren managed to cast slow fall spells upon themselves but watched in horror as the barbarian and ranger fell helplessly. Chuck swung his greataxe out, managing to dig it into a wall to slow his fall. He watched the ranger fall past him, before she vanished from sight. Camilla took a deep breath as she positioned herself to take the fall. A sharp pain filled her right arm, but her fall stopped. Turning to look, she saw a red clawed hand had grabbed her arm.

"Human flesh… so tasty." Something growled as the claw tugged at Camilla. The motion was painful for the ranger as the claws easily began ripping through the muscles in her arm, drawing out blood.

Her mind blanked; a sudden wave of fear clouded her rational mind. She remembered the tunnels from before, the fiendish lizard people. Their claws. Their teeth. Their hungry eyes. This clawed creature reminded her of the moment. The moment when she felt most helpless. Her free arm twitched as she grabbed her shortsword. She slashed at the creature holding her. A loud screech filled the chasm as it dropped her. Camilla managed to reposition herself as she fell. She felt the pain shoot through her left arm as she landed roughly on it. With ragged breaths, she stood and waited for the others to make their way down the chasm. Cautiously she looked around, trying to gauge how far down they had been forced to descend.

Blood continued to drip from the wounds on her right arm. "Hey! Let me patch that up," Azura said as she reached the bottom and rushed to the ranger's side.

Camilla nodded as she held out her bloodied arm for Azura to look over. The young sorceress began tending to the wounds and healing the damage. "I think we're dealing with some sort of demon or devil-like creature down here," Camilla said as she kept watch. Soon they heard the cleric and barbarian finally make their way to the bottom of the chasm, reuniting the group.

Warren held his morningstar at the ready. "Whatever it was, it's big," he said as he looked over the claw marks on Camilla's arm.

"Chuck fight big monster! Chuck ready fight!" the barbarian roared as he hefted his greataxe.

Azura finished tending to Camilla's wounds then looked around. "How far down do you think we are?" she asked as she timidly moved closer to the ranger.

Camilla shook her head and began walking. "Hard to say, but it's warm down here," she noted as she paused and looked down. She had felt something squishing under her boots as she walked. The rest of the party looked at the ground, all of them instantly regretting such. All around them were the remains of various humanoid creatures. Elves, dwarves, orcs, humans, goblins, halflings and many more scattered remains were thrown about the chamber. Chuck swallowed slightly then began sifting through bodies, taking anything, he deemed of value.

Warren hesitated at first but soon joined the barbarian in the act. Azura wanted to puke. She wanted to scream but nothing came out. She shuddered as she stayed close to the two men, fear of what might be lurking in the shadows kept her frozen. Camilla shook her head, walking along the stone walls of the massive chamber. She paused when she came upon a stone with very specific runes carved into it. She stared for a moment; the runes seemed familiar but as though from a distant memory. "Hmm…" she hummed before pressing her right hand against the wall. In response, the wall made a click before a door was revealed. The ranger stepped through the door and began investigating the other room, without the rest of the party.

Inside she found what she could only describe as a hide away. There were tattered books scattered about the room along with shredded bedrolls and non-combat relevant gear. As she walked further in, she found herself staring at a damaged table. Sitting upon the table were a series of glass vials and various jars with assorted items inside. There was a damaged book next to such with detailed notes about what was laid out. "A potion crafter must have been here at some point," she murmured, opening the small box that was next to the book. It was large enough to fit fifty potions, and there were forty-three potions on the table. Camilla nodded and loaded up the potions into the box, organizing based on their use. The last potion was a dark blue in coloration, and there were no notes in the book. She hesitated but moved to put it in the box.

"Hey, Hood, where are you!" Warren called loudly from the previous room.

Camilla jumped slightly, the glass vial breaking in her left hand. It burned and she rushed to get the potion off. She emptied the water from her waterskin on her left hand and began blowing on it. After a moment, the pain subsided leaving the ranger questioning what it was. She sighed before wrapping her hand in bandages to prevent anything causing further discomfort to her already wounded hand.

"Camilla!" Azura called as she walked through the main chamber. She was worried. She did not want to be left alone with the two men. As she walked, she came upon the hidden door that Camilla had gone through. "Camilla?" the sorceress began as she poked her head into the room. The ranger was silent as she walked over, causing the sorceress to sigh in relief. "Thought I'd lost you, ag—" She stopped in mid-sentence, quickly covering her mouth.

"Hmm? Lost me, again?" Camilla arched an eyebrow as she spoke. While it was true, Camilla had lost her liege, Lady Azura Vaughan, she could tell this was not the same Azura. She rubbed the back of her head, giving the blue haired sorceress a soft smile. "Listen, Azura, I'm not the same Camilla Windstride that you knew. But then again, you already knew that," she said trying to put things gently.

Azura nodded slightly then frantically began shaking her head. "Wait. Wait. Wait! It's not like that! I mean, yes, I know you're not the same Camilla from my world. But… Oh geez, forget I said anything," she responded, waving her hands frantically.

"Uhm… Alriiight, then, I guess," Camilla said slowly, trying to process the sorceress's strange behavior.

"Hey! Hood! Girl! Where'd ya go!" Warren called loudly from the main chamber.

"Be right there, Warren!" Azura hollered back before glancing at Camilla. "Shall we?" Camilla nodded in response to the question before following Azura back to the main room. Warren and Chuck were waiting at the center of the room, both held bags full of gear they had scavenged from the various remains. "Anything of use?" Azura asked, quite surprised she would even ask that.

Warren smirked. "Big guy can't tell useful from useless, but thankfully you have me. We got us lots of armor, probably make a quick sack of gold; some broken weapons, may not be useable but sellable. And of course, some gold," the cleric stated proudly.

"Chuck think tiny man wet blanket," the barbarian grunted.

Camilla smirked slightly trying not to chuckle hearing the barbarian's words. Warren glared at Chuck; his gaze narrowed. "Excuse me, Big Man?"

Azura shook her head. "He means you're too uptight and thinking too highly of yourself," the young sorceress pointed out as she watched the others.

Everything after those words happened so fast. Warren swung his morningstar at the sorceress. But the blow never connected. Standing between them was the ranger. Camilla had her right arm extended behind her, having pushed Azura out of the attack. Her own left hand had managed to grab part of the morningstar's handle. Everyone was silent. "Don't you touch her, ever." Camilla's voice was dangerously low, feral sounding even. Her yellow eyes gleamed eerily in the low light.

Warren, for the first time in a long time, felt a chill run down his spine. Chuck swallowed hard nervously upon seeing how easily the ranger was able to react and stop the attack. Azura stared for a bit in silence, amazed by the display of speed and strength. No one moved for the longest time. Camilla finally made the next move and flung the cleric back before walking off. Her head felt like it was splitting causing her to rub her forehead with her right hand. She had rarely shown emotions around others, her time in the wilds taught her emotions were a weakness. One that she needed to lose as quickly as she could in order to survive.

It took a moment before anyone else moved to follow but they did. Soon the four came upon a dark tunnel. Camilla put her dark-vision goggles on before continuing, part of her wishing the others would leave her be. And part of her enjoyed having them follow her. All was quiet as they went through the tunnel. No one felt comfortable talking, and oddly enough there were no creatures about. As they stepped out into the next room, they noticed the size of the chamber and once again, the lack of light. The only light consisted of faint trickles from the outside world through small cracks in the ceiling and an exterior tunnel. "Outside world here we come," Warren began as he started walking. Camilla held out an arm blocking him. "What's the big ide—"

"There. On the far side and on the ceiling," Camilla stated quietly as she pointed with an arrow.

Azura stared for a moment, trying to size up the coming fight. "Pit demons," she whispered as she recalled these creatures from what her brother had taught her. Quickly glancing about, Azura began trying to assess the situation. "Their weakness is light, but it only stuns them for a brief amount of time," she spoke as she looked about.

Camilla nocked an arrow as she drew her longbow. "Chuck, you and I take point. Warren, Azura, you two try to find a way we can bounce light around to stun them," she instructed as she watched the two pit demons.

"Don't tell me what to do!" Warren yelled before rushing forward to engage the two monsters in battle. In one hand was his morningstar and the other grasped his tower shield.

Chuck let out a war cry then charged. His greataxe drawn. Camilla cursed under her breath as she pivoted slightly. "Azura, make a break for the tunnel out. Those things likely have a potent magic resistance or magic reflection," the ranger stated as she kept her back to the sorceress. Three arrows fired in rapid succession, each one missing their target. The pit demons used their wings to easily fly about the open chamber and avoid any attacks from the group. One of them had grabbed Warren and was dragging him along the wall. The other blocked Chuck's greataxe before tearing the weapon from his hands.

Camilla knocked another arrow on the bowstring. She took a deep breath as she steadied herself. The arrow flew from the bow. Silence. It was silent for a full fifteen seconds before a loud screech was heard from a pit demon. The creature turned its attention to the ranger, a look of pure hatred in its ruby eyes. "Come on! I'll take you both on!" the ranger challenged as she shouldered her bow and drew her shortswords. Both pit demons exchanged glances before lunging for the ranger. She skillfully dodged in and out of their strikes, using her shortswords to go on the offense when there were openings. She glanced to the barbarian and cleric, hoping that they would be able to recover enough to run.

Azura glanced back, her eyes darting around as she heard Camilla fighting the pit demons. "Wait. I think I got an idea…" she murmured as she studied the area again. "Warren, use your shield! Bounce that faint light off your shield and aim it at the pit demons!" she called over.

Warren grumbled as he got to his feet. He saw small pockets of light and nodded. His desire to survive outweighing his desire to work alone. He ran to the nearest pocket of light trickling down and raised his shield. The cleric aimed his shield around, trying to bounce the light off of it and strike the pit demons. "Come on, come on, come on," he muttered as he angled his shield.

Chuck watched the scene unfolding. Camilla was fighting two enemies at once; her arms were bleeding from repeated claw attacks. He charged forward, shoving one of the pit demons into the light reflecting from Warren's shield. The creature shrieked as the light struck its skin. Its movements had become sluggish as it tried to break away from the barbarian. He swung out with his greataxe, clipping both wings off. Chuck kept swinging his greataxe, dealing big hits to the pit demon. Between the sluggish movements from the blast of light and barbarian's onslaught, the creature soon met its end.

Camilla ran her shortswords through the remaining pit demon, causing it to bleed. As she brought her blades around for the next attack, she saw the beam of light hitting the creature causing it to howl in agony. She lunged forward, pressing the advantage. "Enough is enough," she said lowly before beheading the final enemy. Her yellow eyes looked more ruthless than before as she watched the corpse fall to the ground.

"Camilla! Chuck! Warren! This way!" Azura called from the tunnel leading out.

The other three rushed over, quickly rejoining with the young sorceress. In one final sprint, the four made their way out of the cavern and came upon a lush and wide-open field. None of this made sense to them, but who were they to judge what was making sense and what did not. "Warriors of the Outrealms, welcome to Bridging Field. In order to advance to the gateway between worlds, you must reclaim the four jewels of heart. One in the northern mountains. One to the far western canyon. To the far east, you'll find the beyond housing the third. And in the depths of the southern sanctum the fourth resides in the aether." A voice echoed before them.

"Who are you?" Warren demanded.

"Seek out the jewels of heart if you wish to learn the truth," the voice stated before everything went silent.

Camilla looked onward to the north. "Well, let's get this adventure under way," she said before heading north.

"Don't forget about me," Azura said as she followed the ranger.

"Chuck want fight," the barbarian growled as he sprinted to keep up with the ranger and sorceress. Warren rolled his eyes before going after the other three. Like it or not, he was stuck with them.

Chapter 2 – The Way Ahead

The four had been traversing the field for what seemed like weeks as they tried to reach the northern mountain. They came upon a small town; the people all looked sickly and exhausted. Warren shook his head in disgust. Chuck ignored every person they passed. Azura's eyes reflected pity and wishing she could help them. Camilla watched as every person in the town looked at them as though gauging what to steal. Eventually the group came upon a tavern. Deciding to enter, they found themselves sitting at the counter and ordering drinks as they planned their next course of action. "How're we supposed to find this northern mountain with no map?" Warren complained as he shook his head.

"Chuck not think exist. Chuck say we ravage town," the barbarian chimed in.

Azura took a deep breath trying to think and plan. "Maybe we just keep going north until we find the mountain. Seems like a simple option."

"Keep going north? Girl, we'd eventually run out of place to travel. And it's unlikely that this damn mountain is that easy to find," Warren quickly spat out the words. He hated the idea of following anyone's ideas.

Camilla shook her head as the others argued. Looking across the tavern, she saw a reptilian-like creature watching them. She stood then made her way to his table and gestured to the seat across from him. "This seat taken?" she asked.

He looked her over. His ruby eyes sizing her up. "Nay, milady," he replied. Camilla took a seat then sipped from her tankard. "Aye, you seek Ner Mountain? Err, was it Harmony Mountain? Aaaaah, it's been so long since I travelled 'at fer north," he spoke.

"Tell me, good sir, do you have a map of these wilds?" Camilla asked as she slid a gold piece across the table to the reptilian man.

He picked up the coin, looking it over. "Map? Nay, milady. But I have an impressee memory. Scribble, scrabble, eh, whatever ye do to make yer map," he said as he rubbed his chin.

Camilla pulled a piece of parchment from her bag along with an inkwell and quill. The reptilian man began talking, describing the wilds to the far north. Camilla making certain to jot down notes and make rough map sketches to follow. Once finished with her rough map, she showed it to the reptilian man. "Yeh, yeh, that's yer north mountain. Need thy western canyon?" he asked while frantically flailing his left hand.

"If you'd be so kind to tell," Camilla replied as she pulled out another sheet of parchment. As with before, she listened to him rattle on about the area in question and made notes to match his words. She sketched out the area and detailed out the paths he spoke of. Once finished, she set the sheet to the side. "You wouldn't happen to know about the beyond or aether, would you?"

"M'hmm? Beyond and aether? Never hear of 'em," he said as he leaned back in his chair.

The ranger nodded as she looked the parchment sheets over, waiting for them to dry. "Thank you very much, good sir, for the aid you have provided my group and I," she said before looking up. Nothing. She was alone at the table. The gold piece she had slid across earlier remained exactly where she had left it. But the reptilian man was nowhere to be seen. "Was he real? Or was I seeing things?" she wondered as she stared at the empty chair across from her.

"You alright, Camilla?" Azura asked as she approached the ranger. Camilla did not answer; she continued to stare across from her at the empty seat. She glanced at the maps she had drawn before returning her gaze to the empty seat. "Camilla?" Azura began as she gently patted the ranger's shoulder.

"Huh? Oh, sorry, I must have zoned out for a moment," Camilla replied.

"You've been sitting here by yourself for over an hour. Warren and Chuck said you were just brooding," the young sorceress said calmly as she looked at the table. She arched an eyebrow before gesturing to the maps. "You made these?" Azura asked as she began studying the maps. "Wait… How can you know where these areas are?"

Camilla shook her head as she stared for a moment. "I've been here alone? That's not possible. There was a reptilian man here. He was sitting right there," she responded as she pointed to the seat across from her.

"Sounds like Hood's lost her mind," Warren stated as he and Chuck joined the girls.

"Hmm? You four talking about the ghost?" the barkeeper asked as he looked at the four. They turned to look at him, each one with a confused expression. "It's just a story in these parts, but there's a man of many faces who appears and disappears without a trace. Course it's just a story crazed adventures use to hide their madness," he added.

"What exactly did you see?" Azura asked Camilla, concern lining her voice as she looked into the ranger's eyes.

Camilla shook her head. "It doesn't matter. Come on, let's get going. I keep getting weird vibes from this town," she stated as she stood and headed for the door. The rest of the group followed, exiting the tavern.

They made their way through the town, ignoring the people that stared at them. Some of the townsfolk attempted to talk to them. Others ignored them all together. "Coin for the poor?" an elderly man asked as he sat slouched against a building. He had reached out a worn cup as he asked them.

"Keep your filth to yourself, mongrel," Warren responded as the group walked. He drew his morningstar. "Any of you filthy creatures come near us, I'll bludgeon in your skulls," he threatened, glaring at the townsfolk.

Camilla remained silent as she pulled her hood up, covering her head. Chuck let out a war cry, challenging the townsfolk to try something against the group. Azura shook her head, not wanting to imagine the violence that would take place if the barbarian and cleric had their way. As they reached the edge of town, the group heard movement behind them. Turning to look, Warren and Chuck both cracked a smirk. "Looks like we get to fight after all." Warren laughed.

The townsfolk had all begun shambling toward the four adventurers. They were armed with basic iron swords and iron lances. Some had pitchforks, others torches. Chuck let out a war cry before rushing them and swinging out his greataxe. Warren laughed sadistically as he entered combat and bludgeoned villagers with his morningstar. Azura tensed up, uncertain what to do. Camilla arched an eyebrow, shaking her head. "This is all wrong," she murmured as she shook her head again. "Wait a moment…" She paused and began to think over the recent events. Everyone had been short-fused since the tavern. She had seen something that was not physically there. "The drinks were spiked… " she murmured as she shook her head, trying to clear it. "Azura, how much did you and the guys drink?"

"I had maybe two tankards. Warren and Chuck… I lost count," Azura replied.

Camilla looked back at the slaughter going on. The townsfolk were running in terror; they only had simple farming equipment in hand. Chuck and Warren brutally killed them even though the people were running. "I barely drank any of mine," she muttered before rushing forward. Chuck brought his greataxe down, about to split a young boy in two. His greataxe was blocked by a shortsword. Camilla stood between the barbarian and the child. "Run," she said to the child as she struggled to hold back the half orc's brute strength.

"Puny ranger! Why stop Chuck's fun!" Chuck demanded as he flung Camilla aside.

"Chuck, Warren, listen to me. Those drinks at the tavern were spiked with something. It's making you see things that aren't real," Camilla explained, trying to remain calm. She leapt back, barely dodging the morningstar from the cleric.

"Says the one who spoke to a lizard person that didn't exist," Warren remarked as he swung out with his morningstar, aimed at the ranger's chest. She managed to dodge the hit before countering with her shortsword to his thigh. "Cheap trick," he grunted as he tried to move but felt his body suddenly feel heavy. "What's…" he mumbled before collapsing.

Camilla sighed in relief then glanced at Chuck. "Ok, big guy, what's it going to be? Hear my words or yield to my combat?" she asked as she deepened her stance.

Chuck let out an impressive roar as he charged the ranger. She leapt back, barely dodging the greataxe. "Chuck want fight! Fight Chuck!" the half orc roared as he swung out his greataxe.

Camilla leapt over the swings, landing nimbly on her feet a few feet away. "Fine I'll fight," she said before bobbing to the side. Her short sword meeting the barbarian's thigh drawing a line of blood. The half orc swung his axe out, colliding with the ranger and sending her several feet back. She struggled to move but saw the half orc continue the slaughter. The screams haunted the ranger, each one making her cringe.

A fireball struck the barbarian, drawing his attention to the young sorceress who was shaking. Her hands each held another fireball at the ready, but her composure was easy to read and intimidated. "Chuck, please. Please stop this senseless killing," she wept as she watched the massive barbarian. In return, he growled deeply as he charged at her, his blood-covered greataxe glistening. Fear gripped the sorceress as she found it impossible to move, the fireballs dying down and leaving her helpless. She felt a pinch; someone had grabbed her arm. Before she could react, Azura felt herself be thrown to the side out of harm's way. She shook her head, trying to clear it. She sat up from the hay bale and quickly turned to look in the direction she had come from. Blood sprayed across, covering her face as the horrific scene unfolded.

Camilla's right arm was split in several spots, blood running freely. Chuck seemed frozen, but as Azura looked closer, she saw the ranger's short sword embedded deep in his gut. "This… this is all wrong. We're supposed to be a team," the young sorceress whimpered as she crumbled to her knees in tears. Her hand clutched her head as her body trembled. "Why is this world… why is it—"

"Hey."

Azura looked up upon hearing the greeting. Gazing down upon her were the haunting yellow eyes of the ranger. Camilla was badly wounded, blood soaked through her clothes and her lavender hair was sticky with the red liquid. "Camilla…" Azura began.

"I didn't kill them. The boys will be awake in about an hour. Just some poison to knock them out for a little while," the ranger stated before holding out a hand to the sorceress. Azura hesitated but took the ranger's hand, allowing herself to be pulled to her feet. Camilla gave the sorceress a warm smile. "I may not be your Camilla, and you may not be my Azura, and yet I feel as though I must protect you," the ranger explained as looked away, the intimidating feel in her eyes replaced with a comforting warmth. She pulled away from the sorceress and began tending to her wounds.

Azura swallowed the lump in her throat as she dared to look at the countless bodies that littered the ground. Her hands were shaking as she brought them up to cover her mouth, her eyes wide from the horror before her. Men, women and children, all slaughtered by the cleric and barbarian. Her eyes went to the ranger who had just finished patching up her wounds. The yellow-eyed young woman motioned for Azura to grab one of the men. "We need to get out of here before anyone sees us. Come on," Camilla stated as she hefted Warren over her shoulders. Azura nodded numbly as she dragged Chuck, following Camilla.

"Where do we go from here?" Azura asked softly, her voice barely audible. Silence. Camilla did not answer as she led the sorceress away from the town. After what seemed like several miles of walking, they came upon a cave. The ranger slumped the cleric against a stone wall before moving to the front of the cave mouth to keep look out. Azura dragged Chuck to the side and looked to Camilla, waiting. She was not sure what she was waiting for, but she knew the ranger was being the cautious one.

"Get some rest, Azura. I'll keep look out," Camilla said as she sat at the entrance to the cave, her longbow ready should she need it. Behind her, Camilla heard the sorceress shift slightly, clearly uncomfortable. The temperature was chilly at best and only getting colder as the night progressed. Camilla removed her cloak and tossed it backwards.

"Huh?" Azura questioned as she felt the cloak land on her lap. She looked at Camilla, her eyes marveling at how stoic the ranger could be at times.

"You're cold, are you not? You can borrow my cloak for the time being," Camilla responded without even looking at the sorceress. She continued to look out, ignoring the group behind her. Azura had finally nodded off, wrapped in the ranger's cloak. The ranger sighed as she removed her left glove, finally examining her bandaged left hand. It felt like it was on fire but tingled at the same time. She arched an eyebrow as she noticed the claws that had replaced her fingernails. Where her skin had once been was covered by thick dark blue scales. "What's happening to me?" she whispered to herself as she looked over her clawed hand. Behind her, she heard the boys beginning to stir and quickly rewrapped her hand and put her glove on once again.

"What the hell happened?" Warren mumbled as he rubbed his head.

"Chuck no feel right," the barbarian added as he sat up.

Camilla gave both a warm smile as she looked over to them. "You both alright? No killing frenzy mindsets?" she asked as she stood and walked over to the ground.

"Noooo…?" Warren was very confused. He remembered leaving the tavern with the others, but everything after was a blur. Chuck shook his head then winced regretting even moving his head.

The ranger took a deep breath before exhaling. She calmly but quickly filled the boys in on what had transpired after the tavern. There was shock upon the cleric's face but not much expression from the barbarian. Silence was between the adventurers as Camilla finished. No one wanted to speak for a while. The nightly chill began to get the better of everyone and made them all shiver slightly.

Warren shook his head and looked to Camilla. "Alright, so we still need to reach the northern mountain? So which way?"

Camilla unfolded the map she had drawn. "If this map is correct there are two routes we can take. An overworld route which would likely take us through villages and towns. And an underground route, which we know nothing about."

"With the track record we have, we should go underground," Azura chimed in, now fully awake and watching the others.

"Chuck say we stay above ground!" the barbarian belted.

"I agree with the big guy," Warren noted as he looked over Camilla's map.

"And I disagree. If you boys have another outburst, we're likely to end up in deeper trouble than we're already in with guards and such," Camilla responded. She looked over the map again. She knew there was no persuading the boys to listen to her or Azura. "Alternatively, we can split up. You guys can stay above ground and head north along this route. While Azura and I go underground, along this road and hopefully use some tunnels to make it there," she commented as she indicated the routes on the map.

"Alright, Hood, I can agree to that. Last one there has to pick up everyone's bar tab at the next sane village!" Warren laughed as he took off. Chuck roared as he sprinted after the cleric.

Azura shuddered but looked to Camilla. A faint wave of relief washing over her, knowing she was in good hands with the ranger. "We'll head out as soon as you're rested," Camilla said softly as she leaned back against a stone wall. Azura opened her mouth to say something but stopped when she heard Camilla chuckle. "Besides, I sense a storm coming in, and I don't want to be out while its downpours."

As though on cue, a downpour of rain began. Camilla sighed slightly, a smile on her face as she sat beside the young sorceress. Azura hesitated but moved closer, until she was practically snuggled up next to the ranger. She pulled the cloak tightly around herself, shivering from the chill in the air. Camilla said nothing; she merely sat in silence allowing the sorceress to curl up next to her. What started as a light rain soon turned into a heavy downpour. Camilla's eyelids felt heavy as she struggled to stay awake. "You should get some rest, I… I can keep watch," Azura said softly.

Camilla arched an eyebrow. "You sure?" she asked, trying to hide her fatigue. Azura nodded as she looked into the ranger's tired eyes. The ranger waved things off, chuckling slightly. "Alright, but you wake me if anything happens." Azura nodded again as she watched the ranger begin to fall asleep. The night was quiet aside from the downpour of rain; the sorceress hated the sounds and found it unsettling. She found herself questioning how easily the ranger was comfortable with all this.

"She must've spent a much longer time in the wilds than around civilization," Azura murmured as she watched the ranger. She shook her head trying to clear it. *"Stop it, Azura. She's not your Camilla. Stop thinking she is,"* she thought as she looked away.

Hours passed, and nothing noteworthy happened during the night. As the sun's rays began peaking over the horizon, Camilla's eyes instantly shot open. She leapt to her feet, accidently knocking Azura over in the process. "Whoa! Easy Camilla!" Azura called out as she got to her feet.

Camilla was breathing heavily; she shook her head as though shaking away some horrible thought. "Sorry, Azura. Just a nightmare. Nevermind, let's get going." She was quick to shut down the thought of talking about it. Before she headed out, she saw Azura hold out something to her. "Huh?"

"Your cloak. Thank you for letting me borrow it last night," Azura said as she handed the cloak to Camilla. The ranger nodded before taking the black cloak and putting it on. They soon headed out from the cave, their destination in mind as they moved out.

Chuck and Warren found themselves going through a vast field. There were no signs of wildlife, or anyone. They walked onward, both groaning as they made their way through the field. "Chuck bored! Chuck want fight!" the barbarian yelled in frustration as they walked.

Warren rolled his eyes as he walked, Chuck following. "Maybe we should've stuck with the girls. Maybe there'd be some excitement then," he noted as they marched. Both were still drenched from walking all night in the rain. There was nowhere they could camp, and they kept moving onward. The weather had turned to their favor as it had been storm-free for the entire morning. The field seemed endless, but they pushed onward. At one point they stopped to catch their breath from all the walking.

"Chuck wonder if girls fighting," the barbarian said as he looked around.

Warren shrugged; he honestly did not care in the slightest. He was growing bored and tired of the never-ending field. All he wanted was a break from the empty fields. He sighed before continuing. He withdrew his spyglass from his bag and looked ahead, his eyes lighting up with excitement. "Good news, big guy, there's a massive town ahead. Maybe we can get some ale and see if anyone knows how much further this mountain range is," he noted as he took the lead. Chuck followed behind, growling to himself as they marched.

Camilla paused when they reached the access to the tunnels. She nodded to Azura then began working her way through the first set of tunnels. The ranger reached to pull her goggles over her eyes but paused when she realized she could see in the darkness clearly. It was odd, she had always needed them before, and now her vision was fine without them. Shrugging it off, the ranger continued ahead, the sorceress behind her.

"You think these tunnels will be faster?" Azura asked as she followed close behind the ranger.

"I don't know. Maybe. Honestly, I just wanted a break from the boys," the ranger replied as she walked. She held her short swords at the ready; the not knowing what to expect made her more cautious than normal. Her senses were on high alert as she and Azura walked. In the darkness, her yellow eyes gleaming catching even the slightest movement.

They came to a stop, a few rocks shifting catching their attention. Azura tightened her grip on her spell book. She kept her back pressed against Camilla's back, ensuring neither would be attacked on their vulnerable spines. A creature that resembled a human shambled forward. Its empty eye sockets were haunting; blood covered its mouth and hands as it shambled forward. The skin was deathly gray; no clothing covered it. "A ghoul…" Azura whispered as she watched it shamble about.

"And it's not alone," Camilla said very quietly as nine more ghouls shambled out. They shambled right up to Camilla and Azura, their claws lashing out wildly. Camilla did not miss a beat; she pushed Azura down before going into a whirlwind, slashing all ten ghouls. None of them stopped. They shrieked loudly as they staggered then lunged forward again. Azura chanted something before unleashing a cone of flames, scorching five ghouls. Camilla quickly attacked again with her whirlwind movements, slicing through the five that were not on fire.

Azura shook her head as the ten ghouls fell to the ground. She sighed in relief as she looked to Camila. "You alright?" she asked the ranger.

"Yeah, you?" Camilla replied, keeping her guard up. Azura nodded. "Then let's get going," Camilla added as she headed further into the tunnels, Azura behind her. They came upon a dead-end in the tunnels.

"This doesn't make any sense," Azura noted. She paced for a moment before feeling Camilla grab and yank her back. Camilla winced as she dropped the shortsword from her left hand. Blood trickled down her left arm as she looked up and around. "Camilla!" Azura called seeing the blood.

"I'm alright, but whatever it is, it's big," Camilla stated as she winced. She felt the blood dribbling from the wound. "And it's likely the thing blocking the tunnel," she added, slight fear in her voice.

Azura watched closely looking for whatever this creature was. Some sort of aberration appeared; it was pitch black and looked like a floating cloth with a red hook hanging from the bottom. The sorceress gasped before blasting the aberration with a light magic sphere. Camilla turned and slashed with her short sword, knocking the cloth aside. A gray-blue scorpion-like creature lunged from under the cloth, its red pincers grabbing at Camilla's short sword.

She barely managed to keep a grip on her blade as she wrestled with the scorpion creature. Azura threw another orb of light magic at the creature. Camilla pivoted on her heel just in time to see another one of these creatures lunged forward. She moved without thinking, her right arm bleeding profusely as it took the hit for Azura.

"What's the plan, Camilla?" Azura asked, panicking.

"Stay calm. Your light magic is the key to this victory. No matter what happens, I'll endure whatever they attack with. You focus on attacking those things," the ranger replied as she winced from the blood loss.

Camilla lunged forward again, blocking the assault from the two creatures. Azura nodded, trusting Camilla fully. She charged her light magic and waited for an opening. As the first opening appeared, Azura sent the magic at the still cloaked creature. Knocking its black cloth aside and leaving a serious wound upon the scorpion-like creature. As the two creatures were wounded, they began to merge and mutate into something far worse. They resembled some sort of giant mouth connected to a massive ooze with tentacles. The teeth were massive; each tentacle ended in a sharp serrated edge. Azura began shaking in fear. Camilla rushed forward to protect the sorceress. She was terrified herself, but she had to be brave for the young sorceress. She drew her longbow and fired off forty arrows in rapid succession, praying to the deity Patroklos that the arrows would hit their mark and bring this beast down.

Seeing no progress with the arrow volley, Camilla grabbed the sorceress and ran. She saw the tunnel they were trying to reach and pushed herself to run as fast as she could. A tentacle slashed out, leaving a deep gash in her leg. Camilla winced, screaming in pain as she threw Azura down the tunnel. Her leg gave out, causing the ranger to collapse. She winced as she looked to the sizable wound in her leg. Before the creature could attack again, Camilla drew forth her longbow, chanting something in a different language before firing a single arrow. She dragged herself towards the tunnel, praying the arrow hit its mark. A loud bang was heard above as rock began falling. Camilla winced as she dragged herself into the tunnel before fully collapsing. Behind her she could hear the shrieking of the monster as it was buried under the rockslide, the tunnel now fully blocked off leaving the pair the only way to go as forward. The ranger felt her vision getting foggy as she laid on the ground. Her eyes felt heavy before they closed.

The tavern was rowdy as can be. Chuck and Warren both drank themselves to the point of seeing blurs. It had been quite the walk, but they made it to the town and were now enjoying some hard-earned ale. They laughed as they watched the live entertainment of the small band of bards. One was playing an accordion; another had a flute and the third had a violin. The music was very upbeat and had most of the folk in the tavern dancing to the music. Warren turned to face Chuck. "Well, this is more like it!" he cheered as the two clanked their ale tankards together. He downed the amber liquid and watched the various folk dancing. "This, this is living!" he cheered as he signaled for one of the barmaids to their section of the counter.

"Boss says you boys are cut off," the barmaid stated as she flicked her tail under Warren's nose, teasing him. She had red skin, two curved horns upon her head and a long slender tail. Her hair was black as coal, and her eyes shone like topazes in low light. Her bosom was buster than most women, the busty melons exposed by how her shirt clung to her skin and was unbuttoned a bit. She was a race known to most as half devils. They were rare to be sure, but wherever they went, chaos usually followed. She strutted past Warren as she walked hastily to the next table.

Warren leaned out, pinching the woman's large bubble butt. The action earned him a glare from her. "Let's get something straight, girlie. My friend and I aren't done yet. When we order another round, we get another round," he blurted in his drunken stupor.

"Hailey, ignore the drunk dastard," the tavern keeper called as he looked over before serving out ale to a couple of travelers that had just entered. Hailey, the half devil, nodded to the keeper before walking to the table where a minotaur and his crew sat. The tavern keeper was rather well built. His muscles rippled with each action he took. He was a half ogre, his ash-colored skin was covered with scars from many fights. His mouth had a distinct underbite with two large fangs protruding out and visible to everyone. "Ye boys are cut off. 'Til you pay your tab out anyway," he stated as he flicked a rag over his left shoulder.

Chuck roared at this treatment. Did these tavern folk know who they were dealing with? He was Chuck Bloodscourge, feared throughout his lands. A terror and menace to societies. He stood and walked to the counter section where the tavern keeper was. Chuck slammed both his fists down on the wooden counter splintering it as he roared in the ogre's face. "Chuck want more! Pay later!" he roared.

The ogre was unfazed as he stared at Chuck. "You'll get more when you and yer bud pay yer tab," he said.

Warren grumbled; he knew there was no talking either of them at all. He knew there were two outcomes. Fight or pay the damned tab. He sized up the tavern employees and shook his head, clearly not liking the odds they had. His hand went to his coin purse and withdrew several gold pieces and placed them on the counter. "That should be enough for our current tab plus two more rounds each," the elf stated as he watched the ogre.

The ogre counted the coin and nodded. He poured two more tankards for each of the men then went back to serving other customers that had trickled into the tavern. Chuck growled before sitting beside Warren again. "Chuck had under control," the barbarian snarled as he sat beside the elf.

Warren rolled his eyes. "Big guy, there's more of them than even we can handle. Besides between his brute strength, the various barmaids and the bards, we'd each be fighting at least six opponents," he noted as he downed his two tankards. "Now then, shall we head back out. Don't want the girls beating us to Harmony Mountain," he added as he stood. Chuck growled but finished his tankards and followed Warren. They headed out walking toward what they assumed was north. Warren in truth was not sure if his compass was working the same in this world. They reached a vast chasm, but it was the only way forward.

Chuck took the lead, with Warren barely five feet behind him. They were surprised by the lack of monsters. Instead, they found themselves dealing with several puzzles and riddles. Chuck groaned in protest, clearly hating the lack of fight. Warren read the text upon the stone table in front of them. "To cross the gate, four hearts must join." He paused looking at the next piece of text. "In each a strength, but each strength a weakness." He glanced at the next text. His heart rate rose as he took everything in. "Alone they fall, together they… " There was nothing else inscribed. He sighed as he walked to the next stone object in the ground. A stone tablet. The highborn elf read it over a few times before speaking aloud. "The heart of harmony is corrupt and filled with greed.

The valor heart is senseless and predictable. Mystical heart is filled with fear and lacks initiative. But the instinctive heart is the most troubled, it has forgotten why it exists."

Warren looked to Chuck. "The hell does any of this mean?" he yelled as he flung the stone tablet aside. They walked forward and pushed through a stone door. Before them was a long bridge with nothing below. Both swallowed nervously before crossing. It took them hours to reach the other side of the bridge. As they stepped off the bridge, they heard the ropes holding the bridge snap, leaving them with no retreat. "Onward," Warren said calmly as he took lead, the various texts still ingrained in his mind.

Camilla slowly opened her eyes as she felt magic coursing over her wounds. She inhaled sharply, wincing as she tugged away. "Take it easy. You got hurt pretty bad," Azura said softly as she continued to tend to the ranger's wounds. The lavender-haired woman was silent as she slumped against the rocks. Her body ached and wounds littered her body. "Thank you, for keeping me safe," Azura added as she patched the last of Camilla's wounds.

"Don't mention it. Seriously don't. I can't have anyone thinking I've gone soft," Camilla replied as she looked over her gear. She saw the short sword she had dropped and arched an eyebrow. Reaching down, she collected the blade and sheathed it upon her belt.

"One of us must've kicked it during all the chaos," the sorceress noted as she looked from the weapon to the ranger.

Camilla stood, brushing herself off. "We've still a way to go. So, let's get going," she stated as she began walking once again. Azura followed close behind, her feet lightly pattering across the stone.

As they reached the end of the tunnel, they came upon a massive chamber. Standing, blocking their only way out was a stone golem, with four crystals embedded in its shoulders. The moment the golem sensed their movement it sprung to life and turned a vibrant red. Flame gleamed across its body as it readied to fight. Camilla saw the flames beginning to rush forward and brought both her short swords up, spinning them to deflect as much of the fire as she could. "Azura! What can you do about fire?" she called as she blocked the flames.

Azura quickly thought about her spells before casting her Blizzard spell. Ice shrouded the fire golem, and while the ice itself was useless, it became water which doused the golem. As if on cue though, a different crystal began to glow, and the golem's coloration was altered. It was gray in coloration as it unleashed rushes of wind, sending any magic back at the pair. Camilla was blown aside, her body slamming hard into a stone wall. She winced as she tried to stand. Azura was between the ranger and the golem. She swallowed hard as she used her magic to put up a barrier, trying to deflect the golem's barrage of attacks.

Camilla shook her head as she stood and rushed forward again. Her blades did little to the golem but forced its attention upon her. Azura quickly readied her next spell before canceling. "Any magic I cast will be blown back or worse," Azure muttered as she tried to think up a plan. She saw both short swords clatter to the ground as they were knocked from the ranger's grip.

Wincing, Camilla glanced to her left hand and pondered the option. She nodded and knew she had to try. Removing the bandages from her clawed hand, she rushed forward. Her claw gouged out chunks from the golem, causing breaks in its armored body. Azura saw the openings and unleashed cones of magical energy, each one hitting its mark. Camilla smirked seeing the golem wither in pain. She quickly followed up with a series of quick slashes from her claw, shattering the golem completely.

"When did you get that!" Azura exclaimed seeing the clawed hand.

The ranger quickly moved her left hand behind her back, now realizing the mistake she made. "Uh… It's… It's complicated," she stated trying to hide her clawed hand from view.

Azura shook her head then took a step toward the ranger and yanked the clawed hand back into view. "Your hand… How? When?" the sorceress stammered as she looked the ranger over.

"It's not important. And I'll tell you when the time's right. For now, please keep this just between us," Camilla replied as she yanked her hand free and bandaged it again. She collected her short swords then began walking once again. She heard Azura following but keeping her distance. Before long, Camilla arched an eyebrow as her nostrils twitched. "I can smell something on a breeze. Breeze means there's a way out," she said with a grin as she pushed onward, her pace quickened. Azura sprinted to catch up, soon both making it to the side of the mountain ridge. Both looked at one another before laughing for a moment. “We made it!” Camilla cheered.

“Yeah, we did,” Azura added her grin beaming brightly.

“Hey! Looks like we’re the late ones…” Warren mumbled as he and Chuck sprinted over. The four all shared a laugh before looking at the mountain. “Well, I suppose we should get started,” Warren said before heading towards a large stone gate. The others followed, each one excited to start things off.

Chapter 3 – Harmony Mountain

As the four warriors pushed past the stone gate, they found themselves in a massive entry chamber. Stone walls around on all sides and a single door on the far side of the room. They looked about trying to assess the situation and how to go about things. Warren took the first step forward, clearly wanting to get things quickly. Once he was about twenty feet from the others, he dropped to his knees, suddenly overcome with pain. "Warren!" Azura called as she began to rush to help. She felt someone grab her arm and hold her back. Looking behind her, she saw the cold yellow eyes of the ranger. "Let go, he needs help!" she yelled as she tried to tug free from Camilla's grip.

"Traps. Lots of them," Camilla responded in an even tone as she pulled the sorceress behind her. She crouched and proceeded slowly to the cleric. Her movements mirror that of a wary and cautious animal as it stalked its prey. Camilla came upon the cleric who was trembling in pain and looked for the source of such. She noticed something off about the ground and proceeded to take a closer look. Reaching into her bag, she withdrew a pouch of tools. "I've seen these before. Let's just hope I can get this disarmed," she muttered as she began working over the trap with the tools. It took a few minutes but the distinct click and the cleric finally finding solace, let the ranger breathe a sigh of relief.

Azura and Chuck rushed to Warren and Camilla's side, both following the exact path the ranger had used. "How many more do you think there are?" Warren gasped as he allowed the barbarian to support him.

Camilla shook her head, not knowing. She stayed low to the ground as she proceeded through the room. Her yellow eyes glistened as she looked for any traps that could hinder the group. Each step was taken with caution as the ranger made her way through the room. Every so often she stopped and disarmed a trap, while also dropping a piece of chalk, ensuring the others would be able to follow. As she reached the other side, the ranger let out a breath. “Ok, step exactly where I stepped!” she called back.

Azura nodded as she and Chuck began walking, both helping support the cleric. They moved slowly and stepped in the exact spots where the ranger had stepped and left chalk pieces. Everyone was silent as they moved, each one trying to keep their focus as they moved. Soon they caught up to the ranger who had begun examining some of the text inscribed on the walls. “It’s Drake tongue,” Azura noted as she examined the walls and read through the text.

Warren looked over, still being supported by the barbarian. “Help me over to the wall they’re looking into,” he requested as he glanced up at the barbarian. Chuck growled but assisted with moving the cleric to the wall. Warren read over the text and shook his head. “It’s not Drake tongue. That’s the language of celestial beings,” he commented as he began reading. “Wish to proceed? Thy need the Harmonic heart to enter,” he translated as he read things over.

“Harmonic heart?” Azura questioned.

Warren staggered for a moment before limping toward the door and looking it over. “I read something about four virtues earlier. There’s four of us. So, each of us has a virtue,” he stated as he put his hand against the door. There was a wave of silence before the door opened and granted the four access into the rest of the dungeon. “Guess that means I’m harmony,” he stated as he limped further in.

As Warren began, he felt someone grab his shoulder and pull him back. “Let me take point. You’re still shaking off the effects of that trap,” the ranger stated as she stepped past the cleric, her short swords drawn. It was a long narrow hallway; the group had to move in a line one by one, each one being careful as they stepped. Once everything opened up a bit, they were met with a massive chamber. Stepping out to get a better look, Warren noted the pristine condition of everything. The four made their way down a series of stairs into the chamber and looked about.

Before any of them could react, they were ambushed by six impressive looking demon-like creatures. The first was covered by what seemed like a black mist. Second one more closely resembled a black dog that walked upright with fire in its eyes, around its muzzle and within its ribcage. The remaining four were all red-skinned, with massive gaping mouths, lined with sharp teeth. They were short and had stubby wings, but they were equipped with razor sharp claws.

Chuck quickly swung his axe, trying to hit all six targets. His attack however failed, and the mist demon easily knocked him aside. Camilla slashed out with her blades, but as with Chuck, the attack failed. This time it was the dog-looking demon that lunged forward and easily knocked the ranger to the ground. Snapping its jaws wildly, it was attempting to grab the ranger's throat. Azura had frozen up in fear, her body trembling. The four remaining demons all lunged for her. The sorceress flinched back, unable to do much else in fear. None of the attacks connected. Warren stood between the demons and the sorceress; his shield held in front of them.

Warren began chanting something in elvish, as the words left his lips, his morning star began glowing with a golden aura. He swung out, dispatching the first two demons with no effort. Wasting no time, he rushed forward and dealt with the other two jaw demons. Chuck was struggling to keep up with the black mist demon and was unable to land a hit at all. Camilla, on the other hand, had several burns covering her arms and hands. She was barely managing to keep the dog demon from grasping her throat. The cleric turned to the sorceress. "Snap out of it! Magic and magic aligned weapons as all that affect these things! We have to help them!" he snapped at the young blue haired girl.

She looked at him, trembling. "I… I… I can't…" she muttered, unable to move.

Warren cursed under his breath as he turned his attention to the other two. Without thinking, he rushed forward, his morning star colliding with the mist demon and sending it a few feet back. "You are nothing! Nothing compared to the might of the righteous Celethian!" he called out as his morning star effortlessly landed hit after hit against mist demon. Chuck watched in a mix of confusion and awe as the cleric made the demon seem much easier than it appeared.

Chuck turned to check on the ranger. His eyes narrowed when he saw the amount of burns she had suffered. Charging forward, the barbarian threw himself at the dog demon, knocking it off of the ranger. Camilla winced but quickly got to her feet, drawing her bow as she stood. She breathed heavily as she knocked an arrow and steadied her aim. Chuck and the dog demon were exchanging blows, neither making it easy for the other. The ranger watched and waited for a clean shot. The arrow flew from the bow, splintering through the dog's skull. Chuck took the opening and swung his axe, cleaving the head clean off.

Warren glanced over, chanting something before a small beam of light shot from his shield, annihilating the dog demon. He turned and easily took out the mist demon. The cleric breathed a huge sigh of relief before dropping to his knees. "You alright?" Camilla asked as she walked to the cleric side. She shouldered her bow and held out a hand to help him up.

The cleric rolled his eyes, batting the ranger's hand back. "I don't need your help," he grumbled as he stood. Camilla said nothing as she walked away. Chuck growled at the lack of his axe being able to do anything. Each tended to their own wounds before heading deeper into the dungeon.

Stone lined the floor, and nothing else seemed to be amiss in the dungeon. The four warriors trekked down a narrow hallway before coming upon a massive door. Warren examined the door, noting how there was a damaged and rusted keyhole. "Huh… I doubt any sort of key or lockpick can get through this."

Azura glanced over. "I bet my magic can bust through it," she stated as she readied a spell.

Chuck hefted his axe. "Chuck smash!"

"Hang on, big guy. Let's do this carefully," Azura tried to convince the barbarian.

Soon the barbarian and sorceress were arguing about how to go about breaking through the door. Warren leaned back against a wall, shaking his head. He looked up seeing the ranger crouching by the door, examining the rusted keyhole. Groaning the cleric rolled his eyes. "Didn't you hear me? Thing's not going to budge to some keys or lockpick tools."

Camilla remained silent as she checked it over. She pulled her lockpick kit from her bag and began to slowly ease one of her tools into the lock. Carefully and slowly, she jostled the tool until she heard the faintest click. She continued working the lock over, slowly but surely getting the lock to turn.

After a moment, she glanced at the barbarian and sorceress. "Both of you need to be quiet. I'm trying to work here, and this is very delicate," she commented. The two turned, silence. They were astonished that the ranger had managed to work the lock as she had. Now that it was quiet, Camilla continued. After another faint click, the lock finally came undone. "And we are in," Camilla said softly as she pulled her tools out and tossed them back into the kit. She slid the kit back into her bag before standing and pushing the door open.

Another massive chamber awaited the four warriors. This one, however, was only lit up with torches ignited by green flames lining the walls. Sleeping in the middle of the room was a massive dragon, its green skin glittering like emeralds in the dim light. Quietly the group made their approach. Camilla stayed in the shadows, her longbow ready. Chuck was in the front lines, Warren beside him. Azura hung back, trying her best to not show how intimidated she was.

Unfortunately for the group, the sounds of Warren's heavy armor clanking about, woke the dragon from its slumber. The great beast roared as it leapt up, its roar causing everyone to stagger and feel like the sound itself was damaging their bodies.

"Who enters the lair of Emelic the Great!" the emerald dragon roared.

Warren quickly assessed the situation. He knew the only way forward was to fight this massive creature. Without another word, he nudged Chuck and pointed. The two nodded before rushing forward, great axe and morning star colliding with the dragon's chest. With an outraged roar, Emelic swung out with his claws, sending both men to the side. His roar caused a series of rock slides within the chamber. Azura quickly began casting her magic, firing off two mystical orbs hitting the dragon in his left side. Camilla assessed the scene unfolding and began to formulate her plan. She nocked three arrows and fired each one before nocking another three and firing. All six arrows hit their mark, causing the dragon to bleed.

"Where's the one with dragon blood!" Emelic roared as he twisted his head around, trying to see each member of the party.

Azura took the distraction as her opening and fired off another series of mystical orbs. Chuck rushed the dragon with his greataxe, while Warren swung out with his morning star. All the attacks hit and caused the massive emerald dragon to refocus his attention. With a mighty roar, he began to bring the chamber down upon the group. Warren muttered something in elvish, a protective dome surrounded him. "Everyone, get over here!" he called as rocks fell and splintered the ground.

Chuck growled as he joined the cleric, dragging the sorceress with him. Camilla sprinted over, diving into the protective field as more rocks buried the area. After a few more quakes, the ground and walls seemed to settle. Warren looked out, assessing the damage. Their foe was buried under rocks, only part of his head was sticking out. Unfortunately, the four were also buried with the only thing keeping them from being crushed was the magical field. "So, what's the plan?" Azura cautiously piped up.

"There no plan. We die," Chuck angrily roared as he flung his axe at the barrier.

Warren hated to admit it, but Chuck had a point. While his plan kept them alive, there was no way out. He arched an eyebrow when he saw the ranger investigating the rocks around. "Something on your mind, Hood?" he questioned.

"Yeah, can you expand part of the barrier? If Chuck's willing, I think we can tunnel out from this mess," Camilla replied as she shouldered her bow and pressed against the edge of the barrier.

Warren nodded. "Ok, but I don't get how—"

"Just expand this spot here, not much. We would only need a few inches," Camilla interrupted as she tested the rocks with a light push. "Chuck, I'm going to need your help as I'm not strong enough." Chuck nodded and walked over. He had already seen what the ranger could do but knew she was right, they needed strength. "Ok, Warren, now."

Warren nodded and expanded the barrier a little bit. He and Azura watched as the ranger and barbarian began clearing a path by removing the stone. As they cleared a path, the cleric and sorceress moved to follow with the cleric adjusting the barrier's location every so often. Chuck moved quicker than the ranger, his brute strength coming into play as he easily shoved through the stone and tunneled. It was a long ordeal, but eventually they reached a door. As with most other doors it was locked.

"We don't have much time left on the barrier," Warren said as he strained to keep his magic going.

"Chuck, this one's all you," Camilla responded as she took a few steps back allowing the barbarian to do his thing.

Chuck roared happily as he brought his greataxe around and easily smashed through the door. Once everyone was through the doorway, the barrier that Warren had been maintaining dropped. Everyone was breathing heavily as they slumped over. "Warriors from the Outrealms, heed my call."

Upon hearing the voice, all four began looking around in confusion. Before them stood what appeared to be the spirit of the emerald dragon they had just fought. His eyes reflected a sense of respect and his position shifted as he sat before them. "Your teamwork is poor. But your strength is apparent. The future of this world rests with the four of you. I leave you the Hamonic Emerald. Use it to access the truth," he roared as his body began to fade away. Where the dragon sat, a small emerald brooch remained.

Warren picked up the small trinket and looked it over. "That's one virtue down and three to go," he calmly stated.

Camilla stepped forward, unfolding the map she had drawn up. "I think we should try to find this Western Canyon. Might hold clues about why we're here. And what Emelic meant," she replied as she showed the others the map. Everyone nodded in agreement before heading for the location marked on the map.

Chapter 4 - Valor Canyon

The four adventurers had stopped, taking a break to rest and collect themselves after the ordeal at Harmony Mountain. "What do you think he meant? The future of this world rests on the four of you. What does that even mean?" Azura asked as they sat around a small campfire.

"Not sure. But I've a sinking feeling that we're going to be fighting more gemstone dragons," Warren noted as he looked over the emerald brooch. He wondered why he was chosen as Harmony. His entire life, the life he hid from his new travel companions, he always caused discord. Was this a message that he needed to set his life down a new path?

Chuck grumbled as he checked his bag. "Chuck hungry. Chuck need food!" the barbarian growled.

Camilla smirked as she stood. "I believe that's my cue. I'll be back. Try not to get into too much trouble," she teased before heading out into the wilderness.

The other three sat in silence for a bit, each of them reminded about their hunger from the sounds of their rumbling bellies. They hadn't a chance to collect any food items prior to being brought to this world, and despite the towns they had stopped, they never thought about buying rations for the road. In the faint distance they heard the sounds of some sort of animal yowl in pain before it was silenced.

"Think Hood caught something?" Warren asked, finally breaking the silence.

"If she's even half the shot the Camilla from my world was, it's very likely," Azura noted as she sat, staring at the flames.

Chuck merely grunted as he tossed another piece of wood onto the flames. He hated waiting; he was hungry and wanted food right this moment. In the past, the barbarian had eaten other humanoids for survival. This was no different. He would perish if he did not eat. The sorceress was easier to bring down; all he had to was simply get a hand on her. But the cleric looked like he had more meat on him. The half orc stood and eyed the other two from the group. Before he could make his move, a dagger stabbed the ground by his feet. All three jumped in surprise as they turned their gaze.

"I've seen that look before. Hell, I've probably had that look a handful of times," Camilla said as she dragged an elk carcass over to the flames. She was silent again as she pulled the dagger from the ground and began skinning the massive animal. Everyone gazed in silence as the ranger got the animal tied to a lengthy log and positioned it over the flames. She wiped a bead of sweat from her brow before looking at the barbarian. "You're a big guy, mind turning this? Slow and evenly," she commented as though telling him despite phrasing as a question.

Chuck knew better than to anger the ranger; she had already best him repeatedly. Another would likely damage his ego more than he could take. He turned the log every so often, getting a sear on the meat and bringing the smell out. Warren shook his head. "No seasonings, Hood?" he questioned looking to the ranger that sat to the side sharpening her blades.

She paused mid stroke and glanced up, her yellow eyes barely visible in the low light. "If you've a problem with the meat, with how it's prepared, by all means hunt something for yourself. I've had about enough of your bullshit," the ranger said in the most even tone she had used.

Chuck shook his head. "Chuck think, tiny man not fight scary girl. Chuck think, scary girl win fight," he said as he continued to roast the meat.

Warren grumbled before standing. "Our group clearly needs a leader. One who won't shy away from a challenge. I think I'm best suited as I'm a king where I'm from."

"Chuck think, tiny man bad leader. Chuck say, tiny man not strong," the barbarian responded. He pounded a hand against his chest. "Chuck be leader. Chuck strongest."

"Hang on, being a leader is more than strength," Azura chimed in. "A leader also needs to be smart, knowledgeable."

"And you're that? You're a bloody coward," Warren taunted.

The three bickered about it, none of them willing to back down from their views. Camilla remained silent as she watched the flames dance. She shook her head as she tended the abandoned meat, making sure it did not burn. While the group argued, Camilla finished cooking the elk and began carving it up. She sat listening and watching the argument, eating her portion of elk and taking a drink from his waterskin every once in a while. Rolling her eyes, she finally decided to speak. "None of us are fit to be a leader," she finally stated. All three turned to look at her. "Chuck, you're not that bright. You'd likely lead us into unneeded fights. Azura, you're a coward relying on everyone else. You're likely to run when a fight gets rough. Warren, you lack people skills. You leading would lead to us getting on the wrong side of townsfolk. And me, I don't trust anyone. Can't lead a team if you can't trust them," she stated.

They were silent again. Camilla shook her head, collecting her thoughts again. "For now, let's get our bellies filled, get some rest then head to the next town. We'll need to resupply before taking on whatever is in the canyon," she commented finally getting everyone to see reason in the situation.

The rest of the night was silent as they ate then rested. Warren was restless and unable to let his mind relax. While he did not require sleep, he did need time to let his mind unwind. He could not shake Camilla's words from their leader argument. It was unnerving that she saw through all of them. They had only been together as a team for a few days, and yet she was able to find their biggest flaws like it was second nature. "*Has she survived this long in the wilds because of that? Because of her preceptive nature? And just how is she able to read all of us like that? Just who the hell is she!*" His thoughts danced about his mind as he tried to find some level of rest.

Chuck snored every so often. But his snoring was the least of the strange noises he made. The barbarian also had a habit of smacking his lips in his sleep. There was also the occasional grunt as he rolled over in his sleep. Azura was the quietest as she slept. Her dreams were nothing but emptiness. Every once in a while, she rolled over before curling up tightly, much like a prey animal when at rest.

Then there was Camilla, who seemed to be in a very uneasy rest. She kept tossing and turning, mumbling even, in her sleep. Whatever was going on, it seemed to cause the ranger a mix of pain and fear. Warren arched an eyebrow as he listened to the ranger's uneasy rest. *"What could possibly be causing her that much distress?"* he thought as he listened a bit longer. It finally got to a point where he had to know. Quietly he approached the ranger and put a hand on her shoulder. "Hey, Hood," he began before pausing. He noticed as soon as he had touched her shoulder, Camilla stopped thrashing and seemed to calm down. It was the strangest thing, but he decided to let it go this time. He removed his hand and walked away, sitting back down upon the log where he had been.

Hours passed, and soon everyone was awake and packing up. They were all silent with one another as they headed for the next town. It was smaller than most towns, and the people were mostly elderly or sickened. Warren made his way to the tavern, Chuck following alongside him. Azura spotted a nearby bookshop and went to check it out. She was wanting to expand her knowledge of spells and knew the bookshop likely had what she was looking for. Camilla walked the streets for a while before coming upon the blacksmith's shop. She needed arrows and lots of them. She purchased twelve bundles and hoped it would be enough.

At the bookshop, Azura sifted through dozens of spell books. She knew what she was looking for, but it was a rare spell. While she did not find the one she was looking for, she did find several books that focused on healing magic. She collected the books she desired and went to the counter to make her purchase.

Meanwhile at the tavern, Chuck was once again eating. He devoured plate after plate of food, leaving nothing but bones and inedible scraps. Warren sat at the counter, his right hand wrapped around a glass. His gaze focused on the amber liquid within the glass. He kept seeing visions, memories of the things he had done in his past. Was he really someone who could save others? If their roles were flipped, would he have been so inclined to help if someone had tripped a trap? He chugged down the liquid then signaled for another. A second drink was placed in front of him, and he stared at it, a distant gaze upon his face.

"Only time I've seen someone drink like that is when they're running away from something," the tavern keeper said as he watched Warren. The keeper was an elderly human but looked like he could still fight at a moment's notice. Warren was silent as he continued to stare at the glass. "Young man, if you don't change the error of your ways, you'll always be on the run. Something to think about," the tavern keeper said before going to check on another patron.

"There you boys are!" Azura exclaimed as she rushed over to Warren. She noticed the distant look in his eyes. "Warren, you alright?" she asked as she sat beside him.

The high-born elf turned his attention to her. "Azura… Why? Why do you care about others? What is it that makes you care?" he asked, his voice sounding a bit distant.

Azura thought for a moment. "Well, I might be a coward, have been since I was a child. But my brother, Henry, once told me, you don't have to be brave to have a heart that can care about others. He said I was perceptive on sensing the feelings of others around me. And that I could leave the fighting to him if I focused on healing the hearts of those I met. I try to care for others because it's really all I can do to help. I'm not strong like Henry or Chuck. And I'm not brave like he was, or like you are. And I certainly don't know much about the wilds, like Camilla does. But if I can help heal someone's heart, then I'll do what I can to help. And sometimes, caring for another is all you can do." She paused before glancing to the high-born elf and meeting his gaze. "Sorry I rambled a bit."

Warren merely nodded. He thought about her words, clearly trying to understand better what she meant. To care about another was something she was good at; it was second nature to her. But to him, he lacked that. He lacked the ability to connect with others on equal ground, that much Camilla was right about when they argued the previous night.

Chuck stomped over a low rumble escaped him. "Chuck think caring is weak. Chuck say only strength matters. Chuck seen it before, strong live, weak perish," he stated as he sat on Warren's other side.

"But at some point, something has to stop the flow. Someone has to stop the cycle of the strong praying upon the weak," Azura argued.

"Chuck say doing such breed only weakness. Chuck think, weak must become strong or be prey," the barbarian protested.

Warren shook his head. "It's clear you both have different ideals on this. But surely there must be a middle ground. Is there not?" he muttered under his breath. The other two continued their disagreement, causing Warren to shake his head but smirk slightly. "Guess not," he mumbled.

Camilla walked the streets alone, her mind constantly drifting. She sighed as she sat down on the stone surrounding the central fountain. "I keep having these visions. A life I once lived perhaps? Or a life yet to come?" she spoke softly. She had seen a desert, sandstorms everywhere. The scorching heat was so real, she felt like she had been there. She looked toward the tavern when she saw her traveling companions make their way out.

"Ready to go?" Azura asked, seeing the ranger.

With a small nod, the four headed out. They started their adventure west, knowing whatever was ahead for them was in the western canyon. It was a long journey across ravaged fields and ruined villages. Each one felt something different as they traveled. Soon they came upon what they could only assume was the western canyon. "How do you suppose we enter?" Azura asked as she looked along the rough ground.

Warren studied the terrain for a moment. They would need rope, a very sturdy one at that. He looked to the group; it was likely that the only one who had rope was going to be the ranger. They never saw eye to eye, and worse off, whenever they spoke to one another, they argued. "Hood, any chance you got rope?" he asked.

Camilla looked over before digging through her backpack. She pulled out two large bundles of rope. Each one looked sufficient for the trek below. "About two hundred fifty feet per bundle," she stated as she walked over to Warren. She followed his gaze and nodded. "Understood," she said before setting up two climbing rigs. Chuck growled; if it were up to him, he would have charged down and already been in the heart of the canyon. Camilla tied everything off then nodded to the others. "Should be able to go two at a time down this canyon."

"I'll go first," Warren responded as he approached one of the rigs. "My armor is the thickest. In case there's a fight waiting for us, it'd be smart for the guy who's mostly armor to be the first one down."

"Hard to argue with that logic," Camilla noted as she walked over and began tying things off to the high-born elf. After a few knots and loops, everything was ready. "Right rope gives you more slack and lets you slide down quickly. Left rope will ease your descent and hopefully make things less bumpy," she said as she handed Warren the two ropes. He nodded then began his slow descent down. Every so often, he felt the slight tug of one of the others easing the slack more so he would get snared.

Warren felt his feet touch the bottom and nodded. "Alright, I'm untying myself!" he called up to the others.

Above the others looked back and forth. "Azura, you're next," Camilla said as she got the sorceress ready on the second rig. As she finished, she repeated the same message she had given the cleric. "Right rope gives you more slack and lets you slide down quickly. Left rope will ease your descent and hopefully make things less bumpy," she repeated as she eased more slack for the sorceress to start.

Azura mostly used the left rope, a slow and steady descent not wanting to slip. She noted how the canyon walls looked as she travelled slowly down the side. It took about twice the time Warren took, but soon Azura joined the cleric at the bottom. "Made it!" she called up to the ranger and barbarian.

"Alright, your turn, Chuck," Camilla said as she got Chuck situated on the first rig. "Remember, right rope for speedy descent, left rope for slow and steady," she repeated as she got everything tied off. As he started down, Camilla collected the rope from the second rig and tossed it into her bag. Carefully she eased more slack for the barbarian before feeling the overwhelming tug. He was impatient and constantly using the right rope. Camilla managed to keep up and let out more slack.

"Just you left, Hood!" Warren called up as he and Azura helped get Chuck out of the rig.

Camilla nodded as she got herself situated in the rig. It was going to be tricky without someone at the top to loosen things. She had given out plenty of slack before starting her descent. As she made her way down, she noticed the rope was fraying in certain spots. Not a good sign. She shook her head not wanting to think about the frayed rope. It would be easier if she focused on the task at hand. Thankfully she reached the bottom without much hassle. Warren and Azura helped her out of the rig. Chuck on the other hand was pacing up and down the canyon base.

Camilla nodded her thanks before giving the rope a firm tug to the far left. Almost instantly the rest of the rope came spiraling down. She quickly began bundling the rope back to a single manageable bundle while the others started exploring. "Found our way in!" Warren called from somewhere deep in the canyon. The others rushed to catch up, but once everyone had reached him, Warren indicated a stone with a slot for a hand print. "Just like Harmony Mountain," he stated as he glanced at the others.

Chuck grew even more impatient and slammed his fist against the stone, trying to punch it down. As though resonating with him, the stone gave way and revealed the dungeon ahead. Upon entering the dungeon, the group was greeted with an intense heat. "Hate to break it to you guys, but this heat is likely to kill us if we don't hurry," Warren said as he cast a spell to allow him to watch over everyone's condition.

Camilla nodded. "So, let's do this quickly," she added as she cast an endure environment spell on everyone. It was not much, but it would at least buy them a little more time.

They were in a large round chamber. Nothing looked out of the ordinary, and there was a single door on the far side of the room. Lining the walls were torches lit with orange flames. As Chuck began to stride forward, he felt someone on either side grab his arms stopping him. Warren was on the right, gripping the barbarian's arm, while Camilla was on the left doing the same action. Warren indicated the ceiling. Looking up, everyone noticed the massive ruby dragon hanging above the room. It was hard to tell if it was asleep or just waiting.

Roaring at them, the dragon made it clear that he was ready for combat. "Well, there goes sneaking into the area," Warren noted as he drew his morning star and tower shield.

Azura thought long and hard before readying a blizzard spell. Chuck wasted no time and rushed forward, letting out a war cry as he did so. Camilla drew her bow and nocked three arrows. The dragon dropped down, its claws easily flinging the barbarian to the side. Warren sprinted as fast as he could and put up his shield just in time to block a massive flame spire from hitting the barbarian.

"Arrogant mortals! You do not deserve the gift of life that the great ones have given you! To intrude upon another's domain, with no respect! Such a vile act shall be dealt with without any hesitation," the ruby dragon roared before slamming his front left claw against the ground. The ground shook, and flame spires shot up from parts of the ground. Warren and Chuck were dodging in and out of the spires.

Azura studied the room before unleashing her blizzard spell, hoping to freeze the massive beast. The spell never connected, and the dragon was upon her in a heartbeat. As he reared up to attack, three arrows pierced his chest. A shrieking roar escaped the great beast as he turned his attention to the ranger as she nocked another three arrows. Camilla held her gaze upon the ruby dragon, watching as it launched itself into the air and began circling. Warren growled under his breath as he detected everyone's vitals drop significantly. "Everyone, form up on my position!" he called as he began preparing a healing spell.

Chuck ignored the cleric and instead threw his greataxe at the dragon. "Chuck want coward to land. Chuck want fight!" the barbarian yelled loudly as he drew another greataxe.

Camilla glanced to Azura and nodded. "Get to Warren. I'll cover ya," she stated as she fired off arrows any time the dragon approached her or the sorceress. Azura hesitated but sprinted to the cleric's side; she had already prepared another spell as she reached him. Camilla waited then sprinted down to the others.

"Chuck! Chuck, get over here! If you keep going, I may not be able to heal you!" Warren called out to the barbarian. Chuck ignored the cleric and continued to try to bait the dragon down. With a low growl, Warren shook his head and used the healing spell he had prepared. Once he felt their vitals return to a mostly stable level, the cleric cast a healing field around himself and the area within ten feet of him.

Camilla quickly nocked two arrows and fired in rapid succession of each other. A loud roar was heard from the ruby dragon as it was forced to the ground. "Go for it, Chuck!" Camilla called out as she watched the dragon try to regain its footing.

Chuck rushed forward, his greataxe in hand as he closed the distance. With one mighty swing, he cleaved the dragon's head clean off from its neck. Blood covered the barbarian, and the group watched as the dragon's body collapsed. The ruby dragon was no more. Where its body had been now shimmered a ruby amulet. Chuck growled at the trinket but collected his prize all the same. The ground shook, and the door to the far side of the room opened. Collecting themselves, the four adventurers rushed ahead. The intense heat of the dungeon having taken its toll on them.

As they reached the outside, they felt the rush of cool winds beat down upon them. They looked across the horizon seeing a bright blue flash in the distance. "The far east seems to be next," Azura noted as she glanced at the lands before them.

Chapter 5 - Mystical Beyond

How long had they been traveling? It felt like the western canyon was months ago. Still the adventurers pressed on, over the massive plains that seemed to never end. And through the underground caverns. When they finally arrived at the far eastern region, they were met with a sight that all seemed confused by. It was a lush waterfall with a surreal feel to it. None of them could explain what they were seeing.

"If seek… thy… the Mystical Beyond… present that of the mystic heart," a voice faintly called out to them.

"Just like the previous two," Warren noted as he looked around.

"But I don't see any dungeon entrances," Azura commented as she looked around.

Camilla glanced over from where she had been sitting, her yellow eyes gleaming. "Azura, hold out your hand. Doesn't matter where," she said as she thought about what the voice had said.

Azura hesitated but did so. The area in front of her shifted, revealing a watery looking passageway. "Nice thinking, Camilla!" Azura cheered as she looked ahead.

"Only the mystic heart and one other of their choosing may enter. The others must remain out here," the voice stated.

The sorceress turned to the others. "What do you guys think?"

"It'd be wiser to take Warren," Camilla said reluctantly. "He has healing magic for his focus and his thick armor makes it hard for anything to put a dent in him."

Warren nodded. "As much as I hate agreeing with Hood, she's right."

Azura nodded and stepped through, Warren following behind her. As they emerged on the other side of the watery rift, they found themselves in an elegant looking castle. No words could describe how ornate everything was. Tall pillars acted as supports for the ceiling, and the walls were lined with artifacts that reminded the pair of the sea. As they walked through the hallway, they came upon a balcony. Sitting looking out onto the horizon was a woman, clad in a deep blue dress resembling sapphires; her hair was long and pale sky blue. "Welcome, travelers. This is the Mystical Beyond," she greeted with a warm, motherly smile.

"This place is beautiful," Azura said as she looked around before her eyes met those of the woman.

Warren nodded. "I've never seen anything like this in all my travels," he chimed in.

"You both speak with empty words. I can sense what lies in your hearts. If you wish to claim the sapphire bracelet, you need only complete my trial," she stated as she turned her attention back to the horizon.

"So, we have to best you in combat?" Warren questioned.

"Heavens no! Nothing so barbaric. No for this trial, you needn't do anything. Clear your minds. Empty them of all thoughts. Only then can the trial begin."

Warren and Azura looked at one another before finally agreeing. They closed their eyes and tried to calm their thoughts that had been racing. After several minutes they both heard movement from the woman. She chuckled slightly. "The trial of Taylla the distant has begun," she whispered before listening to their heart beats.

All three were silent for some time. The only sounds were their heartbeats and their breathing. Taylla shifted slightly, clearly picking up on something. "Why do you want the sapphire bracelet?" she asked.

Warren opened his mouth to speak but found he had no voice. Azura hesitated before answering, "We wish the sapphire bracelet in order to proceed with our quest."

"You speak truth and yet your words waver. What is your quest?" Taylla asked.

Azura thought long and hard. She had not the slightest clue what their quest was. She did not even fully know if they needed the sapphire bracelet.

How could she answer with truth but sound confident? "I know not our real quest; we are four adventurers from other worlds. Brought here by some wings of fate, perhaps. But we seek a way home."

Silence filled the room. Azura wondered if she made the right choice in her answer. What other answer was there if she was to speak the truth? "Azura Vaughan, you may open your eyes." Upon doing so, Azura saw a vast castle and dark clouds looming over it. "This is the Abyssal Castle. Long has it been sealed away by the four guardian dragons. Emelic the emerald to guard the north and with it the emerald brooch. Vulcan the ruby dragon was to protect the west and defend the ruby amulet. To the south is the domain of Sharon the topaz and with her is the topaz ring. I am Taylla the sapphire, guardian of the east and holder of the sapphire bracelet," the woman stated as she gazed off into the distance towards the castle.

"Why was Abyssal Castle sealed away?" Azura asked as she followed Taylla's gaze.

"Within the Abyssal Castle is the gateway into the true realm. The realm you and the others have been exploring thus far has been nothing more than an illusionary world to test your hearts and confirm you are the heroes we need to save this world. I believe in your group's strength, teamwork, and wisdom. But your courage has yet to be tested. That would be Sharon's trial." Taylla paused and held out the sapphire bracelet. "Take it, Azura. Find the last guardian and prove yourselves to her. Then and only then can you find the truth," she stated as she watched Azura reach out and take the bracelet.

Azura felt a haze wash over her as she and Warren awoke back where Camilla and Chuck were. "You two ok?" Camilla asked as she checked them over.

The sorceress nodded as she held up the sapphire bracelet. "Next stop is south. One more trial," she said softly.

Chuck grunted not liking the idea of another trial. Warren looked over the etched maps they had been making of the land and pointed. "Looks like we can follow the river south," he noted as he traced his index finger along the river marked on the map.

"Then let's be on our way," Camilla murmured as she shouldered her longbow. She glanced to the river; the glistening water rushed down but there were no traces of life in it. The four adventurers gathered their belongings and headed south, following the river.

Chapter 6 - Instinctive Aether

After following the river for about a week, they finally reached a point where the river vanished. Met with scorching sands, and harsh sun, the four found shelter in an underground cavern. It was too hot to be above ground, but they suspected the underground may also not be inviting. Camilla was on first watch as the others rested. She was paranoid about the desert region. Memories of the last time she was in the desert flooded her mind. The abandonment. The betrayal. It was all still fresh in her mind as she looked around. There was also the constant smell of decay from within the cavern. Rotting corpses did not help with the nightmares she tried to forget. If it was not for needing some artifact from this region, she would have left by now.

"You alright, Camilla?" Azura asked as she walked over. The ranger hesitated but gave a very small nod. "You're lying." The sorceress could easily read Camilla. This was the first time she had seen Camilla genuinely uncomfortable with an area. She wanted to help the ranger but how could she? "Something you want to talk about?"

Camilla hesitated again before answering. "Last time I was in the desert." She paused collecting her thoughts and keeping her emotions in check. "I was to be abandoned by my old team. They were all for it. I… I had outlived my usefulness to them. Ever since, I've always found deserts, any area that resembles one really, makes me very on edge."

Azura reached out, putting a hand on Camilla's shoulder. "That's not going to happen. We're a team. The four of us," she said.

"I've been fed that lie before too. It was by a half lizard person named Roy," the ranger responded sharply.

Silence. It was that awkward silence. Warren sat to the side, listening in and making mental notes to himself. "So, abandonment issues, huh? No wonder you're a loner, Hood," he stated, finally drawing attention to himself. "Anyways, I think there's something further down that we should check out."

"Something as in?" Azura began.

"As in, I think I found our next area to explore," Warren replied. The others nodded as they packed up and moved to follow Warren deeper into the cavern. After about ten minutes of walking, they came upon a large drop off. "On the other side is an opening into some other area. But I can't figure out how we'd get across. I've tried magic but something cancels out my spells," Warren noted.

Camilla studied the emptiness below and area across. She reached into her bag and pulled out several small pieces of chalk. "I wonder..." she murmured to herself as she walked to the edge and reached out with the chalk and tossed a single piece. Sure enough, the small object appeared to be suspended above the ground. "An invisible path?" she noted with curiosity as she took a step. Her foot made contact with something solid. She tossed another piece of chalk, watching as it disappeared into the abyss below. Rotating slightly to her right, Camilla tossed a third piece, this one remaining suspended above the ground. The ranger proceeded to step onto the area where the chalk piece was. Below her, she could hear the rushing of water, as though there was a massive lake below.

Warren, Azura and Chuck watched on as Camilla continued to toss chalk pieces to locate the invisible path. Warren glanced down, his vision barely picking up on something moving in the chasm below. "What is that?" he muttered as he watched the movements.

Azura leaned over, watching the movements. "Whatever it is, it's big. And looks like it's getting ready to—" Before she could finish her sentence, Azura and Warren saw some massive reptile-like creature leap up from the abyss below and knock into the platform where Camilla was. "CAMILLA!" Azura called as she looked to the ranger.

Camilla had been knocked off the platform but had managed to grab onto the edge of it. She reached her other hand up and attempted to pull herself up. But before anyone could react, the platform was struck again, causing the ranger to lose her grip and fall into the watery abyss below. "CAMILLA!" Azura called in horror as the ranger disappeared from view.

Warren pulled Azura away from the edge and put his shield up blocking whatever beast had lunged for them. "Stay focused, we've got a fight on our hands!" he called.

Chuck drew his greataxe and stood ready. "Chuck fight!" he roared as he readied for combat.

The creature sprang forth; it looked vaguely like a gecko but with gills and its size was massive in comparison. Standing roughly twelve feet tall and close to forty feet long the reptile was ready to fight the travelers. Chuck rushed in first, his greataxe leaving a gash in the gecko's front right leg. Before his second swing could connect, the mighty barbarian was thrown back by the lightning-fast tail of the gecko. Azura quickly began casting a barrier spell to block out harm that the beast was capable of. Warren drew his morning star and swung, attempting to hit the beast's body. A sickening crunch was heard, the morningstar had broken a bone.

Chuck was on his feet rushing forward to fight once again. His greataxe swung out taking one of the legs clean off the gecko. A loud shrill roar in pain reverberated throughout the area. Despite the loss of a limb the gecko seemed ready to continue.

Camilla managed to drag herself onto a low resting shore, coughing and spurting as she spat up water. She took a few ragged breaths before looking up toward where she could barely hear combat. Her body ached but she managed to stand. Looking around, Camilla tried to gauge how to proceed. Climbing would take hours. The water was dark and unsettling as there was no way to tell what was swimming around. A faint distorted light caught the ranger's attention. It looked like a ripple, much like the one she had entered when she came to this world. Sticking a hand through, she felt the temperature on the other side was cold. Freezing cold. She pulled her hand back, noticing the snow that had quickly accumulated.

She hesitated, weighing her options one more time. Before she made her decision, a massive claw reached out from the ripple and grabbed the ranger. She was dragged through the ripple, coming face to face with a topaz dragon. The dragon snarled as it looked her over.

"So, you've come for the ring, have you? And alone. Brave but very foolish." The topaz dragon snarled. It pinned Camilla against the ground as it let out a massive roar. She winced; Camilla would have covered her ears had she been able to. "The challenge of riddles has begun."

"What?" Camilla questioned as she arched an eyebrow.

"A hillful, a holefull. Yet you can't catch a bowlful. Of what do I speak?"

Camilla thought for a moment. "Fog."

"Your turn, mortal," the topaz dragon stated.

"Echoes from a shadow realm, whispers of things yet to come. Thought's strange sister dwells in night, is swept away by dawning light. Of what do I speak?"

"Dreams." The topaz dragon laughed. It thought briefly. "She wields the broken sword, and separates true kings from tyrants. Of what do I speak?"

"Mercy," Camilla said with confidence. She had heard that riddle but could not recall from where. She thought for a moment before speaking. "You can touch me. You can break me. You should win me if you want to be mine. Of what do I speak?"

The Topaz dragon laughed. "The heart." It flicked his tail as it adjusted itself. "No mortal has solved this one. I cannot be bought. But I can be stolen with a glance. I'm worthless to one. But priceless to two. Of what do I speak?"

It took the ranger a moment. She murmured the riddle to herself as she thought. "Love." The dragon's disgruntled snarls told her she guessed correctly. She only knew one more riddle. And if the dragon could answer it, that was the end of her. "You have me today. Tomorrow you'll have more. As your time passes, I'm not easy to store. I don't take up space, but I'm only in one place. I am what you saw, but not what you see. Of what do I speak?"

The topaz dragon was taken back. Had she finally stumped the topaz dragon? It snarled deeply as it thought. Its claws clicked against the ground. Its eyebrows showed its agitation. It thought again. "Could you repeat the riddle?" it asked.

Camilla nodded. "You have me today. Tomorrow you'll have more. As your time passes, I'm not easy to store. I don't take up space, but I'm only in one place. I am what you saw, but not what you see. Of what do I speak?" the ranger repeated.

The topaz dragon snarled. "Dreams, again," it said, though its tone lacked confidence.

There was a small smirk from the ranger. "Memories," she corrected.

A defeated growl escaped the Topaz dragon as it lifted its claw from the human. Its scales shimmered brightly before its massive from disappeared. Resting in the snow, where the dragon stood was a ring, silver band and a single topaz encrusted into it.

Camilla slowly stood; she picked up the ring and sighed in relief. Behind her, she could hear the rippling of the portal. Upon stepping through, Camilla was returned to the area where the rest of the group was. "Camilla!" Azura exclaimed as she rushed to the ranger's side.

"Well, I'll be damned, you survived that fall," Warren said as he looked over.

The ranger nodded before pulling the ring from her pocket. With a smile she turned to the group. "Looks like we got the treasure from this area."

"Wait! You found the topaz item?" Warren exclaimed in surprise.

Camilla nodded slowly. Before they could discuss the matter further, the area began distorting and shifting. When it finally stopped, the cavern they were in had been replaced. They were standing outside a massive black castle. Gargoyles adorned the exterior and there were various spikes upon balconies and towers.

"I guess this is the next area," Warren said as he walked ahead.

Everyone followed, the four travelers soon coming upon a large door. There were four idents in the stone. In response, the treasures they held began glowing. Looking over the door, they placed the treasures within the idents. The emerald brooch was placed in the top ident. There was a bright green glow, indicating they were on the right track. Azura looked at the sapphire bracelet before putting it in the right ident. A blue glow began shimmering from the ident. Chuck growled as he stepped forward with the ruby amulet and slammed it into the left ident, causing it to glow a deep red. Camilla was last as she stepped forward with the topaz ring and placed it into the bottom ident. In response it began glowing yellow. Once all four idents were glowing the travelers could hear a humming from the door before the massive stone door opened.

Inside was poorly illuminated, making it difficult to see. Azura was readying a spell when she felt someone put a hand on her shoulder. "Save your magic for whatever's inside," Camilla said as she reached into her bag. She withdrew a small bronze rod; cautiously she snapped the end piece causing the rod to illuminate with light. They could see maybe thirty feet into the corridor but past that was darkness.

"You had those this entire time and you still chose to wear those ridiculous goggles?" Warren questioned.

"I only have a handful of sunrods, and they have a set duration," Camilla argued. She held the sunrod in her left hand, while drawing one of her shortswords in her right. "I'll take point, Warren you—"

"Don't tell me what to do!" the cleric snapped.

Azura rolled her eyes as she moved out of the cleric's way, watching as he took point. Camilla did not protest and merely shook her head before being pushed to the side by the half orc who also wanted to take point. "Have at it, boys," Camilla muttered as she stood next to Azura. She flashed the sorceress a confident wink. "Don't worry, I'll protect you," she said quietly.

"Didn't you once say, *I'm not your Camilla, you're not my Azura*, or something like that? What changed?" Azura teased softly. Camilla just rolled her eyes, not having a good answer.

Chapter 7 - Abyssal Castle

The corridor seemed to stretch for miles as they continued walking. Warren and Chuck stayed in the front, neither of them ever flinching or wavering. Azura walked behind Warren, maintaining a slight bit of distance in case of traps or enemy attacks. Camilla walked beside the sorceress, her left hand still carrying the sunrod, but the light was dimmer than when they started. Finally, they came upon a large room; there were paintings lining the walls and statues of heavily armored warriors. Warren shook his head. "Just like any other noble castle. These paintings are probably of the owner's lineage." He snorted in disgust.

"So, you're saying your castle doesn't have paintings of you or your ancestors all over the place?" Azura asked.

Warren paused. "My ancestors were powerless, weak fools. They lived in fear. I embraced strength and became the most powerful elf in the land. I hang paintings of those who are strong."

"So just himself," Camilla whispered to the sorceress.

Chuck growled as he smashed a statue. "Chuck think noble stupid. Chuck want fight!" he roared loudly.

"Welcome to my master's castle. We hope you enjoy your stay. Allow me to show you to your rooms," a grotesque being stated as they approached. They had a massive hump on their back and walked with a limp. One arm was significantly longer than the other and was covered with warts and his skin appeared to be peeling in some spots. His head was down, and he had several lumps on his head. His ears were elongated and twisted, the right ear looking like part of it had been cut off. His clothing was little more than rag, a green piece of cloth covered his torso and brown pants covered his legs.

As he approached the group, Warren drew his morningstar. "Back you wretched vermin!" he yelled as he readied for combat.

Azura waved her hand, trying to detect any magic about this disfigured man. She flinched back and hid behind Warren. "He's either a more powerful caster than I and able to hide his magic. Or he was born this way and no magic was used," she whispered.

Chuck swung his greataxe threatening to cleave the man. As the weapon came down, the group heard a distinct metal screech. Warren narrowed his gaze. Standing between Chuck and the disfigured man was none other than Camilla. She held her shortswords blocking the greataxe but clearly straining to do such. "He has done nothing to wrong us," she snarled as she deepened her stance slightly. "Perhaps this sir was merely born this way and is in no way against us," she added as she finally managed to push the greataxe back.

The grotesque man bowed politely to the ranger. "I thank you for acting upon my defense. Now please, allow me to show you to your rooms," he said before limping up a flight of stairs.

Cautiously the adventurers followed him. Each making note of the paintings lining the hallway. Upon reaching the first room, the man came to stop and looked to the group. "For the large burly orc," he said as he unlocked the door then handed Chuck the key. Chuck entered the room and looked about. It was large bed chamber, fancy furniture everywhere. As he turned to look to the others, they were already gone.

The next room was about half down the hall from Chuck's and across the hallway. He unlocked the room and handed the key to Azura. "For the beautiful lass," the grotesque servant stated before continuing. Azura's room was spacious and lined with beautiful blue drapery and as with the previous room, large furniture. Azura flinched at how much it reminded her of her room back at House Vaughan.

Warren and Camilla continued to follow the servant as he led them further down the hall. He unlocked another door and handed the key to Warren. "I hope you find the room suitable, good sir," he commented before limping off.

Camilla glanced to Warren, neither showing any regard for the other's safety. Warren's room was huge. It was adorned with gold-colored linens and the bed looked like it was meant for someone twice his size. He made a mental note as to how it reminded him of his room back in Frothcrest.

The final room was at the end of the hall and was the only one with a balcony. When the servant unlocked it, Camilla put her hand on his, preventing him from opening the door. "What's your name? And how did you know we were coming?" she asked but kept her tone civil.

"I am merely a servant. I have no name, kind lady," he replied with a smile. "And my master was expecting you. I was instructed to wait at the stair until our guests arrived. He said there would be five, but I only counted four."

"Just the four. No one else. Will we have a chance to speak with your master?" she responded, returning the smile. Though it was easy to tell her smile was forced.

"In time. He is finishing up one of his experiments but will meet with all of you at dinner in an hour," he said before slowly turning the doorknob. The room was smaller than the others and simpler looking. The balcony overlooked a large garden and had a perfect view of the sunset. Camilla was taken back by the view and simple nature of the room. She looked to the servant and saw him offering her the key.

"Thank you," Camilla said as she took the key. She heard the servant begin to leave and called out. "You said you have no name. What sort of master doesn't allow you to have one?"

"I haven't needed one," he replied humbly.

"If it's alright, might I give you one? I'd hate to be calling you by other terms," Camilla spoke, her words hinting to some level of emotions she was containing.

"I do not require such, but if it will put you at ease," the servant replied.

"You remind me a lot of someone I once knew. I'd like to call you Darios, if that's alright," she hummed.

He said the name to himself a couple of times before smiling. "A name I shall wear with honor. Thank you, kind lady," Darios said before bowing and taking his leave.

Each of the adventurers settled into their room; it was nice to have a bed and not be sleeping on the ground again. About an hour later, they were called to the dining hall and led there by Darios. The dining hall, like many of the other rooms, was massive and fancifully decorated. Huge draperies hung from the ceiling, each depicting some sort of warrior or battle. Darios went around pulling the chairs out for the group and pushing them in once they had sat down. He even offered to tie their napkins around their necks for them. Warren and Azura both took him up on such. Whereas Chuck growled and slammed his fists down upon the table. Camilla politely declined and chose to have her napkin rest on her lap.

Darios bowed before them and took his leave. After a few very short minutes a noble looking man entered. He was clad in white and gold attire, a fancy shirt, long pants and brown boots. He wore an impressive white and gold coat over his shirt. "My apologies for not meeting with all of you sooner. I ask that you forgive such. My name is Arl Uldritch Von Varley," he introduced as he took his seat at the head of the table.

"Finally, the noble of this manor graces us with his presences," Warren sneered as he looked over. "I'm King Warren Couseland, hero of Frothcrest and leader of this band of misfits," he added.

Azura politely bowed her head as she had been taught to do. "I am Lady Azura Vaughan, soon to be queen of Kardax with the fall of the Blood Circle."

Chuck growled before slamming his fists against the table. "Chuck want food! Chuck hungers!"

"Soon, my friend, soon," Uldritch replied as he signaled to one of the dining staff. "How much longer on the food? We don't want to keep our esteemed guests waiting."

"Five more minutes, your grace," the woman said as she went into the kitchen.

Uldritch turned his attention to Camilla and smiled. "My apologies, young miss, I failed to have heard your name."

Camilla felt uneasy. She was never one to partake in fanciful dinners with nobles. She recalled always being like the servant woman, tending to the affairs of the food and preparing for such but never taking part. "Camilla, no last name or title. Just Camilla," she replied as she slowly inched her chair back. "My apologies, Arl Varley, I must take my leave. I am not feeling quite right and should rest it off," she said as politely as she could before taking her leave and departing from the dining hall.

"I do hope you rest off whatever aliment. I'll have Servant bring you something much easier on the body for food." Uldritch called as he watched the ranger depart. His attention returned to the group. "Was there a fifth? My vision said there would be five of you."

"Nay, good sir. Just four," Warren chimed in.

An extravagant feast was brought forth and laid out upon the long table. The servants served food and drinks to the adventurers and the Arl. Everything was loud with Chuck noisily devouring food and drink. Uldritch, Azura and Warren talked politics and social standings. "I see, so the group known as the Blood Circle plagued Kardax and nearly brought the kingdom to its knees," Uldritch said as he listened to Azura's tales.

"Henry, my brother, was supposed to be the one to take up the throne, but Narcian killed him before he could. Narcian killed many, including several dukes, the king, Henry and Camilla," Azura explained.

"I don't understand? You say he killed Camilla, and your travelling companion—"

Azura held up a hand cutting off Uldritch. "They are different Camillas. It's been confusing to wrap my head around, but her actions are very different from my Camilla."

"I see. And you. Sir Couseland, I'd like to hear about your endeavors," Uldritch stated.

"Ah, where do I begin? My homeland, Frothcrest, was plagued for hundreds of years by a blue dragon. This beast was so massive he could consume entire towns by merely inhaling them. My clan lived in fear and refused to get involved. Then our leader was murdered by the dragon's champion. I took up my morningstar and with countless others set off to end the dragon. However, only myself and Thomas Hemmington survived the ordeal. I was named king and Sir Hemmington became my elite guard."

Uldritch nodded his head. "I see. Such courage and strength, I must admit that sounds like what was best for your homeland if you were the only one to rise up. I believe when tyranny takes hold, it is up to the people to rise up and fight," he explained.

"You've heard our stories, mind telling us yours, Arl Varley?" Azura asked.

"Certainly, Lady Vaughan. Let's see, I suppose I should start at the beginning. I was a young noble training and studying to take up the title of

Arl when my father passed. But before that could happen, the kingdom fell into chaos. War broke out and between the starvation and killings, there was no way I could make an effective ruler. So instead, I trained in combat and joined the military. My twin sister took up the studies to be the political head. But she was slain by the very villagers she was trying to help. When the war ended about ten years after such, I took up the title of Arl and served the crown where I could. Many of the other provinces had no nobility to survive so those lands became part of the Varley province. As it stands, only the king and royal family house more power than the Arl Varley," Uldritch explained as he sat back. He shook his head and smiled. "Enough about me though. What brings you here? I'm sure none of you would've left your lands and titles behind to start this adventure."

Azura, Warren and Chuck glanced at one another before all turning to Uldritch. "We were each brought here upon hearing different promises," Warren explained. "I was promised a land where I could test my strength and not be bored."

"Chuck told he get fights!" Chuck roared proudly.

"And I was promised a chance to make right the wrongs that befell Kardax during the Blood Circle's siege," Azura said.

"I see. These are unusual promises. Perhaps the work of the dark wizard, Arcanist. He's been known to promise travelers various things, but none have ever succeeded in his tasks and end up dead. Please feel free to stay as long as you wish. My staff and I shall accommodate you as much as we can. If you'd like, I can send word to the king and perhaps we can get you all home," Uldritch said before taking a drink from his goblet.

"We would appreciate that, Arl Varley," Warren spoke on behalf of the group.

"My liege, it is time," a servant in a suit stated as he knelt before Uldritch.

"My apologies, friends, but I have matters to attend to. Eat as much as you wish and when you are finished, the servants will clean up. Feel free to explore the castle, I only ask that refrain from exploring the basement. It is where I conduct matters for the king," Uldritch said before leaving the three adventurers.

Camilla could not shake the feeling; it was one she knew well. The feeling of being led astray. She felt as though her mind was in haze as she walked back to her room. She paused when she saw Darios making his rounds. "Darios?" she questioned as she approached him.

"Kind lady, I apologize if I have startled you," Darios replied politely with a bow. "Master Uldritch asked me to do my rounds as I always do. And I cannot refuse my master."

The ranger nodded. "It's alright, I could use some company back to my room. I'm not feeling quite right and do not wish to take a wrong turn within this castle."

Darios smiled as he limped ahead. "Right this way, kind lady."

"Please, just call me Camilla," she replied as she followed the disfigured servant. As they walked, neither attempted to make any sort of talk. Camilla could not shake the feeling the entire time. When they reached her room, she unlocked the door and entered. "Thank you, Darios."

"Always a pleasure to serve. And Camilla, do be careful, this castle is a very different place when the moon rises," he said before departing.

"What do you mean?" Camilla called after him.

"You'll see," Darios replied as he limped away.

Camilla entered the room and locked the door, her uneasy feeling gnawing at her even more. Part of her was starting to believe it was merely fatigue from the travels and the stress of being with another party and wondering when they would leave her like the rest had. She collapsed onto the bed and closed her eyes trying her best to just rest and ignore the feeling gnawing at her mind.

It was late when the others retired to their rooms. The moon was illuminating the night's sky and flooding through any windows. The castle was eerily quiet. At some point Warren left his room, the quiet bothering him significantly. He walked about until he found himself confused and distorted. He heard a voice beckoning him so he stepped forward. He pushed open a door and found himself in a completely empty round room. Warren rubbed his eyes as he looked around. A single mirror caught his attention. It had not been there before. As he approached it, he heard a voice nagging him forward.

Looking into the mirror, Warren saw only his reflection. But there was something very wrong. The skin was purple, the eyes were red. Waren gasped, falling backwards. The reflection did not fall; it stayed standing, looking down at him as he tried to move away from it. Then the reflection stepped forward, coming out of the mirror causing the mirror to vanish.

Warren climbed to his feet and drew his morningstar and tower shield. The shadow did the exact same thing. Its weapons looked identical to his own. He began casting an aura of healing around himself. The shadow smirked as it lunged forward, the morningstar slamming into Warren's side. He winced as he brought his shield around and used a shield bash to force some space between himself and the shadow. To his horror and disbelief, the shadow had not moved; it countered his shield bash with one of its own, keeping him on the defensive.

The cleric was not so easily swayed. He collected his thoughts before launching another attack. This time his morningstar smashing into the shadow's stomach. He heard the sickening squelching of organs being damaged. As he moved to strike again, the shadow was already attacking, the morningstar slammed into wrist. The sound of bone breaking resonated within the chamber. Warren cried out in pain as he dropped his morningstar. He ducked behind his tower shield and grabbed the weapon with his left hand. He was not used to fighting left-handed but had little options.

The shadow lunged forward again, this time slamming its shield into Warren's chest. He winced but managed to counter with his morningstar colliding with the shadow's ribcage. Bones splintered as he made impact. He winced and glanced at his wrist; there was a distinct rot look to it and he knew he had to end this fight quickly. Warren lashed out frantically swinging his morningstar at the shadow. He managed two solid hits before stumbling back. The shadow howled in pain as it limped back. Warren smirked as he rushed forward. His morningstar dealt a finishing blow, crushing the shadow's skull.

He breathed heavily as he swayed. The rot was taking a toll on him. His healing aura could keep his stamina up, but the rot tore through his body's stamina faster than it could be restored. Warren collapsed, a heavy thud as he hit the ground. His vision was fading in and out. The last thing he saw before everything went dark were a pair of brown boots.

"One."

Azura awoke with a sickly feeling in her stomach. She sat up and breathed heavily. Was it a nightmare she saw? No. She knew something was wrong. Cautiously she opened her door and left the room. As she walked, looking for somewhere to relieve herself, she heard a voice calling her. "Warren, is that you?" she called as she followed the sounds. "Warren?" she called.

After some time of walking, Azura found herself in a large square room with a single mirror at the center. She looked around puzzled as she stepped further in. One step in front of the other, Azura approached the mirror and stared. Looking back was her reflection, but there was something very wrong. Staring back at her were deep red eyes and the skin of her reflection was a deep purple. Azura screamed as she fell backwards in shock. To her surprise the reflection stepped out of the mirror and held a bloodlust look in its eyes. Azura quickly fired off a Magic Bolt. It was a basic spell, but it was the first one she could think to use.

The shadow took the attack but seemed unfazed. As Azura rolled to the side and got to her feet, she was hit with a Cone of Flames. She winced and countered with her own Cone of Ice. She and the shadow fought, exchanging spell blasts back and forth. Azura unleashed the newest spell she had learned and was still practicing. Hellstorm. It was a complex spell, but she managed. Fire, ice, lightning, acid and sound blasts rained down, striking the shadow. Azura clutched her sides in pain from the recoil she took from the spell's side effect. She smirked when she saw the room was empty. It, however, was short lived as the shadow clapped slowly stepping out of a barrier field. The shadow smirked at its exhausted foe and retaliated with its own Hellstorm. Azura cried out in pain as she was bombarded with fire, ice, lightning, acid and sound blasts. When the smoke cleared, Azura was on the ground, unconscious and badly wounded.

"Two."

Chuck was roaming the corridors of the castle. He was restless and wanted to fight something. He smashed a few statues as he explored. "Master Uldritch asks that refrain from destroying the statues," Darios said as he approached Chuck.

"Chuck want fight! Chuck restless!" the barbarian yelled loudly, his spittle sticking to Darios's face.

The servant withdrew a handkerchief from his tattered green shirt and wiped his face. "Such droll behavior. I'll ask you again, please refrain from—"

"It's alright, Servant," Uldritch said as he walked over. He nodded to the servant. "Leave us," he stated as he waved the servant away. Once Darios had limped off, Uldritch returned his attention to the barbarian. "So, you wish to fight? I do have a training room; you can fight to your heart's content against the other warriors who train there," he said with a friendly smile. Chuck nodded and followed Uldritch. Once they reached the room, Chuck stormed past Uldritch and charged into the room, not even taking time to look about it. Uldritch smirked as he closed the door and walked away. He could hear the door lock behind him as he walked.

Chuck slammed face first into a single mirror in the room. When he shook off the slight daze it caused him, he saw his reflection dragging itself out of the mirror. He roared a battle cry at the shadow and drew his greataxe. The shadow returned the war cry and drew an identical greataxe.

The barbarians fought, their greataxes slamming against one another. Blood spraying across the room and covering the floor. Chuck lunged forward but was met with a clean swing hitting his abdomen and sent to the ground. As he tried to get his feet under him, the shadow brought its greataxe down hard on the half orc's back. Blood sprayed from the wound, covering the shadow's face. The shadow brought its greataxe down again, this time forcing Chuck to the ground completely. Chuck tried to get up one more time only to feel the greataxe plunge into his back a third and decisive time. "Stay down!" the shadow roared.

Chuck's eyes felt heavy as he collapsed. The last thing heard was a familiar voice. "Three."

Camilla could not sleep. She laid awake staring at the ceiling when a knock sounded from her door. She stood, grabbing one of her shortswords as she did so. "Who's there?" she asked, keeping the closed.

"My apologies, Camilla, but I have some grave news," Darios spoke.

Camilla arched an eyebrow. "Speak, Darios," she responded, still not opening the door.

"Your friends have been captured. My master intends to experiment on them, possibly even kill them. He wishes the same to you. I'm warning you, because you were kind to me," Darios stated.

Camilla stood in silence for a moment. That feeling she had earlier, it was accurate. She walked to where she had left her bag and grabbed it. After putting on her green tunic and gloves, she quickly put her boots on and slung the bag over her shoulder. She finally opened the door and looked at Darios. "Where are they? My traveling companions," she demanded, her voice reflecting no emotion.

Darios hesitated but led Camilla to a tunnel that descended to the basement. "He tricked them each down there where they were captured. Please, reconsider this choice, Camilla. You needn't be captured as well," Darios pleaded.

Camilla walked down the tunnel until she came to a door. She kicked the door open and entered the triangular room. She pulled her goggles over her eyes, allowing her to see a little better in the darkness. There was a mirror at the center of the room, but other than that it was empty. She took a deep breath before murmuring something in the other language she had been prone to using. As the words left her lips, a blue glow formed around her bag, clothes and weapons. She set her bag and weapons to the side, before undid her tunic and other garments leaving her in nothing but her small clothes. She left her clothes with her bag and approached the mirror.

As she looked, she saw a reflection of herself staring back. Purple skin, red eyes and a very angry expression. "So, this was how he captured them?" Camilla murmured as she watched the reflection. The shadow shambled out of the mirror, naked aside from small clothes, just like her. Camilla darted back, avoiding a punch. She smirked as she said something under her breath in the other language. On command, her clothes, gear and weapons flew to her and easily were exactly where they should be. The shadow looked confused, realizing it was suddenly at a disadvantage. Camilla wasted no time and lunged forward using her shortswords.

The shadow wailed and howled in pain as it was easily bested. Upon seeing the shadow collapse, Camilla breathed a sigh of relief. She arched an eyebrow when the shadow's body bubbled and blistered. Soon where the shadow human had been now stood a massive dragon. The beast roared at Camilla as lightning began shooting from its mouth. "You've got to be sodding kidding me!" Camilla yelled as she barely dodged the lightning. She rolled under the claws of the dragon and came up under the beast.

Without thinking, Camilla dug her shortswords into the dragon's exposed underbelly. The deafening roar echoed through the chamber. A tail strike sent the partly dazed ranger into a wall. As she recovered, Camilla saw a lightning blast heading her way. She brought her shortswords up, barely managing to block the worst of the attack. She staggered, her body showing some electrical burns on her hands. The dragon lashed out with its claws trying to cut down the ranger. She was fast, barely avoiding the assault. She was unable to get in close to deal damage with her shortswords. Every attempt she made was met with claws and bite attacks.

Pushed to the edge of the room, Camilla drew her longbow and smirked. "Whatever it takes!" she called as she unleashed a volley of arrows. The dragon roared as sixty arrows pierced its skin. Camilla saw her second chance and went for it. She readied her bow and unleashed another volley. "I'm not about to stop here," she muttered before releasing the bowstring. Another sixty arrowed peppered the dragon.

The air was still. A wave of silence lingered heavily. Finally, the sound of several small explosions was heard, each arrow detonated within the dragon's flesh, blowing it apart and leaving a shadowy mist in the room. Camilla breathed a sigh of relief as she watched the mist fade. She shouldered her longbow and studied the room. To the far side was a single door, opposite from where she had entered. She made her way to the far door and shoved it open.

Ahead of her was a long and narrow bridge suspended above what seemed to be an endless abyss. Carefully the ranger made her way across the bridge.

Below she saw the flickers of green flames. On the other side of the bridge was a portal which seemed to be the way out of this castle. She glanced down toward the green flames again. Against her better judgment, she leapt from the bridge. The fall was not as far as she thought it was and she easily landed on her feet. Looking around, she found herself in a large room. Her yellow eyes gleamed in the dimness as she took in everything. Standing at the far side of the room was a hulking colossal sized creature; it was hard to tell in the dim light, but Camilla could see distinct claws and wings. In front of it was a humanoid looking creature; even at a distance, it looked about Camilla's own height. She drew her shortswords, steeling herself for the fight. Behind the pair, chained to the wall were the other three from the group. She took a step forward causing the humanoid to turn to look.

Though his clothes were different, there was no mistaking the man. It was Arl Uldritch Von Varley. "I didn't expect anyone to be able to defeat their shadow selves. And yet you did. You warriors of the Outrealms believe you can be heroes? Why, because you saved your worlds! This world doesn't need heroes! It needs order! My master entrusted me with ensuring they don't need to get their hands dirty. Allow me to demonstrate my power. Then you can decide if you want to fight or flee," he stated as he touched the ground.

Camilla leapt back narrowly dodging the rearranging floor. She landed with ease on her feet as she watched the scene unfold. The floor had completely rearranged to resemble spikes and began shooting every which way. Camilla skillfully brought the shortsword in her left hand up and spun it quickly deflecting the assault. Once the debris cleared, she saw the cold look in Uldritch's eyes. "Final warning," he said as he watched her.

"I didn't come this far to back down. Release the others!" Camilla responded as she deepened her stance.

Uldritch laughed before glaring at Camilla. "These flawed warriors? They don't deserve the right to exist! I will use their powers to exterminate any future outrealm warriors," he stated before unleashing another wave of splintering spikes.

Camilla barely dodged the spikes this time, the fight had begun. She knew everything was on the line here and now. It was not new for her, the rush of combat. The heart racing of kill or be killed, she knew this feeling too well. Her senses heightened; her blood raced. She rushed in close and unleashed a flurry of whirlwind like strikes using both blades. She watched as each strike drew blood from her foe. He in turn would use point blank Splinter Spikes to pierce vital areas on the ranger. Her right side, near the lung. It would bleed out quickly. Her left thigh. It would slow her movements, and her speed was vital to her attacks. Her stomach. The most critical wound, it was a death sentence for even the strongest adventurers.

The ranger leapt back, before rushing again. Both shortswords shredded through the defense Uldritch tried to mount. He smirked at her, as he touched the blades, instantly shattering them. Camilla's gaze narrowed as she rolled backwards to avoid the next attack. As she came up in a crouch, she drew her longbow. Her breathing was ragged at best as she knocked three arrows and fired in rapid succession. Uldritch dodged each arrow before unleashing his Splinter Spikes again. Camilla was hit hard; spikes had ripped through most of her body, blood pooling everywhere as she struggled to stay on her feet. She brought her bow up, using it to shield herself from Uldritch's grasp. The bow splintered at his touch, leaving the ranger weaponless. Uldritch smirked as he kicked her to the side.

"Do you see how weak you really are?" he taunted as he watched her struggle to her feet. All injuries he had instantly healed as he touched his wounds. "You see, I can put myself back together faster than you can hurt me."

Camilla got her feet under her before muttering a spell under her breath. Having grown up in the wilds, she had learned to be self-reliant, which meant knowing some level of magic. Her stomach and thigh wounds healed, the two most critical ones no longer playing a factor in this fight. She watched as the floor splintered again and again. Her movements were slowed from the blood loss, but she managed to dodge the worst of the attacks. *"How do I win this? No weapons, and he heals so fast. One hit, gotta do this with one hit,"* she thought as her eyes darted around and she dodged in and out of each attack.

Uldritch unleashed another wave of Splinter Spikes. He laughed as he watched the ranger struggle to keep ahead of his attacks. He managed to land a few hits to the ranger, nothing critically life threatening but they would certainly hinder her fighting ability. "Let me make it clear. You're going to die down here." He cackled as one of his Splinter Spikes impaled Camilla's left side just below the lung.

She staggered, coughing out blood. Everything was hurting and she was losing a lot of blood. Camilla glanced down at her gloved hands. "*It might be my only option. Embrace those...*" she thought as she returned her attention to the sorcerer. Another rush of Splinter Spikes put Camilla on the defensive. She dodged in and out, trying to close the distance between her and Uldritch. "*One hit. I have to do this with one hit,*" she reminded herself. As she moved, Camilla ripped her gloves off and rushed forward. "You're finished!" she growled as her right claw lashed out, tearing through Uldritch's throat.

He struggled; his breathing was weak. Camilla ripped her claw upward, her fist wrapped around bone. As she did so, Uldritch's spine was torn from his body. The body went limp, dropping to the ground as the ranger mercilessly tore the rest of the spine out. She was breathing heavily, blood soaked most of her clothes. Her claws wavered, dropping the spine before she collapsed. Her body felt heavy, her eyes struggled to stay open. Camilla heard someone yell her name, but she was too tired to recognize who it was. Her yellow eyes closed as she accepted what was to come.

The sound of birds chirping filled her ears. Then there was the bright sunlight coming in from a window. Was she alive? How? Camilla slowly opened her eyes and glanced around. Her body was covered in bandages, but she was in fact alive. "Camilla!" Azura's voice broke the softer sounds. The young sorceress was ecstatic to see the ranger was awake.

"What happened? I remember defeating Uldritch, but after that—"

"You really should be resting," a brass-colored dragon-like person stated as he walked over. His silver eyes shimmered in the light. "I am Arcanist, the one who summoned the four of you here. You were able to brave the cardinal dungeons and Uldritch's Abyssal Castle. You're brave and strong, I will give the four that."

"It's thanks to Arcanist that you still draw breath, Hood," Warren chimed in. He walked over then paused, rubbing the back of his head. "We got a lot of questions for you though. Starting with those," he added as he pointed to the still exposed claws.

Camilla flinched slightly. "I'm still not sure how to explain them. But it was early on, our first adventure to be exact."

Warren clearly did not like the answer but accepted it as much as he could. "Alright, I suppose we can accept that. So then, how about how you dealt with your shadow and Uldritch? The rest of us had a hard time with our shadow copies."

"I can answer that one, young man," Arcanist cut in. Everyone turned their attention to the brass reptile. "Did any of you ingest any food or drink from Uldritch or his staff?" He paused, watching at Warren, Azura and Chuck nodded. "Then I'll assume Camilla did not." He received nods. "The last set of adventures, Uldritch had poisoned the food and slain them using shadow versions of themselves. It's a trick he uses. And before you ask why I could not do anything about him, his magic prevents anyone from entering his domain unless he wishes them to or unless they gathered treasures from the cardinal dungeons."

"Arcanist, I'm assuming you've a lot of magic," Camilla began.

"Yes, very skilled with such."

"Can you use magic to reforge my weapons?" Camilla asked.

Arcanist's brows furled but he nodded. "It will take time, but I can. You should consider yourself lucky that your companions collected the pieces of your blades and bow before getting here. Otherwise, we'd be starting over from scratch on your weapons."

"So, you summoned us here, why?" Warren questioned.

"Yes, about that. There is a being known as Timer Eater; they rule this world, and if they have their way, they'll rule or destroy all worlds. Time Eater has the ability to distort time and space; they've been bringing worlds together and either destroy them or fuse them into this world. My magic is useless against Time Eater. The only thing I can do is summon heroes from other worlds to fight on this world's behalf," Arcanist explained as he grabbed a book from one of the many bookshelves. He thumbed through before setting the book on the side table.

"Time Eater did not originate from this world. No, their power was brought about by fusing with other versions of themself from other worlds. But they were once a hero I summoned to help end the reign of the first tyrant who seized control on this place. Unfortunately, Time Eater became obsessed with power; they managed to summon versions of the being they were from other parallel worlds and fused those other versions into themself. And before long the power-hungry Time Eater was born. It's been so long, I've forgotten Time Eater's true identity," Arcanist added as he showed them the book.

Warren shook his head. "So, you expect a powerhouse cleric, an idiotic barbarian, a—"

"You want a warmongering cleric, a power-hungry barbarian, a timid sorceress and distrustful ranger to defeat a being who is basically a god?" Camilla interrupted.

Arcanist sighed. "I knew it was a longshot, but you're all I've got. Please. If Time Eater succeeds, it will be more than this world consumed. It will be all worlds."

"Looks like I'm saving Frothcrest, again," Warren said.

"Chuck want fight! Chuck fight time god!" Chuck roared.

"I can't let Kardax be destroyed. I'll fight for my people," Azura added.

Camilla hesitated. She did not owe anyone anything. She let out a sigh. "Fine, whatever. A battle between a god and mortals, sounds like fun," she responded, trying to suppress a grin.

Arcanist smiled. "Thank you. As I said, it'll be some time before I have Camilla's weapons ready again. You're all welcome to stay and explore. I have many books about the land, I'd advise you all to read up and get familiar with things so you're prepared when the time comes."

Chapter 8 - A World's History

It had been two weeks since they came to Arcanist's tower. Camilla had finally made a full recovery and was sharpening her shortswords while Arcanist addressed the group. "In order to defeat Time Eater, you'll need to find the five legendary weapons, the six relics and the eight virtues. They won't be easy to find I can assure of that. While I have no information on where any of these can be found, I'd assume they would be well protected. Hopefully Time Eater's forces haven't found any of them, otherwise all hope is already lost," Arcanist stated as he unrolled a map onto the table where they were gathered.

"Hang on, legendary weapons? Relics? Virtues?" Warren questioned as he glanced down at the map.

"Yes. Five weapons, six relics and eight virtues. I know there are areas scattered about the land protected by otherworldly magic. I've been able to pin down one location but not much else about it," the brass reptile stated as he placed a green block on the map. Looking over the map, the location was well hidden in a deep forest. "I don't know what you'll find there, but it would be worth investigating. You'll have to travel either across mountains or under those mountains to reach that particular forest."

They studied the map again, planning out their options. Warren shook his head. "Across and over mountains is more dangerous and takes much longer. We'd be better off going under the mountains and through that area," he stated as he looked things over.

Camilla looked over and nodded. "Agreed. Underground we don't have to worry too much about the weather of the mountain region. Any nearby villages or towns where we can prepare and supply up for such?"

Arcanist nodded. "If you take this route," he paused as he pointed out a set route, "you'll pass through three small villages and one fairly decent sized town. Should be able to resupply as you travel to the forest," he added as he placed four small blocks along the route."

"Chuck hope there fight! Chuck want combat!" the barbarian roared as he pounded his chest.

Azura closed the book she had been reading. "Thanks to Arcanist's library, I've picked up a few more spells. Hopefully I'll be more useful now," she added as she set the book to the side.

Camilla cleaned off her shortswords then sheathed them. "So, we head out come daybreak, yes?" she asked looking to the others.

"Sounds like a plan," Azura said as she went to pack her bag.

Warren nodded in agreement then left to check his supplies. He made notes of what he would need to resupply along the path to the underground. Chuck grumbled before sulking off to check over his few supplies. Camilla looked over her longbow, doing maintenance upon it. She sighed as she turned to her bag and checked over her supplies.

Arcanist smiled and nodded at how the adventurers had a plan. He pulled a thin stone from his robes and handed it to Warren. "Here, this will allow me to contact you as I gather more information as to the locations you'll need to investigate."

Warren took the stone and slid it into his pocket before returning to his gear and ensuring it was in perfect condition. He saw everyone was doing the same and nodded at the team's dedication to the task. He noticed Camilla step outside and decided to follow the ranger. He needed to know what she was up to.

Camilla looked over the targets that surrounded the exterior of Arcanist's tower. She tested her longbow's draw strength and nodded to herself. In rapid succession nocked and fired three arrows. Two hit their marks at the center, but the third arrow was off and missed. She collected the arrows then performed the same actions, adjusting her stance slightly. The first and third arrows made their marks, but the second missed.

"Your left shoulder wavers slightly. Meaning the muscles are still recovering," Warren said as he walked over.

"Huh?" Camilla looked over and stared at the cleric.

He walked up and placed a hand on her shoulder, a pale blue glow leaked from his hand into her shoulder. Warren scoffed slightly before pulling away and turning away. "Try shooting now," he stated.

Camilla nodded and once again in rapid succession knocked and fired three arrows. This time all three hit their marks. She smirked as she turned to the cleric. "Thanks, Warren," she said as she bowed her head slightly. He scoffed as he walked away. "I really can't read you at times. Sometimes, I swear you're looking out for everyone. And other times, you don't give a damn," she noted.

Warren paused and iooked over his shoulder. "I don't give a damn about you, Hood. But we're travelling together, which means you'll be watching my back. An injury could lead to death. Which means one less set of eyes watching my back. Think of yourself as my side kick," he growled.

Camilla began laughing as she shouldered her longbow and collected her arrows. "If that's what you need to say to keep you feeling better." She paused her laughter and gave the cleric a faint smile. "I think you really do care about everyone," she said as she turned to go inside. Her footsteps paused and she looked over her shoulder at Warren. "Don't worry, I'll keep your secret," she added before going back inside.

He glared in the ranger's direction before rolling his eyes and turning away. "Damn it. She's wrong. I don't care. They're just pawns," he added before kicking at the ground. He shook his head before thinking back to when he was chained to the wall at Uldritch's castle.

"Why is she fighting so hard? She can't win against him," Warren said as he barely managed to keep his eyes open.

"That's just how Camilla is. Even the Camilla I knew, she would fight to her last breath to protect others. While they're different people, that much is still the same," Azura replied, her voice greatly strained as she tried to lift her head to look.

Warren could barely see the fight ongoing. The spikes impaled the ranger's left side. He winced watching. He knew that blow, on top of everything else, that would be the blow that ended things. "She's lost too much blood. She should just retreat," he murmured watching the ranger continue to fight, continue to struggle.

"Damn it! Is it because I owe her?" he yelled as he shook the memory from his head. Warren angrily entered the tower and saw everyone was turning in for the night. They all needed to be well rested if they were going to start this journey. He walked to the bed he had been using and collapsed. There were too many thoughts racing through his head.

Azura was already sound asleep. Chuck's snoring indicated he was sleeping very soundly. Camilla was laying on her bed, but she had yet to find sleep. Her eyes were closed, but the pleasant sleep refused to come. She kept seeing the dragon she fought after defeating the shadow copy. Why a dragon? It plagued her thoughts. As she slowly began to drift into sleep, it was not a peaceful state.

Harsh desert winds, raging sandstorms. The intense heat. And yet none of it bothered her. She walked along, dragging something behind her. She smirked as she walked, clearly proud of whatever had been done. She came upon an underground dwelling and entered. There were bones littering the ground. Not just animal bones but human bones as well.

Camilla sat up, rubbing her forehead as she did so. She was panting heavily. Another nightmare. Though she was beginning to question if they were nightmares or if they were something else. Slowly she laid back upon the bed and tried again to find sleep. She closed her eyes and hummed to herself until finally she fell into a light slumber.

It was early; the sun was just starting to rise. Warren was the first one awake and ready to head out. He woke each of the others and waited. The group met up with one another outside the tower. They exchanged nods then headed out towards the forest that Arcanist wanted them to explore. Their route was already planned; it was just a matter of getting there now.

By midafternoon, they reached the first small village that had been marked on their map. "This would be much easier if we had horses, or some sort of stead," Warren grumbled.

"I agree. Maybe we see if there's a stable in this village looking to sell," Azura suggested as she looked about.

Camilla looked at the sundial in the village's central area. "Meet back here in an hour? Warren, you and Azura see about steads. I'll check into gathering up some supplies. And Chuck." She paused as she saw the barbarian. He was sitting to the side sleeping. "Nevermind. I'll gather supplies and rations," she said before heading off.

Warren and Azura walked in a different direction from the ranger. They looked about as they walked. The cleric could not help but find himself more at ease around the sorceress. It was strange and foreign to him, but he enjoyed her company. Azura pointed. "There, looks like they do have a stable," she said as they walked over.

"Aye, g'afternoon travelers. What can we do ye fer?" the stable master asked as he looked up from a book. Likely used to track the horse and their value.

"We're looking to purchase four horses. They need to have a lot of stamina, where we're going is far," Warren stated as he began looking over the magnificent creatures within the stables. There were half a dozen horses, most were dark brown in coloration. A black horse moved further into its pen, avoiding the elf. And the only white one was whining nonstop once Warren glanced and her.

"Hmm… Young man, these horses sense something off about ye. No, that won't do at all. No horse will choose you as its master. Best of luck elsewhere," the stable master said as he watched how his six horses behaved erratically the moment Warren glanced at them.

Azura approached the whining white horse. "Easy girl, easy," she whispered softly as she stroked the large animal's head. The stable master looked over and arched an eyebrow at what he was seeing. Azura continued speaking softly to the horse and stroking it. Much to his surprise, the white horse calmed down and nuzzled Azura's hand. "That's a good girl," the sorceress said as she smiled.

"Young lass, ye ever ridden one?"

"No, but my brother taught me how to handle horses when they get unruly. He said while they might be able to speak through words, they speak through the heart," Azura replied.

"Aye, that they do." The stable master looked torn. He rubbed his chin and thought before speaking again. "Tell ye what, if the other two in yer group can handle these horses like ye did, I'll sell ya three horses."

Warren nodded. "That sounds fair. We'll be back in an hour," he said before leaving the stable, Azura following close behind. Once they had some distance, he came to a stop and looked to the sorceress. "Do you think Chuck and Hood can handle horses like you did?"

Azura shook her head. "I don't know. Chuck seems more likely to kill the animal. And Camilla's, well, she's been a bit of wildcard."

The cleric nodded; if he struggled with animals, he had a feeling the barbarian would also struggle. And the ranger was hard to gauge. They made their way back to the meeting spot and waited.

Camilla stopped by a blacksmith shop she found and looked about his wares. "Good afternoon, miss. What can I do for you?" a large man wearing a red apron asked as he walked over. He was covered in ash and soot from working his craft.

"Good afternoon, I'm looking for a few things. I need arrows, lots of them." She paused as she pulled the list from her belt pouch. "Arrows, a couple of daggers, a shortsword, two hand axes and ball-chain," she said looking over the weapon list everyone provided.

The blacksmith scratched his chin. "That's a lot of weapons for one, miss."

"I'm buying for a group," Camilla explained.

He nodded as he turned to his wares. "Blades will be on the south wall; axes will be next to those. Arrowheads will be at my desk. I don't sell arrows, my apologies. And a ball-n-chain will be with the exotic weapons on the west wall," he informed the ranger.

Camilla nodded her thanks and went to have a look. She picked out two hand axes that looked about right for what Chuck had described. Then four daggers, one for each member of the group in case they were ever without their primary weapons. She looked over the shortswords but stopped when a longsword caught her eye. It was heavier than her shortswords but would provide more power in combat. The blade glistened with a blue glow; the pommel and hilt were simple. She looked for a price tag but could not find one; it was still a nice blade, and she could not pass up the opportunity to pick up a new blade. All that was left was the ball and chain Warren requested. She found one that felt about the right weight and chain length.

The blacksmith wrote the weapons down in his book and their selling prices. He added everything up and turned to ranger. "Will you be purchasing any arrowheads today?" he asked.

Camilla was looking over the arrowheads. The weight was off, they lacked the sharp edge she needed and were far too rough. "I'll give those a pass, thank you though," she replied as she withdrew the coin pouch she had.

"It'll be seven hundred wendells," he said as he added the prices up. He arched an eyebrow seeing the longsword. "Huh, never seen that one in my stock, not in my books either. Well, still seven hundred wendells for the daggers, handaxes, ball and chain."

The ranger nodded and checked her coin pouch. She had five hundred wendells. Not enough to make the purchase. "Any chance I can haggle you down some?" she asked looking up.

The blacksmith laughed. "Young miss, you've made me laugh. Tell you what, I got a few targets out back. If you can hit all of them within sixty seconds, I'll give you the most expensive weapon from your list free. That'll bring your cost down to four hundred seventy-five wendells."

Camilla liked the challenge. "Deal," she said as she drew her longbow and followed the shopkeeper to the back. The targets were small as can be. And the bullseyes were barely visible.

"Remember you got to hit all thirty targets in sixty seconds," the blacksmith reminded and he got the hourglass ready.

"What's the percent of people who've succeeded?" Camilla asked as she studied the location of the targets.

"Zero." The blacksmith laughed as he set the hourglass down. Camilla nocked her arrow and fired. She repeated the simple action twenty-nine more times. There was no pause from one target to the next; she never paused her movements. It was as though something otherworldly had taken hold as she adjusted her aim as she moved to focus on the next target. To the blacksmith's shock, all targets had been hit in the bullseye in mere forty-five seconds. He looked slack-jawed as his eyes darted from the targets to the purple haired ranger.

"So that weapon free?" Camilla asked with a subtle smirk.

"How? I…" He was at a loss for words. The blacksmith coughed a couple of times. "I'm a man of my word. You get the ball and chain free. I'll even throw in some arrowheads. Just uh… tell me how you did that?" he stammered.

Camilla collected her arrows before following the blacksmith into his shop. "Lots of practice with a bow and living in the wilds," she replied as they returned to the weapon pile. He nodded and marked the price down to four hundred seventy-five wendells. Camilla handed him the coins then loaded the weapons in her bag and departed.

"Camilla! Hey!" Azura called as she ran up to the ranger. "I know it hasn't been an hour, but Warren and I ran into an issue trying to get the horses."

"Alright, what happened?" the ranger replied calmly.

"The horses began behaving erratically when Warren approached. So, the stable master won't sell to him. He said if the other travelling mates can calm the horses, like I did, he'd sell us some horses. Otherwise, no deal," Azura explained. Camilla slowly nodded; she was not the best with domesticated animals. Wild animals were no issue to her. She followed Azura to the stable and saw Chuck trying to calm a horse but horribly failing.

"Aye, that's two of ye bad with animals," the stable master stated. He looked over when Azura returned with the fourth party member. "Another lass? Alright, let's see ye have a go."

Camilla looked at the horses; the black horse was the one that caught her eyes. She felt drawn to him. As she approached, the black horse began behaving more erratically than he ever had. The ranger instantly took a step back. "Probably best I don't try," she said as she heard the other horses beginning to whine and thrash in their pens.

"Well, I'll be damned. The purple-haired lass riles them up worse than anyone else," the stable master noted. "Sorry, travelers, I won't be selling ye any horses. They're excellent judges of character. This behavior, it ain't normal for them."

The party left the stable and walked to one last shop to check into. A general store that sold various adventuring gear and rations for the road. As they entered, everyone within the general store stared at them. Warren remained silent as he went about picking up anything they needed. Azura stayed close to the cleric and helped him collect anything they needed for the journey. Chuck snarled at all the other folks within the shop. He would not be intimidated. Camilla stated near the door they entered the shop from and was looking over everyone. Sizing them up and gauging any weapons they had.

Warren brought over everything they intended to purchase to the front desk where the shopkeeper sat. No words outside of the price for everything were spoken. The cleric did not argue with the price and paid the shopkeeper. As he walked back to Camilla and Chuck, he finally spoke. "Move with haste, meet outside of town," he whispered.

Chuck growled as he watched the shopgoers begin to draw weapons for no reason. Camilla rested her right hand on her shortsword. "There's no need for violence," she said looking at each shopgoer.

Silence. Warren shook his head. He knew there was no reason with people who wanted violence. He was the same as they were, and he knew it. The cleric and sorceress left the shop, both moving at a brisk pace and continued such pace until they were clear of the town. They waited a bit, and soon the barbarian and ranger joined them, blood stains visible on the barbarian's greataxe. No one spoke as they continued their travels.

It took another two weeks, but they soon came upon the underground passage they had planned to use. They set up camp, deciding to rest before heading into the underground. Warren had gathered plenty of firewood for them, and Camilla had hunted some prey as to avoid using their rations. "What do you guys think we'll be facing in that forest?" Warren asked, breaking the tense silence.

Azura shuddered. "I don't know, but we've been able to overcome just about everything so far. I don't doubt we can do this," she said before returning her attention to the food. It was some sort of wild game, but no one bothered to ask the ranger.

Chuck growled. "Chuck think fight. Chuck hope for lots of fight," he said, his voice surprisingly calm and not loud like it normally was.

Warren looked to Camilla; she had been silent. "Hood, what do you think?"

She glanced up from the bowl of the stew she had prepared from her catch. "No telling what we've gotten ourselves into. All we can do is look out for one another," she said then finished the stew. Camilla was uneasy again and was not sure why. She shook her head, brushing it off as simply being the idea of going underground.

After their meal, everyone turned in for the night. They took turns keeping watch and ensuring nothing snuck up on their camp. When morning came, they quickly packed up and headed into the underground passage. Camilla pulled a sunrod from her bag and crackled the tip to illuminate the area. There was a lot of writing on the walls as they made their way through the narrow pass. Chuck looked it over and shook his head. "Why write when smash?" he growled.

Warren ignored the comment as they went further. Soon they came to a large open room. Everyone looked about, noting anything they saw to each other. Camilla lifted the sunrod a little higher to illuminate things better. What they saw took them back. There were no monsters or other creatures. The walls were lined with various colored crystals. Warren stepped forward first, his tower shield in hand as he walked. Camilla looked around again, making certain they did not miss anything.

"I think this is gemstone mine," Warren finally said as they walked.

"Looks that way," Azura added as she followed behind him.

Chuck slammed his greataxe against a large crystal breaking it off the wall. He hefted the massive crystal over his head, belting out a war cry as he did so. As quick as he cut it down, the barbarian threw the crystal into his bag. "Chuck have trophy!" he roared proudly.

Camilla brought the rear, her sunrod the only source of light for the group. As they left the crystal cave, they found a split path. There was a sign scribed in what appeared to be ruins. "Dark realm runes," Warren said as he looked it over. "Right path leads to riches, left for safety."

Chuck instantly began running down the right path. "Chuck, wait!" everyone called before he faded from view.

"Damn it," Warren muttered. He looked to the girls and shook his head. "Guess we're taking the right path like it or not," he said as he took lead position. Azura followed behind him, with Camilla bringing up the rear.

Warren drew his morningstar as they walked, uncertain of what they would find. He could hear the ranger draw a weapon and assumed a shortsword. The deeper into the tunnel they went, the more they regretted the choice they had made. Even with the ability to see in the dark, both Warren and Azura were struggling to make out shapes of the environment. Camilla held the sunrod a little higher, trying to give them additional light, but it seemed that was not enough to pierce the darkness ahead.

"Chuck!" Warren called out as loud as he could, hoping for an answer.

No answer. They continued walking, each becoming more paranoid the deeper they went. Camilla came to a stop and looked over her shoulder. "We're being followed," she whispered to Azura and Warren.

Both stopped and looked back. They did not hear anything, and they failed to see anything. Camilla's gaze was fixed on the section of tunnel they had come through. Her longsword began to alight with a red aura. Bane. An enchantment that was common for rangers to have on their weapons. It alerted them to when something they hated was approaching. Camilla handed the sunrod to Azura and drew a shortsword in her left hand.

Lunging from behind were four frenzied dwarves. They had a bloodlust look in their eyes as they attacked with hand axes. Camilla was quick on her feet. She parried the attacks and retaliated as best she could. "Beautiful voice! Sing! Sing!" the dwarves all yelled as they attacked again.

Warren drew his ball and chain and began spinning it. "Azura, Hood, duck!" he yelled.

Both girls dropped, dodging the massive steel ball as it flew over their heads. The dwarves were sent back a few feet giving the travelers room to breathe. Warren began pulling his weapon back in to wind it up again. Camilla rushed ahead and slashed wildly to keep the dwarves tripped up. The ranger did not miss a beat as she kept the pressure up. Behind her, she heard a fireball being cast.

"Camilla, drop!" Azura called, hoping the ranger could react in time. The fireball hurled from the sorceress's fingers and flew down the tunnel. Camilla barely managed to avoid getting scorched and watched as flames exploded around the dwarves, keeping them at bay. She remained low as the massive steel ball went over her head and knocked the dwarves further back.

Warren reeled the ball back to him and threw it back in his bag. "Come on, they should be staggered enough we can make an escape," he said as he began heading further into the tunnel, his tower shield in arm again.

Camilla sprinted back to the sorceress and cleric and followed them as they made their way deeper through the tunnel. They came upon another room; it was large, but nothing illuminated the room aside from the sunrod Azura carried. Standing on the opposite side was Chuck. His back was to the group when they entered. "Chuck?" Warren called seeing the barbarian.

Chuck slowly turned to face the group, his greataxe drawn. "Sing! Sing!" he roared as he lunged for the group.

Warren brought his shield up, managing to block the impact. "Chuck! What's gotten into you!" he yelled.

Camilla rushed forward, her fast movements forcing the barbarian back. "You both try to figure out what's causing all this. I'll keep Chuck busy," she said calmly as she adjusted her posture.

The cleric nodded and continued further into the tunnels. Azura dropped the sunrod and raced after the cleric. Camilla eyed the barbarian who roared at her, ready to fight to the death. "Chuck, knock this off!" she yelled. No response. He swung his greataxe again forcing Camilla to dodge back to avoid being hit. *"Connard! Je-seison battue vu avantic!"* Camilla growled in her other language as she stepped back.

Warren and Azura found themselves in another large chamber. As they walked through, they heard what sounded like a woman singing. They exchanged glances before looking around. Warren shook his head a few times; his mind was slightly foggy compared to earlier. "Warren?" Azura asked.

"I'm alright," Warren responded as he shook his head trying to focus. He heard Azura cast a spell and felt a warm session overtake him. His mind was clear again. "Thanks," he stated as he nodded to the sorceress.

They looked around again, this time spotting what looked like a woman sitting in the middle of the room. Her back was to them, and it sounded like she was singing. The language was unfamiliar to them, but they figured she was the source of the dwarves and Chuck's crazed state. "Excuse me, miss," Warren began.

The woman turned; her face was haggard in appearance. She had empty eye sockets; her nose was removed, and her lips were missing. She let out a screech followed by a deafening wail. Warren and Azura were forced to cover their ears from the sound. Azura shook her head and unleashed her Hellstorm spell, raining down fire, ice, acid, lightning and sonic blasts upon the creature. There was another ghastly wail, causing the two casters to cover their ears again.

Warren ran ahead, his morningstar in hand as he swung out. His attack connected with the woman's chest, bones splintering from the impact. She heaved a few times before a shriek was heard. Warren was sent flying from the volume of the sound and landed hard on his back. He winced and struggled to move.

Azura flung two fireballs in rapid succession hoping one might work. "Azura, aim for her throat! Damage her vocal cords!" Warren called from where he had fallen.

She nodded as began casting one of her newer spells. Three dagger-like illusions formed and were hurled at the woman's throat. The first two were batted aside with no effort. But the third hit and tore through the vocal cords. As the woman went to shriek again, no sound came out. Azura took the opening to unleash a Cone of Ice, freezing the woman solid. Warren managed to stand despite the pain he was in and rushed forward. He saw the woman trying to free herself from inside the ice and smashed the ice with his morningstar.

Ice blocks were flung about, each containing a part of the creature they had just fought. Both Azura and Warren were breathing heavily as they stood. They turned, hearing movement coming from the tunnel they had come through. Camilla stepped out, a few new scars but nothing serious. Behind her she was dragging Chuck.

"Sorry, tried to catch up to you. Guess you had it under control though," Camilla said as she left Chuck to the side.

Azura rushed to Warren's side and began tending to his wounds. He nodded his thanks and stayed still for the sorceress to work. They stayed in the room for a while, at least until they were healed up and Chuck had woken up. Camilla explored a little way ahead and came back with news. "There's a way out. We continue through this last tunnel and then it's nothing but forest outside the tunnel." Everyone nodded hearing the ranger's report. They stood and began to make their way through the last tunnel.

They found themselves in a dense forest. Not far from where they had emerged from there was a faint ripple like distortion. “Well, let’s see what there is on the other side,” Warren stated as he went through the distortion. Azura and Chuck soon followed, with Camilla bringing up the rear.

Chapter 9 - Memories Of Frothcrest

As they materialized on the other side of the portal, the adventurers found themselves standing outside of a large white colored castle. There were statues of angels along with other peaceful looking creatures decorating the exterior. Warren visibly paled as he looked around. He stood stunned as the group took in the environment. "Warren, you alright?" Azura asked, noticing the cleric's unusual behavior.

"This… this is… It's Frothcrest… My homeland," he said as he looked onward. "That's my castle. I recognize everything; it looks no different than the day I left," he added as they began walking. As the group entered the grand hall, everyone, excluding Warren, were met with a painful sensation in their muscles. "What's wrong?" he asked as he noticed the pained looks of the other three.

Azura was using her quarterstaff to help keep her balance. "Everything hurts. I suddenly feel weak," the sorceress stated as she leaned on her quarterstaff.

Chuck growled as he struggled to lift his greataxe. He removed it from his back and began using it as a walking stick. The barbarian was having a hard time moving without the greataxe being used as such. Camilla took a deep breath; she staggered a bit and leaned against a wall. "Let's get through this quickly," the ranger murmured.

Warren winced; his head suddenly hurt. His mind felt like there was a haze coming over it. "Agreed," he stated as he continued walking.

"Welcome, Master Couseland," a voice familiar to Warren stated as a figure materialized. Everyone turned their attention to the coming figure.

"Thomas Hemmington." Warren was taken back upon seeing a ghostly visage of his servant.

"So, you do remember my name? I should be honored, and yet I'm not. This world is not your Frothcrest. No, this is the world as it should have been," Hemmington stated as he paced in front of the group. The group looked on and saw a high-born elf clad in white robes walk past them. He moved with such grace it took them back. Warren's eyes widened seeing the crown resting on the elf's head. It was his crown, the one he had been given after the fall of the evil dragon that was consuming Frothcrest.

Camilla watched as the high-born elf greeted his people. He spoke with a confident and compassionate tone. Standing beside him was a human who looked like the ghostly visage that had greeted them. The ranger watched as the king turned his attention to the guillotine that was in front of the crowd. Waiting to be executed was Warren. Or at least a version of him.

Warren, the real one, dropped to his knees in broken sobs. His head was hurting worse than it had been. His mind was becoming hazier. Azura looked over, hearing the broken sobs of the cleric. It pained her to see him like this. "Warren, it's not real. It's not true. Whatever this is that we're seeing, it's not real. You saved Frothcrest, not whoever that is," she said as she knelt beside the cleric and placed a hand on his shoulder.

"That… That's my father, our clan leader," Warren stated as he looked to Azura. Tears rolled down his cheeks. "He was killed by the blue dragon because I failed to find my courage the day that beast attacked us. I turned and ran. My father was killed because of me." He choked on the words as he felt more tears fall.

Camilla watched the scene unfold. The blade came down and the head fell into the basket. Standing, cheering in approval were a group of three other elves, two humans and a lone dwarf. They cheered as the headless body was removed from the guillotine. Her attention turned to the broken cleric.

"But you were the one who slew the dragon. Not him. You were the one who lead a group and found victory," Azura tried to get through to the cleric.

"Your travelling companions, they all died. Didn't they?" Camilla asked as she walked over. She saw Warren give her a weak nod. "How did it happen?"

"I... I... I betrayed them. I didn't outright kill them! I led them astray when they questioned my leadership. I led them to their deaths. I'm responsible for the deaths of six of Frothcrest's greatest warriors!" he cried out.

Azura was taken back hearing this. She was not sure how to respond. She had put her trust in Warren, just as the six had. Was he going to lead them astray as well? Had he already done such?

THUD! THUD! THUD!

Warren felt someone grab him by his chest plate and yank him to his feet. "Chuck say enough! Chuck think you pathetic! Chuck say fight!" the barbarian roared in the cleric's face.

Camilla blinked a few times. She nodded. "Chuck's right. Enough feeling sorry for yourself. You can't change the past. You have to move forward," she stated, her yellow eyes narrowing slightly.

Azura nodded as well. "So, you let your pride and arrogance blind you. Oh well, sure it's hard to hear that you lead six people to their deaths. And yeah, my trust in you is a little shaken, but you're part of our team now! So, get ahold of yourself!" the sorceress said loudly.

There was a laugh from the ghostly visage of Hemmington. He shook his head as he watched the group. "Feel free to explore the castle grounds, though I doubt you'll last long against any of the heroes," he said before disappearing into a mist.

Warren did not want to move. He just wanted to collapse into the ground and give up. His head was throbbing at this point and his mind was deep in a haze. It was hard to think about anything. He felt two of his traveling companions on either side, supporting him. "Come on, Warren, we're going to get through this," Camilla muttered as she supported Warren on the left side.

"They're weakened. Struggling to move. And yet they're helping me? Why? Do I actually mean something to them?" Warren thought as he felt Camilla and Azura supporting him on either side.

Chuck walked ahead, still leaning on his greataxe to steady himself. There was not much to be found within the castle. No treasures or coins for them to take. Warren shook his head trying to focus. "The throne room. We need to go to the throne room," he muttered. Lifting his head, he looked about and studied the layout. "Take the left-hand corridor all the way down then make a right. Should put us in the throne room," he added as he relied on the girls to steady him. As they walked, something in Warren stirred. The words his companions spoke echoing in his head.

Before long they had reached the throne room. "I knew you'd make your way here," the king stated as he stood from the throne. He was clad in gold armor and held a tower shield just like Warren's. In his right hand was a massive morningstar, much more impressive looking than the cleric's.

The six heroes from earlier appeared, joined by Hemmington. It was eight against four. The odds were not looking good for the adventurers. Camilla eased Warren to be seated against a wall. She drew her longsword and a shortsword, readying to fight. Chuck stood beside her, his greataxe drawn despite the weakened state he was in. Azura hung back but readied her spells.

"Seize them!" the king ordered.

The seven rushed forward engaging Camilla and Chuck in battle. Chuck focused on using powerful swings to knock back the foes. He tried to keep his enemies back, but with each swing, the greataxe felt heavier and heavier. Camilla stayed in a defensive stance, her blades being used to block, and she only launched an attack when an opening presented itself. The weakened state was catching up to her as well. Azura unleashed a wave of spells only for it to be blocked completely by a barrier spell.

"Are you going to sit idle? Let them fight for you? Let them die," a voice echoed in the back of Warren's head.

He looked up, seeing how despite their weakened conditions, the others still fought. The pain in his head was starting to break. His mind was finally coming out of the haze. He was not sure what caused the sudden spur, but he drew his morningstar. Slowly he stood, his shield raised and his morningstar ready. *"I won't run. I will prevail!"* he thought as he rushed past his group and lunged for the king.

"Warren!" Camilla and Azura called out seeing the cleric rush headfirst into the fight.

"No regrets! Never again!" Warren thought as his shield was struck by a powerful blow from the king's morningstar.

"What's this? Finally brave enough to fight your own battles?! I'll honor you with a fight, but it will be your last," the king stated as he brought his morningstar down, shattering Warren's shield.

Warren only smirked as he swung out with his morningstar and smashed through the chest plate the king wore. "Thanks for that. Now I'm lighter on my feet," the cleric said before swinging again while the king was still recovering. The sickening crunch of bones echoed in the chamber.

"Sire!" the seven guards yelled before moving to protect their king.

"Don't think so!" Camilla growled as she moved between them and their target. She endured the onslaught of attacks, her blades blocking and parrying each new attack. Chuck roared as he rushed over and swung out with his greataxe, knocking the seven off the ranger. Azura followed up with a Cone of Flames, trapping three of the guards. Chuck had grabbed the fourth by the throat and was crushing his neck. Camilla remained in a defensive position, opting to guard Warren's back.

Warren dodged the attack from the king and countered with his own. He saw the king's shield splinter from the impact. "Your defenses are dropping, Highness. Sure, you want to continue?" he asked as he watched the last of the gold armor hit the ground.

"I brought you into being, I can end such as well," the king said with no emotion.

The three guards trapped in the Cone of Flames finally broke free. As they moved to take down the sorceress, Chuck countered with a massive swing. Two dropped to the ground, slain. The third joined the other three who were engaging the ranger. Camilla smirked as she muttered something under her breath. "El, ava, iteo, saato." Her longsword began shimmering brighter. "Time to even the odds," she added in common as her blade pierced the four guards. Three dropped to the ground dead. Hemmington was the only one remaining of the guards.

Warren was forced back from a big hit. He leaned against a wall trying to recover. Hemmington made his move, as did the king. It was a two-pronged assault. As the bastard sword and morningstar closed in, Warren flinched knowing there was no dodging or enduring the hit. He saw a quick flash of a blade then felt the warm blood hit him. The ranger had thrown herself into the attack to shield him. "Camilla..." His voice shook upon seeing the bloodied ranger. As she fell backwards, he reached out, catching her in his left arm. He swung out with more aggression than he thought he possessed. His morningstar hit its mark, crushing Hemmington's skull and shattering the king's rib cage.

Silence. Everything was still. There was a sudden flash and the group found themselves outside the front of the castle. Warren still held Camilla, but her injuries seemed to be fading as though they never were. Floating before them was the king's morningstar. It drifted up to Warren as though beckoning him to take it.

"I am Ironvice. One of five legendary weapons. You have proven your resolve and will to change. I grant you my power to aid you upon your adventures," a voice echoed, seemingly coming from the weapon.

Warren glanced down to Camilla, who had started to move again. "You alright?" he asked as he watched her slowly pull away from him. No words, just the confident smirk. With a nod, Warren shouldered his morningstar and took Ironvice's handle. Another sudden flash went off. When everything cleared up, the group found themselves back in the forest from before. Their wounds fully healed and any damages their gear had taken was gone.

They all heard a clicking sound drawing their attention to the stone in Warren's pocket. As he withdrew the stone. "Ah, good I was able to reach you. I have some new information to report," Arcanist's voice came from the stone.

Camilla unrolled the world map she had scribed while they were at Arcanist's tower. She saw Azura ready with a quill and ink jar. Warren nodded. "Let's hear it, Arcanist," he said.

"To the far north of that forest there's a huge field. I'm sensing a disturbance over there. Maybe it's worth investigating. Along the way there, you'll likely encounter many villages and people who could use help. Perhaps lend them a hand and see about earning some coin and information about locations to check out. That's all I have to report. Best of luck, travelers." With those last words, the stone was silent.

Azura had marked the map with the new location and looked up. "We don't have a lot of options for routes. Straight through the forest, and we should come upon the plains and eventually the field he mentioned," she stated as she looked over the map.

"Right, then let's go," Warren said as he headed north.

CHAPTER 10 - An Unstoppable Force

They had been wandering the forest for days without any signs of towns or even the field they had been looking for. Warren remained quiet as they marched. Camilla had taken the lead as forests and wilderness were home to her. The cleric glanced at the sorceress, that feeling he had forming again. His heart was beating faster; his palms were sweaty. Why did she make him feel this way? What was it about her? Perhaps it was the unconditional trust and friendship she had shown him. Even after learning of his dark past, Azura still seemed to see Warren in the same light she had. For some reason, he could not explain, Warren wanted to be a better person. He wanted to better himself for Azura.

Camilla came to stop a little way ahead of the group, drawing her longbow as she did so. Everyone stopped and waited. "What is it? What do you sense?" Warren asked as he approached, his shield in hand.

The ranger tilted her head slightly as she listened to the sounds around them. After a moment, she shook her head and shouldered her bow. "It's nothing, just my imagination," she said before turning to Warren. She leaned closer, making the cleric uncomfortable. "Steady your heartbeat. If I can hear it, any predator can as well," she whispered before returning to scouting ahead.

Warren took a deep breath before exhaling. His heartbeat. That was all this was. He tried to calm himself and steady his nerves as he walked alongside

Azura. He had told the group, it made sense for the most armored and shield based of them to stay by the person who was most vulnerable. No one questioned him; they all just agreed with his sound logic. When in reality, he just wanted to be closer to Azura.

Chuck was second in the lineup, his strides just barely behind Camilla. The barbarian wanted to be near the front of their formation in case a fight broke out. He wanted blood and combat; he wanted to be slaughtering his foes and butcher anyone he could. Though he hated to admit such, he followed the ranger because she seemed more knowing of the forest.

After another half day of walking, they finally came upon a small town. It looked rundown and like everyone was struggling to make ends meet. Warren indicated the nearby inn. "We can probably check in and see about getting a room for the night," he suggested.

As the group walked toward the inn, several missing posters caught the group's attention. Camilla looked them over before turning to a tired looking merchant. "What's the story here?" she asked bluntly.

The merchant looked up at the sound of the ranger's voice. "Oh those? Local orphanage has been ransacked by unknown attackers. And every time, a child is taken. Though a couple of children in the posters are from families living here. Not all are orphans. Sheriff has quite the reward for anyone who can bring the children back, alive and safe," he explained.

"Camilla!" Warren called from the inn's entryway. The ranger hesitated before jogging to catch up to the rest of the group. "Everything alright?" he asked.

"Children taken in these numbers, it's not normal. Last time I saw this, the Blood Circle was abducting young casters trying to find one who could use some sort of dark tome. At least that was what Ned told us," Camilla murmured.

"Ned? Who's that?" Azura asked, hearing the exchange.

Camilla paused; she had said too much. They were not in Kardax, this was not her Azura. And most importantly, they were not the supposed Guardians of Kardax. She shook her head. "It's nothing. He's not someone to worry about," she replied as she tried to cover things up.

"If you change your mind and want to talk, we're here for you," Warren said, trying for once in his life to be open minded to the needs of others.

They entered the inn and got three rooms as it was all the inn had left. Warren and Chuck each had their own room, Camilla and Azura had opted to share a room. Each were laying out their gear on the provided armor and equipment stands. Azura arched an eyebrow as she watched the ranger shoulder her longbow and tie her quiver to her belt. “Going somewhere?” Azura asked.

“Yeah, out. I don’t need you or the others slowing me down on my tracking. I’ll be back before daybreak,” Camilla reasoned as she tied her boot laces tighter. Before Azura could argue, Camilla had already headed out the door.

“Warren’s not going to like this,” Azura muttered before going down the hall to the cleric’s room. She knocked and waited.

Warren answered the door and was surprised to see the young sorceress. “Azura? Everything ok?” he asked, genuine concern in his voice.

“Camilla’s being reckless and going off on her own again,” Azura said as she met the cleric’s gaze.

He cursed under his breath as he went back into his room. As quick as he could, the cleric was in his armor and had grabbed his tower shield and morningstar. “I suppose we should grab Chuck on our way after Camilla,” he said as he walked down the hall to the barbarian’s room. He knocked loudly, earning him an agitated grunt.

Chuck opened his door, his nude body showing every muscle, every scar and just how well-endowed the barbarian was. “Chuck want know what want,” he snarled.

“Ranger’s gone off on her own again. Want to join us in going after her? Might be some fights for ya,” Warren said trying to appeal to the half orc.

Chuck roared happily before going back to grab his axe. He raced down the hall in nothing but his birthday suit. Azura averted her gaze as the barbarian charged past her. “If he has that effect on us, hopefully anyone he fights has a similar reaction.” Warren tried to make light of the situation. Azura nervously chuckled as she followed behind the cleric.

Camilla had been poking around and checking the area around the orphanage. Any tracks she found were old, showing the attacks were some time ago. She followed what few she found into the forest. She stalked the forest but had the uncanny feeling that she was being watched. There was someone else out here. Shaking her head, Camilla remained on her task of finding out where the tracks were going.

A scream caught her attention and got her to look over. She instantly hid behind the trees near her and listened. It was a child; they were screaming and struggling as they were dragged along. A man's voice snapped; his language was foreign to the ranger as she listened. This was likely another abduction. She followed close enough to keep them within earshot but remained hidden in the dense tree cover.

The man came to a stop; he looked around. The uneasy feeling of being followed had hit him. He looked about again, trying to assess where his follower was. Then without warning, a massive greataxe came down and split him in two. Camilla rolled her eyes. She had told them not to follow and yet here they were.

Chuck roared in triumph as the remains of the man hit the ground. Azura rushed over and collected the child, a young girl. The sorceress tried her best to comfort the child, but the little girl pulled away and ran. Warren easily caught the child and held her. "It's ok, we're here to help," he whispered trying to calm the girl. She stopped fighting and just looked up at the cleric, her amber eyes meeting his light blue ones. With a gentle smile, Warren continued. "I'm Warren. What's your name?" he asked.

"May." The girl sniffled.

"That's a pretty name, May. Why don't you tell us what happened?" Warren kept his voice calm and friendly as he comforted the girl.

May nodded weakly. "He said he knew where my brother was taken. I followed him. Then he said I'd make a delicious snack."

Warren gently cut May off and just patted her shoulders. "Let's get you back to town."

Camilla remained hidden, hoping none of the others noticed her. Once she heard the three and the child head back toward town, the ranger emerged. She checked the remains of the man and found a slip of paper. It had a location scribbled down and a map to such. She took off again in pursuit of such.

After an hour of tracking, the ranger came upon a rundown looking house in the forest. It looked like it was falling apart and in disarray. She swallowed the lump in her throat and headed into the building. Inside there was a lot of blood covering the walls and floors, there were also what appeared to be human remains scattered about the floor. Camilla did her best to contain herself as she continued deeper.

As she came to a cellar door, she yanked it open and was stunned to see many of the missing children from the posters. "Come on, let's get all of you out of here," she said as she helped the children out of the cellar. They whimpered but followed her commands. Chains bound them and kept the children from separating from one another. Camilla opened her belt pouch and pulled out her lock picking tools and began to work the locks that were on the cuffs binding the children. She was about half down the line when she heard a sickening laugh. A massive pit fiend lumbered forward, blood dripping from his fangs and claws.

"You dare steal my food?" He laughed as he lunged forward.

Camilla barely managed to dodge the assault and came up on a crouch, bow in hand. She fired three arrows in rapid succession trying to pin the monster. He lumbered forward again, his claws slashing wildly. Camilla dropped her longbow and drew her longsword and a shortsword, barely blocking each assault. One claw strike got through and left a scar down the ranger's face. She winced from the pain but pushed through such.

"If you insist on starving me, then you'll be my prey," the monster's voice boomed as he overpowered the ranger. His claws wrapped around her, pinning her arms against her sides.

Camilla struggled trying to free herself. She glanced at the children. "Run! Go!" She yelled as she finally managed to break free from the monster's grip. The children were frozen in fear. The ranger was breathing heavily as she gripped her longsword tightly and steeled herself. "All of you run. I won't let him past. I won't let him get at any of you. So just run," she said, her voice even. Blood was running down her arms from the Pit Fiend's claws; the left side of her face was bloodied up from the wound she had been dealt.

Camilla rushed forward again, delivering another flurry of attacks, keeping the Pit Fiend off balance. He roared loudly as he tried to use his impressive strength to overpower the ranger. Behind her, Camilla could hear the children running. A smile formed on her face as she fought. She felt the Pit Fiend's claws rack her midsection, spilling more blood. This one was clearly more skilled than the ones she had faced prior. At the least it was smarter. His thick tail knocked her off balance and into a wall.

She remained motionlessly, trying to think up a plan. Camilla knew this fight needed to end fast, but her movements had been slowed by all the blood loss. As she managed to stand, she saw the massive Pit Fiend was already standing before her. "I must admit, I've never had a meal make me work so hard," he growled as he eyed the ranger.

"Get away from her!"

A fireball forced the Pit Fiend back, before he could recover from the attack a massive morningstar slammed into his chest and knocked him back. "Sorry we're late, Camilla!" Warren said as he flashed the ranger a smirk.

Chuck ran past the cleric and slammed his greataxe into the monster's back. A roar of pain was heard as the beast staggered back. Warren began tending to Camilla's wounds, trusting the rest of the team could handle the fight. Azura flung another Fireball at the Pit Fiend, knocking him back. As he was trying to recover, he was caught up in a Cone of Ice. The sound he made as he fought against the ice was otherworldly. Chuck grunted as he swung his axe, taking the monster's head clean off. The room was silent only to be broken up by the wet *thunk* of the body hitting the ground.

Azura and Chuck nodded to each other before going over to where Warren was. Camilla was badly wounded, many injuries leading to massive blood loss. Warren's magic was giving off a warm glow as it sealed the wounds shut and worked its way through the ranger. He gave Azura and Chuck a smile as he took the ranger in his arms. "She'll be alright, just needs a lot of rest. Good thing you got us, eh Azura?" he noted.

The sorceress breathed a sigh of relief hearing the cleric's words. They made their way back to town and took the rest of the night to rest. Much to their surprise all the children that were still living had returned to the town.

The next morning, the Sheriff met up with the group and paid them a small reward for rescuing the children. He also handed them a small ruby. "I don't know what it is, but every merchant says it has no value. Maybe it'll help you with your adventures," he said before bowing.

Warren, Azura and Chuck were gathering any supplies they could and figured they would need. The cleric made his way to the ranger's room to check on her. Camilla was still resting from the ordeal, but her eyes opened and looked to him as he entered. "I guess I really do owe you and the others my life," Camilla said softly. She was ashamed of herself for being so reckless and thickheaded.

He laughed as he checked over her wounds. "Ah, don't worry so much. Think of it as us paying you back for saving us from Uldritch," Warren noted as he finished changing the bandages. "Still, you're lucky to be alive after that kind of fight. I don't know how you do it, Camilla, but somehow you survive despite overwhelming odds."

She shook her head. "Wish I could explain it," Camilla replied slowly. She watched the cleric finish tending to her wounds and nodded her thanks again.

As Warren departed from the room, he met up with Azura and Chuck. The barbarian looked disgruntled while the sorceress looked distressed. "What's wrong?" the cleric asked worried about his comrades.

"We recently heard a report about a massive army converging on this town. And there's a lone warrior fighting on behalf of the town. From what the townsfolk say, the warrior's been fighting for three solid days to protect the town," Azura replied trying to steady her voice.

Warren looked over his shoulder as he saw the ranger emerge from her room, geared up and ready for combat. "Then what are we waiting for? There's a fight to be won, so let's go," she said as she pulled some of the bandages off. "Can't have these hindering my movements. And with your magic, I'm as good as new," Camilla added as she walked past the others.

They made their way to the large field that was at the other exit to the town. As they rushed forward, they saw a heavily armored figure fighting off wave after wave of undead soldiers. Camilla quickened her pace, as did Chuck. Warren began casting healing auras upon them and Azura followed up with casting her Speed spell. Chuck was first onto the scene, his greataxe cleaving through many undead warriors in a single swing. Camilla soon joined him, her longsword slashing through the undead and her short sword parrying attacks.

The armored figure seemingly glanced to the newcomers but continued to assault any undead beings that clambered forward. They did not miss a beast as their bastard sword easily ripped and tore through countless shambling monsters. Chuck snarled as he brought his greataxe down upon what he assumed was the leader. The creature was far larger than any of the others and roared loudly as it turned to face the barbarian.

Camilla saw the armored figure stagger briefly, an undead lizard person closing the distance on them. Without thinking, she lunged forward, her short sword parrying the assault and her longsword split the creature in two.

Azura and Warren soon caught up to the fight and readied themselves for anything. Warren quickly studied the situation and began casting heal spells to restore Camilla and Chuck. Azura on the other hand began throwing Fireballs at the onslaught of enemies. Chuck was still battling the Chieftain, determined to kill the biggest and baddest thing on the battlefield. They exchanged axe strikes, and soon Chuck found an advantage. His greataxe was clearly heavier. He took a step forward, bringing his axe down, splintering the skull of his foe.

Chuck soon joined the others in dealing with the other smaller, zombie-like monsters. Camilla stayed near the tiring armored warrior, ensuring they had some support. Azura rained down another storm of fireballs, ending the remaining monsters. "What were those things?" Azura asked as she looked over the rotted and burning corpses.

"They're called Horrors," the armored warrior stated as they removed their damaged helmet, letting it drop to the ground. "They're created from the malice that dwells within the hearts of those who are living."

"Wait, you're a woman?" Warren was taken back seeing the long auburn hair flowing from the armored warrior.

"Is that so uncommon?" she asked as she sheathed her bastard sword.

"So then, these were once people? People who could not find salvation?" Warren spoke as he examined the bodies.

"Yes, it's more common than you might realize," she added as she watched the cleric.

"Chuck want fight! Chuck demand more fight!" the barbarian roared as he swung his greataxe.

Camilla leaned against a lone tree that was overlooking the battlefield. "So, what's your name, stranger?" she asked looking at the auburn-haired fighter.

"I am Amelia Lucia, daughter of Duke Lucia of Highever," she introduced herself before pausing slightly. "Not that Highever matters, it was lost as was the rest of the kingdom. Everyone was slaughtered during the War for the Chalice," she added more somberly. She looked at the lavender haired ranger. "And yourself?"

"Name's Camilla. I hail from Kardax," Camilla responded as she watched everyone.

The two stared at one another in silence for a moment. It was as though they had met or knew one another. But that was impossible for they came from different worlds. "I'm Azura," the pale-blue-haired sorceress chimed in. She pointed to the barbarian. "That's Chuck. And," she paused before indicating Warren, "this is Warren." She stepped forward. "May I check your wounds, Amelia?"

"That's not necessary," Amelia tried to reason. Before she could give a reason, Azura was already checking over her body for wounds.

"How is that possible? You've been fighting for three days straight, and yet you haven't a single wound," Azura said, noting the lack of injuries upon the newcomer.

"Because I'm already dead," Amelia replied as she gently tugged away from the sorceress.

"Come again?" Warren asked, wanting clarification.

Amelia simply shrugged as she looked at the cleric, her piercing scarlet eyes meeting his. "My heart hasn't beat for a thousand years. I'm already dead," she said again.

"Then that would mean—" Azura began.

"I'm half vampire, half werewolf. Stronger than both," Amelia finally admitted. Camilla nodded slowly from where she was standing, taking everything in.

Chuck stomped up to Amelia, greataxe in hand. "Chuck want fight! You fight Chuck!" he demanded, as he brought the weapon down upon the half vampire.

Amelia was fast; her blade was instantly drawn and easily blocked the attack. In turn, she countered and easily sent Chuck to the ground, her blade leveled at his throat. Everyone was stunned seeing the lightning reflexes she had. She pulled her blade back and sheathed it again before glancing at Camilla then to Azura. "Your friend's awfully quiet. She your familiar? Or perhaps a demon you summoned and bound to you?"

"What? No, no, no! Nothing like that. Camilla's normally just the silent type. She usually speaks with her actions rather than with words," Azura tried to explain.

Warren finally stepped forward; he had enough of this. "Let's get back to town. There's an inn we got rooms at earlier; you're more than welcome to join us. Best we bunk down and get some rest," he said.

Everyone nodded in agreement. Chuck however was still bitter about losing the fight. Still, he followed the others back to the inn. Once they arrived, Azura had opted for a room change to be with Warren. She felt safer around him than anyone else, given the current circumstances. It was determined that Amelia would bunk in the same room as Camilla. The ranger having the most rational head to things regarding the half vampire.

Once everyone was settling in for the night, Amelia looked Camilla up and down. She was clearly sizing up the ranger and trying to study her. "There's something otherworldly about you," she finally said breaking the tense silence. Camilla hummed curiously in response but gave no other acknowledgement. "I can't put my finger on it, but I sense some sort of dark magic all over you," the half vampire added.

"Sure you aren't just paranoid?" Camilla questioned as she glanced over. Her yellow eyes, void of any emotions. It was as though she was not human but was some sort of primal creature.

Amelia's gaze narrowed as she saw the emotionless gaze of the ranger. "Unlike the others, who were frightened and their heartbeats quickened when I stated I was already dead, you, your heartbeat remained the same steady rhythm," she growled slightly.

Camilla gave an ominous smirk; she enjoyed riling up others. It was something that she could never explain why she loved it but she did. "Wouldn't be the first time I was in the presence of someone who's technically undead. And I highly doubt it'll be the last," she responded while maintaining her even tone. She saw the half vampire about to speak further and merely waved her hand slightly. "It's late, and while you might be undead and not requiring sleep, I do. We can continue this little fuss in the morning if you so please."

Silence. Camilla knew she had won this round with the newest member of the team. Sleep came quickly for the ranger, but it was not restful sleep. She shifted again and again, clearly bothered by her dreams again. Amelia watched, a mix of concern and awe on her face as she watched the ranger toss and turn in her sleep.

Lost in the loneliness

It was hot, and very dry. She felt like she was moving forward but was uncertain where she was going. The sky was dark, but the heat did not let up. Sandstorms were whipping around on all sides. The ground was littered with destroyed human settlements and the scent of death was clear in the air. Looking down, there was blood covering her claws? *She had claws? Distinct claws, not the same as the ones coming off her hands. No, these were full scale covered claws. But why?*

Camilla sat up right and was panting heavily; sweat rolled down her face. She breathed heavily; eventually her breathing became steady again. "Bad dreams?" Amelia asked as she watched the ranger. Camilla hesitated but nodded slightly. "Want to talk about it?" the half vampire continued. Camilla shook her head.

The ranger laid back once again, trying to get back to sleep. It was hard, but eventually sleep came again. She was plagued with another series of broken and horrible dreams. Despite such, she managed to remain asleep. When morning came, everyone met up in the small lobby of the inn. Warren, Chuck and Azura looked well rested. Amelia looked no different than the day before. And Camilla looked exhausted. Warren handed over the room keys to the innkeeper and paid the fees they had.

Warren looked to Amelia. "So, what're your plans, Amelia? We could always use the extra help, but we won't force you to join us," he said.

Amelia nodded; she had sized up most of the party the previous day. And while most of the party feared her, she had accepted such. The ranger was the unusual one, which in turn had piqued her curiosity. "I'll be joining your group, with permission of course," she replied with a smile.

The cleric turned to the rest of the party. Azura nodded, giving her approval. Chuck was disgruntled about it, but he nodded. Camilla gave no obvious answer, but the soft and well-hidden smirk was answer enough. Warren nodded seeing the team's response. "Welcome to the team, Amelia," he spoke up. Slowly he pulled the map from his pack and unrolled it. "According to Arcanist, our next area to explore is going out to that field where we met Amelia last night," he added as before rolling the map back up.

Camilla checked over their supplies and nodded. "We should have the supplies to get there and back, easily. I've plenty of arrows for prolonged combat," she noted as she twirled an arrow between her fingers.

They headed back to the field from the previous night. It was quiet, unnaturally quiet. No wind. No wildlife. No anything. It made everyone uneasy, but they pushed onward. Once they were about halfway across the field, they came upon a ripple in the area. "Just like before," Azura murmured as she looked the distorted area over. Chuck snarled before rushing through the ripple as though something was calling out to him. Warren turned to the others and nodded. Everyone dove into the ripple, not knowing what to expect.

Chapter 11 - Memories Of Crest

One by one they came to the other side of the ripple. They found themselves in a large field, fires burning the land on all sides. The scent of blood, of death hung heavy in the air as they looked around.

"Chuck home?" Chuck growled as he recognized the land. It was Crest, a land that was built upon savage and barbaric nature.

Warren felt sick; his body shuddered under his armor. Azura and Camilla recognized the feeling they had. Both of them had to steady themselves before trying to move. Amelia's legs felt weak as she tried to steady herself. What was this feeling she suddenly was overcome with?

"Wel kin travelers." A voice caught their attention, causing all five in the party to look over.

Chuck froze. He knew the woman too well. "Gurk," was all he managed to say.

Standing before them was an ethereal orc, a pale blue glow surrounded them as they floated before the group. "This be Crest, land 'uilt on strength. Seek thee the legend of ol', find the hidden valley and explore the destruction that waits," she stated as she floated a few feet away, waiting for them to follow.

Warren put a hand on Chuck's shoulder. "No matter what you did, who you were, we're here for you," he stated, only receiving a grunt from the barbarian.

They followed the woman and soon found she had led them to a vast valley that was burning and littered with bodies. Chuck smirked seeing such.

He roared happily as he hefted his greataxe high into the air. "Bloodscourge Valley! Chuck home!" he belted proudly.

As the travelers walked through the valley, they came upon a hidden hole as though someone had tried to hide something. Chuck took lead as he entered; behind him were Camilla and Amelia walking side by side. Azura and Warren brought up the rear. The scent of rot burned their noses as they entered the tiny hole in the ground. Gradually it opened up to a series of tunnels, each illuminated by dull torch light. The deeper the went the more rancid the stench of death became. Azura gagged a few times from the rotting smell in the tunnels. Warren was uneasy but did his best not to show it. Camilla's gaze narrowed as she studied the layout of the tunnels they walked. She occasionally dug an arrow into the wall, using such to guide them should they get lost in the tunnel network. Amelia was unfazed by the smells, being undead herself she was never affected by rot smells.

Finally, the tunnel opened up a massive underground chamber. Bodies littered the ground. A spectral version of Chuck was seen walking amidst the bodies as he added more to his collection. There were several children-sized skulls littering the ground. And plenty of adult male-sized skulls and bone fragments strewn about. Chuck, the real one, smirked remembering this. How he loved to kill and keep his trophies. As they watched the spectral version of the barbarian, they noticed the bones began to shake, some flying up only to fall to the ground again.

All at once, the bones sprung up each one shaping a new creature. They collected together, becoming a horrible monster. The beast was made entirely of bone, its massive head and gaping maw looming over the spectral version of Chuck. The creature's arms swung out as it dug claws into the ground. Azura and Warren flinched seeing such a horrific sight as the monster lunged forward devouring the spectral version of the barbarian. Camilla rested her right hand on her longsword, ready to draw the blade at any moment. Amelia had already drawn her bastard sword, her tower shield floating beside her. Chuck took a step back; for the first time in his life, he felt a twinge of fear. The beast turned its attention to the group, letting out a shrill roar as it readied to lunge.

Camilla drew her longsword; the blade was glowing with a white light. Ghost Contact. The enchantment allowed her to damage the undead and incorporeal beings. Amelia moved to put herself between the charging monster and the group. As the bone beast came upon them, Amelia was already slashing in a controlled fashion, trying to break some of the bones off the beast. Camilla rushed forward to aid their newest team member. Chuck was frozen in fear. He had never felt this in his life. A being with his strength should never feel fear. But here he was, scared out of his mind.

Amelia winced as the weight of the monster's claws came down, threatening to crush her. She saw the ranger pinned in the monster's jaws. When had that happened? How had that happened? Warren shook his head as he began casting, he locked onto Camilla and was trying to use a warp spell to get her out of the monster's jaws. Azura unleashed her fireball spells, trying to deal some damage to the monster. There was an unsettling roar, and the monster dropped the ranger from its jaws. Camilla barely had a chance to register her fall, coming up in a very dazed crouch. Her ears were ringing from the roar as she tried to focus.

"Amelia!" Camilla managed to call out. The paladin looked over, now free from the claws thanks to the spell casters intervening. "Think you can give me a boost?" the ranger asked as she wore the most serious expression she had all mission. Amelia nodded and steadied herself, her tower shield coming to her. She gripped the shield, bringing it over her head as she bent her knees slightly. Camilla ran with every bit of strength she had. She jumped, her feet pressing against the paladin's shield. Amelia shoved her shield upward as she felt the ranger's weight land upon it.

Camilla was launched some distance up, landing on part of the bone beast's neck. While not ideally where she wanted to be, it was close enough. She dug her longsword into the segments of bone at the base of the monster's skull and began to force the blade down. A shrill howl escaped the monster as it bucked and trashed around, trying to force the ranger from its back. The longsword dug deeper, starting to split through magic holding the bones together. Warren and Azura used their magic, trying to weaken the monster. Amelia used her shield and bastard sword to chisel away at the monster's claws.

Soon a pop was heard as the skull fell from the beast's neck, landing on the ground before the group. Camilla held on as the body soon crashed to the ground. She staggered as she stepped out from the mess of bones. "Odd that a bone beast would be found here, a place only filled with humanoid bones," Warren noted as he looked around.

"Not all that here. Chuck kill many creatures. Chuck leave bones as trophy. This trophy room," the barbarian stated as he slowly walked over to the others.

"So, you were a ruthless killer, like me," Warren duly noted as he looked around.

Chuck nodded as he walked to another tunnel. Everyone turned and followed the barbarian as he led them to a side tunnel that led to a smaller chamber. Inside were seven caskets, each bearing different decor upon them. "Who are they?" Azura asked slowly as she studied the room.

"They Chuck's seven wives." The barbarian stayed as he looked everything over.

"How did they die?" Warren asked, almost afraid to hear the answer. Chuck did not answer, just stared at the caskets. It was all the cleric needed to figure out the rest. "Why did you do it?" he asked.

"They not strong. They each weak. Strong all that matter," Chuck growled, trying to defend his views on things. As the words lefts his mouth, the seven caskets began to open. Everyone jumped in surprise as they stared intensely at the caskets, waiting. Slowly, rising up from each casket were decayed, undead female humanoids. One held a massive greataxe that was more impressive than Chuck's. The next held a quarterstaff. The third carried twin scimitars. The fourth one lacked noticeable weapons and instead carried a spell book. As their attention reached the fifth, they saw a warhammer. Next one down, the sixth held an impressive longsword. And finally was the seventh who had spiked gauntlets.

Warren moved between the seven undead beings and Azura, his shield brought up and ready to protect. Amelia and Camilla were already weapon drawn as they watched. Combat erupted in the small chamber, five against seven. Chuck was fighting with the one that carried a greataxe; she was clearly the leader. Warren was in combat with the one who carried a longsword. Amelia fought with the one wearing gauntlets as well as the one that carried a quarterstaff. Azura was matching the caster, spell to spell. Camilla fought the one with the scimitars and the one with a warhammer.

Chuck felt a wave of unease as they fought; his body shook from the feeling. It was like something was sapping his will to fight. As he glanced to see the other fights, he noticed he was the only one being affected. Amelia's shield took a battery of blows from the gauntlets as the undead orc punched repeatedly. Her bastard sword barely kept pace with the quarterstaff wielding human. Warren was having a difficult time with the longsword attacker; she was fast and able to move between his attacks. Camilla had drawn her shortsword in her left hand, now fighting with two weapons trying to match the scimitar swinging undead elf. She was sent reeling as the warhammer struck her exposed left side.

"Camilla!" Azura called overseeing the ranger hit a wall.

"That's going to leave a mark," Camilla responded as she got to her feet.

Twin scimitars came around, nearly taking the ranger's head from her shoulders. The loud metallic clank resonated through the chamber as the attack was blocked. Amelia's tower shield was hovering between the scimitars and the recovering ranger. Camilla smirked and kicked the shield, causing it to collide with the undead elf and force her back. "Thanks for the save, Amelia!" Camilla called before rushing back into the fight.

Amelia nodded as she plunged her bastard sword into the undead human. One down. She turned her attention to the brawler with spiked gauntlets. She rushed forward, her armor showing no signs of damage as the brawler punched metal repeatedly.

Warren began pressing for an opening against the longsword aggressor. He finally saw what exactly he was fighting and shook his head. "Chuck, man! The heck! You did a lizard person?" he questioned.

"Chuck not care about race. As long strong, all Chuck want," the barbarian shot back as he parried an axe swing from the undead orc.

"Break it up, boys!" Amelia called out as she shield bashed the brawler.

Azura took a deep breath letting it out slow. Her cone of ice shot forth freezing the opposing caster. "Warren!" she yelled over before flinging a fireball at the lizard person.

"On it!" Warren replied as he rushed the opposing caster. His morningstar smashing the frozen caster into several chunks. Two down.

As the lizard person recovered from the fireball, it was thrown to the ground by the gauntlet wielding wolf like being. Amelia smirked as she pushed the advantage. She had managed to overwhelm the brawler and knocked them into one of their allies. Pushing forward, Amelia brought her bastard sword down, cleaving both enemies in two. Four down.

Camilla backflipped, narrowly dodging the scimitars. As she glanced over, she saw Warren strike the undead half giant. The morningstar colliding with the warhammer. She pressed her attacks further on the undead elf, trusting Warren to handle the half giant. Amelia moved to support the cleric as he fought. The two dodging between warhammer swings and countering where openings presented themselves. "Amelia, go for it!" Warren called out as he pinned the half giant against a wall, his morningstar pressed against the undead being's chest. Amelia rushed forward, her blade tearing through the jugular and sending the severed head to the ground. Five down.

Chuck was in a bad spot; he was barely matching the undead orc's greataxe swings. He staggered as he tried to regain his footing. She lunged forward, another vicious swing of her greataxe threatening to cleave the barbarian. Warren and Amelia were faster. They both managed to get between the assault and their staggered ally. The greataxe collided with both tower shields. Azura began casting again, her ice spell connecting and freezing the orc in place. Chuck lashed out with his greataxe, finally ending the orc. Six down.

Looking back to the ranger, Camilla was disarmed. She lunged forward, her claws slashing wildly like a frenzied animal. A sickening squish like sound was heard as the undead elf finally dropped, claws marks gashed into the rotting flesh. Camilla collected her weapons and walked over to the others.

"So, what now?" Warren asked as he looked at the mess before them.

The greataxe floated up from the ground and hovered in front of Chuck. "I am Crusher the Greataxe. One of five legendary weapons sealed within nightmares. I will bend to your strength as you are worthy." A voice echoed. Chuck took the greataxe in hand, hefting it proudly as he let out a mighty war cry.

The world around them twisted and shifted; soon the adventurers found themselves back in the field where they had entered the ripple. "Weapons sealed in nightmares?" Amelia asked as she arched an eyebrow.

"Yeah, it's a long story," Warren began as he shouldered his morningstar. Amelia twitched her eye before waving for him to continue. "We don't actually know but call it a theory. There are five hidden weapons that are the keys to defeating the being that governs this realm. The nightmares are likely encounters with our old realms and as such, our old adventure parties," he reasoned.

"Which means we'll be visiting Kardax twice as well as your home realm, Amelia," Azura added as she looked around.

"We best find somewhere to camp. Town's too far, and it's already dark," Camilla chimed in before pointing to part of the nearby tree line. "There. It's out of direct sight and we can use the tree branches to stay off the ground," she added as she began heading off. Everyone nodded and soon followed.

Chapter 12 - Tales Of Our Pasts

Once everyone was secured and set up in the tree branches; the group huddled close to one another. Warren shook his head, finally breaking the silence. "So, you guys have seen where I'm from. And we've seen where Chuck's from. What about you three?" he asked. At first there was silence. "Any stories from your home realms?"

Azura took a deep breath, slowly letting it out. "I come from Kardax; I believe I mentioned such when we were having dinner at Uldritch's estate. But I'm to be the queen of the realm. My story, however, has a lot of blood to it." Everyone was silent waiting for the sorceress to continue. "My brother and my retainer were both slain in combat against an evil warlock and his undead blue dragon. Narcian. I'll never forget that fight." She trailed on.

"Camilla!" she called out as she watched the magical blast strike. It was unlike any spell she had seen. No fire, ice, nor lightning. No, this spell was much like a large beam of darkness. The ranger collapsed, a hole through her chest. Azura ran to her side, dropping to her knees beside her retainer. "Camilla! Camilla, don't leave me!" she screamed as she looked over the wound. She did not know healing magic, what was she to do? She felt a hand pat her shoulder. Azura looked up, seeing Camilla's

weak smile as she bled out. Why was she smiling? How could she smile? She was dying! "Camilla… no…" Azura felt the tears stream down her face.

"Azura, look out!" Henry yelled as he parried a lizard person's greatsword. "AZURA!" he screamed when he saw the beam of darkness collide in the same area as his sister.

Azura had flinched back. She knew she was going to die from the attack. She felt no pain. Slowly opening her eyes, she saw her retainer, Camilla, shielding her. The ranger's body was already on the verge of death and yet she used what remained of her strength to shield the young sorceress.

Azura wiped the tears from her eyes. Just recounting the battle was enough to get her in tears. "I lost my best friend that day. I lost her because I was too weak," she said somberly. Everyone was silent trying to process what had been said. Azura shook her head. "But losing Henry soon after, it made me want to give up. I wanted to die."

Azura, Henry and Frederick fought a long hard battle scaling the castle. They were finally engaging in the final battle for Kardax's freedom. Narcian and his summoned undead blue dragon were all that remained. Narcian, the same warlock who had killed Camilla merely a week ago. Henry was keeping the warlock busy while Frederick and Azura handled the undead monster. The knight had been knocked aside, leaving the sorceress alone to fight the undead blue. The claws came down; she froze in fear.

Blood splattered onto her face, breaking the sorceress from the trance like state. Her eyes darting around uncontrollably as she realized what had happened. Henry smiled as he ruffled her hair, blood running down his face, his back and dripping from the corner of his mouth. "You can do this, Azura. I'll always be right there, with you, every step of the way," he said, still boasting the strong smile. Slowly he turned, Azura's eyes widening as she saw the claw gashes in his back.

"He shouldn't be standing from all that! There's no way!" Narcian yelled as he unleashed the beam of darkness.

Henry's smile never faltered. He parried the dark beam and rushed forward, his blade leaving deep wounds in the undead dragon. As the beast came down to bite him, Azura watched as her brother's blade took the dragon's head clean off its neck.

"What is he?" Narcian snarled. For the first time since the fight had begun, there was fear in his voice.

"A hero," Azura said under her breath as she watched Henry stagger. He smiled at her; one final smile before he finally collapsed.

"Milord!" Frederick yelled as he rushed to the dying swordsman's side.

"Henry always smiled. He never showed weakness. His smile was a beacon of hope for others as he said. He once told me that—"

"If you smile while saving someone, it lets them know you're alright. Which in turns means everything will be ok," Camilla interrupted as she thought back to her Kardax. Her Henry said the exact same words when they were younger. It was his way of always trying to boost the spirits of everyone in the village.

Azura nodded before smiling. "Guess our Henrys were more alike than anything else from our versions of Kardax," she said. Camilla just nodded.

Warren looked to Camilla. "What about you? Any stories worth telling?"

Camilla looked at the sky, her thoughts going over each adventure she went on with the supposed Guardians of Kardax. "Well, the old group I travelled with, we had some wild adventures. I suppose I might have one," she said before looking to the group once more.

The undead crawled the desert labyrinth. Everywhere they turned there were more of the undead abominations. Roy had kicked over a few tables to give the spell casters and the archers some cover. He, Thrall and Vanessa were the front-line offense, trying to keep the waves of monsters back.

"Roy on your right!" Lun called out.

The half lizard person barely had time to bring his shield up to block the attack. He nodded his thanks back as he kept up the attack. "They're breaking through!" Gemma called over the sounds of combat.

"Stay calm we can take them!" Roy shouted, rallying his party's morale. Then the hit came. The half lizard roared out in pain as an enemy blade had torn deep into his sword arm. The longsword, Starfang, fell to the ground. Gemma drew her rapier and moved in to cover Roy as he fell back to be healed. Camilla nocked three arrows, letting them fly, covering the demon-like being as she advanced. Roy nodded his thanks to Gemma as she took his position on the front lines. Lun healed Roy's arm as the fight raged on.

Gemma let out a grunt in pain as an enemy caught her off guard and dealt a serious wound to her. "Gemma!" Lun yelled as she and Roy rushed to the demon-like being's side.

Camilla glanced to Dragom, the wizard making no motion of doing anything. She shook her head and leapt over the barricade, joining the main fight as she drew her shortsword. Soon the fight was over. Lun moved to heal Gemma but was caught by surprise when the rogue turned and lashed out with her rapier.

"Lun, lookout!" Camilla hollered as she lunged forward, taking the strike meant for the cleric. Blood stained her green tunic and brown leather vest.

"Gemma, calm down! It's us!" Roy tried to reason with the berserk rogue. It took some convincing but eventually the rogue had come back to rational thought. Lun patched everyone up, everyone aside from the ranger who had taken the rapier strike.

Camilla was silent, her eyes narrowed on her own wound. Carefully she used what little magic she knew from years in the wild to heal the wound. She looked back to the group, seeing they barely noticed how much danger the cleric had been in. No, they treated it like nothing.

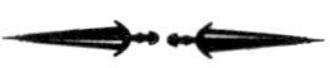

"Wait, so you threw yourself into an attack meant to kill another?" Amelia asked, completely taken back.

Camilla nodded as she watched the sky. She took a deep breath, slowly letting it out as she gave a subtle frown. "I valued their healer's life. None of the others did though. And while I was healed, it was through my own magic, not theirs," she finally spoke.

Warren shook his head. "So, you've always been willing to shield others… " he said slowly, recalling the nightmare battle they had in his realm. He recalled Camilla putting herself in harm's way to shield him.

The ranger was silent as she stared at the sky. Her gaze reflected a somber mood. "Obviously I left that group. And I have no regrets," she noted before glancing at the group before returning her gaze to the sky. She could tell they had more questions, but she did not want to talk about it. "It's not important why I left. And it's not like I had a choice either."

"You always have a choice," Amelia stated.

"Do we?" Camilla questioned as she looked to the half vampire. "Or is everything predetermined, and we are given the illusion of choice?" Everyone was silent, thinking over the words. Camilla shook her head as she looked away again. "Did you have a choice in becoming what you are? Or were you given the illusion of choice and it was if you didn't you'd suffer worse?" she questioned, her tone distant, cold even.

Amelia shook her head. "I had a choice. I chose to let my mentor infect me with the vampiric curse. My choices were become a mindless beast, a werewolf, or let Balthazar bite and infect me. I kept my mind; I made a choice," she reasoned.

"Doesn't sound like much of a choice," Camilla duly noted. She heard Amelia shift slightly. "Be infected with the vampiric curse and become half vampire, half werewolf and keep your rational mind. Or don't be bit, and become a mindless monster, losing all semblance to who you are."

Everyone was silent again. Choice. The more they thought, choice was becoming more of an illusion than something they had. They each chose to come to this world. But returning home, Arcanist did not give them a choice. It was do this task, this quest for him, and then he would send them home. They did not get a choice in returning home.

"We should get some rest. It's been a long day," Warren finally said after a few long moments of silence. Everyone nodded in agreement before calling it a night. The cleric was keeping first watch; he was unable to shake the talk they had just had. Choice. Illusion of choice. Which was it? He believed they were free to choose, but now he thought more and more. And the more he thought he became conflicted.

The next morning the adventurers were up as the red-orange sun was just beginning to rise. Each took their time. Slowly they made their descent from the tree branches and onto the ground. Warren unfolded the map and laid it out for everyone to see. "We have no idea where to go from here. So, any suggestions are welcomed," he said.

Amelia tapped a part of the map where there looked to be some sort of mountain range. "There's a few small settlements there. Maybe we can explore and ask the folks there if they know anything about these ripples," she calmly spoke.

Azura pointed to any area near a lake. "We could also investigate this lake," she chimed in, for once allowing herself to be heard.

Warren looked to Chuck and Camilla. "Any other suggestions?"

Chuck pounded his chest, letting out a war cry. "Chuck not care where go! Chuck only want fight!"

The cleric looked to the ranger. She was oddly quiet this morning. "Camilla?" he asked, waiting for a response.

"I think we should try contacting Arcanist and see if he has any new leads for us," the ranger noted as she looked over the map.

Everyone looked to the communication stone. Warren gripped it slightly as he brought it up to his face. "Arcanist, are you there?" he asked.

"Adventurers! Good to hear your voices!" Arcanist cheered from the other end.

"We were wondering if you had any new leads for us to pursue," Azura chimed in as she stood on her tiptoes.

There was a moment of silence. It was as though Arcanist was having to check something. Finally, he spoke up. "I have two leads for your group. The first is located in Faraway Lake, and the second is in the Spiral Mountains. I can't say for certain anything more past that. My apologies, adventurers." With those words, the communication stone went dark.

The group looked at one another before looking at the map in between them. "Spiral Mountain and Faraway Lake. Those were both areas we had intended to go. So, which one first?" Camilla asked as she looked up from the map.

Warren shook his head. "We should put this to a vote," he calmly reasoned. "All in favor of Faraway Lake, show of hands," he stated. Azura and himself raised their hands. "And those in favor of Spiral Mountain?" He paused as he watched both Amelia and Camilla raise their hands. "Chuck, you're the tie breaker here." He turned his attention to where the barbarian had been standing and arched an eyebrow. "Chuck! Ah, where'd he go?"

Azura, Camilla and Amelia looked around each trying to figure out where the barbarian had gone. Camilla checked for tracks, her senses on high alert. Azura glanced toward where Amelia had been, and her eyes widened. "Did anyone see Amelia walk off?" she asked.

Camilla glanced over, her face showing the same calm demeanor she always wore. "I have no traces on Chuck. No tracks, it's like he just vanished," she stated. As the words left her mouth, both she and Azura saw Warren seemingly vanish as well. "What in the heck is going on?" she questioned. Then she vanished.

Azura looked around, completely scared. She had never been alone before. It was unsettling. Before she knew what to do, a flash of light swallowed her up. No traces remained of the adventurers.

"If they want to split up, then I'll happily grant such!" A dark and sinister voice laughed, their voice echoing within the forest.

Chapter 13 - Faraway Lake

Warren slowly opened his eyes as he sat up. He saw both Chuck and Azura lying not too far from him and rushed to Azura's side. "Azura! Azura, say something!" he pleaded as he shook the young sorceress. She coughed a few times, before slowly opening her eyes. "Thank the gods." Warren breathed a sigh of relief before turning his attention to the barbarian. "Chuck, come on, big guy. Let's get you up," he said as he shook the muscular half orc.

Chuck grunted but eventually started to wake. He let out a deep growl as he sat up and looked around. "Where we?" he asked, his deep voice showing a slight bit of concern.

Azura pointed before them. "Looks like we're at Faraway Lake," she said as she stood. She brushed herself off and looked around again. "Arcanist said there was a ripple here. Guess we should investigate," she added as she began walking along the shore line.

Warren and Chuck nodded as they walked along the shore line looking for different clues. "Any signs of Camilla or Amelia?" Warren asked as he looked around for the ranger and knight. Both Azura and Chuck shook their heads. "Keep your eyes open. I pray both of them are alright," he added as he continued searching along the shore. After a few hours of walking and finding nothing, they decided to try to locate any nearby towns. Warren had a feeling they were going to have to get their feet wet if they wanted to find the ripple but hoped he was wrong as he was not a strong swimmer.

It was nightfall by the time they reached the town, if it could even be called such. Thankfully both the tavern and the inn were still open and accepting travelers. They tried the tavern first trying to gather any information they could. Upon entering they were greeted with the familiar stench of ale and urine, along with incredibly foul body odor. Azura gagged slightly as she waved off the smell. Chuck immediately ran to the counter and demanded ale. Warren surveyed the area and made a mental note of everyone in the grungy environment. There was a large pot-bellied man sitting in the corner playing on a piano, his left hand missing, replaced with a hook hand. Sitting near him was a much shorter dwarf playing an accordion as well as an elf playing the violin. To the far back of the tavern was a lizard person, wearing a cloak and smoking a pipe. With him was a minotaur sharpening her greatsword.

Sitting at the bar counter were three other adventurers. The first was a human clad in leather armor with a sword and shield on his back. The second was an elf wearing a black longcoat; he appeared to be reading some sort of book, ignoring the scene around him. And the last of the trio was another human; she had ebony hair and wore simple black robes that were very revealing in many spots. Warren found her to be the most unnerving character in the tavern.

As the cleric and sorceress approached the bar counter to join the barbarian, they listened to any ongoing conversations. The trio mentioned a missing prince but past such was no important information. The lizard person and minotaur were discussing the sudden disappearance of fish and how it was going to affect the livelihood of the people in the town. The instrument trio were joined by a fourth who sang about heroic tales of old. No new leads. Chuck had ordered a triple ale for himself and a double ale for Warren. They sat at the bar counter, discussing what their next course of action should be.

"We didn't see any ripples at the lakeshore. Think we should try in the lake?" Warren mused as he sipped his ale.

Azura shook her head. "I don't know. Seems risky to just dive into the water without knowing if there's even a ripple down there," she stated, trying to be the voice of reason.

"Ripples you say?" The elf who was reading looked up from his book. He placed a red bookmark then closed the book.

"Darean, my fated one, why do these ones interest you?" the creepy, scantily dressed woman asked as she followed his gaze.

Darean, the elf, ignored his companion as he held his gaze on Warren, Azura and Chuck. "You must be talking about the time ripples, yes?"

Warren and Azura looked to one another then to the elf in the longcoat. "Time ripples? What do you know about them, good sir?" Warren asked.

"They started showing up randomly all over the place. Rumor has it, only a select person can enter. Anyone else enters without that special person and something horrible happens," Darean explained. He rubbed his chin thinking for a moment before continuing. "But if you're really wanting to explore the time ripple, you'll need to first dive down into the depths of Faraway Lake. Last I heard, there's a time ripple somewhere down there."

Warren and Azura exchanged glances, both had the same look, fear. Neither were strong swimmers. "Anywhere we can purchase some gear to proceed with such an adventure?" Warren asked, looking back to Darean.

"You'll have to wait until morning, but try the fisherman's guild," the creepy woman chimed in as she rested her hands on Darean's shoulders, clearly very possessive of the elf.

"Thank you for the information," Azura said calmly as she turned her attention fully to Warren.

"Let's head to the inn and call it a night. We'll need our rest if we're doing this without two of our team," Warren stated as he paid for the ales then stood. Azura followed close behind. Chuck grumbled under his breath before finishing his ale. Once finished, he followed the cleric and sorceress out the tavern and across the way to the inn.

They checked into a single room, no one wanting to be alone with everything going on within the unfamiliar town. Chuck was the first one asleep; his snoring was loud and long. Azura laid upon her bed and stared at the ceiling trying to make sense of everything. She could not stop thinking about the warning they were given. Sitting up she looked to Warren, who was also still awake. "I can't shake that warning we were given," she finally spoke up.

"About how something bad will happen if we enter without the person meant to enter the ripple? Yeah, I've been thinking about that too," Warren noted as he leaned back against his bed. He slowly sat up and looked across from him, his eyes meeting Azura's. "Think we should find Amelia and Camilla first?"

"We don't even know where they are. Or if they're even alive," Azura murmured, fear in her voice.

"I'm sure they're alive, neither seems like they're the type to die easily," the cleric stated as he gave the sorceress a soft smile.

"I think we should take the risk. We don't know how long these ripples are active for. And we have a one in three chance of everything working out," Azura noted.

Warren nodded slowly. "Alright, guess it's settled. Now get some sleep, Azura. We both need it." Soon after their talk, both cleric and sorceress fell asleep.

The next morning, the trio made their way through town to the fisherman's guild. It was a rundown looking shack, anchors and other boating gear scattered about the front. Upon entering the door, they were greeted by a large man who wore an eyepatch over his right eye. "Aye, what can I do for ye land walkers?" he greeted as he walked over to the desk in the corner of the room.

"We were looking to purchase some gear to aid us in an underwater expedition," Azura spoke up.

The man arched an eyebrow as he looked the group up and down. "Underwater, with that?" he asked as he indicated Warren who was in full armor.

"Yes, sir. It's very important that we make haste," Azura explained.

He took a deep breath then let it out slowly. "Alright, lass, alright. First, you'll need some breathing apparatus and proper diving armor," the large man stated as he indicated the wall lined with armors made from fish scales and other marine creature flesh. "Then you'll need a boat," he added as he stood from his table. The large man measured each member in the trio and fitted armor to them as well as got the right sized breathing apparatuses for them. Once they were suited up, he showed them to his boats and made a recommendation which they went with.

"Thank you very much, kind sir," Azura said as she paid for everything then headed to leave.

"Aye, lass, just be careful. No knowing what lies in wait in the inky darkness of Faraway Lake," he added as the group left his shop.

They made the long hike back to the lake and got the boat in the water. "You alright, Warren?" Azura asked, seeing the nervousness of the cleric.

"Yeah, I just uh… can't swim well," Warren admitted.

Chuck laughed a little as they paddled out to the center of the lake. "Chuck strong swimmer. Swim not hard. All able to swim at early age," the barbarian stated.

"I never learned," Warren added.

"Guess we're going to be doing some quick learning," Azura said as she smiled nervously.

Once they reached the center of the lake, they dropped the boat's anchor and jumped into the water. It was frigid at best, all of them regretting this choice. One by one they dove underwater and swam as best they could deeper and deeper. Chuck was in the lead; as the strongest swimmer, he found it easy to move around. Azura and Warren stayed close to one another as they dove deeper. Resting at the bottom of the lake was a sunken temple. Seeing no signs of the ripple, they made their way to the temple.

As they surfaced in the temple, what they saw took them back. It was massive on the inside. Large marble pillars supporting the ceiling above them. At the center of the room was in fact a ripple. They all breathed a sigh of relief as they removed the fish scale armor and re-equipped their normal gear. Warren looked at the series of glyphs on the archway that rested surrounding the ripple. "Enter those with the magic imbued heart. Enter the one with twin souls," he translated from the glyphs.

"Twin souls? Sounds like someone from two worlds," Azura noted.

"Both you and Camilla came from different versions of Kardax. Maybe it's a reference to the two souls in the different Kardax versions?" Warren reasoned. With a nod, Azura stepped through. Chuck and Warren followed close behind her.

Upon coming out the other side of the ripple, each of the three adventurers felt a strange sensation overtake them. It was a dull pain, a mild shock rather. When the haziness in their minds cleared, they realized something was very wrong. Warren was the first to realize something was wrong. He felt weightless, like his armor was missing. Turning his head to look, he then noticed what looked like himself stumbling to the side. "Hey!" he called but found his voice coming out much higher pitched. As he covered his mouth, he noticed his hands were more feminine.

Azura shook her head as she cleared the last of the haziness from her mind. Upon doing so the realization set in very quickly. "Uh… I think we have a serious problem," she said but her voice sounded several octaves too deep. Looking at what she assumed would be her reflection, she found herself looking at the face of the barbarian. "What sort of magic is this!" she hollered out as she stepped back in shock.

"Chuck want know, how move in armor?" Chuck yelled, trying to move. The heavy armor he was suddenly clad in proved to be a challenge to move in.

Warren pinched the bridge of his nose, as he thought back to the words spoken to them at the town. "Damnit. Looks like we stumbled into one of those curses, the *if we don't have the right person present, something bad happens*," he muttered as he looked over the others. "Alright, so who's mental self in where?"

"Chuck here!" Chuck growled as he raised a hand, the thick armor making it feel heavy again.

"I'm Azura, but looks like I'm in Chuck's body," Azura responded as she waved slightly.

"And I'm you, Warren here," Warren said as he indicated Azura's body. He never wanted to be a woman; it was uncomfortable to say the least. And then there were the massive things on his chest. "How do you balance like this? These damned things are huge!" he complained as he had to steady himself.

"I should be asking how does Chuck not feel cold, or heat like this! And why only the loincloth?" Azura practically growled.

Soon the trio was bickering with one another as they tried to assess what to do. Warren shook his head, the light blue hair getting in his face. "Alright, enough! Let's just try to find a way back and maybe that will reverse things," he reasoned. Disgruntled about the situation, the three agreed as they began looking for the portal again.

While there were no signs of the portal, they began taking in their surroundings. Instead of the underwater temple, they had been transported to a ruined town. As they made their way through the remains of the town, each had their own set of difficulties adjusting to whose body they were now in. At the center of the town was a massive altar that was on fire. Lying across it, blood staining the stone slab was a young girl. She looked maybe sixteen in age. Warren felt uneasy; was he feeling this way because he was now in Azura's body? He glanced to Azura; it was so strange to be looking at the barbarian but knowing it was the sorceress inside. She did not seem fazed at all. She stared at the altar, expression blank.

"What do you suppose happened here?" Azura asked as she began walking again.

Chuck had taken the lead; his heavy armor clanked with every step he took. "Chuck not sure. Chuck not sure if want to know," he responded as he looked around. Bodies littered the ground; many were ripped apart as though attacked by animals.

As they made their way to the far side of the town, they found a ruined church. "We should take shelter for a bit. Maybe regain our wits a little," Warren suggested. He hated how meek his voice sounded coming from Azura's body. While he had his resolve, the words carried little weight.

"I think we should keep searching. Stopping is only going to slow us down," Azura nearly snarled, her voice coming out much more aggressive than she intended.

Before any of them could discuss the topic further, the bodies they thought dead began twitching, spasming. One by one they stood; some were just undead remains of the people they had once been. Others began sprouting thick fur. Werewolves. Azura drew the greataxe that rested on her back and let out a fierce battle cry. She had observed Chuck enough to feel comfortable fighting in his place. Warren took a step back, he felt helpless without his armor. He shook his head and began casting. Chuck stumbled a bit but drew his tower shield and morningstar.

Each inwardly hoped the others knew how to fight as whomever they had been transferred to. Azura rushed forward, charging some of the werewolves, the greataxe splintering bones as it swung. Chuck rushed forward next; the heavy armor prevented him from gaining much ground, but it provided a great defense from the bites and claws of the werewolves he had engaged.

Warren unleashed three fireballs in rapid succession trying to deal with the undead villagers. "Chuck, use your divine skills! Should be more effective on the undead than these fireballs!" he called over the sounds of combat.

Chuck snorted. "Chuck not like be told what do!" he shot back as the morningstar crushed a werewolf's skull.

"Put your ego on hold and listen to him!" Azura yelled at Chuck, clearly annoyed with him. She hated not being able to use magic. It had been all she had ever known. In terms of melee combat, that was her brother's specialty, but he always used a shield and longsword. Shaking her head, Azura cleared her thoughts and continued to fight as best she could as the barbarian.

Despite everything, with a bit of luck at their side, the three had managed to survive the encounter. Breathing heavily, they regrouped before each started laughing a little. "Guess you know Chuck's fighting style better than I thought." Warren laughed.

"Yeah, and you've been watching what I cast." Azura chuckled.

Chuck just grunted as he pointed at Azura. "Chuck see new scars," he muttered.

"Sorry about that. New scars for the collection?" Azura tried to redirect things.

As Chuck reached out, a small blue light danced from his hands, healing the wounds Azura had received. "Chuck not earn them. Chuck not want them on body."

"Teehee! You three are so funny!"

Everyone spun on their heels to figure out where the voice had come from.

"But this isn't a fun playtime when I can't mess with all five."

They looked around, panic setting in a bit.

"Wishy and a wash, I send you back through the ripple."

Everything grew hazy again. When they awoke, they were at the lakeshore. Warren felt his chest and breathed a sigh of relief when he felt the heavy chestplate. "Thank the gods," he muttered.

"Yes, thank the gods indeed. I didn't have to look far for you."

As they turned to look, three massive shields slammed into each of their heads, knocking them out instantly. Standing over the three adventurers were six men, each clad in heavy armor and armed with tower shields along with various weapons. "Master Timer Eater will be most happy with this. There's still two out there. But we'll find them soon enough," the leader, armed with a massive hand axe, stated.

"I have a better idea," a seventh member of the group stated as he stepped from the tree line. He was not clad in heavy armor. He wore blue colored armor; over such was a worn and badly damaged black coat. He smirked when he saw the leader arch an eyebrow. "Perhaps, use these three as bait to draw in the other two? Saves you the hassle of looking across the lands," he suggested, his voice carrying a level of sinister intent. He looked younger than all the other men, but it was clear he had a mind for strategy.

"An excellent idea. We'll take them to the keep at Forlorn, schedule an execution. And send out word as far as the messengers can carry it. Surely that would lure out the remaining outrealm warriors," the leader stated. He nodded to his men as they restrained the three adventurers. "Will you be joining us, Wintersong?"

"Nah, Hugo, I have other matters to attend to. I do wish you luck," Wintersong, the blue armor clad one, stated before taking his leave.

"Alright, men, let's move out. We wouldn't want to fail the Master," Hugo ordered as he climbed onto his horse that awaited nearby.

It was a five-day travel to Forlorn Keep. The entire way, Azura, Chuck and Warren had been blindfolded, their ears covered and hands bound. Escape was impossible. They were stripped of their weapons, armor and anything that the six soldiers deemed of value. When they reached the Keep, each were thrown into a different dungeon cell. No light trickled into the cells. No sounds could be heard from anywhere. They were each alone, isolated to whatever cell they were tossed into.

Chapter 14 - Spiral Mountains

"Hey, wake up! Come on, darlin', wake up!" Camilla slowly opened her eyes when she heard the voice. As she opened her eyes, she saw the paladin crouched over her. Amelia breathed a sigh of relief as she saw Camilla's yellow eyes open. "Glad to see you're awake," she added as she stood. She held out a hand, offering it to the ranger.

Camilla took the hand, accepting the help as she stood. "Where are we exactly?" the ranger asked as she brushed herself off then looked around.

"Based on the vast mountains, and the constant sensation of something spinning, I'd wager we're at the base of the Spiral Mountains," Amelia replied as she looked around.

The ranger nodded as she looked around. "Anyone else, or just us?"

"You were the only one I was able to find when I awoke. I theorize that Warren, Azura and Chuck were dropped elsewhere," the paladin noted as she pointed. "There's a small village down that way, maybe we can check into it and get some information about this place."

"Yeah, that sounds like a good plan," Camilla agreed fully with the idea. She drew her longsword in her right hand and one shortsword in her left. It was quite the walk, and she was already on edge. This was never a good sign. She heard Amelia draw her bastard sword and tower shield, both of them were on edge.

Slowly they trekked through the winding path that led them downward. It was an eventful walk, but they were even more on edge than when they started. Coming upon the small village, the paladin saw a grisly sight. She had hoped there would be people they could talk to and get a better idea of the area. Instead, they came upon a completely ruined village. Everyone was dead. Houses were ruined, clearly burned to the ground. Camilla walked past the paladin, her yellow eyes taking in the environment. At the far side of the village was what appeared to be a small schoolhouse.

Camilla paused as she ripped the notice from the door. “By order of our grand and merciful ruler, Time Eater, this village is to be burned and the people put in their place. Kill them all and let Patroklos sort them out,” she read aloud as she looked over the notice.

“So, this Time Eater, they clearly worship some divine being. What do you make of that?” Amelia asked as she walked over to the ranger.

“They worship the god of healing, of light. And yet they order this village and its people destroyed. Whoever this Time Eater being is, they are one very twisted being,” the ranger replied as she filed the notice into her bag. She shook her head then looked around the ruined village again. “We should lay low here for the night. Too dangerous to make our way back up the mountain path. And it’s late, I could use some rest,” she added despite the uneasy feeling she had.

Amelia nodded then pointed out the best in shape looking building. “Our best bet is going to be that one. Looks like it was the only building that was spared,” she explained as they began their walk. When they reached the building in question, Amelia arched an eyebrow. “Duskridge Orphanage. Does this Time Eater being have a soft spot for orphans?”

Camilla pushed the door open and noted how pristine everything looked. It was as though this one building was intentionally spared. She took a slight breath and let it out slowly. “Then that’s one thing I can agree with Time Eater on. Sparing those who lack parents. Who lack family.”

“You’re an orphan yourself, aren’t you?” Amelia asked clearly, already knowing the answer. Camilla nodded as she set her bag down in a corner and sat beside it. The paladin took a moment but soon joined the ranger. “What happened to your parents?”

The ranger barely looked up from her makeshift camp. She shook her head slightly then looked away. “I don’t know. Never knew them. My earliest memories are of serving House Vaughan; prior to that, I have no memories.

And those earliest ones, I was six, maybe seven. I remember Henry welcoming me into the estate and his sister, Azura, hiding behind him. That was my first memory. Nineteen maybe twenty years ago."

Amelia said nothing; she merely listened and tried to understand what the ranger was saying. "It's strange, I feel a kinship with you. Being what I am, I can see into the souls of others."

"I thought vampires lacked souls," Camilla interrupted.

The paladin chuckled slightly, flashing a fanged grin. "We do. And yet we can see into the souls of others. While we lack souls, we don't fully lack them. And I've seen many a vampire with souls cleaner than any human. As I was saying though, I feel a kinship with you. You lack a soul, like me. So, I have to wonder, what was worth the price of a human soul? What was so important that you gave up your soul?"

Camilla shook her head. "Can't say I remember. Must've been something in the long-forgotten past," she said calmly, her voice even as can be. She turned away, clearly trying to silently convey she had no interest in continuing this conversation.

Amelia merely nodded as she looked toward the door they entered from. "I'll keep watch, you get some rest," she finally said, clearly picking up on the ranger's desire to rest.

As Camilla slept, she was plagued by horrible dreams again. She kept dreaming of darkness, the entire world was dark. She felt cold, alone and broken. She wandered aimlessly for what felt like days. Everything was the same though. Bleak. Empty. Nothingness.

Many hours later, the ranger felt someone shaking her awake. "Camilla, wake up, it's morning," Amelia spoke softly as she tried to rouse the ranger.

Camilla's eyes opened slowly as she looked around. She nodded as she sat up then pushed herself to be standing. "Guess we should investigate Spiral Mountains," she said as she brushed herself off. Amelia nodded and followed the ranger's lead.

The two began their trek back up the long winding path back to the base of the mountain. Neither had the uneasy feeling they had the night before. Perhaps it was misplaced paranoia, or perhaps whatever trouble had passed. As they came upon the base of the mountain, both withdrew their spyglasses and began looking for any traces of a ripple. They studied the layout of the mountain range many times before finally looking to one another.

"Straight up this path and then veer left," both said at the same time. They shared a mild chuckle as they realized how in-tuned to the other they were. As they started up the path, Camilla had taken point while Amelia walked behind the ranger. The paladin could not help but smile when she thought about how well she and the ranger were getting along. This was the first time in a long time that Amelia felt like someone understood her. She tried hard to ignore the voice in the back of her mind, the voice that reminded her that Camilla had yet to see her during her worst moments.

"You alright?" Camilla asked, breaking Amelia from the thought. Amelia hesitated but gave a nod. "You hesitated. What's wrong?" the ranger asked, a faint bit of concern in her voice.

"It's nothing. I'm fine," Amelia quickly responded trying to put the concern at rest. Camilla gave a slow nod; it was clearly she was not convinced but was not going to press the matter further. They continued up the path before veering left as they had planned. Upon arriving at the summit, they saw a ripple much like the one they had seen in the field.

"Shall we?" Camilla asked as she indicated the ripple before them. Amelia nodded as she stepped forward. The pair took a deep breath before entering the ripple.

When they emerged on the other side, both felt immense pain. Camilla winced, her hands clutching her head. Glancing over, she saw Amelia was in worse shape. The paladin was leaning forward, her arms wrapped around her midsection and her breathing was shallow. "Don't worry, I'm fine," Amelia quickly stated before the ranger could ask.

Camilla slowly nodded before feeling some relief in her head. She took two big deep breaths, letting each one out slowly. Looking over her hands as she released the grip she had on her head, she noticed that her gloves were shredded and both hands were now covered in blue scales, sharp claws replacing her fingernails. She winced again as she felt something aching in her lower back. As she turned to check, she noticed a blue tail had torn through her clothing and hung low.

The ranger looked to the paladin, a look of genuine concern in her eyes. Amelia was breathing heavily as she tried to focus on anything other than pain. Her fangs had become more pronounced; claws were visible where her hands had been. Her ears were slightly more elongated and pointed back, but the most concerning part was the snout that had replaced her nose and jaw. "Amelia?" Camilla asked finally, her voice coming out with a bit more of a snarl than she anticipated.

Amelia looked over; her breath was labored as she tried to focus on the ranger. Both glanced at the sky, as though something had been heard overhead. Hanging in the night's sky was a blood red moon. Amelia's eyes went wide with horror. "Stay back!" she yelled to the ranger.

"Amelia!" Camilla was more than concerned now.

"I don't want to hurt you! And I don't know if I can..." Before the paladin could finish, she felt the unbearable pain in her abdomen. She let out a blood curdling howl as she dropped to her hands and knees. She was sweating profusely as her inner beast began taking hold of her. As she looked to Camilla, her eyes were a deep crimson. She snarled, not recognizing the ranger.

Camilla stared at the paladin. It made sense in her head, and yet she was still in a state of mild shock. The red moon, a blood moon, it held power over werewolves and vampires alike, and Amelia was both. The ranger watched as the paladin stood, her gaze one of pure bloodlust sizing up the ranger. "Amelia," Camilla began. She should run. She should draw a weapon. But she did not. Even in this state, it was still Amelia. "Amelia, I know you can hear me," Camilla attempted to reason. Her voice was calm, no traces of fear.

Amelia snarled as she lunged at Camilla, swinging out with her claws. The ranger took a step back, narrowly avoiding getting slashed by the claws. She took a deep breath as she dodged another slash from Amelia's claws. "You can hear me, I know it!" Camilla called out, a bit more forceful this time. A claw strike connected, sending Camilla skidding back a few feet. She wiped the blood from her cheek as she looked to see Amelia moving in for another attack. As Amelia was about to lash out with another claw strike, she showed some hesitation. She took a step back, clearly trying to fight back against her nature.

"You recognize me! I know it!" Camilla called as she took a step toward Amelia. She saw the paladin take another step back. "Come on, control yourself!" Camilla tried to get through to the paladin; she did not want to fight. For once she found someone she did not wish to fight. She only hoped her words would reach the paladin's mind.

A loud blood curdling howl was heard causing both ranger and paladin to look around frantically. On the ridgeline were several black werewolves.

Camilla cursed her luck. A one on one with Amelia might have been manageable but painful. Trying to fight an entire pack of frenzied werewolves, that was a whole different endeavor.

The werewolves ignored the paladin and closed in on the ranger. Each making faints, trying to bait the ranger into behaving recklessly. Camilla drew her shortswords from her belt. She had no qualms with fighting werewolves, but drawing her weapons would likely cause Amelia to lose what little control she had. As the werewolves lunged repeatedly, Camilla blocked and parried the claws as best she could. It was difficult to avoid being ripped apart by the werewolves; defensive tactics were all she could manage.

Amelia watched the fight ongoing, her red eyes darting back and forth watching each attacker. The human was on the defensive, easy prey. But the pack of eight proved to be a challenge to maneuver around. She snarled as she lunged forward, grabbing one of the werewolves by the upper jaw. The beast howled in agony as she pulled and ripped the upper jaw and much of the head from the beast. Each of the seven werewolves turned their attention to the paladin. Their attention shifted from hunting the prey to avenge the fallen.

Camilla breathed heavily as she watched the seven werewolves begin to attack Amelia. She studied their movements briefly before nodding, her mind making a plan. The ranger rushed forward, knocking two werewolves away from the paladin. She drove her shortswords through their skulls, killing them in an instant. Turning to engage the next foe, she saw Amelia was slashing wildly at the remaining five. Even in her feral state, five on one was hardly welcoming odds. Camilla rushed into the fight again, this time managing to force four werewolves to break off from the assault on the paladin. She glanced back, noting how it was the alpha that was still fighting with Amelia.

She turned her attention back to the four she had forced back. They slashed wildly, their jaws snapping, trying to wound the ranger and regroup with their alpha. Camilla winced as claws tore her left arm open. She slashed out with her shortswords, making quick but decisive hits. Behind her, she heard a loud snap. The attacks came to a halt and only then did the ranger turn her attention to the scene behind her.

Amelia stood, blood running down her fangs as she snapped down hard. The lifeless body of the alpha werewolf fell to the ground, chest ripped open and heart missing. The paladin's jaws lurched a few times as she consumed the heart of the alpha. There was clearly some hesitation, but the four other werewolves took off in a full sprint, fleeing the area.

Camilla breathed a sigh of relief as she sheathed her blades then focused completely on Amelia. The paladin was clearly still in a feral, bloodlust state of mind. She snarled at the ranger, a warning. "It's ok, Amelia. I'm not going to hurt you," she said softly as she tried to reason with the paladin. She gave a friendly smile as she held out a hand. "It's me, Camilla, you know me. I know you recognize me."

Amelia took a step back, her ears twitching slightly. Her mind was hazy, but she heard the words clearly. And more than the words, she heard the calm steady beating of the ranger's heart. It was not beating in fear, nor in aggression. It was calm. It was steady. She closed her eyes, focusing on the ranger's heartbeat. After a few moments, Amelia slowly opened her eyes, both having returned to their normal scarlet coloration. She took a few deep breaths, letting each one out slowly.

Camilla smiled and walked over, standing at an arm's distance from the paladin. "You alright, Amelia?" she asked, concern in her voice.

"Yes, I believe so," Amelia replied as she slowly met Camilla's gaze. "Camilla, I—"

"It's alright. No harm done," Camilla interrupted as she patted Amelia's right shoulder. She winced slightly before remembering her arm injury. "Hang on a sec," she added before tending to the wound. After a healing spell, the wound was sealed up and mended. "Blood moons always rile you up?" she asked.

"Blood moons, full moons, and lunar eclipses. Eclipse is the worst, but blood moon is a close second," Amelia explained as she rubbed the back of her head. She felt horrible. In her berserk state, she attacked her only friend. And yet, Camilla did not seem to be phased by such. "Camilla, I… I…"

"It's alright, Amelia. I know you didn't mean to slash my cheek," the ranger cut in with a smile. She patted the paladin's shoulder again. "Just remember, no matter what happens, I'm with you. Blood moon, full moon, eclipse or normal situation, I've got your back. I don't know why, but I feel a kinship with you just as you said you felt with me. You go berserk again; I'll be right here to snap you back."

"Camilla…" Amelia was taken back; never had she ever had anyone offer such. Never had she grown to feel friendship toward someone. She nodded her head, a faint smile visible. "Thank you," she responded.

The two shared a laugh before continuing to explore the area. No matter where they searched, they could not find any traces of a dungeon to explore. They came upon a small village. All the inhabitants claimed to be people yet looked like beasts. Some looked like taller versions of a normal animal. Others looked like they were disfigured beastmen.

"What can you tell us about this place?" Amelia asked a beastman.

"This is Duskridge, village of the setting moons." he replied.

Camilla arched an eyebrow as she looked from the beastman to the map she carried. Duskridge was the same village at the base of the Spiral Mountain. Was it possible this was what became of them? Time Eater's punishment to them was to send them into a void like space where they continued to live but had no idea what had been done to them?

Amelia noticed the ranger's expression and decided to ask for more information. "Can you tell us where Spiral Mountain is?" she asked.

The beastman nodded before pointing. "It's up and yonder that way," he stated calmly. He tilted his head as he looked the two travelers over. "Hey, can I ask a favor?"

Camilla stepped forward. "Certainly."

"My daughter's gone missing. She was playing in the field west of here. But never came home, the fighters who protect the town said they can't make time to look for her. And I can't leave my three other children. I promise I'll reward ya nicely if you bring my daughter home," he said.

Amelia nodded. "We'll find your daughter and bring her home." She looked at Camilla, who also nodded. The two set off for the fields mentioned by the beastman and began investigating. "What do you suppose we're dealing with?" Amelia finally asked.

"Time Eater making Duskridge an example. Probably some sort of magic that keeps them living, but they're isolated from the rest of the realm. And they don't even know it," she reasoned as she checked for tracks. Camilla paused when she found a small boot. "No tracks but this must be a boot belonging to the girl."

"Let me have a whiff. You're not the only one who can track," Amelia retorted as she reached for the boot. Camilla nodded and handed over the object. The paladin sniffed the boot a few times, her sharp werewolf nose picking up the scent easily. "Follow me!" she called before sprinting off. Camilla smirked and chased after her partner.

The two raced across the field before coming to a cave. It was clearly manmade, or at the least creature made. Amelia sniffed the air and nodded. "Whoever took her went into that cave," she added as she looked into the cave. She hesitated but saw Camilla begin heading into the cave. Nodding to herself, Amelia followed the ranger.

It was dark and damp within the cave. It smelled of rot. Both pushed onward despite how uncomfortable this made them feel. As they came upon a large chamber, they spotted the girl they had been looking for. Neither rushed over, both suspecting a trap of some sort had been laid out. They looked about trying to determine if there was in fact a trap. Camilla pointed to a few unusual markings on the ground, clearly a trap.

Amelia nodded and pointed to the ceiling of the chamber. Hanging from the ceiling was a massive creature that resembled a cross between a bat and a wolf. Its fangs and snout were wolflike, but the eyes, ears and wings were from a bat. The creature hissed before swooping down at the adventurers. The paladin brought her tower shield up, blocking the attack. The ranger had leapt backwards, her longbow drawn as she fired three arrows in rapid succession.

It let out a shrill howl as it leapt back, arrows lodged in its chest and wings. Camilla nudged Amelia and pointed at a clear path to the girl. "I'll cover ya, you get the girl out of here," the ranger instructed as she took aim again. Amelia nodded and took off in a sprint. She heard arrows being fired swiftly as the ranger barely took any time to adjust her stance. The creature hissed as it lunged for the ranger, clearly wanting to end her.

Camilla took a step back, shouldering her longbow and drawing her longsword. She took a deep breath to steady herself as she slashed out twice with the blade. A loud screech was heard as the bat-wolf creature was forced to land. Its wings were bleeding from all the gashes in the membrane. With a howl, it rushed the ranger, snapping its jaws. Camilla barely managed to avoid the teeth but was knocked back by a claw swipe. She winced as blood trickled from the wound. She looked over and smirked when she saw Amelia had gotten to the girl. The paladin was already sprinting back, ready to leave the cave as soon as they were able to.

The ranger nodded, trying to tell the paladin to head back to the village. Amelia nodded, understanding what the ranger was saying. She sprinted past the ranger and kept running. Camilla took one more slash at the bat-wolf monster, forcing it back. Once there was some space between them, the ranger reached into one of her belt pouches and drew forth a stone with a lightning bolt on it. She threw the stone toward the creature's feet then began running away. A loud bang was heard followed by a bright flash. There was a screech from the creature as it fled deeper into the cave, disoriented from the sound and light.

Amelia was breathing heavily as she escaped the cave. She glanced over her shoulder in time to see the ranger come running up to her. Both shared a brief smile before sprinting back toward the village. They were struggling to breath from fatigue as they reached Duskridge.

"Papa!" the girl cried as she spotted her father.

"Daisy!" the beastman called out as he rushed over.

Amelia gently set the girl down and watched the reunion. She breathed a sigh of relief before sitting on a nearby bench. Camilla stood near her and arched an eyebrow. "You alright, Amelia?" she asked.

"Just a bit winded. I'm not used to running in this heavy armor. Not meant for running either," she commented as she leaned back.

"You. Both of you kept true to your word. You brought my daughter home," the beastman stated as he walked over. "Here, take these. I don't know what use they'll be, but I'm sure they'll serve you better than me," he added as he handed each of the adventurers a small rock.

"Thank you, good sir," Camilla replied before giving a slight bow. Once the beastman had walked away, Camilla and Amelia looked to each other then the rocks they were given. Amelia's was a ruby but at the center was a strange marking. Camilla's was a diamond also with an unusual marking in the center. "What do you suppose they are?" Camilla asked, looking at the paladin.

"Not sure, but probably going to be important later," Amelia reasoned as she placed the ruby in a bag she had on her belt. Camilla nodded in agreement as she slid the diamond into her belt pouch. They looked at the sky and chuckled slightly. "I suppose we should find a way back to the ripple, shouldn't we," the paladin said before standing.

"Probably should," Camilla answered as she looked toward the mountain nearby. They had originally found the ripple at the summit; it was fair to reason that the same would be said here. They began hiking up the mountain path, stopping every so often to catch their breath. Upon reaching the summit, the ripple was in fact waiting for them. Neither hesitated as they dove through the ripple.

When they emerged from the ripple, they found themselves back at the summit of Spiral Mountain. They breathed a sigh of relief as they had returned to the main realm as they knew it. Amelia felt along where her fangs had been pronounced earlier, another sigh of relief as she felt they had recessed back a bit. Camilla checked herself over, a sense of dread filled her as she still had the tail and her claws were still very pronounced.

"It's alright, it doesn't change who you are," Amelia tried to reassure the ranger. Camilla nodded numbly as she tried to shake the thoughts from her mind.

"Two random travelers? Not likely. Heroes from the Outrealms more likely," a man clad in full plate silver armor snarled as he approached the two. He held a large steel shield in his left hand and a battle axe in his right. Around his waist was a red sash.

Amelia did not hesitate; she drew her bastard sword and tower shield. Clearly ready for a fight. Camilla in turn drew her longsword and one of her shortswords. The man rushed forward, his axe swinging out in slow but powerful attacks. Amelia used her shield to block the attacks and keep the focus of the man on her. Camilla saw the opening and rushed in, her longsword piercing the chinks in the man's armor. He hissed in pain as he tried to catch the ranger in one of his attacks. Amelia smirked and thrust forward with her bastard sword. Blood spilled out the armor from the attack. He took a step back, clearly reconsidering engaging the pair in combat.

Before he had time to fully reconsider, both adventurers were on him. He attempted to block both but only managed to block the ranger's attacks. The paladin's blade cleaved through the armor and took the man's head from between his shoulders. As the body collapsed, the pair shared a quick glance to one another before turning their attention to the man's corpse. Camilla searched for anything that might indicate who he was or at least who sent him.

"Find anything?" Amelia asked.

Camilla held a piece of parchment and unfolded it. "There's going to be an execution of three warriors of the Outrealms. In three days' time at Forlorn Keep," she said as she looked over the note.

"Warriors of the Outrealms? What does that mean?" the paladin questioned.

"It's Azura, Chuck and Warren. When we were summoned here, Arcanist called us heroes of the Outrealms. This notice is about their execution. And judging by the date on here, I'd say we have two days to rescue them," Camilla said as she shoved the notice into her pocket. She shook her head as she looked over her map. It was a long journey; they likely would not be able to stop to rest but time was of the essence. She looked at Amelia. "Let's make sure we get there in time. Come on," she said before sprinting off.

Amelia nodded and sprinted after the ranger. "Got a plan for when we get there?"

"I'll make one as we go!" Camilla called back to the paladin.

Chapter 15 - Lightning Rescue

It took a day and a half for the pair to each Forlorn Keep. Both were breathing heavily. It was not just the physical exertion of running the whole way, but also the mental fatigue of not having rested in order to arrive in time. Amelia turned to face Camilla, her scarlet eyes silently asking the question. What is the plan?

Camilla studied the layout of the keep as best she could from their position. There were hundreds of soldiers guarding the front. And even more along the massive walls, all armed to fight and kill. The ranger nodded slightly as she formed a plan. "There's two ways into the keep that we can reach. First is the front, second being that drainage canal," she said while pointing. Amelia nodded slightly trying to gauge what the ranger wanted. Camilla flashed the paladin a smirk; clearly she had a plan. "How big of a distraction can you make?"

Amelia looked toward the front gates. "How big do you need? I can make as big as you need," she replied, having a vague idea of the plan. The paladin looked at the ranger and nodded slightly. "Let's see if I understand correctly. I make a distraction, and you're going to slip in using the drainage canal."

"Soon as you're able to, bullrush your way into the keep through the front. Try to clear out as many of the soldiers as you can," Camilla added.

"And draw as many in as I can to my position so you can try to find the others," Amelia clarified. She did not like the reckless nature of the plan, but they did not have much else they could do. She hated it but knew this was likely their best option. She trusted Camilla and had complete faith in any crazy schemes the ranger could make. "Alright, let's do this," Amelia finally said as she readied herself.

"Good luck, my friend." Camilla's words were barely above a whisper.

"And you as well," the paladin spoke before charging toward the front gates. She made quite the scene. Her immense strength combined with her bastard sword made it easy to cut and cleave through soldiers.

Camilla took a deep breath before rushing toward the drainage canal. She dove a few feet and rolled, coming up just out of sight. Thankfully there were no enemy soldiers waiting for her. She counted her blessings that Amelia was willing to go along with her plan. The ranger rushed forward, making her way through the canal until she reached a passage that led further into the keep. *"Please be alright, Amelia,"* she thought as she pushed onward.

Once inside the keep, Camilla crept from one shadow to another, trying to remain out of sight as she moved. What she would give for anything that could make her invisible right now. She ducked behind a wall as she heard voices further ahead.

"The front gate has been breached!" a soldier clad in red armor called, his voice filled with fear.

"There's never been a breach in the three hundred years since this keep was built! Send more men to the gate, we can't lose this keep!" a large man, likely a half giant, yelled as he slammed his warhammer against the ground.

"Carden, this is likely a two-pronged attack. You shore up defenses at the front gate, I'll take some of my men and set up a kill line at the dungeons. If it's the remaining Outrealm Heroes, we'll crush them regardless of what they might be able to do," a man clad in silver armor stated as he stood from the table. He walked over to a small desk in the room and opened a hidden drawer.

"Hugo, you can't really be considering using that!" Carden yelled as he stepped toward the smaller man.

"I am. We can't lose this keep, nor can we lose those prisoners. With this, I'll be able to crush whoever tries to take Forlorn Keep. For the glory of Time Eater," Hugo stated as he removed an emerald from the desk. It was glowing with an otherworldly light as Hugo held it. He slammed the emerald into his chest plate and watched as it radiated a pale green glow into his armor. "Let them come. I'll show them real power," he said as he headed for the dungeon.

Carden nodded as he left for the front gate. Camilla waited and took a deep breath. Based on what she had heard, she and Amelia would both be in for some intense combat very soon. She made her way to the now emptied room and gave it a quick search. There was nothing useful to aid in this mission.

Amelia had broken through the gates and made her way into the keep. Her bastard sword made short work of the soldiers that flooded the entry. They were weaker than she anticipated, but that only put her on edge even more. She feared for Camilla's safety knowing the ranger lacked the same level of thick armor she had.

"You! You and me, one on one. I do not wish to see any more of my men slain!" a man clad in red armor yelled as he made his way to the front entry. At his commands, the soldiers backed down and moved clear to give him a path. "I am General Carden, second in command of this keep. And you are?"

"Amelia Lucia of Highever, and I accept your terms," she stated as she came to a stop. She watched as Carden approached, an impressive warhammer in his right hand and a massive shield in his left. On his back was a huge lance that looked like it was meant for much larger game than her. "What rules are we to fight by?" she asked as she held her bastard sword and tower shield.

"A standard fight to the death. No dirty tactics, one on one." Carden's words were strong as he waited. He turned to his men. "Should I fall, you will flee. I am a man of my word, and you men are in my service."

"Yes, sir!" all the soldiers responded as they stood to the side, spears at their sides.

Carden turned to face Amelia. "Are you ready, lass?" he asked.

Amelia nodded. "Ready."

The two circled briefly, clearly sizing each other up. Carden lunged first, his warhammer hitting and making a loud thud as it impacted Amelia's shield. Amelia kept her shield up, Carden moved fast and aggressively, giving her no opening to launch a counterattack. She had to give the man credit; he was honorable, and it was clear that he cared about his men. She barely had time to avoid a side swing of the warhammer as he came around to hit her right side. It was an opening, a risky one, but she would take it. Lunging forward, Amelia drove her sword into the man's barely exposed armpit. She watched as blood rushed forward. A clean hit.

Carden winced slightly but lunged forward again, his warhammer hitting Amelia's midsection, sending her staggering. He smirked as he moved in again, another hit, this time to the paladin's left side. Amelia brought her shield up, barely blocking the third attack. She managed to take in a shallow breath as she collected herself. Shallow breaths were all she could manage; her ribs were cracked despite the armor and padding. She needed to end the fight before Carden got another attack like that off.

Amelia waited patiently behind her shield, letting Carden unleash a fury of attacks. She waited for the exact moment. "*Now!*" something called out to her as she lunged forward, throwing all caution to the wind. Her blade caught the general along the throat, tearing through flesh and arteries. Blood sprayed her face as she finished the opposing general. Carden coughed a few times as he slumped backwards, collapsing. As he bled to death, Amelia knelt and gingerly closed the man's eyes.

"Let whatever deity you worship take you into his embrace. You've earned such, Carden. Rest now, rest off the wounds of eternity," she prayed softly as she stayed by his side.

Camilla had made her way to the dungeons and saw a sight she was praying she would not see. Several soldiers and a general. She stayed just barely out of line of sight. Hesitantly she drew her longbow. She might be able to pick off some of the soldiers with her bow, but the general's thick armor would be an issue no matter what tactic she used.

She nocked three arrows while speaking in a different dialect. The bow shimmered with a black aura before returning to normal. In rapid succession the three arrows were released; each one split into five additional arrows before splitting again into another twenty-five arrows a piece. It was a bloodbath; the soldiers were ripped apart by the volley of arrows, leaving only the general.

Camilla quickly shouldered her longbow and drew her longsword and shortsword. “Stand aside, I’ve already bested all your men,” Camilla said as she approached.

“Come at me you wench!” Hugo snarled as he steeled himself. His battle axe was impressive to say the least. He easily closed the distance on the ranger. As he swung the weapon out, Camilla narrowly dodged under the attack. The wall where she had been splintered and crumbled to the attack.

Camilla winced seeing such strength; if she was hit even once, it was likely a death blow. Swallowing hard, the ranger lashed out with a whirlwind of attacks from both blades. It was unlike he felt such, but it was all she could manage. This was very much a speed vs power type of fight, and such battles were never favorable to the speediness of the ranger. Each swing of the battle axe forced Camilla to fight defensively as she leapt back, tumbled or ducked trying to avoid being hit. She looked for any chinks in the armor that she could use to make a solid offense.

Hugo swung the battle axe again, this time forcing Camilla into a corner. It was right where he wanted her; there would be nowhere to dodge. As he lashed out with another fierce swing, he took great joy knowing this would connect no matter what happened. Camilla had nowhere to tumble to, nowhere to leapt toward. The axe was angled in a way that even if she ducked, she would still be hit. She brought her blades up, barely catching the powerful attack. Her arms shook from the strength needed to keep the attack at bay.

“What’s wrong, too much for ya?” Hugo laughed as he pressed forward, adding more of his weight to the attack.

Camilla nearly dropped her guard from the added strength. She wavered slightly as she tried to think up a plan. She had one chance, and only a single attempt. Her tail poked out from under her coat and lashed out at the man. Her tail wrapped around his ankle and pulled, causing him to take a forced step backward. Camilla smirked, knowing this was the only moment she had. She lunged forward, striking the man’s right wrist with her shortsword.

He howled in pain as his hand fell to the ground, separated from his arm. The added strength from the emerald meant nothing in that moment. He lunged with a left jab, colliding with the ranger’s sternum. Camilla felt the air rush from her lungs as the sternum and ribs were forced inward. The pain was beyond anything she felt. As she tried to recover, she felt the man’s hand grab her by the throat and lift her off the ground. The pressure was on as he put on the squeeze. "Nowhere to run, no more tricks. You lose." Hugo laughed.

Camilla felt her mind becoming hazy as Hugo tightened his grip. She tried to free herself from his grip, but nothing came of it. As everything began to blur in her mind, she heard the familiar heavy clanks and smiled slightly. "Get your hand off of her!" Amelia yelled as she charged and slammed into the enemy general. Hugo grunted as he dropped the ranger and was forced to the ground. Amelia collected herself and threw her full weight upon the general. "Camilla! Camilla, are you alright!" she called over.

The ranger coughed a few times as she slowly got to her feet. "Yeah, thanks for the save," Camilla said as she grabbed her longsword and made her way over. "Move the chainmail from his neck. We're finishing this."

Amelia nodded as she reached and removed the chainmail from Hugo's neck, exposing the delicate area. She glanced up at Camilla as the ranger approached. Camilla raised her blade and brought it down in rapid succession, five hits. The head rolled to the side, separated from the body. Amelia quickly stood and rushed to the ranger's side to steady her. "I've got you, don't worry," Amelia said as she supported the ranger against her. The two looked further down the hallway and saw the holding cell. The paladin nodded as she carried the ranger over.

"Amelia! Camilla! You're both alright!" Warren exclaimed upon seeing the pair.

Camilla observed the lock then proceeded to attempt to pick it. She frowned as she shook her head. "I can't pick this one." she muttered as she withdrew her lockpick tools. Amelia looked around seeing if there was a key nearby. Camilla coughed slightly as she steadied herself and walked back to Hugo's body. She reached down, taking the general's battle axe. "Everyone, stand back," she stated as she limped back to the cell. *"Please, great and mighty Patrokolos, let this work,"* she prayed in her head as she brought the battle axe down on the lock.

With a stroke of luck, the lock fell to the ground. "Great job, Camilla!" Azura cheered as she watched the ranger. Camilla and Amelia were both exhausted as they opened the cell then undid the ropes that restrained their teammates.

"Are all of you alright?" Amelia asked as she finished.

"Chuck fine. Chuck mad that Chuck miss fight though," the barbarian stated as he stepped forward.

"Aside from being humiliated by being captured, I'm alright," Warren responded.

Azura nodded that she was fine and quickly began healing Camilla's wounds. Warren tended to Amelia's wounds; both ranger and paladin needed a lot of healing, but they looked like they could manage. "You two are both in rough shape. Best let Chuck, Azura and I take the lead," Warren added as he finished tending to Amelia's wounds.

"We need to find your gear," Camilla countered as she winced from one of the heal spells.

"Sorry, that'd be your sternum. Almost got crushed based on the healing needed," Azura apologized as she continued patching up the ranger.

"Yeah, about their gear." Amelia paused as she untied three bags from her belt. She took quick glances at each bag before handing them off. "I found it while I was rushing down here," she added as she watched the other three reequip themselves. "Camilla, you're in the worst shape, best you hang back. Chuck, you and I, we'll take point. Warren, you stay in the center. Azura, rearguard and help support Camilla." The paladin was quick to take over as the leader.

Everyone nodded as they took their position in the lineup. Camilla paused as she went back to the general's corpse. She grabbed the emerald and ripped it from the armor before stuffing it into one of her belt pouches before rejoining the others. Azura slipped under the ranger's arm and helped support her as they made their way out of Forlorn Keep. Chuck and Amelia fought through any of Hugo's remaining men, Warren healed them as needed.

Once out of the keep, the group made their way into an underground tunnel system to rest. "How did you know we needed help?" Azura asked as she eased Camilla to be sitting down.

"After our brief adventure at Spiral Mountain, we ran into a guy who had a notice about an execution. Heroes of the Outrealms. Camilla said it was referring to you three, so we rushed as fast as we could to stop the execution," Amelia explained before drinking from her waterskin.

Warren nodded. "Regardless, thanks for saving us."

"Any luck at Faraway Lake?" Camilla asked as she leaned back.

"No, we found a ripple, but when we crossed through it, there was no dungeon," Azura explained.

"Same with Spiral Mountain," Amelia chimed in.

Camilla nodded. "Well, now that we're together again, which one should we hit first?" she asked as her eyes drooped slightly.

"You need rest, Camilla. We can sort that out after we've all had some time to rest," Amelia scolded the ranger.

Everyone was silent for a moment before sharing a small laugh. It was good to be together again. Even if they were only separated for at most a few days, it was still good to be reunited. Camilla nodded. "Fine, I surrender. We'll discuss it more in the morning." She laughed before laying out her bedroll to sleep.

Amelia looked at the others. "All of you as well. I'm undead, don't need to sleep. You four do."

Warren nodded. "Anything happens, don't hesitate to wake us up," he stated. Amelia just gave the cleric a thumbs up.

Chapter 16 - Memories Of Shadow

The next morning, everyone had woken up early to discuss the next course of action they needed to make. Warren unrolled the map and tapped a spot. "We're here at Forlorn Keep. Spiral Mountain is about a two-to-four-day journey going east. Faraway Lake is about a five-day journey going south and west. Let's hear it, which area do we want to pursue?" he asked, stepping once again into the role of the leader.

Amelia looked over the map then looked across to the sorceress. Camilla walked over and took a seat with the others, handing out a packet of rations to each member of the band of misfits. Azura was silent, she looked over at the paladin, the two silently gauging the other's plan. Chuck was noisily enjoying the quick meal that had been provided.

The ranger finally spoke up after staring at the map. "I think we should head to Spiral Mountain. Supply wise, I've got plenty of food to last us and can easily hunt if rations start running low. It's closer for the time being. Trying to double back to it would prove difficult as there isn't anywhere to resupply before making the journey," she said as she finished her rations.

The paladin nodded in agreement. "I agree with Camilla. We're supplied at the moment and can easily make that journey," she added before starting to eat her rations.

Warren looked to Azura. "You up for this?" he asked, concern lining his voice. She looked up at him and nodded. "Right, once everyone's finished eating we'll start the trip to Spiral Mountain. And likely to whatever memory or otherworldly thing awaits Azura," he added. It was a hunch based on the information they had from the fishing town. If neither Amelia nor Camilla came to a memory event like he and Chuck had, then it meant Spiral Mountain was harboring an event meant for Azura. He wondered what hellish world awaited them as they crossed the ripple this time.

After another five minutes, everyone was ready to head out. Camilla and Chuck took point, leading the group as they travelled. Azura and Warren were at the center of the formation and Amelia was to be rearguard. An hour into the journey and Camilla came to a stop, clearly on high alert. Her right hand rested on the pommel of her longsword as she looked around. Chuck had already drawn his greataxe and was sniffing at the air, like an animal. Amelia turned her back to the group as she looked behind them, hoping to ensure they were not going to be snuck up on. Warren had drawn his tower shield and waited, he positioned himself in a way that he could easily shield the sorceress.

"Talk to us, Camilla. What is it?" Amelia called from the rear of the group.

Camilla looked at Chuck, trying to gauge if he sensed it. The barbarian shook his head, clearly not smelling or sensing anything. Camilla looked around again. "I thought I sensed someone approaching us from the shadows of that boulder field," she stated as she indicated the boulder field to the left of her position.

All eyes turned to the boulder field. It was well shaded, even with the sun overhead. Easy for an ambush attacker to get the jump on them if they chose. There was no indication of anything amiss though. Was the ranger just jumpy or was there something she was sensing that no else could? Azura threw a fireball into the boulder field, illuminating it enough for everyone to see. Nothing. It was still. No attacker. No signs anyone was ever there.

"Sorry, guess I'm just on edge after everything," Camilla apologized as she turned her attention back to the trail they were walking.

Returning to their positions, the group began making the journey again. Hours passed, and soon the sun was setting on the horizon, causing the adventurers to set up camp. Everyone set up their tents and rolled out their bedrolls. Camilla checked her bag and nodded as she withdrew some dried meat and a few other small rations and set them to the side for everyone. Each one grabbed a small portion ensuring everyone would be able to eat.

Amelia sat beside the ranger and looked her up and down. "What happened back there? It's not like you to falsely sense something," she asked, wanting to check on the ranger.

Camilla looked around briefly before looking at Amelia. "I'm not certain, but I felt like I'd been at that boulder field before and the group I was with was ambushed. Like a memory that's not mine but put me on edge," she explained, trying to make sense of her own words. Camilla shook her head. "Forget I said anything," she said as she looked down.

"A false memory?" Azura asked, catching part of the conversation. She sat with the ranger and paladin; her sense of wonder piped with interest. "It's not unheard of, just very rare. I read about such things back home. False memories can occur when someone is exposed to an otherworldly version of something they would normally be used to. Or when the self exists in two points in the same plane, they begin to share memories."

"Otherworldly, are you suggesting that perhaps because both of you are from Kardax but different events happened, perhaps that might be causing false memories?" Amelia questioned trying to get a better understanding of the sorceress's words.

Azura nodded. "It could be the case. But then I'd likely be having similar, where I remember things that I didn't actually experience," the sorceress reasoned.

Camilla shook her head. "Let's not dwell on such. I'd rather just move on from this," she cut in, clearly not liking either explanation they had.

Amelia sighed and nodded, letting the topic go. "Try to get some rest, we don't need you having more false memories," the paladin spoke gently to the ranger.

Everyone retired to their tents, leaving the half vampire paladin to keep watch. She thought about Azura's words more. *"If two selves exist in the same plane, that can cause false memories. Shared memories. And if that's the case, where is the other Camilla? Or could they be real memories from the past she's claimed to have forgotten?"* Amelia thought as she looked about the area.

It was secluded, dark green grass under them with large stone monuments around them obstructing the view from the trail. It was a good defensive position with there being no way to ambush them. But it still had its share of risks. The one way in and out of the camp made so there was no retreat if something happened. Both an advantage and a death trap. Amelia shook her head as she listened to the night's sounds. The howl of a wolf pack in the distance. The hoots of owls in the nearby tree line. And the whisper of the wind. She was not as in tune with nature as the ranger, but she was more in tune with the night than any.

Cautiously Amelia felt her fangs. They were sharper than before. Almost like the night in Duskridge, where she almost killed Camilla. Shaking the thought from her mind, the paladin looked up at the sky. It was a crescent moon, not full nor a blood moon. She breathed a sigh of relief before sitting back against the stone. What would the others say when they learned the truth? Yes, Camilla still accepted her and said she would stay by the paladin's side. But what if Chuck, Warren or Azura learned the truth? Would she be hunted? Exiled? Or perhaps condemned?

She shook the thoughts from her mind as she focused on the present. It was eerily calm. The hoots had stopped. The wolf pack could not be heard and even the breeze came to a still. Amelia was on edge as she grabbed her bastard sword. Nature never just comes to a halt on the sounds, something was very amiss. She heard one of the tents unzip and glanced over to see the sorceress step out. "Couldn't sleep?" Amelia asked.

"Not really. I'm worried. Worried about Camilla and these false memories," Azura explained as she sat down not too far from the paladin. She rubbed the back of her head. "Amelia, am I a bad person for wanting something?"

"Depends what that desire is," the paladin said.

Azura paused, thinking about how to word things. She took a deep breath, letting it out slowly. "When this is all over, when we return to our home worlds, I want Camilla to return with me. I don't want her to go back to her Kardax. When we first met here, I could tell Camilla was running away from something. From her past, from someone, I don't know, but I felt it. I don't want her to return to that. If she went to my Kardax, if she returned home with me, she could have a peaceful life," the sorceress reasoned.

Amelia shook her head. "I don't believe that makes you a bad person. However, whatever happened in her Kardax, Camilla is the type to return and sort things out. She doesn't just turn her back on things," she said, a faint smile on her face. "I believe, deep down, everyone in this group is a good person, but may have been misguided at some point and gotten lost. Maybe we were all called here, not because we're some sort of heroes, but to find ourselves," Amelia added as she looked at the sky.

Azura nodded as she followed Amelia's gaze to the sky. "Maybe when this is all over, we can each visit each other's home. I don't want to say goodbye to anyone in this group. Honestly, you four are the best friends I've ever had."

Amelia flashed the young sorceress a smirk. "I'd like that. Travelling and visiting everyone's home realm. Though my home realm has nothing to offer in sites or anything really. Most of my home was destroyed during the War for the Chalice. I don't feel I've a home to go back to when this is all over."

"I don't particularly want to return to my home realm. I'm hated for what I became," Warren stated as he stepped out of his tent. He walked over and sat with the others. Taking a small breath, he looked at the ground. "Back home, I'm a king. But I'm seeing the error in how I rule. Azura, you lead with kindness and compassion, something I know nothing about. Back home, I rule with an iron fist. I made people fight and kill each other for my amusement," the cleric added as he stared at the ground. He shook his head. "Thing is, I don't know how to be someone else. I treated my adventure party back home the same way. And I'm frightened that when this is over, when we are to return to our home realms, any memories we have of this place, any life lessons we've learned, will simply be left behind as part of the Distortion."

"Warren…" Azura began, this was not the first time she had seen him doubting himself. She remembered the night in the tavern that seemed like weeks ago. She remembered the first ripple they went through. "Sounds like it's something we'll have to ask Arcanist. I don't want to forget everything I've learned here either. All of you have taught me so much. How to be brave. How to fight for what I believe in. I don't want to forget such."

"Chuck learning. Chuck want learn more," the barbarian stated as he stepped out from his tent. "Chuck home, Chuck feared by all. Chuck not have friends home. Chuck have four friends now," the barbarian added as he packed his bedroll and tent.

Amelia chuckled slightly. "Sounds like all of us have something we've gained by coming here," she commented, feeling at ease around the others.

Azura and Warren began packing up their gear as they would likely be moving out soon. Camilla yawned as she stepped out of her ten. "Geez, if I oversleep again, feel free to wake me," she said as she quickly began packing up her gear.

"We figured you could use the extra few minutes of rest," Warren teased slightly as he finished packing. He laughed when he saw the glare the ranger shot him. "Sometimes I swear your glares are more deadly than that longbow of yours."

"Well, now that all of us are awake, and packed, let's get moving," Amelia stated as she shouldered her blade.

They continued the trek to Spiral Mountain, finally coming to the base of the mountain. As they looked over the trails leading up the mountain, Amelia and Camilla noticed the one they had used last time was gone. Warren pulled out his spyglass and checked over the area again. Chuck yawned as he for once waited for the others to make a plan. Azura used her magic to try to detect anything off about the area. Camilla kept a watch on the surrounding environment, making sure they were not falling into a trap. Amelia had her spyglass out and was also looking for a trail. "There!" she called out and pointed.

Warren adjusted his gaze to look at the trail Amelia pointed to. He nodded as he lowered his spyglass. "Let's get going," he said then began the hike. He and Amelia took point while Chuck and Camilla took rearguard, and Azura stayed toward the center of the group. It was about a two-hour hike to reach the summit, but when they arrived, they found the ripple they were looking for. Azura swallowed hard as she approached and looked through it. She was shaking in nervousness of what they would find. She felt a hand on her shoulder and looked up. "Whatever happens, we're here for you," Warren stated as he gave the sorceress's shoulder a reassuring squeeze.

Azura nodded then stepped through the ripple, the rest of adventurers following behind her. As they emerged on the other side of the ripple, they found they were in a fairly sizable village. "This… This is my home village. It's Lowestoft," Azura said as she looked around. The buildings were all intact but there were no people. It was as though the people left without a trace.

As they walked through the village, everyone felt as though they were being watched. Looking around though, there was nothing they could see. Amelia closed her eyes and focused. She pointed to a large estate sitting at the hilltop. "Whatever it is, it's up there."

Azura looked to the hilltop. "That's House Vaughan. My home..." she responded as she began walking up to the hilltop. Warren and Chuck followed close behind the sorceress.

Amelia looked to Camilla and waited. "Camilla?" she asked, waiting for the ranger.

"Lowestoft looks so different in this version of Kardax. It looks peaceful, like the ruination never happened," Camilla noted before walking to the paladin's side. She shook her head then looked away. "Sorry, I shouldn't be thinking like that, this isn't my Kardax after all."

The two caught up to the rest of the party who were standing outside House Vaughan. Warren and Chuck were looking around, trying to figure out where they were being watched from. Azura stepped toward the front door of the estate. Her hand shakily grasping the door handle and pulling the door open. Inside, everything looked pristine. Whatever sorcery was done, preserved everything in the estate. "Hello? Is someone there?" Azura softly called out.

"Wel... me... trav... This is..." The voice was struggling to speak. Azura closed her eyes, focusing on the source of the voice. She began chanting something in a very foreign dialect before casting a spell. Standing before them was a young man, human in appearance. He wore golden full plate armor, a longsword on his belt, on his right arm was a large steel shield. Around his neck and draped behind him was a red cape. His red hair looked like fire and his deep blue eyes were piercing to say the least. Despite how real he looked, the group was still able to see through him as though he was not fully there.

"Thank you, sister. Welcome, travelers. This is Lowestoft of Kardax. My name is Henry Vaughan, and I'm to guide you to what you seek," the ghostly image stated as he floated toward the group.

"Henry..." Azura began, tears forming in her eyes as she looked at the ghost. She noticed details no one else seemed to see. The scar on his face, the hole in his chest. To her his skin looked rotted.

"Fear not, Azura, it's alright. Death is a part of life. I proudly laid down my life for yours. And I would do so again if I were able to," Henry spoke as he gave the sorceress a warm smile. He turned and began floating further into the estate. "Come, travelers, we must make haste," he added as he moved.

Azura saw the gash in his back, the very same that was caused by the blue dracolich. She covered her mouth as she tried to steel herself once again.

Despite how long it had been, she still blamed herself for Henry's death. If she had been stronger. If she had been more skilled with magic

"Do not fret over the what-ifs, sister. For they will cloud your judgment." Henry's words were kind as he glanced over his shoulder at the sorceress.

Azura sniffled slightly as she wiped the tears from her eyes. She nodded slowly as she moved to follow the spirit. She could hear the others following behind her. They made their way to the top of the estate. It was far above the village and only had small slopes to allow any storm waters to flow downward. Azura saw the spirit of Henry stop and indicate a quarterstaff at the center of the arena like set up. She looked at him and saw the concerned face he wore. "We have to fight something, don't we?" she asked as she looked toward the quarterstaff.

"Yes, I wish I could aid you, but I cannot," Henry said softly. He smiled at Azura and gently rested his hands as best he could on her shoulders. "Azura, I know you can do this. I may not be with you anymore physically, but I'm always with you. In here," he said as he pointed at her chest, right above her heart. "Keep me close in your memories, in your dreams, but please move forward. Move past my death and do not blame yourself. I want you to live for me, in the world you shape," he added with a smile. Both siblings looked toward quarterstaff as more spirits began to materialize.

Standing at the center were a warlock, a ranger, a knight, a rogue and a paladin. Azura took a deep breath as she looked ahead, their faces becoming clearer as time passed. They were Narcian, the warlock who killed many of her allies; Frederick, the knight that served her brother as his retainer; Arthur, the rogue and her eldest brother; Lord Vaughan, the paladin and father who sought her executed after she showed prowess with magic, and finally a dark and twisted version of Camilla, the ranger who had been her best friend.

Warren instantly stepped forward, his tower shield and morningstar in hand. Chuck rushed forward, his greataxe drawn. Amelia moved to cover Chuck as she drew her bastard sword and tower shield. Camilla, the real one, drew her longbow and nocked three arrows. Warren nodded to Azura. "Chuck's got the paladin handled, Amelia's going for the rogue. Camilla's got their ranger in her sights. I'll deal with the knight. Think you can handle the warlock?" He went through the strategy.

Azura nodded. "Narcian's mine. I killed him before; I can do it again," she said under her breath. It was the first time since Henry's death that she held any confidence in her voice during combat.

Warren rushed past her and engaged the knight in combat. He glanced about the battlefield and saw everyone had engaged their respective foe. Arrows and spells were sent across the battlefield, each countering one another and ending in attacks canceling out. Chuck roared loudly as he struck the opposing paladin hard with his greataxe. Had it not been for the thick armor the man wore, it would have been a killing strike. The barbarian spun on his right heel avoiding the paladin's onslaught of attacks and countered with another swing from his greataxe.

Amelia was probably having the easiest time. She landed three hits on the rogue before shield bashing him. As he staggered, she closed in and ran her blade through his chest, piercing his heart. One down. She quickly rushed to aid Chuck; the opposing paladin was powerful and the barbarian would need any help she could provide to break through the armor. Camilla launched arrow after arrow trying to gain some ground on the evil version of herself. After about the fifth arrow exchange, the ranger shouldered her bow and sprinted at the evil ranger. The evil Camilla merely smirked as she drew two shortswords and charged to meet the longsword and shortsword pair of the light counterpart.

The two struck one another repeatedly, sparks flying from their blades as they fought. Camilla rolled under the doppelganger's attack, coming up behind her in a crouch. "Sorry but I'm the real Camilla. The only one," Camilla stated as she ran her longsword through the evil version's heart.

Warren held his shield firm as the knight's greatsword pounded away trying to break through. He smirked slightly. The rush of combat getting to him. "Alright, big guy, let's go!" Warren called as he popped out from behind his shield and slammed the morningstar against the knight's chest. It forced the foe back a few feet allowing the cleric to get the opportunity he wanted. Lunging with speed and powerful hits, Warren's morningstar crushed the knight's armor around him until he slumped to the ground. Two down.

Amelia and Chuck were easily pivoting around and making their attacks on the paladin. Her bastard sword stuck through the paladin's stomach causing him to stumble. "Go for it, Chuck!" Amelia called.

Chuck roared loud and proud as his greataxe split through the paladin's scalp, piercing the rest of the head with ease. "Like melon!" the barbarian snarled as he looked across the battlefield. Three down. It seemed like only Narcian remained.

Narcian and Azura exchanged spell blasts again, both putting everything they had into their attacks. The warlock took a step back, clearly fatigue was setting in as he tried to end the fight. He glanced over and held out a hand. "Rise, death dragon of Null! It's time you fulfilled your blood oath!" he yelled.

Camilla winced at his words before looking behind her. She saw the evil version of her stand despite the wounds. "Azura, stay on Narcian! Warren, back her up! Amelia, Chuck, form up on the dragon!" she called out as she rushed to fight the undead blue dragon that had materialized where her evil counterpart had been. *"That's twice now. Twice I've fought a version of myself and both times it turns into a dragon of some kind!"* she thought as she dodged a lightning blast.

Warren rushed to Azura, barely making it to her in time to put his tower shield up for defense. Narcian's dark beam struck the shield and pushed the cleric back a few feet. "That's his signature spell. But he can only use it three times. We've got him in a corner if he's using it." Azura said as she ducked down, using Warren's shield for cover.

"Got a plan?" Warren asked as he held firm. His shield was starting to show signs of damage, but he knew it would hold.

"Yeah, I've got one. Can you provide cover and get me in close?" she asked as she held a spectral dagger in her right hand. Warren nodded as he got ready to move. "Coming from a family of mostly rogues, I can use a dagger easily enough. Henry once told me to combine my spells to make touch weapons. Any armor Narcian has, it won't do him any good against this," she added as she gripped the spectral dagger tightly.

Warren nodded as he shouldered his morningstar and held his tower shield with both hands. It gave him better grip and he would need such for the sorceress's plan to work. "You ready?" he asked as he took a step forward. Azura nodded as she stayed behind the armor-clad cleric and his shield. "Then let's do this!" Warren called as he began sprinting toward Narcian.

"What idiotic ruse is this?!" Narcian sneered as he unleashed another dark beam.

The cleric winced slightly as he kept rushing forward, his body aching from the attack. His shield was straining to hold up against magic. There were cracks forming in the metal. "*I won't waver! Never again!*" Warren thought as he continued to press forward. His shield shattered from the overload of magic. They were not close enough for Azura's plan. He needed to get her closer. Warren brought his arms up in front of him and continued his press forward. The armor covering his arms began creaking as he was blasted repeatedly by spells. "*Almost there. Almost there. Just a little more,*" he thought as he closed the distance.

"Warren!" Azura's voice was filled with fear. She saw the shield shatter. She watched as Warren's armor began cracking.

"Don't worry, I'll take everything he throws at us. I'll make sure you get close enough," Warren said as he deepened his stance slightly.

Amelia brought her shield up, blocking a claw strike. She saw Chuck rush past her and cleave through the dragon's claw. The beast roared in pain as the greataxe made contact. Chuck landed surprisingly gracefully and turned to attack again. Camilla had closed the distance where she needed and slashed out eight times, alternating with longsword and shortsword. They were not powerful strikes, but the volume added up and chipped away at the dragon's scales. "Now!" she called out.

Chuck and Amelia both lunged forward, their weapons cleaving through the dragon's chest. The paladin dropped back and crouched, raising her shield over her head. "Camilla!" she called.

The barbarian hacked his way deeper into the dragon's chest, keeping the beast's focus on him. Camilla ran and jumped. Her feet pressed against the shield and she felt Amelia push up as she jumped off. It was just enough height for the attack. Camilla curled herself up slightly as she held her blades tight. Her body whirled forward as her blades made contact. She landed behind the dragon, rolling and coming up in a crouch. "Amelia, go!" Camilla called out as she glanced at the other fight ongoing. Amelia glanced over her shoulder and sprinted toward Warren and Azura. She trusted Chuck and Camilla could handle the dragon.

Chuck swung out with his greataxe as the ranger slashed wildly with her blades. Both hit their marks as they attempted to fell the dragon. The beast roared loudly as it tried to use its lightning breath. The barbarian barely had enough time to dive out of the way. He watched as Camilla ran under the dragon, thrusting her longsword upward as she ran. The blade pierced the decaying flesh of the undead beast, ripping through flesh as the ranger ran. Another loud roar echoed as the beast began to collapse. Chuck sprinted full speed toward the ranger, he was not going to let the dragon crush her as it died. He gripped his greataxe by the bladed end, blood running down his hands as he reached the wooden handle out.

Camilla saw the barbarian and sprinted to his greataxe. She dove, barely grabbing the butt of the handle. Chuck smirked as he swung around and flung the ranger clear of the collapsing dragon. She rolled as she landed and wobbled slightly as she came up. She smirked at him and gave a thumbs up, he returned the gesture as he smirked. They looked to the now dead dragon. Four down.

Narcian unleashed his final dark beam. Surely it would end the cleric. “Now you die!” he yelled as the beam shot from his hands. Smoke and debris obscured his vision as the attack connected. A smirk formed as he waited. Surely they were dead. As the smoke cleared, he saw a tower shield that shone brightly. “What!” he growled seeing only the paladin standing where the attack had hit.

He sucked in a deep breath as he felt something pierce his left side, getting right between his ribs. He looked down, horror on his face. The spectral dagger pierced through and hit its mark. “You lose, Narcian. This time, my friends and I prevail,” Azura said as she pushed the spectral dagger deeper. Warren stood a little way back, his armor heavily damaged. Narcian coughed, bloody gurgles coming from him as he took a step. Azura created a second spectral dagger, this one piercing the warlock’s throat.

Narcian collapsed; he had been bested. He coughed a few more times before finally succumbing to his wounds. Azura breathed a sigh of relief as she watched the warlock’s body begin to dissolve. She turned to face her teammates who had gathered up after the fight. “Thank you, all of you. I don’t think I would have had the courage to do that without all of you watching out for me," she said as she smiled at them.

Warren only chuckled as he gave a thumbs up to the sorceress. Amelia nodded, not being one for words most of the time. Chuck only let out a hearty victorious roar. Camilla smiled as she looked over the group. They were all roughed up and needed to fix something in their gear or required healing, but they finally fully worked together.

"Azura," the sorceress turned to face where she heard the voice come from. Standing less than arm's length from her was the spirit of Henry. He smiled at her as he attempted to hug her. "Azura, you've done well. Keep pushing forward, keep growing stronger," he said as he held her. Azura tried her best to hug the spirit, but her arms failed to make contact. Henry smiled again as his form began to fade. "When I fade, take the item I leave. It will help you in your endeavors to save the world," he added before fading away.

Azura tried to suppress her tears, knowing Henry would not want to see her sad. She cupped her hands as several gold-colored sprites of light gathered within them. A bright light shone and sitting in her cupped hands was a topaz. She let a few tears fall before placing the topaz in one of the pouches on her belt. "Thank you, Henry. Be at peace now," she said softly before turning to the group.

As the five stood, the quarterstaff began glowing before flying to Azura. "I am Infinite the quarterstaff, one of five legendary weapons hidden within the nightmares. I shall grant you my magical prowess as you have proven your courage and resolve." The words seemingly came from the quarterstaff.

Azura reached out, taking the quarterstaff in hand. As she did so, everything blurred around them and soon they found themselves back at Spiral Mountain. They checked themselves over, finding their equipment repaired and wounds healed. Each looked at one another before they all spoke. "To Faraway Lake!" all five adventurers called out as though on the same page for once in a long time.

Chapter 17 - Into The Abyss

It was a minimum nine-to-ten-day journey to Faraway Lake, even for the most able adventurers it would prove difficult. After about the fifth day, the group stopped in a small town to get some much-needed rest. As they entered, all five of them could tell something was very wrong. Warren looked over the map then the outpost sign. "Same place as on our map. Must be right," he murmured.

"The people look estranged. They look unwell," Amelia commented as she saw the starved and depraved looks in their eyes.

"Welcome to Darktowne," a man stated as the adventurers entered. He laughed slightly before it turned into a raspy cough. "Best see the mayor before you do anything around the town. He'll treat ye right." He coughed before collapsing, his skin pale and blistered all over.

A woman walked out from a nearby vendor stall and handled the recently deceased. She shook her head before throwing his corpse onto a wagon filled with other deceased townsfolk. "Might be best if you don't stay. Wouldn't want to catch the plague," she said to the travelers before going to dispose of the bodies.

"We find the mayor, find out what's going on. Might leave soon after," Warren whispered to the group. He did not like the idea of abandoning the town when they clearly needed aid, but he did not want to put the lives of the group at stake if a plague was sweeping the area.

Camilla nodded in agreement. "Judging by the layout of this place, I'll assume that's the mayor's office. Only building that looks fortified," she reasoned as she pointed.

The group quickly made their way to the building and were escorted inside by two heavily armed guards. While their armor left much to be desired, their weapons looked capable of causing serious harm. They sat in the waiting lobby for a few moments before a short stocky looking man came out to greet them. "My apologies about the reception. Ever since Darktowne became infected, we've been cut off from the outside world. I am Mayor Itchiban the second," he introduced as he sat across from Warren.

Warren nodded politely before speaking. "Mayor Ichiban, what happened here? On the map, Darktowne looks much larger and well more."

"Ah yes, as I said there is a disease rampaging the town. It started about two months ago. And has been destroying us left and right. When we've tried to request aid from the king, our request was never answered. We've been left to solve the issue ourselves," the mayor stated as he frowned.

Camilla arched an eyebrow. "Two months ago? Did perhaps something happen?" she asked as she pulled out a small journal she had been keeping.

"Lord Uldritch showed up and demanded we pay him royally. This of course wasn't a payment of gold. No, no, he demanded the first born of the Emel children. Not sure why he wanted young Eoden though. The boy doesn't have any special talents," Ichiban recounted.

"Uldritch? As in Uldritch Von Varley?" Camilla was hoping it was just a coincidence in the name. But seeing the mayor nod, her blood ran cold. She looked down at her journal and shook her head. "That's not possible. Uldritch Von Varley was slain three months ago."

"And how would you know that, lass?" Ichiban asked.

"Because I'm the one who killed him. I tore his spine from his body, I saw him die. I felt his blood, his bones," Camilla said, trying to keep her emotions in check.

"You're certain the encounter at Abyssal Castle was three months ago?" Azura asked, looking at Camilla.

Camilla nodded and pointed to her notes. "I've been tracking time based on the cycles of the moon. Tonight's a full moon, and marks exactly three and half months since I ripped that dastard's spine from his body," the ranger responded.

"You ripped his spine out, but you didn't crush his heart," Ichiban murmured. He shook his head. "My girl, Uldritch can't be killed so easily. Before he became known as Lord Uldritch Von Varley, he was known as Uldritch the death defier. According to the stories, he was killed twenty-four times in a single night and still he lived. No one knows how he can be slain. Some say he has to be killed at sunrise after a blood moon. Others proclaim the removal of his heart. And some say he can only be slain by the true king of the Alibi."

"Alibi?" Azura questioned. This was the first they had heard a country name being used.

"You mean to tell me; you've been travelling three months here and didn't know the name of the kingdom?" Ichiban asked, arching an eyebrow. He shook his head. "That's not important. Anyways, we theorized that Uldritch is the one behind the plague. But we're so few able bodies to fight him. Darktowne will be entirely claimed by the plague by the next full moon."

"Mayor Ichiban! Mayor Ichiban!" a woman screamed as she ran into the building. Her hair was a mess, her clothes hardly more than rags. Her skin was covered in ash and mud. She panted heavily as she looked at the mayor. "Mayor Ichiban, it's my son! He's missing!"

"Persephone, we've been over this. Eoden has guards round the clock. There is no way he can simply go missing," Ichiban said calmly.

"But he is! And his guards are dead! My two younger children were murdered, their bodies splattered against the wall!" the woman wept.

Camilla moved to comfort the woman. She was not sure why, but she felt she had to do this. "Persephone was it?" she began. The woman nodded shakily. "How much time has lapsed do you think?"

"I don't know. I left my children with the guards so I could travel to visit my sister in Duskridge. When I returned this morning, they were dead or missing." Persephone was in hysterics.

Camilla nodded. "If Eoden is still alive, I will find him and bring him home. I swear it," the ranger said before standing and departing from the building.

"Why did Uldritch want this child?" Amelia asked, looking at the mayor.

"Eoden has magical abilities unlike anyone ever born to Alibi. He can cancel spells and enhance them. But most importantly, he can cast any spell he's read about without any training," Persephone said shakily. She sighed slightly, trying to collect herself before shaking her head. "It's likely Uldritch wants him for the enhancing another caster."

"We need to find them and fast," Amelia said as she stood.

"Wait for us!" Warren and Azura called as they ran to catch up with the ranger.

Amelia and Chuck soon followed. "Think it's Uldritch?" Amelia asked as she caught up to the ranger.

"Without a doubt," Camilla said as she began walking to the house where a handful of guards were investigating. There was blood everywhere, but more alarming was how brutally not only the two guards but also the two children were killed. Camilla surveyed the scene, trying to spot any tracks or anything that could be used to pick up on where Eoden would have been taken.

"Camilla, not to alarm you, but you said it's a full moon tonight," Amelia began, watching for any sort of reaction from the ranger.

Camilla nodded. "Yes, I know. I also have faith that you won't go berserk," the ranger said as she checked over the scene.

"Berserk?" Warren asked, looking at Amelia. He looked her up and down. "What do the two of you mean by that?"

Amelia let out a frustrated sigh. "Being what I am, half werewolf and half vampire, I sort of go into a blood frenzied, or berserk state once in a while. Blood moons, full moons, lunar eclipses, that sort of thing," she explained. She mentally kicked herself, this was what she feared, them finding out.

"Remember what I said to you. No matter what happens," Camilla began as she investigated something.

"You're with me no matter what happens," Amelia finished, feeling a little calmer.

Warren nodded slightly. "Alright, I trust Camilla on this. I hope you'll forgive me though if I have to knock you out." Amelia just nodded at the words.

"Find anything?" Azura asked as she observed Camilla. Chuck, surprisingly, stood to the side giving the ranger room to investigate.

"I got tracks. They're very faint but I can track them," Camilla responded as she took off in a sprint. The rest of the adventurers were hot on her heels as she led them out of Darktowne and into a nearby forest. She did not slow down even slightly as she sprinted through trees, narrowly dodging branches and thick mud. She finally stopped and looked back seeing Warren, Amelia and Chuck caught in the mud.

Azura was already casting spells from safety, trying to get them out. "Keep going, we'll catch up!" Warren called from the mud that was chest level with him. She hesitated. "Go! Time is of the essence if Uldritch is involved!" Warren hollered as he nodded to the ranger.

"I'll make sure you can track my path!" Camilla yelled back as she took off again. She hated leaving them behind like this, but she knew Warren was right. There was no telling how much time they had. As she bounded through trees and the area, she shot the occasional arrow making certain the others could find her.

The tracks she pursued took her into a grisly site as she came upon what could only be described as a heavily damaged mausoleum. She hesitated slightly, fear actually gripping her. Flashbacks ran through her mind as she thought back to Kardax.

The desert heat was intense even in the old jail. Roy had collapsed in battle, having tripped over his own tail. Camilla whistled to Flannel and ordered the wolf to drag Roy to the protective aura Lun had crafted. Thrall and Vanessa fought the massive army of undead that continued to flood the room. Gemma and Camilla had been using their bows to snipe anything that got past the other two.

Tremors began shaking the floor as two huge golems made of rotted flesh lumbered forward. Camilla felt her heart race as she shouldered her bow and drew her shortsword and dagger. "Guys, we got big ones!" she called out to the rest of the party. Thrall growled as he dealt with more tiny undead things that shambled forward.

Vanessa dropped back to help deal with the golems. Between the monk's speedy assault and Camilla's tactics, they managed to drop the golems.

Camilla shook her head and ran into the mausoleum. Her heart was hammering as she pushed onward. She had bested Uldritch once, she could do so again. The tracks became harder to locate as she pursued her prey. She only slowed down enough to catch her breath slightly as she went deeper into the tombs. There was no way of knowing when or where Uldritch would strike, let alone how far down he was.

She listened to the stall air of the tombs hoping to hear anything. As she took another step, she finally started hearing things. Taking a steady breath and letting it out slowly, Camilla knew she was close. She rounded the next corner and found herself staring at Uldritch's back, roughly fifty feet away from him. "Excuse me, Uldritch, but we need to talk," she said as she tried to calm her nerves.

Uldritch smirked as he turned to face the ranger; he gripped a boy tightly by the wrist. "You shouldn't have been able to track me that fast," he responded coldly, as his gaze narrowed.

"What can I say, I'm quite the tracker," Camilla replied, calmly. She held out a hand. "Let the boy go, Uldritch. I might give you a chance if you do."

Uldritch laughed as he glared at Camilla. "You only defeated me last time because you got lucky," he snarled before touching the ground with his free hand.

Just as in Abyssal Castle, the ground reformed and splintered forward. Camilla narrowly dodged the attack; her footwork was about the same as his speed. She drew her longsword and shortsword as she tried to close the distance on Uldritch. Before he could react, the ranger unleashed a quick flurry of blade strikes forcing him away from the boy. Camilla sheathed her shortsword and scooped the boy into her left arm, holding him against her chest. "Don't worry, I'm never going to let you go," she said, her voice reflecting confidence.

The boy, Eoden, winced, gripping Camilla's shirt as he pressed into her. "Why? Why did you come here?" he whimpered.

"My friends and I came to rescue you. I'm not going to let you down. I will get you out of here and back to your mother," Camilla said as she held her gaze on Uldritch.

The warlock laughed maniacally as he reshaped the floor and rest of the room. All possible exits were sealed off and there was more space for them to fight. More surfaces he could use to attack with. "So, going to stand and fight, eh, *Hero*?" he spat the word hero as he took a step forward. He unleashed several splinter waves toward the ranger.

Camilla sheathed her longsword as she held Eoden close. She moved in and out of the reshaped floor, trying to stay ahead of the attacks. At one point she had to lift and hold Eoden overhead to avoid having him skewered. She landed roughly on her right ankle, sending a wave of pain through her. Eoden whimpered as Camilla held him against her. "Please, don't. Just run. Leave me and run," Eoden whimpered.

The ranger shook her head. "I'm not going to let you down. I promise," she whispered to him while giving the boy a smile. Uldritch smirked as he launched several steel bolts from his hands. Camilla smiled again at Eodon. "Sorry about this," she said while pulling her cloak around to obscure the warlock's view.

When Uldritch was able to see again, he saw the boy wrapped in the torn black cloak the ranger had been wearing. He instantly went to shield himself, predicting what was to come. A quick slash struck his cheek, a line of blood visible. "You won't lay another finger on him!" Camilla snarled as she dodged back avoiding Uldritch's attempt to grab her.

"You've gotten faster since our last encounter," Uldritch noted as he took a step back. He touched the ground. "But I know how to get your attention." He smirked as the splinter wave went towards Eoden.

Camilla sprinted, barely getting in position in time. She shoved Eoden back, the spikes impaling her thighs and forearms. *"I need to predict his next move,"* Camilla thought as she collected herself. *"It's clear he has no regard for Eoden's safety,"* she thought, while glancing over her shoulder at the frightened boy.

Uldritch attacked again; this time he knew the ranger had nowhere to run or dodge to. If she moved, the attack would kill the boy she was trying to protect. She might have been faster and stronger than him, but he was far smarter. Camilla brought her blades up, twirling them in front of her, managing to break up some of the attack. Step. Step. She managed two steps towards Uldritch. If she could close the distance, she might have a chance. Step. Step. The attacks the warlock threw were becoming more aggressive, each one pushing the ranger and her weapons to their limits. Step. Step. She was close, just a little more.

The ranger had taken the bait. Uldritch wanted her to try to close the distance. He already had victory in the palm of his hand the very moment the fight began. As Camilla took another step, several splinter spikes impaled her stomach and chest. Her eyes widened as she felt the pain. Her hands were shaking from an overload of the pain. Was this it? Was she going to die here? Blood rushed from the wounds, spilling onto the ground.

"Camilla! Hang on! We're coming!"

A loud explosion was heard as part of the wall was destroyed. Warren and Amelia rushed forward, both with their tower shields in hand. Chuck sprinted past them and swung his greataxe knocking Uldritch back a few feet. Azura was the last one into the room and sprinted to the boy. Camilla smiled at the others. "Get Eoden out of here. That's the mission."

"We're not leaving you behind," Amelia responded as she took a defensive position to protect the ranger. She looked at Warren then focused on the attacker. "Warren, get her wounds patched up."

"Already doing such," Warren responded as he healed the wounds that covered the ranger. He started with the most critical ones, being the chest and stomach. Then moved onto healing the wounds to the thighs and forearms.

Uldritch snarled as he glared at the group. In a one on one, he could easily take them down. But a five on one could be difficult. He smirked before snapping his fingers. Several shadows materialized around him, each one looked like a different sort of beast. A manticore, a serpentine dragon, a griffon, a phoenix and finally a leviathan. He was known for his reshaping matter spell, but he had plenty of other spells up his sleeves. "Rend the flesh from their bones," he ordered, gazing darkly at the adventurers.

The shadow versions of the beasts lunged forward, each with bloodlust in their eyes. "No matter what happens, protect Eoden!" Camilla called as she slashed at the serpentine dragon.

Warren was fighting with the griffon. Amelia took the manticore. Chuck had a hard time engaging the phoenix but did so anyway. Azura used her magic to create a protective barrier around the boy then proceeded to cast a cone of ice in hopes of freezing the leviathan.

"Why? Why are they fighting for me?" Eoden whimpered as he watched the fight.

Amelia managed a lucky hit and took the manticore's head off its body. She turned, drawing a crossbow from her bag as she did so. In rapid succession she fired, grounding the phoenix. Chuck went to work, his greataxe cutting through the phoenix's talons and eventually the head. Warren endured attack after attack from the griffon before countering with a fierce swing of his morningstar. The weapon cracked the beast's skull causing it to howl in pain as it stepped back. "Amelia, help Azura!" Warren called over the heat of battle.

The paladin nodded and rushed to aid the sorceress. Her mind was hazy again, the full moon taking a toll on her. She shook her head as she sprinted to the sorceress. Despite the moon, she still retained control of her mind. She refused to go berserk at a time like this. Chuck drew his handaxe and threw it, embedding the weapon into the griffon's back.

Camilla leapt to the side, narrowly avoiding the dragon's shadow breath. She rushed forward, plunging her blades into the beast's eyes. The shrill roar of pain echoed in the chamber. She was trying to get around the dragon and reach Uldritch but it was proving difficult to do. Sucking in a deep breath, she managed to tumble behind the dragon and reach the warlock. As she slashed out with her blades, she saw the warlock leap backwards. Where was this sudden agility coming from?

"I tire of this game; I will have that brat!" Uldritch snarled.

"Why! Why is he so important?" Camilla demanded as she continued to press up to fight.

"Why do you try to rescue him when you haven't a clue about his value!" Uldritch shot back.

Before any more of the beasts could be slain, the living ones advanced to Uldritch's position. He smirked as they also brought the fallen ones. He reached out, touching each beast, absorbing them into himself and began transforming. Standing where the warlock had been was a massive monster. It had the legs of the griffon, the head of a manticore, phoenix's wings, leviathan's body and the dragon's tail.

Uldritch roared loudly, shaking the entire mausoleum. Warren, Amelia and Chuck rushed to form up on Camilla's location. They would fight as a team. Azura hung back and provided spells to cover them as they made a plan. Uldritch smirked, fire shot from his mouth, unfortunately it canceled out all of Azura's spells. She tried to cast again but found her spells were out. Claws slashed out, ripping through Warren's armor and sending the cleric into a wall. He winced as he tried to get up but found both his legs had been broken.

Chuck, Amelia and Camilla fought onward, all three trying to avoid any attacks that were used. Uldritch's tail swung out, grabbing the barbarian, at the same time his wings flapped hard. Amelia and Camilla were flung back from the gale brought on by the wings. They watched as Uldritch tightened his tail, crushing Chuck.

"Do you want them to die, Eoden! Return to me and I'll spare them!" Uldritch roared as he eyed the boy. His gaze narrowed as he smirked at scene unfolding. "If they die down here, you're to blame, Eoden!"

Eoden was shaking. He took a step forward. "Stop. Please," he whimpered as he took another shaky step. He sniffled slightly, clearly in tears. "I'll go with you. Just please, no more. Restore them too how they were," he begged.

"Eoden, no!" Camilla called as she managed to stand. Her body ached in too many spots. But she refused to sit by and watch as this child was taken. Her legs wobbled and she collapsed; she had taken on too many critical injuries.

Uldritch smirked as he flung Chuck aside and held out a claw to the boy. "Come, Eoden. No one at Darktowne can hone your magic. I can," he said as he watched Eoden step closer.

Amelia managed to stand, her fighting spirit amplified by the effects of the full moon. She held her bastard sword with both hands, leaving behind her tower shield. She sprinted forward, the blade leaving a gash in Uldritch's front left leg. He roared loudly before turning to face the paladin. "Don't you dare lay a claw on him!" Amelia yelled as she engaged the monster in battle.

Eoden watched as Amelia dove between attacks and unleashed sword strike after sword strike. He had never seen anyone willing to fight for him. And here this group of five was, willing to fight, willing to die, all to rescue him. Amelia leapt to the side before lunging forward and driving her bastard sword deep into Uldritch's chest. He roared in agony as he glared down at the paladin. Flames ignited his jaws as he unleashed a rush of blue fire. Amelia hissed in pain as she was forced back, her armor had been super-heated around her, leaving several burn spots on her body. She staggered, trying to stay standing but a slam from the tail sent her into a wall.

Uldritch flexed, forcing the bastard sword out of his body as his wounds healed. "I should kill all of you for that," he snarled. Eoden took a shaky step back.

"Fight back! Fight back, Eoden!" Camilla yelled as she finally got to her feet. Eoden looked over, his gray eyes meeting the ranger's yellow eyes. "Whatever you can manage, just fight back! None of us are going to stop. We won't stop until we get you home!" she called as she tightened her hold on her blades.

"Camilla…" Everyone whispered as they saw how despite her wounds, the ranger was still trying to fight. It motivated them. Chuck got to his feet and rushed the monster again. Warren began casting, trying any spell he could. Azura dragged herself to Warren's side and tended to his legs, using any bandages and splints she had. Amelia managed to stand and drew her crossbow, firing bolts rapidly into the monster.

Camilla darted forward, adrenaline pumping fully. She wiped the blood from her eyes as she closed in on her target. Her blades lashed out as she struck Uldritch's chest. Eoden shook his head as he looked toward the fight. He held out both his hands and began chanting. Several bolts of lightning shot forward striking Uldritch.

The roar was deafening. His eyes showed the hatred he harbored for the outrealm warriors. His form began to change again as he tapped himself. He now stood on his hind legs and sported an even more menacing look. His feet were talon like. His arms were massive and ended in huge claws. His tail remained unchanged. His wings had grown larger. His chest was more muscular and pronounced. His head mutated from a lion-like manticore head to that of a monstrous wolf with horns jutting out from his temples. Uldritch easily towered over the adventurers, his new height a massive sixty feet. The back of his throat lit up just before a beam-like attack shot out, destroying most of the area. Uldritch moved his jaws in a sweep of the area, the beam hitting everyone except for Eoden.

Warren and Azura lay slumped against one another. Neither showing any signs of getting up anytime soon. Chuck was sprawled out on the ground, his eyes closed and breathing shallow. Amelia and Camilla had fallen side by side, both badly injured and fighting to stay conscious. Eoden shook in fear. He did not want to go with Uldritch but it was starting to seem like that was the only way to survive. Uldritch glared down at the boy. "No!" Eoden yelled as he threw several lightning, ice and fire balls at the monster.

"Then perish!" Uldritch roared as he fired his beam attack at the boy.

"Eoden!" Amelia yelled as she saw the attack. She glanced at her side and saw the ranger on her feet and sprinting toward the boy. Smoke and debris went everywhere. When it cleared, Camilla was holding Eoden; the boy was unharmed. Her back was to Uldritch, it was clear she had been badly injured from the blast. "Camilla! Camilla, no!" Amelia tried to stand but could not find the strength to do so. She began crawling, trying to reach her friend.

Camilla's eyes were closed as she held the boy in her arms. "You're not... hurt...? Tell me... you're... ok..." she said, her head down.

"I... I... I'm fine," Eoden said as he looked up at the ranger. He felt the warm red droplets land on his skin and his eyes widened.

The ranger gave him a weak smile. "I'm glad," she whispered before going silent.

"Eoden! Eoden! Whatever magic you have, use it!" Amelia yelled as loud as she could.

The boy looked up and shook with fear when he saw Uldritch preparing another beam attack. He looked at the ranger, he sensed something stirring within her. It just needed something to draw it out. He reached his hands out, pressing them into the ranger's chest. Magic began flowing freely from his hands into the ranger. Lightning began crackling in the air around them. He felt the heartbeats within the ranger quicken. Eoden only prayed this worked, he had never tried a spell so massive before.

Camilla's eyes shot open, both a piercing red instead of their normal yellow. She let out an inhuman sound, almost like a roar as she felt the magic surging from the boy. Eoden winced but kept using his magic. He continued to silently pray that this worked. Lightning sparks crackled in the air before massive bolts crashed around the ranger and the boy. Amelia had to shield her eyes as the bright flashes of lightning went off. When things cleared up enough that the paladin could see again, standing where the ranger had been was a colossal blue dragon.

The blue dragon roared loudly as it lumbered toward Uldritch, a rage burning deep in the dragon's eyes. Eoden had fallen unconscious and was laying on the ground, exhausted from how much magic he had used. Amelia dragged herself to the boy and cradled him in her arms as she watched helpless to do anything.

Uldritch slashed out with his claws, trying to get the better of the dragon. The blue wyrm was not having any of it as it unleashed a cone of electricity from its mouth before slamming its body into the abomination. As Uldritch tried to recover he felt the claws of the dragon slashing through his flesh before feeling another bolt of lightning sear him. He staggered to his feet and took a step back. The repeated attacks he had taken in the previous fights combined with the dragon's assault was becoming too much. He attempted to flee but felt the fangs of the blue dig deep into his tail and drag him down. The dragon snarled as it slammed him into the ground many times over there before unleashing a massive blast of lightning causing the area to become unstable and bury him under several boulders and bricks.

Amelia winced, watching the scene. She zoned out slightly only to be brought back to the present by the massive claws landing in front of her. Hesitantly the paladin looked up and saw the piercing red eyes of the dragon gazing down at her and the boy, its fangs bared. Fear gripped her as she tried to speak. No words came out. She finally managed to shake her head and focus.

The boy began to come to and looked up as well. He felt no fear though; he felt calm. A smile crept onto his face as he gazed up at the dragon. He reached a hand up. "You mustn't let anger cloud your mind," Eoden spoke softly. Amelia looked from the boy to the dragon and waited. The dragon snarled slightly before relaxing its fangs. "Calm your heart and feel. Feel the emotions around you," Eoden added as he watched the dragon.

The blue dragon looked around, as though taking in the environment. It looked down at the boy again, seemingly calmed from its violent state. It took a few steps back, letting out a pained roar as it did so. Lightning began crackling again around the dragon as its size began diminishing. Amelia shielded her eyes briefly as the lightning illuminated the chamber. When everything cleared, the paladin saw the ranger collapsed on the ground where the dragon had been. She looked down at Eoden. "What manner of spell was that?" she asked, her voice filled with fear and wonder.

Eoden said nothing as he began casting what healing magic he knew. It was not much but he managed to heal Warren and Azura before he lost consciousness. Amelia hesitated but left the boy near Camilla before trying to stand again. She winced, clearly exhausted. She dragged Warren and Azura over to where she had left Eoden and Camilla. Once the two casters were in the formation, she moved to secure the barbarian. She dragged Chuck to where she had everyone else positioned before finally slumping down. Her scarlet eyes looked to the boulders, and she prayed that it was the last of Uldritch.

Warren slowly opened his eyes and sat up rather quickly. "Is everyone alr—-" He stopped mid-sentence as he looked around and saw everyone in the huddle. Amelia gave him a tired thumbs up and a nod as she looked over at him. He nodded and began healing everyone. "So, did we beat him?" he asked as he tended to the various wounds his friends had taken.

"As far as I know, yes," Amelia replied as she pointed to the boulders. "He was buried under there, hopefully that's enough to kill the dastard," she added as she sat back, still fatigued from everything.

The cleric nodded as he finished Azura's wounds and moved on to Chuck's. Despite everything, the ranger was not in as bad of condition as he imagined her to be. He was grateful regardless but found it odd that the one who had been in constant combat somehow managed to have fewer wounds than the rest. The cleric paused briefly as he looked at Amelia, still healing Chuck as he did so. "Amelia, I don't know if I can heal your wounds," he said slowly as he looked up and down the paladin's injuries.

Amelia merely waved him off. "You would need magic that normally harms living in order to heal them. It's fine, Warren, just tend to the others," she replied as she sat back. Her body was aching from everything that had transpired. Her mind was spinning from what she witnessed. She had seen the ranger seemingly turn into a blue dragon and back to human. It was surreal, but she wondered more about what spell the boy had used on her friend.

Warren nodded as he returned his full focus on the barbarian. After a few more spells, all of Chuck's wounds were fully healed. The cleric sighed as he rubbed his eyes, tired from everything. "Don't strain yourself. Rest if you need to," Amelia commented, worried about Warren's wellbeing. The cleric was trying to make certain everyone was going to pull through, but he seemed to have little regard for his own wellbeing.

He sighed as he slumped back, the fatigue of using so much magic getting to him. "You know, I don't think I would be doing this if I never came here," he whispered.

"Clearly. You wouldn't have met this merrier band of misfits if you never came here," the paladin quipped.

"That's not what I meant." Warren paused. He looked down at his hands and shook his head. "What I meant was... well, prior to coming here... I... I had no regard for the lives of others. I didn't see anyone's life mattering unless it was my own. I killed for sport; I made others kill each other for my amusement. I think I already said all this though. But prior to coming here, I was ruthless. No better than Uldritch."

"So, you strayed towards a darker path. What matters is you came back from it. What matters is you've acknowledged such and are trying to be better," Amelia replied as she looked around the room. A small smile formed on her face as she looked back at Warren. "I've seen how you care about Azura. Someone truly evil, someone like Uldritch, they would never look at anyone with such affection." She paused as Warren's face turned a deep red from embarrassment. "Don't worry. I won't say a word. Though I'm sure I'm not the only one who knows. My point is, I've seen how you act. You were willing to die against Narcian, you put your life on the line to protect Azura and be her shield. That's the difference between someone like you and someone like Uldritch. You're willing to change and help others."

Warren thought about Amelia's words for a moment before looking over the rest of the group. He made his way to Camilla and began tending to her wounds. He mentally scolded himself. While he didn't see any visible wounds, the ranger was in fact badly hurt. Two broken ribs and broken right arm. He did what he could to stabilize the ranger, hoping his magic would suffice.

Behind him, Warren heard a grunt in pain. "How're you feeling, Chuck?" Warren asked as he continued tending to the ranger.

"Chuck mad. Chuck miss fight. Chuck wanted fight," the barbarian groaned.

Amelia chuckled hearing the half orc's words. "Maybe next time, big guy. Next big monster we fight, we'll make sure you get more fight time," she said as she laid back against the ground.

Another groan was heard as Azura started to sit up. The young sorceress looked around, clearly disturbed. "What happened! Is Eoden safe?" she began, clearly distraught.

"He's unconscious but fine. And before you ask, Uldritch is buried under those boulders," Amelia commented as she pointed to the fallen boulders. She kept quiet about the dragon incident. She would wait until she could talk to Eoden or Camilla before bringing it up.

Warren slouched back as he finished tending to the worst of the ranger's wounds. He took a few deep breaths, clearly pushing himself to his limit through magic fatigue. He checked over Eoden, eyes widening when he saw the boy was completely unharmed. "Guys, believe it or not, but we did our mission really damn well. He's not hurt at all," the cleric said as he slumped back.

It was another few minutes before Camilla began opening her eyes. She was in a lot of pain, but pain let her know she was alive. With a faint smile, she slowly sat up and looked over to the rest of the group. "Are all of you alright?" she asked, wincing from pain in her chest.

"Yeah, but try not to push yourself too hard. While you hardly had any external injuries, you had some really bad internal ones," Warren replied, giving the ranger a thumbs up. He chuckled slightly then met her gaze. "You holding up alright?"

"Well enough,." Camilla shot back as she reached into her bag and withdrew the potion box. She winced as she tried using her right arm. The pain was a bit much so she began fumbling with the box using her left. She withdrew a handful of healing potions and tossed one to each member of the party. "Drink up, we're going to need our stamina if we're heading back to Dusktowne anytime soon."

Azura, Chuck and Warren showed no hesitation as they downed the potions. The flavor was disgusting but it did help in their recovery. Amelia shook her head before tossing the small bottle back to the ranger. "Won't help as I'm undead," the paladin said. Camilla frowned as she put the bottle back in the box. She wanted to help the paladin but lacked any way of doing such. "I appreciate the gesture though," Amelia added, trying to cheer the ranger up.

Finally, the Eoden awoke and sat up slowly; he rubbed his head. "You alright, Eoden?" Camilla asked softly as she looked the boy over for any injuries. He nodded to her before turning his attention to the entire group. He wanted to thank them for everything, to tell them how much it meant to him. But as he went to speak, he could not find the right words. He hung his head. Camilla chuckled as she ruffled his hair. "You're fine. Now, then, let's get you home to your mother," she added as she finally stood.

Chuck and Azura supported Warren, his legs still badly injured despite all the magic that had been used. Amelia was the last one to her feet and turned to face Camilla. Warren nodded his thanks to the others then looked to Camilla. "Call it. What's the formation, Boss," he said. Camilla arched an eyebrow, clearly taken back. For the first time since they arrived, Warren was not arguing about leadership, he was yielding to her. "You call the shots, and I'll follow," he added as he gave her a slight smile. Chuck and Azura nodded in agreement.

Camilla shook her head. "First off, I'm not the boss. Second, as for formation, Chuck, Azura and Warren, you three stay at the center. Amelia, you bring up the rear. I'll take lead," she stated before turning to Eoden. She gently scooped him up and carried him with her left arm. Eoden was not sure how to react, he leaned into Camilla, his head against her chest.

The adventurers made their way out of the mausoleum and back into the forest. It was dark, how much time had they spent underground? Camilla shook her head as she led the group safely through the forest, making sure to avoid the massive mud pit that had ensnared them the first time. They moved at a slower pace than last time. But they eventually made it back to town without any encounters. Each counting their blessings.

Upon reaching the town, they saw Persephone and Mayor Ichiban waiting for them. "Mama!" Eoden cried as he saw his mother.

"Eoden!" Persephone called as she sprinted over. Camilla gently set the boy down and watched as he ran to his awaiting mother's arms. She wanted to smile but could not do such. Persephone held Eoden in a hug, both in tears at the reunion. She looked to the ranger and the rest of the group. "Thank you! Thank you so much!" She wept.

"Just doing what's right," Warren replied, speaking on behalf of the group.

Mayor Ichiban invited the adventurers back to his estate. "Come, stay the night and take however long you need to recover. You've done this town a grand service." He paused seeing the confused looks on their faces. "The plague, it seems to have stopped. No further infections have been reported and everyone who was sick has made a sudden recovery."

"That's great news, Mayor," Azura spoke up this time. She and Chuck entered the estate, still helping Warren. The trio paused glancing over their shoulders at Camilla. "You coming?"

"I'll catch up. Needed to check into something," Camilla replied.

Amelia stood a little way behind Camilla. She looked to Azura and mouthed *I'll stay with her*, reassuring the sorceress. Azura nodded, she knew if

Amelia was with Camilla, they would be fine. But she was still worried all the same. Once the others had gone inside, Amelia put a hand gently on Camilla's shoulder. "Darling, what's troubling you?" she cooed slightly. She always had a soft spot for the ranger.

Camilla glanced over but looked down soon after. She shook her head. "Not here," she replied before starting to walk away. Amelia was disturbed by the ranger's sudden shift but followed all the same. They came to a part of Darktowne that was empty, no houses, no people, just empty aside from a large tree. Camilla sat on the bricks that enclosed the tree, still looking down. Amelia sat beside her, waiting for the ranger to say something. "Back there, at the mausoleum," Camilla paused as she tried to find the words, "I remember what Eoden did. What he turned me into." She paused again, trying to collect herself. "It didn't feel strange or unnatural. The opposite really. It felt normal. It felt like for once, I was in a natural state. Yeah, I lost my head, but everything else felt right," she said, her tone showing how bothered she was.

"I have to admit, you looked pretty darn scary. But you didn't attack anyone, aside from Uldritch. What's this really about?" Amelia asked, knowing there was more to this talk.

The ranger looked up at the tree branches hanging overhead. "When I lost consciousness, after the fight, I... I had another vision. I'm starting to think they're memories," she said somberly yet held a slight smile. Camilla chuckled softly. "It's strange really, to suddenly have memories of a life I'd forgotten," she added softly. "But this time, I was traveling through the desert again. I wasn't alone, there was someone with me. I can't recall his name, but his presence felt calming, reassuring even. Then it went dark and I had a different memory. All I saw was red. Aggressively lashing out at countless people, destroying villages. Then the same man from the previous memory stepped forward. I... I begged him to kill me."

Camilla finally looked at Amelia, tears in her eyes. "Amelia, I don't know what I am. I don't know who I am! Am I Camilla Windstride, retainer to Azura Vaughan? Am I some sort of monstrous beast who only knows killing? Am I human? Or am I something else? What if I am a demon like you thought when we first met?" Camilla broke down into sobs. She let the tears run freely, her head down.

Amelia was not sure how to react. She had grown fond of the ranger. She had grown to trust and care about Camilla. And here her best friend sat, broken. What should she say? What could she say? She did not understand this anymore than Camilla did. Amelia finally reached out and pulled the broken ranger into a hug. “You are Camilla Windstride. And whatever path you decide to follow, you’re not alone. You’ve got friends now—me, Azura, Chuck and Warren. We’re all here for you,” she said, trying to comfort the ranger. Her words were true, but the ranger did not acknowledge them.

“I’ve fought two evil versions of myself. The first was in Uldritch’s castle, the second in that memory event at Spiral Mountain. Both times, after their defeat, they turned into blue dragons! I’m starting to doubt I’m even the real Camilla! What if… What if I… What if I’m some other thing, some monster posing as the ranger? What if I’m the shadow copy from Uldritch’s castle and the real Camilla was slain by my hand?” Camilla snapped. She was clearly unstable mentally.

Amelia clenched her fist before punching the ranger’s right cheek. “Snap out of it! You are Camilla Windstride! The only Camilla Windstride! You’re the real Camilla! Not those fake distortion illusions! You! The only one!” the paladin yelled; she was breathing heavily after her outburst. She flinched realizing she had punched the ranger. “I…”

“No, I needed that,” Camilla interrupted. She rubbed her cheek slightly then looked at Amelia, a ghost of a smile on her face. “Thank you, Amelia. Sorry I got all weird on you,” she apologized.

Amelia just pulled the ranger into a hug. “Know this, if you ever start having doubts, if you ever need to talk, I’m here for you. No matter what happens.” The paladin felt the ranger bury her face against the metal armor before chuckling slightly. “What? Wait, I got you to chuckle. Feeling better?”

“It’s funny, really it is,” Camilla whispered before looking up to meet Amelia’s gaze. “I could’ve sworn we’ve had this talk. But our roles were reversed. And now here we are, exactly how we were.” Camilla chuckled again before pulling away from Amelia. “I’m fine now. Come on, we best get back to the estate. Don’t want Azura or Warren, or Chuck even starting to get too worried.” She laughed as she stood.

The paladin nodded as she stood and followed the ranger. She was not fully convinced that Camilla was better. It was likely just a show, something to try to ease her own mind and lessen her worries over the ranger’s wellbeing. It was just how Camilla was, after all she had been keeping this from everyone.

"You don't need to shoulder every burden alone. We're all here for you," she thought as they reached the estate.

The pair went inside and were soon escorted to the room where the others were staying. Warren was already asleep, as was Chuck. Azura perked up hearing the door open and smiled at the pair as they entered. "You both ok?" she asked as she looked them over.

Camilla nodded before going to one of the beds. She set her gear down beside it, undoing her belt and quiver, leaving them to the side. She laid down, her back to the others as she soon fell asleep. Her mind was racing from everything, but her body was fatigued making it easy to enter a light slumber.

Amelia nodded as well but waited for Camilla to fall asleep. Once she was certain the ranger was sleeping, she turned her attention to the sorceress. "Camilla just needed to vent about some stuff. Do me a favor, in case I don't catch everything, please keep eyes on her."

Azura arched an eyebrow confused and trying to figure out what they spoke about. "Of course, but what's wrong?" the young sorceress asked.

"It's complicated and when Camilla's ready, I'm sure she'll talk about it," the paladin answered as she began removing her armor. She placed the heavy full plate armor on the empty armor stand then sat down on one of the wing chairs and stared into the small fireplace they had. Azura nodded slowly before retiring to a bed for the night.

Stars. The same stars that always shone. Something calming and yet alluring.

"Hey, you alright?" the man asked.

Craning her neck down to look at him, the blue dragon smiled softly. "Yes, just taking in the night view."

He chuckled slightly as he patted the dragon's chest then leaned back against it. "It sure is peaceful out here. Thank you for travelling with me, Celica."

"I should be the one thanking you, Ashe."

The next morning everyone was being checked over by the town healer. She checked over their wounds and tended to any that required additional healing. "You're a good healer. Your team survived thanks to such," she said as she used magic to heal Warren's legs. He nodded his gratitude as he sat there in silence.

Once the healer had finished and left the room, Mayor Ichiban entered. "It's good to see all of you awake and well," he stated while taking a seat before the group. He set a bag on the table and smiled. "It's not much, but it's what we could scrape together as payment," he added as he indicated the bag. The five adventurers hesitated before looking at the bag. Inside were roughly five thousand wendells as well as a pair of boots. "The boots are from Persephone; she said she noticed one of you had rather damaged looking boots and could use a new pair."

Each of them checked their attire. All of them had some noticeable wear and tear, some more than others. Warren's boots were barely anything more than leather barely being held together. His armor had some scuffs and dents. Amelia's armor was dented in a few spots, but nothing a hammer could not handle. Azura's light dress was split in several spots, looking well beyond needing to be replaced. Chuck's loincloth was about the same as it was the day he arrived. He never wore armor nor clothes due to the costs to maintain and replace such. Camilla checked her attire over. Her cloak was torn up and mostly gone, her shirt had several holes and bloodstains and her gloves were frayed.

"Mayor Ichiban, is there a seamstress or apparel shop in town?" Warren asked as everyone had similar thoughts.

"And a blacksmith?" Amelia asked as she looked over her weapons.

"Aye, I'll walk y'all to the blacksmith then to Gracidia's apparel," the mayor replied as he stood.

Everyone collected their gear that needed work as well as any coin they had saved up. It was going to be a long journey to Faraway Lake; they figured they might as well stock up and get everything fixed up. When they reached the blacksmith, they had asked how long everything would need for repairs. He looked over the two sets of armor and the various weapons. "Going to be about four days for the armor and another three for that many weapons," he stated, as he checked everything over again. "I hope you all have some spare armor and weapons, being this isolated our town, even as Ichiban runs it, still has its dangers," he added.

"Yeah, we'll be fine. We'll leave all this in your care," Warren replied with a polite bow before taking the claim number and tickets for each item they left. He handed the tickets to whomever in the group the ticket corresponded to their gear. "Seven days isn't too bad. Means the big guy is confident in his skills," he added.

They arrived at Gracidia's apparel and began browsing the various clothes. A haggard woman sat at the counter observing the group, sitting on her shoulder was a small fairy. "Women's wears are on the upper floor, men's wears on the lower floor. And if you're looking for anything with enchantments, my catalogue is at the desk by the stairs. Lily here can enchant anything in the shop," the woman called out as she sat back in her chair at the counter.

Warren and Chuck wandered the lower level, neither looking for anything specific. Chuck paused when he found an elegant cape made from the skin of a tiger. The head was stitched up to be a hood while the body made up the rest of the cape. He looked over the price then counted his wendells. "Need some extra money?" Warren asked as he looked to the barbarian. Chuck nodded ashamed he was having to borrow from someone. Warren opened his belt pouch and pulled out some coins. "What about enchantments? Might as well splurge a little," the elf stated as he walked to the desk in question.

On the upper floor, Azura, Camilla and Amelia were looking through the wares. Amelia had picked up a fairly modest looking long sleeve shirt and a new pair of pants. She did not need any enchantments, just something to wear under her heavy armor. Azura had grabbed a long sleeve shirt, a leather vest and a pair of pants. Camilla arched an eyebrow. "Trying a new style?" she asked, seeing the wardrobe change.

Azura nodded. "Yes, while I prefer a dress, it doesn't seem practical with everything we've gone through," she replied as she went to meet up with the boys at the desk.

Amelia laughed slightly as she wandered with Camilla a little bit longer. "You never struck me as the type to shop." She chuckled.

"I'm only looking to replace my cloak. But I'm not seeing anything that's functionable and fits my needs," the ranger stated as they went down the stairs.

"Maybe you can see if Gracidia can tailor something specific to you," the paladin replied as they caught up with the others. Camilla rolled her eyes, not liking the idea. "Come on, worst case she says no."

"Fine, I'll ask," Camilla responded as she walked behind the paladin.

Once the group was ready, they went to the counter. Chuck's tiger pelt cape was enchanted with elemental resistances. Azura got her vest enchanted to have increased defenses and her shirt to have element resistances. Amelia stuck with the simple shirt and pants, nothing added to them.

"Miss Gracidia?" Camilla began nervously after the others had finished paying.

"Yes, young lady?" the old woman asked.

"I was wondering, would it be possible to get something tailored specifically for me?" the ranger asked but looked down.

"What sort of garment do you need? I'll see what I can do," Gracidia replied as she stood from her seat and collected a few things to take measurements with.

"I'm looking to replace a cloak I had. But I'm needing something with pockets," the ranger explained as she continued to look down.

The old woman took a few measurements. She made her notes and smiled. "Come back by in five days and I'll have something ready for you," she said before looking over her fabrics. "And did you have a color in mind?"

Camilla shook her head as she turned to leave. "Black or green, stay matching her current attire if we can," Warren said with a soft sincere smile. Gracidia nodded as she looked over her fabrics again. The party thanked the woman before departing from the shop.

"You guys know I'm not picky about the color," Camilla mumbled.

Warren laughed. "I'll keep that in mind next time and tell them to make it pink." He flinched when he saw the glare Camilla shot him. There was a pause then he laughed again. "See, you clearly do care about the color. Anyway, I suggested black or green so it stays blending in with the forest like you always try to do."

"Huh, now that you mention it, yeah, I suppose you're right. Thanks, Warren," Camilla said, her head tilted slightly as she thought about it a little. She shook her head before looking at Warren. "How much coin are we going to need when we return to the blacksmith?"

Warren paused as he looked over his claim ticket. "My armor, shield and morningstar are going to be about three thousand wendells."

Amelia looked her claim ticket over and winced. "Armor, shield and sword are going to be about the same. Three thousand wendells."

Chuck held his claim ticket. "Chuck not read," he grunted.

The cleric grabbed the ticket and looked it over. "One greataxe, about five hundred wendells."

Camilla looked at her claim ticket. "One shortsword, three hundred wendells," she added.

Azura shook her head. "So, we're looking at six thousand eight hundred wendells," the sorceress noted as she looked in her coin pouch. "I've got about two thousand."

Warren was next checking his coin pouch. "I'm at three thousand even."

Amelia shook her head. "I've only got about one hundred."

"Chuck broke," the barbarian growled.

All eyes went to Camilla as she opened her coin pouch. "Five hundred wendells. We're coming up short still," she noted.

"What do you propose we do?" Warren asked, knowing Camilla already had a plan.

The ranger unfolded her map and looked it over before pointing at a few towns marked on it. "Loft Ridge is about a half day's travel from here. Maybe we head there and see about doing some mercenary work."

"I read about Loft Ridge. It's a city full of rich folks who haven't the slightest idea what to do with their money. And the crime rate is very high," Azura chimed in.

"It's not safe for all of us to travel though. What does everyone have armor and weapon wise?" Camilla asked as she began thinking.

Warren pulled out his ball and chain. "This is all I've got left. And my banged up morningstar."

Amelia shook her head. "I've only got my crossbow. No armor though."

"Chuck have damaged greataxe," the barbarian stated as he hefted a greataxe that was barely holding together.

Azura smiled. "I mostly use magic, so I'm still all set."

Camilla rested her right hand on the pommel of her longsword. "I've still got my longsword, a shortsword, a few daggers and my longbow," the ranger replied. She paced for a moment. "Alright, Azura and I will travel to Loft Ridge and see if we can make some fast coin. You three stay here and try not to do anything too reckless," she stated.

The sorceress nodded. "Sounds as good of a plan as any. When do we head out?" she asked.

The ranger handed her coin pouch to Amelia. "Hang onto this for me. And use it if you need to," she said then turned her attention to the young sorceress. "As soon as you're ready, we'll head out."

"Then let's go!" Azura cheered, all too happy to be going on a side adventure.

"You sure you both will be ok, without us, I mean?" Warren asked as he stood awkwardly to the side.

"We'll be fine, Warren," Azura responded as she began heading off.

"I'll keep her safe, don't worry," Camilla added before departing.

Chapter 18 - Hauntings

It was a half day's journey, the ranger and sorceress arriving just before nightfall in Loft Ridge. Camilla studied the layout of the city; it was larger than anywhere they had been leading up to this point. Shops were packed up for the night. Guards did their routine walks, making sure everything was as it should be. In truth it made the ranger uneasy; she had seen this before, back in her version of Kardax. Azura tapped Camilla's shoulder then pointed. "City message board. Maybe we'll find some work there," she said.

The two approached the message board and looked it over. There were dozens of jobs, each one had decent pay, some even had high pay. Camilla took a handful of the papers and looked them over doing the math in her head. "If we can complete these six, we'll have enough wendells for the blacksmith and some to spare," she noted as she looked over the tasks.

"Most of these are gathering random ingredients from the forests surrounding the area. It's like they don't know safe plants from harmful ones," Azura noted as she read over four of the six jobs that the ranger had selected.

Camilla nodded then turned her attention to the next two. "This one is dealing with bandits that have been randomly attacking the city at night. And the last one is escorting a merchant safely and conveniently to Darktowne."

Azura nodded, excited to start. "Then let's get those herbs first," she said before feeling the ranger grab her by the shoulder, stopping her. She spun around to face the lavender haired ranger and arched an eyebrow. She followed the ranger's gaze to a group of bandits who were raiding a small merchant shop. "Oooh! Alright, I get it," she responded.

The ranger nocked three arrows and fired in rapid succession, pinning the bandits to the wall behind them. "Excuse me, gentlemen, I do believe those aren't your wares," she said, voice calm and level.

"Oy! What you think yer doin'!" One of the bandits snarled as he tore the arrow from his cloak and drew his handaxe. He sized up the ranger and smirked. "Two pretty things such as yerselves, ye fetch higher prices than these wares on black market," he snarled as he rushed the ranger.

Camilla smirked as she shouldered her longbow and drew her longsword. If there was one thing that always calmed her nerves, it was combat. She held her blade at the ready before easily disarming the charging bandit. As he turned to figure out what had happened, he felt the cold metal thrust into his stomach. "I was going to talk, but since you charged, I guess talk is wasted." The ranger's voice was low; it was cold. It was more like the tone used by a cold-blooded killer.

Azura looked at the two bandits still pinned to the wall. "You guys can come quietly and turn yourselves in, or my friend here will do the same to you as she did to your friend," she said with a calm and sincere tone.

The bandits looked at one another before nodding. "We surrender," they both said not wanting to meet the same fate.

The sorceress walked over and handcuffed the two men before helping them off the wall. "Good, I knew you guys could be reasoned with," she added as she turned to lead them.

"Azura, wait, stop!" Camilla called out as she moved to rush over.

Azura spun on her heels only to be grabbed by one of the bandits. He had repositioned his wrists so that the sorceress's neck was caught in the chain from the handcuffs. "Lay down yer weapon lassie, or I'll choke the sweet girl," he threatened as he looked at Camilla.

Camilla waited; she watched Azura's expression. Even if this was not her Azura, even if she was not this Azura's Camilla, they had grown close. She waited, waiting for the silent order from the sorceress. Azura knew what Camilla was waiting for and blinked twice. She only hoped it was the same silent code that the ranger had in the realm she was from.

With the two blinks, the ranger nodded. "Alright, you win," Camilla said as she lowered her blade to the ground. She put her hands up and waited. The men stumbled forward, each making it clear they wanted the handcuffs removed. Camilla smirked a sinister look in her eyes. She lashed out with her claws, ripping the throat from the one who held Azura. Her tail wrapped around the other's ankle, dragging him to the ground. Her left claw struck his chest, ripping a hole clean through him.

Azura freed herself from the dead man's grip and winced as she looked to the ranger. She saw the slight red in the ranger's eyes. She knew it was normal when Camilla grew angry. She had seen it before, but it had been several months. "Camilla. Camilla, stop," she said, hoping the ranger could still hear reason.

Camilla glanced over and nodded. "Go get the guards. I'll wait here," she responded, her tone calm once more. Azura hesitated but left to find one of the guards. The ranger sat, waiting. She cleaned off her claws, not wanting the guards to see such. Sure, they would be questioned but Azura generally had a silver tongue and could talk them out of the situation.

When the guards arrived, they looked stunned to see that the bandits had in fact been dealt with. They noticed the violent way they had been put down and grimaced from such. "Young lady, how did you and your friend manage this?" one of the guards asked as he looked at Azura. He noted to himself that neither of the female travelers looked muscular nor capable of close-range combat.

Azura looked down. "Whenever I'm in danger, my friend... my friend receives some sort of divine might and is able to do unimaginable things to save me," she answered, keeping her head down.

Camilla looked over, hoping Azura's lie would work. The guards nodded as they identified the bodies as the three bandits that had in fact been plundering the city. "Well, regardless, you two did Loft Ridge a grand favor. If you'll join us in reporting this to the duke, we'll ensure you get paid," the second guard, slightly shorter than the first, stated.

It was a quiet walk to the massive estate that sat at the far northern side of the city. Upon entering, Azura glanced over her shoulder at the ranger. She got the silent gesture she wanted, three blinks. It was clear to the sorceress that the ranger was agreeing to remain silent unless needed.

"My guards told me the bandits had been dealt with. I didn't expect the source of our aid to be two beautiful young women," the duke said as he walked out to greet the pair. He was clad in a white long sleeve shirt, sand-colored trousers and wore a burgundy vest. His hair was cut short and a deep crimson. His eyes were a deep blue, almost like the ocean. Azura and Camilla both bowed slightly, showing their respect. "I am Duke Ignis, and you have my gratitude for slaying those bandits. They've been running amok since the prince's disappearance years ago," the duke introduced himself.

"The prince disappeared?" Azura asked.

"Aye, many years ago. I believe it was seven years to be exact. His advisor was the top suspect, but no one could find means or opportunity. The man had motive, but that was all he had. At the time I was in the prince's court as his tactical general, after his advisor took the throne, well, Alibi hasn't been herself," Ignis responded as he walked to the large chest in the room. He took a deep breath. "Curious that you didn't know of the young prince's disappearance."

"We're not from around here," Azura blurted out. She sighed slightly as she collected herself. "We were summoned from across the sea by an unseen force. And that was mere months ago."

"I see, then the rumors I've heard about warriors from the Outrealms are true. In that case, I will help you in your endeavors. But that's if of course you're willing to help find the lost prince," Duke Ignis stated as he unlocked the chest and withdrew some coins.

"We'll keep our eyes and ears open. Can you give us a description of the prince?" Azura responded, trying to keep things on friendly terms.

"He was a human, about twenty-one in age. Black hair, green eyes. He stood about six feet and four inches in height and was always seen in his crimson cape. The young man had the makings of being a great king," Ignis added as he counted out the wendells. "Here we are, two thousand wendells."

"The posting was for—"

"Considering your goal, I can spare a few extra wendells. I hope it will help with your travels. I have one more request for the two of you. Tomorrow, a merchant of ours is heading to Darktowne to deliver medicine and sell his wares. I ask that you ensure his safety," the duke requested as he looked the two travelers over.

"We'll see to his safe travels," Azura replied with a quick smile.

"Come see me in the morning before you depart. I'll pay you in full before you leave," Ignis stated.

Azura and Camilla bowed before taking their leave. "Still want to do those four herb related jobs?" Camilla asked as she glanced over her shoulder to the sorceress.

"Yeah, those herbs are used in medicines. At the least, we should help them out and get a few extra coins for it. Never know when we'll need to buy stuff again," Azura replied as she and Camilla walked out the southern exit of the town. They walked aways before finding a small field where several flowers and herbs were growing. To the untrained eye the herbs looked very similar.

Camilla grew up in the wilds. She knew how to tell poisonous plants from medicinal ones. As the pair walked, the ranger picked a few of the herbs and put them in her satchel. There was one remaining from the list, but they did not see it growing anywhere. Azura looked over the list again and paused. "This herb doesn't grow in this area. It's a desert flower. And with how rarely it grows—"

"You're talking about the mirage flower. It's supposedly an herb capable of performing lifesaving miracles. But it only grows once every thousand years. And it's so rare that everyone calls it a mirage as there's no knowing if it exists," Camilla interrupted.

"Yeah, how'd you know about it? I never took you for being one who researched plants for medicinal use." Azura was taken back.

"I don't. Actually, I don't know how I knew about the mirage flower. It's not important. We got all the other ones, should be worth something," the ranger replied as she started walking back toward Loft Ridge.

Azura nodded and skipped behind the ranger. "So do you know the other name for the mirage flower?" she asked as she happily skipped behind the ranger.

Camilla tilted her head thinking for a moment. "Blue's tears?" she murmured. As the words left her lips, the ranger felt an overwhelming pain in her head. She stopped, dropping to her knees and clutching her head.

"Camilla!" Azura instantly dropped next to the ranger, concern plastered to her face.

"They're called mirage flowers or blue's tears. It's rare to find but according to legend this flower can perform lifesaving miracles," the man stated as he looked at the small flower.

"Blue's tears? Why is it called that?" the massive blue dragon asked.

"That's easy, silly. People swear blue dragons can't cry so seeing one cry is akin to seeing a mirage flower. Both are incredibly rare," he responded as he looked up at the blue dragon that towered over him.

"Well, it's a half truth. Because of our bodies acclimating to the harsh environment of the desert, our tear ducts don't function as normal. We can cry, but in doing so we risk harming ourselves. Which is why humanoids rarely see us blue dragons cry," the dragon explained as it sat on its haunches.

"I'm sorry. I didn't mean anything. And if I upset you, I—"

"Peace, Ashe. Your words did not bother me," the dragon interrupted. It looked down at the humanoid and the flower. "So, what are you going to do with the flower? Are you going to take it into town? Sell it to the highest bidder?"

"No. I think it's best we leave this flower here to grow and flourish. Maybe it's so rare because humanoids harvest it when it blooms after hearing what it can do. Maybe if we leave it to grow, it will become less of a mirage," Ashe responded as he collected his gear. He smiled up at the dragon. "Well, Celica, where does our next adventure take us?"

Where does our next adventure take us?

Camilla shook her head as she tried to collect her thoughts. A waking dream? A memory? A vision? "Camilla? Camilla, are you alright!" Azura's voice was filled with concern and worry. She was panicked as she knelt beside the ranger. Camilla nodded, trying to reassure the sorceress before slowly standing. Azura breathed a sigh of relief as she stood. "You just sort of dropped and I didn't know what to do. I..." She paused as she covered her mouth. Her eyes widened slightly. "I'm sorry, Camilla."

The ranger arched an eyebrow, not understanding what was wrong this time. "I'm sorry I didn't react sooner. You're probably still recovering from the fight with Uldritch, I should have known such. I didn't take how you were feeling into account. I should have said we wait a day or two before heading for Loft Ridge," the sorceress cried as she lowered her gaze and her body heaved from the deep breaths and tears.

Camilla blinked a few times before resting a hand on the sorceress's shoulder. "It's fine, I'm alright. Don't worry so much," she said softly before ruffling the young sorceress's hair.

Azura slowly looked up and nodded, sniffling slightly as she tried to dry her tears. "I... I just don't want to see the same thing happen to you as—"

"We've been over this, I'm not your Camilla. Though I do appreciate your concern," the ranger interrupted as she looked ahead at the city. "Come on, we should get back to Loft Ridge and deliver these herbs," she added as she began walking, not wanting to spend much more time in the field. Azura nodded and walked behind the stoic ranger.

They delivered the herbs to the medicine shop, despite not having the mirage flower, they still got a fair amount of wendells. The rest of the night was uneventful as they decided to stay the night in a small inn that was cheap. Neither sorceress nor ranger spoke another word as they both tried to get some sleep before they would be heading out in the morning. It was dawn, the sun just barely coming up on the horizon when Azura felt someone gently shake her awake. "I've already paid the innkeeper. I'll be at the duke's estate, meet me there when you're ready," Camilla said before heading out.

Azura hastily got ready for the day. She rushed after the ranger, soon arriving at Duke Ignis' estate. Outside the merchant was finishing up loading his wagon and getting his horse situated. "Aye, you must be one of the adventurers who'll be escorting, yeah?" the merchant asked as he climbed up and took his seat in the front of the wagon.

"Yup, that's us. Have you seen a lavender haired woman? She's your other escort. Don't worry, you're in good hands," Azura replied with a smile. The merchant indicated the pair coming out of the estate. Azura looked over and bowed slightly when she saw Duke Ignis. "Good morning, Duke Ignis," she greeted, as she tried to maintain her composure.

"And good morning to you, Miss Azura. Camilla and I just finished a brief chat about the route you'll be taking. It's the fastest one to Darktowne, about half a day's journey. Should put you three in Darktowne by early afternoon if there are no interruptions," Ignis replied before handing the ranger a bag. "I doubt I'll be seeing either of you anytime in the near future, so here's the payment for my merchant's escort to Darktowne. I wish the safest travels to the three of you," he added before ensuring everything was in order.

Camilla nodded as she began walking. Azura waited, letting the merchant take the middle position while she brought up the rear. It was still early and there were very few city folk awake at the hour. The three made their way out the southern gates and started the journey to Darktowne. "So, Duke Ignis seemed really fond of the two of ya," the merchant began, wanting to break the ice and get to know his two bodyguards.

"Probably because we dealt with the bandit problem you guys had," Azura mentioned as she looked about the area as they walked. She was nervous. She had gotten used to having Warren, his thick armor and massive shield walking beside her. It unnerved her that she was so exposed.

"Wait, that was the two of ye? Well, color me impressed. Those bandits were a real pain and even gave the guards issues. Though the guards are all about taking troublemakers in alive," the merchant noted as they continued.

"I'm not one for such," Camilla said casually. She glanced over her shoulder at the merchant. "Someone raises a weapon; I go for the kill. Yes, I'll fire a warning arrow, but when it comes to combat, I'd rather come out of such alive," the ranger added as she walked onward, returning her focus to the road.

"I see. Yes, that would be smart and more likely to get results than the guards," the merchant said quietly as he looked around.

They reached Darktowne about midafternoon with no interruptions along the way. Camilla helped the merchant unload his wagon as Azura went to meet up with the others. Many of the merchant crates were marked with various weapons and other wares but a few contained medicine. Once the merchant's wares were unloaded, the ranger took her leave, joining up with the rest of her group that awaited at Mayor Ichiban's estate.

"Welcome back, glad to see both of you are alright," Warren greeted seeing the ranger return.

Camilla nodded before pulling out the bag of wendells she had received from the duke of Loft Ridge. "Good news, with what Azura and I made from a handful of side jobs and two jobs for Duke Ignis, we made enough to cover the blacksmith costs in full and still have some left over," she stated as she began counting out the wendells. She made piles for each claim ticket then handed them off.

A few uneventful days passed until it was time for the adventurers to pick up their gear from the blacksmith. Each was impressed by the fine craftsmanship that had been done. “His armor was damaged the most,” the blacksmith said as he took his payment, watching as everyone got geared back up.

“Thank you for the hard work,” Warren stated as he shouldered his morningstar. Each was grateful for the fine work and impressed with the speed. As they left the shop, they made a stop by Gracadia’s Apparel to pay for the new cloak for Camilla. Upon entering they saw the older woman going through a large crate of new arrivals.

“Welcome, welcome! I was hoping you had not forgotten to visit us!” the fairy, Lily, called from the front desk. Her smile was beaming as she pulled a bundle of cloth from one of the desk drawers. “Miss Gracadia hopes you like it,” she added as she shook the bundle out.

“A longcoat?” Camilla arched an eyebrow seeing the garment.

“Yes, you said you needed something that could act as cover as well as having pockets. As such we made the garment to your specifications,” Lily stated.

Camilla nodded her thanks before taking the coat and trying it on. The fabric lining the inside was soft to the touch while the outer fabric felt sturdy. It was ebony in color with a deep purple trim. Overall, it was perfect, the coat fulfilled the needs the ranger required and it was comfortable too. She turned to the book of enchantments. Lily’s eyes lit up in excitement as she watched the ranger. Camilla wrote down a few enchantments before removing her coat and looking at the fairy. “Can you enchant this to have invisibility, element resistance and increased durability?” she asked.

Lily nodded excitedly. “Of course! Let me see! Let me see!” Lily was eager to enchant the item. It was rare that she got to use her magic. Aside from this group, she hadn’t used her magic on clothing in years. The small fairy said a few spells in Faye tongue before touching the coat. The longcoat shimmered slightly before returning to its normal coloration. “All done. In order for the invisibility to be active, you have to be wearing the hood up. The rest of the enchantments are passive and will activate when you encounter situations in which you require them.”

Camilla nodded her thanks as she put the coat back on and smiled. She withdrew her coin pouch. "How much do I owe you and Miss Gracadia?"

"Your total for this purchase comes to one thousand forty-three wendells," Lily said as she added everything up and marked the sales book they kept. Camilla nodded and withdrew the appropriate coin, placing it on the counter. Lily counted to make certain it was exact before placing it in the drawer they used for money. "Thank you for shopping with us. We hope you return and shop with us again," Lily added.

Camilla looked over at the rest of the group, shaking her head but grinning as she watched them check out the new apparel. Chuck found a belt he liked and pulled it out. Azura had found a circlet and pulled it out. Camilla even found herself checking out the new items. A simple green long sleeve shirt caught her eye. The group took the items they wished to purchase to the front desk then returned to help Gracadia unpacking and organizing the remaining wares.

After a couple of hours, everything was organized and set up in the shop. They returned to the counter to pay for the new garments. Gracadia shook her head. "These are on the house. Least I can do for your help in the shop," the elder woman stated.

Lily checked over the garments the adventurers had collected. "Belt of the Beast King, this belt will give you great strength, but I think it might have a backlash if you aren't careful. And that circlet, it has great magic properties for a caster, though I think it might make it hard to focus," the small fairy stated.

Warren placed the boots they had received days earlier. "Lily, are you able to tell if these have magical properties?" he asked.

Lily nodded as she waved a hand over the boots. "Boots of Faststide, these will allow you to move very quickly over any terrain," Lily stated. Warren nodded his thanks as he put the boots on, anything to increase his speed was something he considered helpful.

The group looked at Gracadia who sat in her chair. "Miss Gracadia, we cannot take the belt nor circlet without giving you something in return," Azura, Warren and Amelia stated at the same time.

The elderly woman shook her head. "Consider them gifts to aid in your travels," she stated with a smile.

Everyone bowed and said their thanks departing from the shop. Amelia paused and went back inside. "I'll be back, five minutes tops," the paladin said as she went inside. She went through a few shelves before finding what she was looking for. Amelia set the items on the desk then quickly read through the enchantment guide. "Can you enchant these to have spells integrated into them?" Amelia asked.

Lily nodded. "Of course, I can." The fairy stated as she withdrew a few stones from the drawer. "In order to enchant spells into them, I'll need to use magic crystals then fuse them into those," Lily explained. She set out the stones and looked at the list that Amelia handed her. Lily nodded and she began enchanting the crystals. After a few moments, the small fairy began fusing the crystals into the garments that sat on the counter. "There, it's done," Lily stated.

Amelia nodded then placed a bag of wendells on the counter. "Thank you, Lily."

The fairy arched an eyebrow seeing the pair of silver bands, one adorned with a blue gem while the other had a red gem. "Rings of bonds? You're purchasing these as well?"

Amelia nodded again. "Yes, if my research on these is correct, they synchronize to a pair and when the two fight alongside one another—"

"The pair will have increased stamina, along with the ability to endure the elements," Gracadia responded as she walked over. She eyed the rings then looked at the paladin. "An interesting choice of items. Rings of bonds are typically used for proposals."

"I'm aware. How much for the pair?" the paladin asked as she held her coin pouch.

Gracadia shook her head. "Take them, no charge. Just be certain the person you give the other ring to is someone you can imagine yourself with, for all of time."

"Thank you, Miss Gracadia," she said before sprinting after the group.

"Everything alright?" Camilla asked as she looked at Amelia. The paladin nodded before handing something to the ranger. "Hmm?" the ranger asked, taken back.

"Your gloves, you need to replace them. You keep shooting that longbow of yours without something to protect your fingers, you'll eventually hurt yourself," Amelia stated as she removed Camilla's frayed and falling apart gloves. She paused, secretly slipping the silver band adorned with the red gem onto the ranger's ring finger, then put the new gloves on the ranger's claws. "There, they look a lot better on you," she added as she put the damaged gloves in her spare bag.

"Onward to Faraway Lake!" Warren called out. Everyone let out a hearty cheer in response as they followed the cleric's lead.

It was a long journey to Faraway Lake, several days of traveling. As the group came upon the quiet fishing town, they felt uneasy. Many of the villagers were strung up and their corpses littered the area. Warren sprinted through town, trying to find anyone still among the living. He heard a faint cough and turned to look. Azura was kneeling by a brutally wounded elf. "Darean, what happened here?" the sorceress asked as she tried to tend to his wounds.

Darean frowned, blood running down his face and chest. "I figured you would return. We all did. General Todo of the north wind came. He slaughtered everyone, said it was punishment for aiding you. He…" Darean winced before coughing up blood. He took shallow breaths. "He took my friends into the caverns. I tried to stop him. Didn't work out so well. He left me here to bleed to death. To send the message to you and the others."

Warren checked over the wounds and pulled Azura away. "There's nothing we can do to treat these wounds. Between the blood loss and infection, we won't be able to treat him in time," he stated, upset by the situation.

Camilla stepped forward and looked over the infection. "This infection, it's not normal."

Darean nodded weakly. "When I die, I'll become a monster. Same as the others did before we had to kill them," he replied weakly as he looked up to meet the ranger's gaze. He coughed slightly. "You have the same eyes as her," he whispered before slumping back against the wall.

"Her?" Camilla questioned.

"Please, kill me, I don't want to cause anyone further harm. Two attacks, one through the heart, one through the head," he begged as his breathing became shallower.

Azura and Warren were shaken. They cursed their luck of being unable to save Darean. Amelia turned away; she did not want to perform the deed. Chuck stomped off, wanting to find the general and fight that would come.

Camilla drew her shortsword and looked at Darean. "Are you certain this is what you want?" she asked. He nodded weakly before mouthing the words *Thank you* to her. Camilla nodded before stabbing the elf through the heart then through the head.

Everyone was silent for a moment as they watched the lifeless body slump to the ground. Warren looked around before spotting a side road that likely led to the caverns. He started walking, not waiting for anyone else.

"Warren?" Amelia asked when she saw the cleric's behavior.

"We're going to find the general, and we're going to kill him. He butchered the town, for no real reason. We can't let someone so inhuman run around," he stated as he continued walking.

Azura followed the cleric as did the barbarian. It was their fault this quiet fishing town had been dealt a cruel fate. Camilla looked over at Amelia, both sharing the same uncertain expression. "I'm going with them. Not because of what was done here. And not because I'm looking for a fight. I want to make sure the person responsible doesn't do this to Darktowne or Loft Ridge." Camilla said as she cleaned off her shortsword then moved to follow the others.

Amelia let out a disgruntled sigh as she followed them. She did not like this at all. The caverns were dark, the stale air made it difficult to breathe. As they delved deeper, they found themselves fighting several undead abominations. Half human, half beast. The faces resembled that of innocent townsfolk, but the attacks were feral like monsters. After they descended a mile below ground, they came upon a large open chamber. Each was already on edge.

The general was clad in dark blue armor as he turned to face the group. He smirked at them as he tossed the head of the creepy sorceress to their feet, followed by the head of the other traveler from Darean's group. "Welcome, warriors of the Outrealms. Glad you could make it. I am General Todo, and by Time Eater's orders, I cannot allow you to leave this place alive," the general greeted as he drew forth a potion. He chugged it down and smirked at the group. His body spasmed as he underwent a horrific transformation.

Todo, if he could even be called that anymore, stood an impressive thirty feet in height. A single eye sat at the center of his forehead; several massive teeth lined his jaws. His arms rippled; the muscles larger than any that had been seen before. His hands ended with claws but had whip-like tendrils around his wrists. His torso flex, the bulging muscles shattering his armor. His legs were thick, much like tree trunks. A roar escaped the monster as he eyed the group.

His whips flung about trying to ensnare the adventures. Everyone dove to the sides trying to avoid being grabbed. "Hope you got a plan, Warren!" Amelia called as she got to her feet.

The cleric did not answer as he drew his morningstar and rushed into battle. Chuck sprinted after him to cover the cleric's right flank. Azura was already casting her storm spell, raining fire, lightning, acid and ice upon the monster. Amelia looked to her left and saw the ranger draw her longbow. "Think you can handle melee point?" Camilla asked as she nocked three arrows before muttering a spell. Amelia nodded as she drew her bastard sword and held her tower shield at the ready. "Cover Warren's left, neither of the boys are thinking clearly and fighting with more rage and primal-like mindset."

"Understood!" Amelia called back before rushing up to help with the melee offense against the monster. She saw the arrows whiz pass her as they began splitting as they closed in on the creature before them. The paladin brought her shield up barely in time to catch a claw strike intended for the cleric. "Warren, calm down and think! We need to all think this fight through!" Amelia lectured.

"Don't tell me what to do!" the cleric snarled as his morningstar struck the hideous creature.

He was not going to listen to reason, the best the paladin could hope for was to defend him. "*Damn it all!*" Amelia thought as her shield endured another claw strike.

Camilla cursed under her breath; the arrow volley seemed to have no effect on the monster. She took a step back as she opened the potion box and looked for any offense-based potions. One caught her eye, a purple potion. If her memory was correct, it should remove any spell resistances this thing had. She poured some of the potion on her arrows and quickly nocked them firing in rapid succession. Three arrows in each small volley, four volleys. Twelve arrows left the ranger's bow before splitting into sixty arrows. Those sixty then split into two thousand seven hundred each hitting its marks on the beast before the party.

A loud roar echoed through the chamber causing everyone to stagger from the vibrations and echoing. A whip tendril lashed out, ensnaring the ranger and dragging her around before throwing her at the paladin. Amelia dropped her shield and blade, managing to catch Camilla. "I think you pissed it off," the paladin whispered before steadying the ranger.

Camilla smirked. "Yeah, I'm good at that," she responded as she nocked another three arrows and fired. As the tendril whirled to hit her and Amelia, Camilla took off in a sprint trying to bait the attack.

Amelia grabbed her bastard sword and tower shield then rushed to attack the same area that Chuck and Warren had been focusing on. The second whip tendril ensnared the barbarian and flung him aside. Chuck rolled, managing to recover without too many bruises from the fight. He shook off before letting out a war cry and charging again. Before he could reach the monster, he felt something heavy slam into him, knocking him off his feet. As Chuck recovered, he saw it was the paladin. Amelia managed to stand, but putting pressure on her right ankle was difficult. "Help Warren," she said. The half orc nodded and charged back into the fight.

Warren was forced on the defensive as both tendrils smashed against his shield. He dropped to a knee, struggling to get his footing back. He heard a shrill screech from the monster as it reared back. Chuck spun his greataxe around, leaving a deep gash in the abomination. A tendril whip ensnared him again and threw him to the side.

Chuck slammed into the ranger, sending both of them to the ground. Camilla shook her head as she fired two arrows from her grounded position. "Warren, look out!" the ranger yelled as loud as she could.

Warren didn't have a chance to react. The tendril ensnared him tightly, constricting his breathing. He could not get a breath and felt his mind becoming a haze. Azura fired off multiple spells in rapid succession trying to desperately free the cleric. To everyone's horror, the abomination began smashing the cleric against the ground repeatedly, his armor shattering in the process. The sickening crack filled the room as his ribs were crushed from the repeated abuse. Blood ran down his face as his forehead split open.

Arrows and spells collided with the abomination, as both ranger and sorceress tried any attack they could. Chuck and Amelia were trying to draw the monster's attention to them as they hacked their way through the beast's flesh. Nothing worked. The creature did not waver. Then a gut-wrenching sound was heard, a snap followed by a bloodied gurgle. Finally, Warren was dropped. He did not move; his chest was not expanding to indicate breathing. Amelia rushed to drag him out of harm's way while Camilla, Chuck and Azura covered her.

"Warren! Warren, can you hear me!" Amelia yelled as she dropped next to his side. She felt along his neck, desperate to find a pulse. Nothing. "No. No no no no, you can't do this to us." Her voice was shaking as she dragged him to Azura's side.

Azura wasted no time trying any spell she knew to revive the cleric. Nothing worked. Warren's body was still, his eyes closed, blood stained much of his front. Amelia rushed to aid Chuck and Camilla in the fight. She failed Warren, she was not going to fail anyone else. Before she was close enough to rejoin the fight, the barbarian was thrown against her, sending them both back.

Camilla reached for another arrow before cursing to herself. "Of all times to be out of arrows," she cursed as she shouldered her longbow. She drew her longsword in her right hand and one of her shortswords in her left. Her attacks were quick but anywhere she struck, the wounds healed instantly. She barely managed to tumble out of the way of the tendrils. Looking over at Chuck and Amelia, Camilla could see they were exhausted. Everyone was on their last leg. And without Warren's healing magic, there were no swift recoveries using magic. "I have a plan, it's risky but it might work," Camilla said as she managed to regroup with the other two melee fighters.

"We're all ears," Amelia stated as she looked at the ranger. Chuck nodded in agreement. He wanted the glory of killing this thing but his desire to survive outweighed such.

Camilla pointed. "If we can gouge out that eye, maybe, just maybe he won't be able to locate us. And we can attack freely."

"There's no way past those tendrils," Amelia noted.

Chuck stepped forward. "Chuck act bait. Chuck force it grab," the barbarian snarled as he looked at the monster.

Amelia looked back to Camilla. "Shield jump?"

"Think you can get me high enough?" Camilla asked. Amelia nodded as she sheathed her bastard sword. "Shield jump is it."

The barbarian rushed in first, drawing all attention to him. Both tendrils lashed outward at him. He dropped his greataxe, grabbing the tendrils and trying to anchor himself. He had one job, to keep the tendrils at bay. He was going to see it through.

Amelia got into position and brought her massive shield overhead. Her task was probably the easiest but also the one that left her most vulnerable. A way behind her, she could hear the ranger running at full speed. Camilla leapt up, her feet landing on the shield. They had done this a few times already, they knew it would work. Amelia forced her shield upward the moment she felt Camilla's weight. The ranger leapt, using the extra lift to get airborne.

Camilla drove her longsword deep into the eye. A loud screech filled the chamber as the abomination thrashed around wildly. Chuck kept his grip, not wavering in the slightest. Amelia rushed the barbarian's side and grabbed one of the tendrils, while he moved to anchor with the other. They held firm as they kept their grips tight, not letting the monster move its arms. The ranger kept a grip on her longsword, using it as something to hold onto while she brought her shortsword up and slashed repeatedly at the eye. Green blood spluttered out from the eye, covering the ranger as she hacked away.

In a fit of rage and adrenaline, the beast lashed out, throwing the ranger from its face. It managed to drag the barbarian and paladin around, throwing them to the side. A massive roar filled the room as the now blinded creature began shaking violently. Its form began shrinking until the battle-worn general was back to his humanoid form.

Todo hissed in pain; his eyes were badly damaged. Blood ran down his face as he tried to sense his prey. They were not making any sound, which meant they were not moving. His forked tongue flicked out as he tried to smell them. It became clear what he was, a lizard person. He was relying on his sense of smell and taste to locate them. He turned, laughing maniacally as he finally smelled one of them. "I can smell your fear," he snarled as he drew a greatsword from his back. He lunged forward, his greatsword striking something metallic.

"Now!" Camilla yelled as she caught the greatsword with her longsword and shortsword.

Chuck sprinted from the left, greataxe in hand. Amelia came from the right, her bastard sword at the ready. Both slashed out, taking the lizard-man's head from his body. All three of them took deep breaths as they collected themselves. They were lucky to be alive. They were lucky to have survived past the first few attacks. They turned their attention to Azura who was in tears, holding Warren's corpse close to her.

"If we can preserve his body, we might be able to get him to a powerful caster for a resurrection," Amelia suggested as she, Chuck and Camilla approached.

Camilla looked around for anything they could use to preserve him with. Azura nodded, understanding what Amelia was saying. She was still in tears but managed to cast a preservation spell on the corpse. "We have maybe two days at best with that spell," the sorceress said as she stood. Chuck picked up the corpse and followed behind the ranger and paladin who had taken lead positions again.

"Nearest caster I can think of who might be powerful enough is Arcanist! If the map is correct, we're about a day and half from his tower!" Camilla called over her shoulder to the others.

"Then let's make haste!" Amelia responded as she ran beside the ranger.

Chapter 19 - Worth

It had been raining the entire journey. They were still half a day at best from Arcanist's tower, and they were exhausted. Still, they pressed on, hoping the brass-colored humanoid reptilian would be able to bring back the cleric. Camilla came to a stop and signaled for everyone else to do so as well. Ahead a few meters from them at the base of the hill they were coming over was a group of soldiers. They had the same emblem on their armor that General Hugo, General Carden and General Todo had. "What's the plan? We need to get past them if we're going to get to Arcanist," Amelia asked as she looked at Camilla.

Azura hissed at the sight. "I can storm blast them and be done with them."

"Save your magic, there might be a better way," Camilla stated as she looked for a general. Standing with the soldiers was an elf clad in thick armor. He stood in the front of the group, as though he was waiting. The ranger looked to the others and withdrew her map. "There's a back trail here, through the forest. You guys go on ahead. I'll try to lure them away and give you a clearing," she added as she handed the map to Amelia. "No matter what happens, get to Arcanist's tower," the ranger finished before heading off, not allowing anyone to argue with her.

Amelia hated this plan but knew it was probably their best chance. The rain weakened aspects of the storm spell and with Azura's emotions spinning wildly, there was also a chance she would be unable to fully control the spell.

The paladin cursed under her breath but led Azura and Chuck to the back trail the ranger mentioned. "We trust in Camilla's plan and make for Arcanist's tower," she said as she took point, alone.

Camilla observed the soldiers and general for a moment. Longbow was off the table as she lacked the arrows. She could try to politely call out for a one on one with the general, but that would likely fail. Cursing under her breath, Camilla pulled her hood over her head, going invisible and moved closer, shortsword and longsword drawn.

"You sure they'll come through here?" one of the soldiers asked as he sat on a log.

The general nodded. "Aye. I'm certain. Time Eater said she sensed Todo had slain one of them. And they would likely try to resurrect their fallen. Fastest route from Faraway Lake to Arcanist would bring them down this road," he spoke as he continued to watch and wait. Rain landed on his armor, rolling down harmlessly as he stood in place. "It's just a matter of when," he added.

"Sir, even if they do come through here, are you certain we can take them?" a second soldier asked.

"Aye. There's four of them and I've all of you. They'll be exhausted, it'll be like sheep to slaughter," he stated as he looked on again.

Camilla was close enough. She darted forward, maintaining her invisibility as she did so. Her blades and agility made quick work of the soldiers, each one requiring only a single strike, slitting their throats. One by one the twenty soldiers dropped, leaving only the general. He turned, drawing his double-bladed sword. "So how many of you am I dealing with? Two or three? Perhaps all four? You'd be a fool to try one on one with me," the general stated as he twirled his blade.

Azura breathed a faint sigh of relief as she saw Arcanist's tower. Both she and Chuck picked up their pace, determined to reach the caster. Amelia took notice of the increase to speed and soon followed. They only slowed when they reached gates in front of the tower. Pushing through the gate, they entered the tower grounds and made their way inside.

"My word adventurers, it's been too long!" Arcanist began.

Chuck set the corpse on the table before collapsing into a nearby armchair. Azura stepped forward. "Arcanist, can you resurrect Warren? He fell in battle about a day and half ago," she said as she stayed by.

Arcanist checked the body over, noting the condition. He nodded. "I can but I need lightning to do so," he responded as he carried the body to the top floor of his tower. Azura followed and offered to help where she could. They set Warren on a large table and placed a strange looking headpiece on him. "I should warn you, Azura, I'm not overly skilled at this sort of thing. In truth, this is my first time performing such a deed. Warren may not be the same Warren when he's resurrected," Arcanist added as he worked.

"I don't care, just bring him back," Azura snarled, her voice low.

The brass reptile nodded as he finished getting everything set up. He turned a wheel, opening the roof up and allowing any lightning to strike the apparatus he had set up. Both Arcanist and Azura watched, waiting, hoping for a lightning bolt to strike. Crashes of thunder resonated as lightning struck the surrounding area. Finally, if by some stroke of luck, a bolt struck the apparatus and sparked everything into whirling and creaking. Arcanist threw a lever as the corpse began shaking violently from the electricity going through it. He began casting, infusing his magic into the corpse. A blue aura surrounded the corpse as the lightning continued. After a moment, Arcanist took a step back, ending his magic. The electricity soon came to a stop as the machines died down and the whirling stopped.

Amelia looked down at the silver band she wore on her right ring finger. She absent-mindedly rubbed the blue gem on it as she took a deep breath. She sighed in relief as the barbarian was too tired to take notice. The paladin looked outside; her scarlet eyes filled with worry for the ranger. She stood and started for the door when the barbarian's grunt made her stop. "I'm going back for Camilla," Amelia stated as she glanced over her shoulder at the half orc.

"Chuck think you wait. Chuck know scary lady fine," the barbarian grunted. The paladin turned to leave again only to be stopped by a sharp wince in pain. "Chuck think you rest. No healed from last fight." He shook his head as he stood and walked over to the half vampire. The barbarian easily overpowered the fatigued paladin, forcing her to sit down. "You rest. Not help scary lady if you die."

"Show yourself!" the general snarled as he swung his double blade out again.

Camilla had stayed constantly moving around, trying to avoid the general's attacks. She needed to get in close. One attack was all she needed. In the distance, the crackle of lightning striking the massive tower, drew their attention. Camilla saw her opening and moved to dispatch her foe. The general sensed the movement and turned, his double blade clashing with the longsword of the ranger. "Found you," he said with a smirk as he eyed where the ranger was standing.

The ranger smirked under her invisibility and pressed into her attack. Her shortsword came up and struck the general's exposed upper thighs. He recoiled back in pain as he tried to block the next strike. The longsword was visible for only a split second before striking down the fourth general they had encountered. Once certain he was downed, Camilla threw back her hood. "Just one attacker," she noted as she watched the life fade from his eyes.

It was a clear path to Arcanist's tower from where she was. Taking a deep breath and letting it out slowly, Camilla took off for the tower. In the back of her mind, she hoped they had in fact managed to restore Warren. That was the whole reason for detouring this far away from Faraway Lake. With the tower gates in sight, the ranger gave one final sprint. She reached the door and made her way inside. Her coat drenched from the rain.

"Camilla!" Amelia began, excited to see the ranger's return. The paladin marched over to her friend, throwing her arms around the slightly short female in a hug. "I'm glad you're alright," she whispered into the ranger's ear.

Camilla merely smiled as she gently pulled free from the paladin's grip. "Any luck with Warren?" she asked, reminding the paladin why they were here.

"Arcanist and Azura took the body up the stairs and—"

Before Amelia could finish a loud crash was heard. Camilla, Amelia and Chuck had all drawn their weapons, on edge and ready for anything. Azura and Arcanist came sprinting down the stairs, both exhausted. "What happened?" Camilla questioned seeing the pair.

Arcanist was breathing heavily, not used to running or any form of physical activity. He looked up, meeting the ranger's stern gaze. "Good news, your friend has been resurrected. The bad news, I'm inexperienced with this sort of thing, and so he's a lich. And right now, he's very hungry. And unless he eats four living humanoids very soon, we're next on the menu," the brass reptilian stated through his panting. He finally caught his breath then pointed. "I've a cellar we can hide out in, in the meantime," he suggested.

"Any chance you left the soldiers or general alive?" Azura asked, looking at the ranger. Camilla shook her head, cursing at herself for not considering such. "So, time to find some bandits," the young sorceress stated. She turned to face Amelia and Chuck. "You two, take Arcanist and hide in the cellar. Camilla and I will go find a few bandits and hopefully be back soon," she added before sprinting off, Camilla hot on her heels.

Amelia, Chuck and Arcanist did as they were instructed and hid in the cellar. All three hoping they would not be found. Azura sprinted ahead to the west path off the property and kept running, behind her, she could hear the ranger sprinting and catching up. "You sure we'll find bandits?" Camilla called out as she followed behind the sorceress.

"Yeah, I mean, neither of us are that impressive looking. Easy prey, am I right?" Azura responded as she came to a stop.

Camilla laughed slightly. "Might want to undo a shirt button or two. Bandits see those, you'll be able to get them to do anything," she teased.

The sorceress nodded. "Not a bad idea," she mused before undoing the top two buttons of her shirt. Her massive cleavage hung out a little, causing Camilla's eyes to widen.

"Dear lord Patrokolos! Those are huge. No, scratch that. They're gargantuan, maybe even colossal." The ranger gaped as she saw the massive cleavage of the young sorceress.

"Jealous?" Azura teased as she winked at the ranger. Camilla could not help but look down at her own chest. She was as flat as flat could get, but it meant she could move more easily. Azura shook her head as she started walking, calmly, trying to locate any low lives.

They were maybe fifty yards from Arcanist's tower when fortune smiled on them. Camped in the shadows of the rocky cliff side were five bandits. Camilla fought her instincts about drawing her longbow, about going invisible. She let Azura take the lead as the young sorceress had a plan. Azura disheveled her hair then turned to Camilla. "Use your coat to go invisible. Don't intervene unless it looks like I've lost control of the situation," she stated. Camilla nodded and did as she was instructed. Azura then approached the bandits. "Oh, thank lord Patrokolos! Some strong travelers. Perhaps you'd be willing to help me out," she pleaded, swaying her cleavage every so often.

A tall human stepped forward, his behavior making it clear he was the leader. His eyes looked the busty sorceress up and down, it was easy to tell he was imagining her without her shirt or other clothes. "And what's a pretty young thing like yourself doing out here?" he asked as he leaned in closer, sniffing the sorceress's hair. He smiled, his husky breath beating against Azura's neck. "You smell divine," he whispered in a lustful tone.

Azura flinched, uncomfortable with the situation. "I came upon a large spire, rumored to have great treasure inside. But I'm just too weak to get the door open," she pouted, pursing her lips slightly. She had the leader hooked, a little flaunting of her feminine woes and he was all over her.

"Treasure you say?" The leader smiled, very interested. He looked at his men and nodded. Within mere moments, their camp was packed and the five bandits were ready to move. "Tell you what, pretty lass, we'll give you a hand finding this treasure. And in return you give us some of that." His heavy breaths made Azura want to squirm. She looked where he was indicating, his finger clearly pointing at her bust. She blushed before nodding shily and looking down. "Alright, men, let's help this lass out. Then we get a nice reward," he barked at the men. There were cheers from the bandits as their leader spoke. "Lead the way, lass." His smile made Azura want to single Camilla for help. But if she did, they would blow their chance. She nodded and led the men toward Arcanist's tower.

Camilla rested her right hand on the pommel of her longsword. A habit she had developed when she was planning or issuing orders. The entire scene made her uneasy, it made her angry. The way the bandits were treating the sorceress, she wanted them to suffer. She hoped whatever lich abomination Warren had become would do just that. Slow, painful suffering. It was all these five men deserved. The ranger followed at a slight distance as they made their way back to the tower.

After a bit of a walk, the gate was in view. Azura mentally sighed in relief seeing the gate and knew she just had to continue the charade a little longer. While she could not see Camilla, Azura felt the ranger's presence and made a small gesture to the door. Camilla saw such and had an idea what was being asked of her. She went a little way ahead of the others, ready to shove the bandits through once they were close enough.

"This is the spire," Azura said as she paused. She waited a moment, trying to feel Camilla's presence. She saw a faint flicker of light by the door and nodded. "Shall we, travelers?" she asked.

The leader stepped forward. "Looks like a nice place," he noted before turning to face his men. He laughed slightly as he addressed them. "Right, here's the plan. We're going to go in and take anything that ain't nailed down," he ordered before turning back to the door. He gave it a hearty shove, and to his surprise it did not budge. With a growl he tried again. Still nothing. "Right, on the count of three." All of his men pressed up against the door. "One. Two. THREE!" he yelled. The five men pushed and shoved, forcing the door open.

Once they were inside and clear of the door, Camilla stepped forward grabbing the door handle and yanked it closed again. She held it closed while placing a lock in place that would prevent anyone inside from opening the door. She threw her hood back and looked over at the sorceress. "You alright?" she asked, voice even. Azura nodded as she breathed a sigh of relief that the plan had in fact worked. Slowly and shakily, she buttoned up her shirt and slumped back.

The pair heard several screams and bloody gurgles coming just on the other side of the door. There was loud banging against the door, followed by the bandits pleading for their lives. Azura covered her ears, trying to ignore the sounds. She had just condemned five men to their deaths. To her it was wrong on so many levels. But she knew this was the only way. Warren needed to feed on living humanoid flesh and she rather it be the bandits than her, Chuck or Camilla.

After a few minutes, the sounds died down and everything was eerily quiet. Camilla looked over her lock before nodding to herself. She undid the lock and placed it in her bag. The ranger took a slow, steady breath before opening the door. Peering inside, Camilla saw blood everywhere. It was a massacre. Various body parts were scattered across the floor and bones were left every which way. Standing about thirty feet from the door was a rather tall looking being. His back was to the ranger, but she could tell he stood at least twelve feet in height. His skin looked rotted in several spots, some areas muscle and bone were exposed. Slowly the tall man turned to look at the ranger. His piercing ruby-colored eyes made the ranger want to shudder, but she forced herself to hold such back.

"Hey, Camilla, where ya been?" the man spoke calmly. He held what looked like part of a leg in his massive right hand, bringing it up to his teeth. He took a bite from the leg, chewing it like it was normal.

"Warren? Wow, you… uh… look really different," the ranger responded as she steadied her nerves.

"Yeah, it's the weirdest thing. I could've sworn I died back there. Ya know while fighting Todo or what that monster that Todo turned himself into. Then I woke up here and had this unusual hunger for flesh," Warren stated calmly before taking another bite of the leg.

"Right…about that, perhaps Arcanist can explain," Camilla said slowly as she turned around and walked to the door. She signaled Azura to come inside. As the sorceress made her approach, the ranger paused her at the door. "Good news, he's still Warren. He's just a little disturbing in his mannerisms," the ranger added before letting the sorceress inside.

"Warren!" Azura cheered happily seeing the massive looming figure.

"Hey, Azura!" Warren exclaimed as he pulled the sorceress into a hug.

While the two were having their moment, the ranger went to find the rest of the group. She knocked at the cellar door indicating it was safe for them to come up. Arcanist, Amelia and Chuck came out from the cellar. The paladin and barbarian were surprised to see the scene before them. "How often is he going to need to feast on the flesh of living beings?" Amelia asked, looking at the bras reptilian man.

Arcanist scrunched his face slightly as he thought. "Likely once a month. And it's four humanoids each time," he replied as he sulked up the stairs. "Now if you would be so kind, I do believe you still have something to attend to at Faraway Lake," he called from the stairs.

"Wait! I have to eat other humanoids every month?" Warren shouted, not liking the sounds of what he heard.

"I'm sure we'll find plenty of bandits and other low lives we can feed you," Camilla stated as she turned to face the paladin. "Well, you've got the map, so guess you're navigating."

Amelia fumbled a bit before pulling the map from her armor. She unfolded it on the table and indicated the route. "We can take this road here to that fishing town. From there it's maybe a couple hours to Faraway Lake," she said as she looked over the group and waited to see their reactions.

"Sounds like an easy enough route," Azura added upon checking the map. She liked easy travelling routes. It made things go smoothly when they had to get from one place to the next. She smiled at the others. "Can we maybe go a bit slower this time? Sprinting for a day and a half was painful enough once already."

The paladin laughed slightly. "Be glad you've only done such once. Camilla and I have done that crazy stunt twice at least."

Warren checked over his gear, making sure he was fit for battle. "Huh? When did my armor get repaired?" he asked.

"I fixed it while we were reviving you!" Arcanist called from higher up in the tower.

"Chuck say we get moving! Chuck want fight!" the barbarian growled.

"Alright, sounds like we're ready," Warren said.

"Let's see what Faraway Lake has in store for us." Camilla breathed as they started out the door.

"Camilla," Arcanist began as he stepped up to her. "You'll need these. Longbow's useless without arrows," he added as he handed her a few hundred arrows for her quiver. The ranger nodded her thanks before departing with the others.

"The way you rest your hand, what purpose does it serve?" the dragon asked as she watched the man.

Ashe smiled as he looked up. "You mean my hand on the pommel? It's in case I need to draw my blade at a moment's notice," he replied as they walked through the vast desert before them. He coughed a few times, as he pulled part of his cloak up to shield his mouth and nose. "Sometimes I wish I had scales like yours, Celica. Would make traveling this desert a lot easier," he added as they continued.

Celica chuckled slightly as she took a few steps forward. Her tail flicked slightly as it moved to shield the man from the whirling sands. "Is this better, Ashe?" she asked as she glanced down at the human who walked slightly behind her.

"Much, thank you my friend," he replied.

"So does that blade of yours have a name?" Celica was just trying to make small talk at this point.

"Yes, as do all my weapons. This blade, it's very dear to me, an invaluable friend on the battlefield. Always at my side." He smiled up at the dragon. "Kind of like a certain blue dragon who's saved my life time and time again." He chuckled.

Celica looked away, a faint redness on her cheeks.

Chapter 20 - Memories Of The Forgotten Kingdom

It took the adventurers about five days to reach Faraway Lake. Amelia let out a low breath. "Think it's you or me?" She asked, looking at Camilla. The ranger shrugged as she looked across the lake. It was dark by the time they arrived and all five of them were tired. "Camp here, then start the dive to the temple in the morning?" the paladin asked.

"Sounds like a plan," Azura said before setting up her tent. She opened her bag and withdrew some food. Chuck nodded in agreement as he set up his tent, climbed inside and went right to sleep. Warren sat on a nearby stone and looked at his reflection in the water. He felt empty. He had no heartbeat, nothing to indicate he was living. He felt Azura put a hand on his arm and looked at her. "Don't worry, you're still the same Warren as before," she reassured gently while giving him a smile.

He nodded numbly before looking down again. "You should get some rest. It's strange, I don't feel overly tired. Guess that's one benefit to being undead," Warren teased, trying to make light of the situation.

Azura giggled at his attempt but nodded. "Yeah, probably. I mean Amelia doesn't need to sleep either," she responded as she looked over her shoulder at where the others were setting up camp. She yawned slightly then gave the undead elf a small smile. "If you never need to talk about anything, know I'm here for you. Even if you're undead, I still care about you. A lot," she added before heading back to her tent. She crawled in and was soon sound asleep.

Camilla stared at the small campfire they had made. She was tired but she did not want to sleep. She knew if she slept, she would likely have more of those visions. The ones she could not explain, they felt real and yet she had no recollection of such places. A yawn escaped her and caused her to reconsider trying to rest. Slowly she made her way to the tent she had set up. Once inside, it did not take the ranger long to fall asleep.

Amelia leaned back and laughed slightly. "I'm not sure how to proceed in conversation. I still haven't gotten used to having someone else on night watch with me," she noted as Warren stared out at the lake.

"Yeah, I'm still getting used to this as well," he responded as he smiled to the paladin. He thought for a bit before finally speaking up. "The lack of feeling, does it bother you?" Warren finally asked.

There was a small sigh from the paladin. "Every day. I miss being able to feel. But deep down, you feel. Even if it's hard to tell. You feel. And it's that, that small bit of still being able to feel that lets us know, we're still somewhat alive. That we are still ourselves," she explained as she looked down.

Warren nodded slightly as he let out a faint sigh. "So, think it's your memory or Camilla's?" he asked as he indicated the lake.

Amelia shook her head. "Not sure. I want to say more than likely, it'll be my memory. In which case, I really hope Balthazar is in a good mood."

"Balthazar?" Warren asked, arching an eyebrow as he did so.

"He was my mentor. The one who taught me how to control my vampiric tendencies," Amelia explained. She pulled back part of the chain shirt that was under her armor. There were two red markings on her neck. "He was also the one who bit me and saved me from becoming a feral and mindless werewolf," she added.

"Were you close to him? As a friend, I mean," the lich clarified.

"Considering I didn't know what friendship was until I came here and met all of you? I wouldn't say he and I were friends. Mentor and pupil but that's probably as far as our relationship got," she explained.

The rest of the night was quiet, only the slight breeze making sound as it blew through the area. When the sun's rays peered over the horizon, everyone was up early and readying for the dive. "Alright, how well can everyone swim?" Amelia asked.

"Chuck great swimmer. Chuck make dive before," the barbarian responded.

Warren removed his armor and tossed it in his water treated bag. "I'm not the best of swimmers, never really learned. But Azura, Chuck and I have made this dive before. Perhaps one of us should lead," he suggested.

Amelia nodded in agreement as she removed her armor and placed it in her water treated bag. "Sounds like a plan. I'm a solid swimmer, so it shouldn't be too bad," she reasoned.

Camilla hesitated. She had never actually been in water deeper than her waistline. She watched as everyone else was already getting into position for the dive. "I've never actually been in water deeper than my hips," she finally said as she began to wade out to the others.

"Don't worry, we'll make it down," Azura tried to reassure the nervous ranger. This was becoming something the sorceress was very good at, reassuring others. Inspiring others.

As they began the dive, Chuck had taken the lead, it was clear he was the most experienced swimmer. Amelia was second, having an easy time with the water. Warren and Azura hung back to make sure Camilla was alright, the three of them, while not the best swimmers, made progress.

Chuck pointed ahead as the temple came into view. Amelia nodded and dove towards the massive underwater temple. She and Chuck made their way inside and into the air pocket that housed the interior of the temple. They looked around briefly before Amelia began re-equipping her armor. A few minutes later, Azura, Camilla and Warren emerged, the ranger coughing and sputtering a bit. Warren re-equipped his armor and began walking about.

Before the group was the ripple they were looking for. It had a faint purple glow to it that it lacked the previous time. Amelia walked over to it and looked it over. "Shall we, then?" she asked while gesturing to the ripple.

They each stepped through one at a time. When they emerged from the other side, they found they were a small farming town. It was unusual to Azura, Warren and Chuck, each taken back by the amount of cattle, sheep and crops that went on for as far as the eye could see. "I remember this place," Amelia began as she looked around. "This was Highever, my home before the attack," she said as they walked along.

Camilla looked around, it was not that she had never seen farming villages, but it had been so long since the last time she had been in one. As the five travelers walked, Amelia knew she heard a voice beckoning her to follow. She looked around before spotting the well. The voice was coming from the depths of the well. "Welcome to the forgotten kingdom!" a voice cheered from within the well. They sounded a mix of cheerful and sadistic, putting most of the adventurers on edge.

"At ease. It's just Balthazar," Amelia stated as she approached the well.

She peered down and sure enough standing at the base of the well was a well-dressed man, wearing a monocle. His attire was fancy to say the least. A white shirt, covered by a black jacket, he wore black pants and black boots that covered up to his knees. His hair was dark brown and well groomed. He flashed the paladin a smirk. "My dear Amelia, it's been too long," he stated, his fangs now visible. He laughed slightly then beckoned the group to follow him. "If it's the legendary weapon you seek, then you'll need to float down here." He gave them the eerie message before going further from the light source.

Camilla looked over the edge of the well. It was a steep drop with no sort of ladder for them to use to climb down. The ranger withdrew a bundle of rope from her bag and began tying it off. "Think we're going to need that pulley system we used at the canyon," she stated as she got everything set up.

Amelia stepped forward. "I'll go first," she stated as she took the ends of the rope. Camilla nodded and got the rig set up. It was a slow process due to the weight of the paladin's gear. Chuck and Warren lent their strength where needed to ensure everything went smoothly. Once Amelia reached the bottom, she untied herself from the pulley. "Alright, whoever's next, it's all clear," she called up.

Camilla turned to the others. "Who wants to go down the creepy well next?" she asked as she adjusted the rig.

Warren stepped forward. "Probably best I go next. That way Chuck can help you if I'm too heavy," he suggested. The barbarian nodded as he and the ranger began getting the rig set up on the lich. As with Amelia, it was slow going due not only because of his armor but also his size. Once he touched the bottom, he undid the ropes and smiled to Amelia. "Not too bad," he said before looking back to the top. "Alright, next person!"

Chuck stepped up; he did not give the ranger time to set up the rig. Instead, the barbarian opted to propel himself down rope, occasionally kicking off the side of the well. It took much less time than the previous two. Camilla turned to Azura. "Your turn," she said as she got the rig set up. The sorceress nodded as she began to descend into the well. It was much faster than the two armor clad adventurers but slower than the barbarian. Camilla remained anchored as best as she could as she let out more slack to allow the sorceress to descend further. The ranger felt the movement stop and sighed waiting.

"Ok, Camilla, just you left!" Warren called up.

Camilla nodded as she loosened the rope slightly and stepped over to the edge of the well. Slowly she began her descent, much like Chuck, she opted to propel herself down. About half way down she heard a sound that put her on edge. The rope had frayed significantly and was coming undone a little ways above her. The ranger cursed as she sped up. Before she made it much further she was in a free fall as the rope snapped.

Below, Warren looked up in time to see the ranger in a free fall. He reached out, hoping he would be able to catch her. The ranger landed hard in the lich's arms, both breathing a sigh of relief from the ordeal. "You alright, Camilla?" Warren asked as he eased her to the ground.

"Yes, thank you," Camilla responded with a nod as she got to her feet.

Amelia pointed further into the labyrinth they would need to enter. "I remember going through here years ago. It's known as the Labyrinth of Truth, there's several dead ends and a lot of undead things down here. I'd say stick together, but the problem is, last time I was here, there was magic and monsters that separated us," she admitted.

Warren nodded as he looked ahead. "What's the plan?" he asked as he took a step forward.

The paladin took the lead, her tower shield and bastard sword drawn. "Try to make our way through the labyrinth as quickly as we can and be ready to fight at all times," she stated as she headed into the start of the labyrinth.

There was clearly some nervousness as the group entered the labyrinth. All around them they heard groans of discomfort and the sounds of shuffling. As they rounded a bend, a bright flash engulfed and separated the adventurers. Amelia was the first to her feet after being warped randomly in the labyrinth. She held her shield and bastard sword at the ready as she took off in a sprint through the massive maze they had to traverse. Elsewhere she could hear combat and assumed it was one of her allies. The paladin rushed further ahead, not fully caring about what was going on within the labyrinth. She only had one goal in mind: get to the end of the maze.

Warren shook his head as he stood before looking around. "Azura! Camilla! Amelia! Chuck!" he called, hoping to hear one of his allies. There was an uneasy silence as he walked through the area. He could barely hear the sounds of combat elsewhere. He recalled what the paladin had said about magic warping people and shuddered. He hoped it was not Azura locked in combat. The lich shook his head and made his way further into the depths of the labyrinth.

Chuck listened for a bit. Silence. The barbarian did not hear anything as he charged through the bends and twists of the maze. He huffed a few times as he reached various dead ends and would charge off in a different direction. The barbarian wanted to fight, he did not care how or when.

Azura sprinted as fast as she could, occasionally shooting spells behind her to throw off the ghouls that were pursuing her. *"Why did it have to be ghouls?"* she thought as she ran. As she rounded a bend, she saw the faint glint of something. On a hunch, the sorceress dropped to the ground, only daring to glance up when she heard the faint movement. Arrows emerged from seemingly nowhere, striking the ghouls and dropping them.

"You alright, Azura?" Camilla asked as she threw her hood back. She offered the sorceress a hand to help her up. Azura nodded as she accepted the help. "Guess we lucked out in being warped not far from one another," Camilla added as she looked around.

Azura pointed. "Nothing but dead ends that way," she stated, indicating the route she had come from.

"Same going the direction, I came from," the ranger replied as she pointed behind her. They looked around briefly, not seeing any other paths they could take. Camilla nocked an arrow and shot it blindly at an upward angle. The pair watched as the arrow eventually went over the towering walls of the maze. "Think your magic can break through this wall?" Camilla asked as she pressed a hand against part of the wall.

There was a smirk from the sorceress. "Of course, I can," she said proudly before focusing on a spell. She launched the spell, breaking a six foot by six-foot hole in the wall. They paused as they heard movement near to where they broke the wall.

Warren heard the sound of something shifting and collapsing. He assumed magic was involved and sprinted to the source. Where there was magic, generally Azura was not far from such. "Azura!" he called as he sprinted towards the sounds he heard.

Before anyone could do anything, there was another warp going off. What progress they each had made was completely tossed to the winds as they had no idea where they were. Chuck smirked when he saw a group of ghouls and fought through them with ease. Ahead of him he heard the heavy clanking of armor and moved to pursue whomever it was. "Chuck!" Amelia was stunned to see the barbarian. Stunned but relieved all the same.

"Chuck fight ghouls. Chuck squish them," the barbarian stated as he and the paladin continued through the maze.

"That explains the sounds I heard," Amelia noted as they rounded another bend.

Elsewhere in the maze, Warren was sprinting trying to find Azura. He knew the others could all handle themselves, but the sorceress was very weak physically. As he rounded a corner he stared blankly as the scene unfolded. A ghoul appeared to be attacking the air before a blade tore through the creature's skull. "Camilla!" he called out.

Camilla looked in Warren's direction, pulling her hood down. "Glad to see a friendly face," Camilla stated as she looked around. She pointed with her blade, indicating the path Warren had come from. "Any open routes over there?"

Warren shook his head. "No, sorry," he replied.

"Then we're stuck until the next warp or we break through and make a path," she noted as she indicated the wall in front of them.

The lich hesitated but knew it was the only way to continue. "Let's see what I can do with my magic," he said as he placed a hand on the wall. Darkness shrouded his hand as he began casting. A massive dark beam like energy shot forward making a path for the pair. Warren looked down at Camilla and indicated the path. "Shall we?" he asked.

Camilla pulled her hood over her head and took off in a sprint. Behind her, she could easily hear Warren making his moves and running. The pair came to a stop as they reached a massive door. Camilla looked the lock over before checking the rest of the door. "Magic seal," Warren stated as he watched Camilla pull her hood down. He pointed to some inscribed text. "Only those proven worth in the eyes of the convenient may enter."

"Then we're to wait for Amelia," the ranger noted.

Warren turned and tried to head back the way they came. As he stepped, he felt something force him back. "What?"

"Guess we really are waiting. Can't go forward and can't go back," Camilla murmured before sitting to the side.

Back in the maze, Azura heard the sound of some sort of loud energy surge and moved to investigate. She saw the damaged walls and the debris littering the ground. She listened intently for any signs of movement. The tombs were quiet all around her as she made her way through the debris. Looking it over, the young sorceress noticed there was a path. Without any hesitation, Azura sprinted down the path, hoping she could find anyone.

"Warren! Camilla!" Azura called as she saw the pair waiting.

"Azura!" Warren responded in glee seeing the sorceress cross the barrier that blocked them from returning. Once she had crossed over, he pulled her into a tight embrace. "I was worried about you," he whispered.

Azura just smiled. "I'm fine, Warren. I've gotten a lot stronger since we started this crazy adventure."

Camilla watched the barrier, waiting. She knew Amelia and Chuck were hearty warriors, but it was a matter of how long they could keep fighting. Neither had any form of healing themselves or each other. *"Please be safe, Amelia, Chuck,"* she thought as she waited.

An hour passed since Azura arrived and joined Warren and Camilla, but there was still no sign of Amelia nor Chuck. Azura looked at Warren, worry in her eyes. "Do you think—"

"They'll be here, any minute now. Those two are stronger than pretty much everyone I've ever met," Warren interrupted. He indicated the barrier in front of them. "Besides, it's not like we have a choice then to wait. That barrier won't let us back through."

The ranger stood from her perch and approached the barrier. Her yellow eyes gleaming as she looked ahead. "I'm going back for them," she stated as she put her hands against the barrier. Camilla bit back a growl as she felt a stinging sensation course through her body.

"Camilla, we've been over this. We can't go back. That barrier won't let us—" Warren stopped his eyebrow arched as he watched the ranger. He noticed a ripple in the barrier where she was pressing. "Back through?"

"You see it two?" Azura asked as she looked from Warren to the ripple in the barrier.

"Maybe we can use our magic to open a small hole," Warren mused as he began casting. Azura nodded and followed the lich's lead.

Camilla snarled slightly as she continued to push forward. Her hands pressed through the barrier and reached the other side. She breathed heavily, the shallow breaths indicated her fatigue and pain. Taking a step forward, Camilla began to force her way through the barrier. She felt the magic the casters were using to open the barrier, or attempt to. It was small, but it was enough. The ranger stumbled forward, clear of the barrier. She looked over her shoulder to Warren and Azura. "I'll find them and bring them back," she stated before taking off in a sprint.

"Be careful!" Azura called.

"You got this!" Warren hollered.

The maze seemed still. No ghouls shambled about. No sounds of armor or other movements. Camilla pulled her hood over her head as she walked through the maze. The eerie silence was getting to her. She sniffed the air, her senses picking up the smell of sweat and unbathed man. Chuck. Camilla sprinted in the direction the scent was coming from. *"When did my senses get this heightened?"* she thought as she rounded a bend. At the heart of the maze were Chuck and Amelia both; they were locked in combat with massive undead ogre.

Amelia blocked the fierce punches using her tower shield. Chuck rushed forward using his greataxe to cleave at the monster's left arm. The ogre roared as it swung out with a massive hammer, launching Chuck several feet backwards. The barbarian was breathing heavily as he got his feet under him. Amelia was also exhausted. "Chuck, make a break for it. I'll keep this thing busy," Amelia said as she gripped her bastard sword tightly.

"Chuck not run from fight. Chuck not leave strong lady," Chuck growled as he readied to rush the undead monster again.

The two were shocked to see an arrow volley hit the ogre and stagger it. They both smirked as they pressed the advantage. Chuck's greataxe hit its mark taking the ogre's left arm off, while Amelia's blade took the creature's head off. Both breathed a sigh of relief before looking around. Camilla threw her hood back, deactivating the invisibility of her coat. "You two alright?" she asked while shouldering her longbow.

"Yeah, thanks for the support," Amelia replied.

Chuck nodded as he gave the ranger a thumbs up. The ranger smiled and returned the gesture to him. "Come on, I found a clear path out of here," Camilla said as she took point. The other two followed behind the ranger as they made their way down a few turns. As they rounded the corner the trio came upon a pack of undead werewolves and another undead ogre. "Another one?" Camilla snarled as she drew her longsword and shortsword.

Amelia ran past the ranger, blocking a hammer swing from the ogre. Chuck sprinted towards the werewolves and twirled his greataxe in a whirlwind attack sending all of the beasts flying. Camilla and Chuck tag teamed the werewolves making short work of the pack of six. They turned upon hearing a loud metallic screech. Camilla's eyes narrowed as she rushed forward, her adrenaline racing as she went after the ogre. Both blades hit their marks as they left deep gashes in the ogre's flesh.

The monster snarled as he stepped back, recoiling from the pain. Amelia took a step back, her tower shield badly cracked. Chuck lunged forward, his greataxe striking the monster's midsection, spilling its innards. Amelia took a deep breath as she slashed out with her bastard sword taking the ogre's head off. "Chuck think shield done," the barbarian stated as he looked at the tower shield.

"Yeah, unfortunately," Amelia stated as she removed her tower shield. It was cracked in several spots and shattering in others. She breathed a frustrated sigh as she dropped the damaged shield. "It's beyond repair. And at this point, it would be deadweight we don't need," she added before walking down the path.

"Why do you not use a shield? Would it not give you more defenses?" Celica asked as she watched Ashe train.

He paused and sheathed his blade. He wore a warm smile, the same one that he always had. "A shield, while great for defense, is also very heavy. Such weight would throw off my fighting style. I prefer to make use of my speed and avoid being hit," Ashe replied as he sat beside Celica's claws.

"I made something for you. I know you hate wearing armor, but please consider wearing this. To give you some sort of defense in case you cannot dodge an attack," Celica stated as she held out a chest to Ashe.

Camilla inhaled sharply as she refocused on the area around. Another waking dream? They were becoming annoying to her. Constant distractions from her mission of returning to Kardax. Did she though? Did she want to return? Alibi was starting to feel like home. She shook her head as she sprinted to catch up to Chuck and Amelia. The trio reached the barrier and stepped through reuniting with Azura and Warren.

"Looks like the party's all here," Warren said with a smile. They all looked at the door, trying to determine the next course of action. "It said something about only those proven worthy by the covenant may enter."

Amelia took a step forward. "Balthazar's covenant. He made anyone he bit pass three trails before they could be initiated into the covenant. And once in the covenant, we were in it until we were felled in battle," she stated as she approached the door. As though sensing her blood ties, the door unlocked, allowing the adventurers to continue.

The air was stale yet held a thick mildew like smell in it. It was pitch dark and there was no way of telling what was ahead of them. Amelia held her bastard sword at the ready, opting to grip it with both hands. Azura looked around trying to find any sort of light source. Warren instinctively moved in front of Azura, his tower shield held in a defensive manner. Chuck growled as he looked around, his greataxe at the ready. Camilla's gaze narrowed as she looked ahead, spotting the same figure from earlier.

"Welcome to my covenant. Amelia, it's been too long, tell me are you still trying to be a knight of some holy order?" Balthazar greeted as numerous candles lit up. Everyone was briefly blinded by the sudden light. Balthazar chuckled as he held out open arms. "Come back to me, Amelia. We shall forgive the crimes you committed against Duncan."

Amelia took a step back, her stance becoming more defensive. "Amelia, what is he talking about?" Azura asked as she glanced between Balthazar and the paladin.

"I wasn't completely honest with you four," Amelia murmured. She knew how this was going to look, how it would sound. But they deserved the right to know. "I was a member of the covenant. But I betrayed one of the high-ranking members, Duncan, Balthazar's right hand. Duncan lorded over several villages; he saw humans as nothing more than cattle. I was already a member of the Holy Order when I was turned. And by order of the Holy Order, I was to kill Duncan and liberate the villages he ruled over."

"Tell them what became of those villages, those peasants," Balthazar taunted as he stepped forward. The paladin hesitated, her head hung low. She could not bring herself to say what happened. "They fell into chaos! They murdered each other! Over population and limited resources lead to each having to destroy one another in order to survive," Balthazar cut in, his fangs visible. A trait that seemed common amongst vampires when they were agitated. "Without Duncan to lead them, to keep them in line, they suffered worse. Your Holy Order did nothing about that."

Balthazar lunged forward, not giving the adventurers any further time to react. His twin scimitars were aimed for the paladin. His fury knowing no limits. To his surprise, a longsword blocked his attack. Camilla's gaze narrowed. "Survival of the fittest. That's how people grow. That's how they establish hierarchies," she snarled as she forced Balthazar back. Her yellow eyes shimmered as her longsword began glowing a faint blue. "Amelia, snap out of it! You did what you believed was right! No one can fault you for that. Now get your head together!"

Materializing from seemingly nowhere, four other vampires appeared. The first bore a striking resemblance to Balthazar, perhaps slightly younger. The second was female, her scarlet eyes reflecting her bloodlust, her pink dress was loose and very seductive looking. Next was another female, her eyes were black as a moonless night and unlike the previous two, she barely resembled anything human. She was closer to a bat with slight human features. Finally, there was a male whose eyes were red as rubies; he was somewhere between being bat-like and humanoid looking.

Balthazar nodded to the group. "Get them, feast on their blood! Amelia is mine," he commanded.

Chuck rushed forward, instantly engaging the ruby eyed vampire. He was fast, easily moving between Chuck's attacks as though the barbarian was moving in slow motion. Warren blocked an attack from the Balthazar look alike, his shield screeching from the claw strike. The lich pushed his shield forward then swung out with his morningstar. Azura began casting, her fireball hitting the pink dressed vampire. To the sorceress's shock, the vampire easily evaded the attack and seemed to have teleported. Camilla shook her head. "I always seem to get the big ones..." she muttered as she engaged in battle with the massive bat-like vampire.

Amelia shook her head as she moved to intercept Balthazar's attack. His scimitars screeched as they grated against the paladin's bastard sword. She held her ground as she moved with his attack, then countered with a pommel strike. He was fast as he quickly moved to attack again. Balthazar smirked as got a few hits off, striking the small chinks in Amelia's armor. "I told you, armor makes you slow. Makes you predictable." He laughed.

Warren's morningstar, Ironvice, came down, crushing the skull of his foe. The vampires had a significant speed advantage, that much was clear. But they were still vulnerable to divine weapons as well as sunlight. He began casting as he watched the battles unfolding. "Hear me, great and mighty Terrain! I ask your favor to grant my allies strength against the undead," he called out.

Chuck's greataxe was shimmering with a white glow as he continued to do battle with the odd-looking vampire. The barbarian felt a surge of energy, his movement increased allowing him to match the undead being's speed. His greataxe effortlessly tore through the space between them and took the vampire's head off. He roared a victory cry.

Azura barely dodged the attack from the female vampire. She was faster than the sorceress and it showed. The young sorceress studied the area before trying her next attack. She took a deep breath, letting the vampire come closer. As the attacker closed in, her bloodlust eyes sizing up the sorceress, Azura made her move. She ducked to the side, taking a small step as she did so. Upon coming up from her dodge, Azura brought up her spectral dagger and dug it into the vampire's heart.

"Your puny dagger is—" Before the vampire could finish her statement, the dagger morphed into a silver stake. It instantly ended the seductive vampire's undead existence.

Camilla backflipped narrowly dodging the claws of the massive, mutated vampire. The ranger was more agile but less powerful than her foe. Nothing new for her. She brought her longsword up in front of her and began casting a spell. It sounded vaguely reptilian in dialect, but the ranger chanted the words with no issues. She smirked as her longsword began glowing a distinct red. "Let's see how you handle this!" Camilla called out as she unleashed a rapid flurry of strikes. She heard her foe hiss before lashing out with several claw swipes. Camilla dodged the worst of the attacks, but one grazed her arm, leaving a thin line of blood.

The vampire reared up to attack again but suddenly stopped. She hissed again before collapsing. Warren stood behind her, the chain from his ball and chain, wrapped around the vampire. The chain was glowing with a white light, disintegrating the vampire. He looked Camilla over, only the one cut on her arm. "You weren't bit, were you?" he asked, worry in his voice. She shook her head. He smiled in response. "Then let's help Amelia and finish this!" he called as he rushed toward the paladin's fight.

Chuck and Azura had already joined the paladin in fighting Balthazar, Warren and Camilla were the last ones into the fight. Balthazar growled as he took a step back, seeing the tide had shifted from a one on one to a five on one. "Guess I should stop holding back," he snarled as his figure shredded away. Standing where the vampire leader was, now stood a massive bat-like monster. It stood on two legs, towering over the group; its wings were huge, draped over its back. The claws on its hands were sharp, getting cut by one would result in a massive injury. Balthazar roared as he lunged forward, his claws coming down. Everyone picked a side and dove out of harm's way barely avoiding the attack.

"Amelia!" Camilla called out. The paladin looked over, knowing the ranger had a plan. "His weakness?" she asked.

Amelia pointed. "That jewel on his forehead. We break that, it'll force him to revert and then we can easily take his head off," she informed the group.

Warren nodded. "Azura, you hang back and cast any supporting magic you have. Chuck, you and I will get his attention. And—"

"No. Chuck and I will get his attention," Amelia interrupted as she pointed at the lich's tower shield. "I haven't got a springboard anymore. This time you'll have to help Camilla," she reasoned.

Chuck nodded. "Chuck like plan," he grunted.

"Alright, we do it your way," Warren yielded to the paladin. He smirked before turning his gaze to the ranger. "What do you say, Camilla?"

"Ready when you are," Camilla responded as she sheathed her shortsword. She only needed one blade to do the task.

Amelia and Chuck both rushed forward, their weapons slashing away at the massive bat beast before them. Balthazar roared as he lashed out with claw and wing attacks, forcing both the paladin and the barbarian on the defensive. Warren sprinted into position and took a knee. He brought his shield up over his head and held it tightly. The rest was up to Camilla. The ranger nodded as she sized everything up. *"Warren's a lot bigger than Amelia. My initial jump is going to need to be a bit higher,"* she thought then glanced at Azura. The sorceress looked over and nodded as though knowing what the ranger needed. She began casting before directing the spell at the ranger. Camilla nodded her thanks before sprinting to Warren. She heard the combat Amelia and Chuck were dealing with, she wanted to join them but that was not her task. She leapt up, her feet landing on the shield.

Warren shoved his shield upward the moment he felt Camilla's weight. She got her second jump off and spiraled toward the brute of a vampire. His roar resonated through the chamber as the longsword pierced the jewel on his forehead. Warren turned to face Amelia. "Are you sure—" he began before he saw Amelia sprinting at Balthazar. "Amelia!" he yelled.

"Something's wrong, I can sense it!" Amelia called back as she slashed at Balthazar's legs. She watched in horror as the massive vampire grabbed the ranger and flung her into a wall. "Camilla!" the paladin yelled seeing the debris. She felt every part of her go into a rage, something that she had not felt in years. "You..." she snarled as she looked at Balthazar. "You're going to pay for that." Her snarls were more feral sounding this time.

Amelia lunged forward, her bastard sword taking Balthazar's right leg off. He staggered a bit before opening his wings and getting airborne. The massive vampire hissed as he flew upward, avoiding Amelia's attacks. He smirked as he saw an opening and lunged forward. The pure blood vampire knocked the paladin off balance. While she was staggered, he disarmed her and flung her to the ground before grabbing her by the back of her armor and dragging her.

Warren and Chuck rushed forward, the barbarian slashing wildly with his axe. The lich swung his morningstar trying to get a clean strike. Balthazar laughed as one mighty flap of his wings sent both into a wall. Azura was trying to maintain her focus on the pure blood vampire as she readied her spell. She flung a fireball at Balthazar. He hissed as he saw the attack but easily moved Amelia to shield him from the flames.

"What's the plan?" Warren called out as he got his feet under him.

"So long as he's airborne, I can't land a spell," Azura responded.

The group heard the distinct sound of a bow before seeing three arrows make their way into the air. Balthazar screeched as the arrows pierced his left wing, before he could recover, three more arrows pierced the same wing, but the attack came from a different direction. Amelia smirked knowing who was attacking. She drew a knife from her belt and slashed Balthazar's arm. He hissed in pain as he dropped the paladin. Another volley, this time sixty arrows pierced his left wing, completely shredding it.

Forced to land, Balthazar rushed Amelia again, knocking her knife aside as he slammed her into the ground. Amelia felt around, trying to find any sort of weapon she could use. She heard Warren and Chuck both rush the pure blood again. As with before they were flung backwards and sent into the walls. Their attack provided what it needed to, a distraction. Amelia noticed the shortsword that had suddenly clattered in front of her. "Thank you, Camilla," she whispered as she grabbed the shortsword. As Balthazar returned his attention to the paladin, he felt a sharp sensation in his throat. Glancing down, he saw the shortsword. Amelia pulled the blade out and made one final slash with everything she had. The pure blood's head fell to the ground as the body staggered before collapsing.

Amelia breathed a sigh of relief as she staggered from fatigue. Before she could fall, she felt someone supporting her. She chuckled slightly as she saw no one around her. "Thanks for the save, Camilla," she said as she accepted the ranger's help. Camilla threw back her hood, revealing herself and merely nodded.

Warren sighed before smiling seeing they had won the battle. "I have to say, he was a powerful foe. And his covenant was just as strong," he noted as everyone regrouped.

The paladin was quiet as she closed her eyes leaning into Camilla. Her armor was greatly damaged, her shield was destroyed but she still had the most important thing to her. Her comrades. "Camilla." Amelia paused, keeping her voice barely above a whisper. The ranger hummed lightly as she glanced down at the paladin in her arms. "Don't go dying on me. Not now. Not ever," Amelia whispered, her head resting on Camilla's chest.

"Not now. Not ever," Camilla replied softly.

There was a low rumble as a statue on the far side turned its head. The shield in its grasp shone with a bright light before separating from the statue. Amelia stood once more as the shield floated to her. "I am Soulfade, the impenetrable tower shield. I am one of five legendary weapons scattered across Alibi. You, holy knight, have proven your strength and your dedication to your oath. I shall lend you my power," a voice came from the tower shield. Amelia held out her left hand and the shield flew right into her grip.

"They all say five. So, one more," Camilla murmured as everyone looked at the new shield. As with past memory locations, the environment rippled before fading away. When they emerged, they were back at Faraway Lake. There was a slight chill in the air as the five let out a deep breath. "Where to next?" the ranger asked, looking the group over.

"Let's head back to the town and get some rest. While it's a ghost town, we can at least use the inn to try to get a decent night's rest," Azura commented as she looked toward the town.

"Sounds like a good idea," Warren chimed in as he followed Azura's gaze.

Amelia nodded as she took point and began heading for town. Chuck was right behind her as they travelled. Camilla brought up the rear, as Warren and Azura walked side by side. Once they reached the quiet fishing village, the five stopped at the inn and made their way inside. Furniture was thrown everywhere, most of it broken from the slaughter a few days prior. The group did a room by room sweep, making sure they were alone. The five set up their lodging for the night in a single room, none of them wanting to be alone. Warren shoved a massive set of drawers in front of the door, ensuring an extra level of safety. Amelia and Camilla barricaded the windows for the added security.

Once everything was in order, the three that required sleep laid back upon a few tattered mattresses. Warren and Amelia kept watch as they had the previous night. "Why don't you tell her how you feel?" Amelia asked, glancing from Warren to Azura.

"I could ask you the same. You and Camilla," Warren countered.

"What Camilla and I have is a friendship. Nothing more," the paladin stated.

Warren scoffed, shaking his head. "Really? All the talk, the closeness, the touching, that's all just friendship? Be true, Amelia. You have a thing for Camilla." He chuckled.

"I do not," Amelia snarled. She looked toward the window, ignoring Warren's further comments. Even if she had feelings for Camilla, it could never work between them. They were friends, nothing more.

CHAPTER 21 - Virtues

It was early; the sun had yet to rise when the group awoke and began readying to leave. As they left the inn, Amelia took one last look around the area. She noticed a faint glow in the soil just south of the inn. Upon investigating, the paladin found a small sapphire. She looked it over briefly before tossing it into her belt pouch and moving to meet up with the others.

Uncertain where to go, the five adventurers made their way back to Arcanist's tower. "Welcome, welcome! I see you've found Soulfade. That means only one legendary weapon remains," Arcanist stated as he thumbed through books.

"These legendary weapons, they aren't from this world, aren't from Alibi, are they?" Warren asked as he looked over Ironvice.

"That's not an easy question to answer," Arcanist replied as he paused and set a book down on the table. He looked over some notes, turning the pages for a bit before stopping. "Ironvice, Crasher, Infinite and Soulfade are all weapons that were used by great heroes from other realms. According to the legends, they are summoned to wherever they are needed most, and they carry within them the souls of their past users," Arcanist noted as he tapped the text within the book.

"And what about the fifth weapon?" Amelia asked.

Arcanist turned the pages again and pointed. "The last of the five, Echoes, is said to have belonged to someone who was not a hero. But the blade was forged with a single purpose, to end an evil that would have destroyed multiple realms."

"And where do we find Echoes?" Camilla questioned as she sharpened her longsword.

"That, I know not," the brass reptilian creature stated. He hummed slightly as rubbed his chin and read over the text again. "The only known detail about the location of Echoes is that it will only reveal itself when someone worthy finds it. Same as the other four. Which means it will likely be in yet another memory tomb."

"That's what you're calling them? Memory tombs?" Azura chimed in.

"Yes, realms created by the memories of those trying to save the realm. Memories that entomb part of your past and attempt to destroy your futures. At this point I would be more worried about locating the virtue stones. There are eight in total and according to legend, if they are brought together, they hold the power to alter the very course of history. They can give their user unimaginable power," Arcanist said as he placed another book on the table.

"And you're just now telling us about these!" Warren hissed as he looked at the book. He studied the drawing in the book. A person surrounded by eight stones, each a different color. The stones possessed a very angular look to them, sharp edges and lots of points. "And where are we to find these?"

Camilla paused her sharpening and looked to the lich. "This is not the first we are hearing about these stones. It was months ago, about the same time that we first met Arcanist," she noted as she looked over her longsword. "Though I admit, I had almost forgotten about such. So Arcanist, where might we find such powerful items?" she asked while sheathing the blade.

"Two reside in a world running parallel to our own. They shine in red and brilliant light," the brass reptile explained.

"Red and brilliant light?" Azura said while arching an eyebrow.

Camilla and Amelia exchanged a quick glance before digging into their belt pouches. "A ruby and a diamond," the ranger responded as she held the diamond and Amelia held the ruby.

"Found in a world parallel to our own. And we did find these in that reverse world," Amelia added.

"One resides within a realm covered in shadows. It shines with a golden light, matching the hero's heart that resides within," Arcanist continued.

"Golden light and a hero's heart," Warren murmured as he thought. He looked to Azura and recalled the gold light particles that flickered off her brother. "Azura, the stone Henry gave you."

Azura withdrew the yellow topaz from her pocket and looked it over. "A realm covered in shadows and gold light of a hero's heart," she mused.

Arcanist paused, seeing the Outrealm warriors possessed three of the virtue stones. He shook his head then continued. "The fourth stone was lost to the quiet town, its light, blue as the sea."

Amelia withdrew the sapphire she had found just before they left the quiet fishing town. "Blue as the sea," she noted.

"The fifth was already found by Time Eater and given to a general. This one cries in a green light," Arcanist continued.

Camilla withdrew an emerald she had taken off an enemy general they encountered. "We took this from one of the generals in Forlorn Keep. Green light, and I'll assume it was given to the general by Time Eater."

Arcanist paused again. "Five of eight. Color me impressed. There are two that will be incredibly difficult to find. One resides in Waray, a village in the far northern desert; it clouds itself in an ebony light. And the seventh is said to be in the World Beneath, whenever that is," he stated.

"Chuck want know, where eight?" the barbarian growled as he pretended to count.

"Yeah, that accounts for seven. Where's the eighth?" Warren added.

"Safe, hidden from all eyes as it can move through dimensions," Arcanist stated as he sat at the table. He looked over the text again before looking at the adventurers. "I suggest you head to Waray and find the sixth stone. Maybe in the desert you'll find clues about Echoes as well."

Warren unrolled the map the party had and looked it over. "The fastest route to the desert is going to be going through these tunnels and popping out here, just outside the desert. From there I guess we'll wander until we find Waray," he said as he looked it over.

Camilla nodded in agreement as she checked over her gear. She always liked ensuring her weapons were in top condition and ready at a moment's notice. "Deserts are my specialty. I've led plenty of travelers through the Dantashi Desert of Kardax, no injuries."

"Then let's get underway," Azura stated as she collected her spell book and readied to head out. Chuck roared loudly as he pounded his chest, excited to travel again. Amelia nodded as she rounded up any last few bits of gear she needed.

Soon the five adventurers were heading out to the tunnels that Warren had marked on the map. Warren was in the lead, Azura beside him. Chuck and Amelia were in the center of the formation. Camilla was rearguard, her right hand resting on the pommel of her longsword. Everywhere the five passed through there was destruction, fires raging and corpses piled high. Was this Time Eater's doing? Or was there someone else responsible?

As they came upon the tunnels, the Outrealm warriors stopped to take a break and catch their breath. Camilla glanced down the entry tunnel, her yellow eyes gleaming and scanning for any threat. "Vision improved?" Warren asked as he looked down the tunnel as well. Camilla glanced briefly at Warren before returning her gaze back to the tunnel and nodding. The lich shook his head slightly. "Not sure how your vision would suddenly have improved but that means we won't need to light a torch and reveal our position in case of the worst," he noted, trying to smile.

Once they had rested, everyone began to trickle into the new formation into the tunnel system. Chuck and Amelia took the lead, Warren and Azura now at the center and Camilla remained in her spot at rearguard. The air was thin, stale and eerily quiet as they moved through the tunnels. Several tunnels were blocked off by various cave-ins or by sudden drop offs. It left the group a single route forward. Amelia signaled for everyone to stop as she looked around. "Anyone else hear that?" she asked softly as her werewolf ears twitched.

Everyone listened, straining to hear anything. "I don't hear anything," Warren finally said.

"Exactly. It's too quiet down here. We should at the least be hearing the movement of rock or some form of debris shifting," Amelia responded as she looked around and listened again.

Camilla turned, looking behind the group as she drew her longsword. "Camilla?" everyone questioned hearing the ranger's sudden movement.

She was silent as she stared back down the tunnel behind the group. Her blade was glowing a faint red, indicating something was in fact coming. There was a long silence before the ranger quickly sheathed her blade and drew her longbow and aimed at the ceiling, firing a few arrows. Several hissing sounds were heard from the ceiling above the group. Everyone drew whatever weapon they had for ranged combat and looked up. Above the group, latched onto the ceiling were several disfigured beings. They had long arms and legs, short torsos and were completely bald. They were ashen gray in color with splotches of red all over them and deep red eyes.

"Ghouls?" Azura questioned as she threw a fireball.

"Horrors?" Warren responded as he searched for a ranged weapon.

"Chuck want fight!" the barbarian growled as he threw rocks at the strange beings.

Amelia shook her head as she loaded a cartridge into her repeating crossbow. "They don't look like ghouls and they lack the stretch of a horror!" she called out as she began firing her crossbow.

Camilla continued to shoot arrows at the unusual beings. They began dropping from the ceiling, their elongated fingers ending in claws, they slashed at the Outrealm warriors. The narrow tunnels prevented the adventurers from using their usual preferred ways to attack. They risked hitting one another if they did so. Amelia drew her tower shield, bringing it up in time to block a claw attack from one of the unusual beings as it slashed at the sorceress. Azura nodded her thanks before throwing another fireball in response.

Fire did little more than annoy the creatures. The young sorceress cursed under her breath as she watched their movements. She shot a lightning arc from her left hand, striking two of the creatures. They withered in agony, their wails echoing in the tunnel. "Lightning magic. They're weak to lightning magic," Azura whispered as she recounted the texts she had read in Arcanist's tower.

"Got an idea?" Warren asked as he began casting some form of dark magic.

"Yeah, I think they're called abyssal guardians. In the books in Arcanist's library, abyssal guardians act as watchers for the desert spirits. They guide those who die in the harsh winds to the afterlife and they rip the souls from those who walk the path of the living. If they touch you with their claws, they will kill you. The only thing that harms them is lightning and weapons that are lightning attuned," the young sorceress responded as she took a step back, narrowly dodging a claw strike.

Warren nodded as he looked to the rest of the group. "Amelia, Camilla, either you have lightning-based weapons?" he asked as he drew his morningstar. He knew he did not have any form of lightning magic in his weapon, but the least he could do was keep the enemies' drawn to him.

Amelia shook her head. "No, my blade is mostly fire and acid based. I'm not much help here," she responded as she loaded another cartridge into her crossbow.

Camilla smirked as she drew her longsword. The blade crackled with yellow sparks as she readied for onslaught. "I've got this," the ranger stated as she steeled herself. The first unusual being shambled forward only to be struck down by a quick series of strikes from the ranger's blade. Chuck growled as he flung a large rock, knocking the next pair of creatures back a few feet, giving the adventurers some breathing room. Azura began casting, her cone of lightning rushing forward and hitting three of the creatures and ending them.

Warren and Amelia kept their shields up and moved to block anytime one of the abyssal guardians tried to claw the group. Camilla darted forward and slashed her way through the various beings until the last one finally dropped. With the tunnels clear, the group continued through the path they had chosen, trying to make their way into the desert. Soon they were greeted with the blistering heat and the harsh winds of the desert environment. Camilla wasted no time as she began casting an enduring spell on everyone, ensuring they would not be hampered too much by the desert's heat.

"Now to find Waray," Warren noted as they looked around. It was bleak. Sand for miles and high above was the scorching sun. They wandered aimlessly for a bit, trying to find the village they were looking for.

"This way. Follow me," a voice drew the ranger's attention.

Camilla looked around; she heard the voice again. It came from the west, somehow the voice seemed familiar, but she could not place it. Without another word, the ranger took off for the western area of the desert.

"Camilla!" the others called as they saw her head off on her own. They exchanged glances but soon followed her. Over several sand dunes and through a raging sandstorm, they followed the ranger.

"Where're you—" Warren began before stopping in mid-sentence. At the base of one of the dunes was a small ruined village. He blinked a few times then looked at the ranger. "How did you know it was here?" he asked, confused as to how they had found the village.

Camilla shook her head. "I didn't. I heard a voice calling to me from here. I followed it, and here we are," she noted as she looked at the village.

They made their way down the dune and towards the village. It was in shambles and mostly buried by the sand but a village nonetheless. Amelia brushed some sand clear of the sign outside the village and looked it over. "Waray Village, last stop before you reach the edge of the world," the paladin stated as she read the sign. "Edge of the world? They make it sound like that's all there is to the land."

"Perhaps at one point in time that was the case," Azura noted as she looked around. On all sides of Waray there was nothing but sand. The people that had once called this village home, had to have been tough to survive in these conditions.

Warren and Chuck were already searching for anything that resembled a stone bathed in ebony light. As they searched the few homes and other structures that remained above the endless sands, they found little more than bones and other remains. "They died horrific deaths," Warren noted as he indicated the position of the bodies.

Many looked like they had been pulled apart or ground to dust. The few that were more intact, were missing teeth and had severely broken limbs. Azura shook her head seeing all the death. "What do you suppose did this?" she asked, to no one specifically.

"One of the generals," Amelia chimed in as she looked over some of the more badly damaged remains. She recalled each of the generals they had fought up to this point. There were the pair from Forlorn Keep; both were strong, but at least one of them was honorable. Then there was the one who slaughtered the people of the quiet fishing village and turned himself into a monster to fight them. And the most recent one was the one who blocked their path back to Arcanist's tower. "They're ruthlessly enough and aggressive to a fault, I have no doubts they did this," she added as she looked over a series of neck bones. They had deep scratches. Something that was not human made such. And was likely whatever the next general they were to fight.

"What do you make of those?" Warren asked, noticing how focused Amelia was.

"These gashes were either made by claws, I'd wager a wolf, maybe a bear. Or by large fangs, could be a vampire, wolf or bear. This separated from the rest of Alibi, I don't think we're looking at a bear or wolf though. Between the heat and environment, it's unlikely," she commented.

"Chuck not think vampire," the barbarian responded as he pointed at the harsh sun beating down.

"Quite honestly, Warren, I haven't the slightest clue what we're dealing with," Amelia admitted as she looked around.

Camilla looked over the remains and studied them for a bit. She sniffed at the damaged bones and felt the various breaks and cracks. "Large reptile of sorts. I'd wager we're dealing with either a lizard person or a demi dragon," she stated as she indicated a claw wound in a ribcage.

"Let's find this virtue stone and get out of here," Warren said as he went back to looking for the ebony stone.

Chuck, Amelia and Azura nodded in agreement as they left the crumbling structure and returned to searching for the stone. Camilla followed them outside, her eyes looking around the environment. *"Have I been here before?"* she thought as she studied the layout of the town. It was oddly similar to one she had seen in her dreams. But were they dreams of the future or the past?

The man walked into the village. Behind him was a young woman clad in blue. He wore blue armor made from the scales of a blue dragon. The two made their way to the town hall, where they requested a meeting with the village leader. A short stocky man greeted them; his gray mustache was clean and well kept.

"Mayor Iducan, we've cleared out the tunnels, as requested," the man stated as he looked at the short man.

"Very good. I trust those creatures won't be bothering anyone," he began.

"Actually, Mayor Iducan, those creatures were no threat. Abyssal guardians, disgusting as they might appear, are harmless so long as their territory is left alone," the young woman stated.

"Watch your tongue, wench. Speak out of turn and my guards will make certain you never speak again," Mayor Iducan stated.

The man stepped forward; his hands grasped the mayor's collar as he hefted the man up a few feet. "And you'd best watch what you say to my partner. Next rude comment from your potbellied figure, and I'll feed you to those creatures," the man threatened before dropping the mayor and leaving.

Night soon came and the pair of travelers had set up camp in the desert. "You didn't need to do that, Ashe," the woman said as she looked to the sky.

"He had no right to speak to you that way, Celica. And I'll not tolerate such. You're my partner, my most trusted friend," Ashe stated as he cleaned his weapons. He shook his head. "Sorry the people of Waray are rude. I guess it comes with living in the middle of nowhere."

Camilla shook her head as the memory faded. Waray. She knew the name was familiar, she had seen this place in her waking dreams. It was the village that Ashe and Celica were constantly using to resupply. She walked toward where the town hall would have been and began digging. "If this virtue stone is still here, I'll bet it was kept in town hall," she called to the others as she dug.

Soon everyone was digging, trying to uncover the town hall. Warren managed to dig down to a window and forced it open. "Hey guys, over here!" he called as he dug a little deeper. Warren slowly slid through the open window and landed inside the remains of town hall. One by one the rest of the group made their way through the window and into the small office-like room. "Looks like the mayor's office, if this town had a mayor," Warren noted as he began going through various artifacts and books throughout the room.

Amelia and Camilla made their way further into the town hall, deciding to check out a different room. The paladin glanced at the ranger, noticing she was acting more distant than normal. She wanted to ask, wanted to say something but also knew the ranger was likely going through another rough patch and needed her *me time*. "I've been here before," Camilla whispered. She heard the paladin pause her search and hum questioningly. "Waray. I've been here before. Or at least seen it in my waking dreams. I can't explain it though," the ranger explained as she glanced at the paladin.

"You said you heard a voice guiding us this way." Amelia began, trying to understand what was going on within the ranger's head.

"Yes, his voice was familiar, also from my waking dreams. At first I was not certain, but the more I reflect on such, there's no doubt, it was Ashe," Camilla reasoned as she looked at the floor. She knew the paladin was wanting to ask the obvious question, *who's Ashe*, but how was she supposed to answer. Camilla paused thinking over her words. "Ashe was a half human, half elf, I think, and he served some deity. I think he was a paladin, like you. But his preferred weapon was a longsword, no shield. He wore armor that looked like it was made from the scales of a blue dragon," she explained.

"So, this Ashe, is he a friend? Someone we can trust?" Amelia asked.

Camilla nodded. "I believe so. In the waking dreams, he's always polite and kind, he's always trying to help others," she added. The ranger shook her head before looking around. "We should find the virtue stone and move on, no telling what lies ahead." She was quick to change the subject.

Down the hallways were Chuck, Azura and Warren. The trio had started investigating another room in hopes of finding the virtue stone. "He said it glowed with an ebony light. What sort of stone is that dark?" Azura pondered as they searched.

"An obsidian," Warren noted as he paused. He moved several books aside, revealing a small box on the shelf. "Maybe?" he questioned as he opened the lid of the box. Inside was a small stone, black as night but emanated an ebony glow. "Found it!" the lich cheered as he carefully removed the obsidian from the box.

Upon hearing the lich's cheers, the group met up in the room, each relieved to have found the virtue stone. "Well, we found the stone, but we're no closer to finding the next legendary weapon," Amelia noted as they made their way back to the window and began climbing out.

"Adventurers, can you hear me?"

Warren grabbed the communication stone he had and held it out for the entire group to hear. "We can hear you, Arcanist. What news do you have?" the lich asked as he looked everyone over.

"It's about a sudden distortion, not far from where you currently are. About five hundred meters north from you is a tear in the distortion. I believe you'll find the last memory tomb there, and with it, Echoes," Arcanist stated. He paused before continuing. "There's more. From what I can tell, Time Eater only has a handful of realms left to destroy by smashing them into Alibi.

Adventurers, we've little over a month to claim Echoes, find Time Eater's lair and kill the corrupted being."

"Thank you, Arcanist," Warren said before sliding the stone into his pocket. He turned to look everyone over, each was nodding. "Everyone ready?" he asked as they looked north.

"Let's find this last tomb and get the final legendary weapon. We're so close to saving the world," Azura stated.

"There's something else you five should know," Arcanist stated. The group paused and listened intently. "It's about Time Eater and why the five of you were the heroes summoned. Four of you have fought and defeated a variant of Time Eater. The fifth from what I can find, it somehow connected to Time Eater's past."

"How is that possible? What do mean we've fought and defeated Time Eater before?" Amelia questioned as she arched an eyebrow.

"I can't be certain. But my summon locked onto four heroes who had defeated a weaker version of Time Eater. And the fifth hero is somehow connected to Time Eater's past," Arcanist stated. He was about to say something else, but the communication stone began to blur and his voice was lost.

"We'll worry about that later. Come on, we've a memory tomb to finish," Camilla said as she headed out for the location they were told about. Everyone else nodded before heading toward the location they had been told about.

Chapter 22 - Memories Lost To Time

Soon the adventurers found themselves looking into a cavern. They had followed Arcanist's directions, and it led them to a cavern rather than a ripple like they expected. Camilla went into the cavern; she could hear the other four follow a little way behind her. Along the cavern walls were paintings, each depicted a point in time. There was a drawing of a large blue winged reptile, a dragon, following that one was the reptile with a human. As they walked deeper into the cavern, the paintings became more telling of their story. The man was killed. The dragon wept. Then there was a painting of a dark mist communing with the dragon.

The man was brought back to the living. But the paintings of the dragon now had a black mist around it. The man killed the dragon. Then he wept. A being depicted in a white light was shown speaking with the man. The dragon was no longer in the paintings. The man now carried a baby.

"What is this?" Warren asked as he looked at the paintings.

Camilla winced, clutching her head as she looked at the paintings. She felt something inside of her burning, demanding to be set free. The ranger dropped to her knees, still clutching her head. She was breathing heavily as she managed to weakly look up at the depictions on the walls. "It's a story. The blue dragon was alone. Then met that man. Together they had many adventures and helped others. Eventually the man was killed in battle. Saddened by the loss, the dragon wept and prayed to any deity to bring back her friend. A deity answered, but not the one she hoped would answer." The ranger paused, taking deep breaths as she tried to focus.

"The god of death, of the underworld, Null, answered her prayers. He brought the man back in exchange for the dragon's soul," a voice stated, causing the group to look around. They were the only five presents but the voice did not belong to any of them. "The dragon agreed and unfortunately became a puppet for Null to control. He used her to destroy villages, slaughter the innocent. Eventually the man had to kill the very friend who gave their soul for him. Upon the dragon's death, the man prayed for five days and five nights. His deity, Patrokolos, appeared before him and granted a miracle."

Camilla looked at the paintings. "Patrokolos revived the dragon but as a human baby," she muttered as she winced again.

"And made the man swear he would raise her. Patrokolos said, if raised true and pure her soul will eventually return as will her memories. But if she grows up with malice in her heart, she will become a puppet to Null once more and purge all of Kardax into chaos," the voice stated before a ghost materialized before the group.

He was about Camilla's height, clad in blue dragon scale armor, on his waist was a belt that held a sword sheath but no blade. His eyes were light blue, and his silver-gray hair was cut short but was rather untidy. His left arm was in a sling, he wore gray pants and brown boots, draped over his shoulders was a light blue cape. And around his neck he wore an amulet that depicted the holy symbol of Patrokolos, a radiant sun.

"You're Ashe. The one I keep seeing in my waking dreams," Camilla finally said as she stared at the man.

"It's been far too long, Celica. I'm glad you've stayed true and haven't lost sight of your path," Ashe stated as he helped Camilla to her feet.

"I think you have her mistaken. Her name is Camilla Windstride," Amelia said as she moved forward, helping to steady the ranger.

"I would recognize Celica anywhere. Even if she wears the hunter's green instead of the noble blue. And even if she has lavender hair instead of the fiery red she once had," Ashe said with a smile. He shook his head before turning to look at the entire group. "I am Ashe Valence, paladin of Patrokolos. And I'm the spirit guide for this area. Be not afraid, I mean no harm to any of you. I wish to thank you four, thank you for everything you've done for Celica. For keeping her heart from becoming corrupted," he added before bowing to the group.

"You say my name is Celica, and yet I don't remember. Why?" Camilla questioned as she slowly released the grip she had on her head.

"What do you mean by keeping her heart from becoming corrupted?" Warren added as he looked Ashe up and down.

Ashe smiled at the group, it was a warm and friendly act, holding no malicious intent within it. "To answer your question, Celica, when Patrokolos brought you back to the realm of the living, he told me that you would not remember your past. That those memories were tied to your soul which Null possessed. The only way for you to recover your memories of that past is to recover your soul." He paused as he ran his right hand through his silver hair. "Though it seems you've been able to recall some fragments of your past. The waking dreams, as you call them, they are memories of moments from your past."

The ghostly figure turned his attention to Warren. "As for your question, in the world that Celica is from, that version of Kardax, her heart was on the verge of being corrupted. The betrayal from House Vaughan, followed by years in the wilds, betrayal of the only group she knew and even her animal companion abandoning her." He paused as he gave a saddened look. "It was all too much, even if you weren't aware, Celica, your heart was becoming corrupted. And if it had, Null would have been able to assume control over you again," Ashe added.

"If I meant so much to you, then why weren't you there? Why was I in Lowestoft orphanage?" Camilla asked, barely managing the words.

Ashe's expression reflected a somber nature as he looked at the ranger. "I wanted to be there for you. Truly I did. Unfortunately, word got out that I was among the living again and King Hubert summoned me away to aid his army with turning the tide against a cult group who sought to bring back their master from a thousand-year slumber." Ashe paused as he wiped tears from his eyes. It took the ghostly figure a moment to collect himself. "As such, I entrusted your care to the people of Lowestoft. I knew they worshipped Patrokolos and thought it was the best course of action. I intended to return but fate had other plans. We had pressed the cultist back, victory was at hand, or so we thought. From the sky, black lightning rained down and wiped out half the army. Nine generals made their move and slaughtered everyone. I was killed in that battle. My greatest regret was not being able to return to Lowestoft to stay true to my promise to you."

Camilla shook her head as she looked further down the cavern. "If this is a memory tomb, then we should push onward."

"You sure you're going to be alright?" Azura asked as she approached the ranger.

Camilla nodded. "Course I'll be alright. We have a mission: get the last legendary weapon, find the last two virtue stones and defeat Time Eater," she stated, her voice unwavering.

Ashe nodded as he began to float deeper into the cavern. "This way, heroes of the Outrealms," he said as he led the group through the maze-like labyrinth of tunnels within the cavern. As they walked, the group was looking at all the paintings that were on the walls. Not just paintings, some text was scribed in a language that they struggled to read.

"It's ancient dragon," Camilla stated as she noticed the group's confusion of the words. She smiled slightly as she continued forward. "Celica kept an ongoing journal of events that happened in the desert. From things as mundane as the winds had a different current to them. To as important as a new traveler entering the desert. I'm surprised a dragon would have done such."

"Especially a blue dragon," Warren noted.

"What do you mean by that?" Camilla asked as she glanced over her shoulder at the lich.

"I've only encountered one blue dragon, and it was a world ending monster. It thought little of humanoids or of any being that was not in its brood," he clarified.

Azura shook her head. "Only blue dragon I've fought was an undead one that served Narcian. It didn't act or think freely, it was just a puppet to him."

Chuck growled. "Chuck fight blue dragon. It kill clan. Chuck and Gurk travel, we kill dragon. Avenge clan," the barbarian snarled.

Amelia came to a stop. "What did Arcanist say earlier?" she asked, causing everyone to come to a stop. Warren and Azura looked at one another then to the paladin. Chuck tilted his head before growling.

"Four of us have fought a variant of Time Eater and prevailed. The fifth is somehow connected to Time Eater's past," Camilla stated as she looked over her shoulder at the others. "Amelia, what happened in your realm?"

"You remember the war of the chalice I mentioned?" the paladin began. Everyone nodded slowly hearing the paladin's words. "It was started by a blue dragon. The dragon and its rival, a brass dragon, were seeking the chalice in order to use it to better their clutches." She paused before shaking her head. "The brass was killed by Balthazar; he had been promised great wealth by the blue dragon. And shortly after, the blue dragon used some form of illusion magic on me. I killed Balthazar believing he was someone else. Eventually the blue dragon was slain by Balthazar's brother and I but in its dying breath, the dragon cursed the land. Eventually no crops would grow. And before long everyone died. Only those who had been tainted by the dragon's magic, used by the beast in some fashion, survived," she finished.

Camilla nodded slowly. "Time Eater's a blue dragon. Four of us have fought and prevailed against Time Eater before. Warren, Azura, Chuck and Amelia, all of you have fought a blue dragon. And one of us is connected to Time Eater's past. I've never fought a blue dragon, so somehow I'm connected to Time Eater's past," the ranger concluded.

"If you're this blue dragon, Celica, then perhaps you're a sibling to Time Eater," Azura reasoned as she tried thinking of possibilities.

"Chuck think that likely. Chuck know dragon have many eggs."

"Come on, we need to find Echoes and move on," Camilla stated as she moved to continue down the tunnel. In the back of her mind, she could not shake the feeling that something was very wrong. She wanted to believe Azura's theory, but something still felt off.

"Here we are," Ashe stated as they reached a massive door. "Inside this room, you'll have to battle those from your past. I know not who or what you'll face off against. I wish you the best of luck, Celica," he stated as he hovered in front of the door.

Camilla put her hand to the door, causing it to open with no effort. The five entered the room and looked around. Each was ready to do battle, weapons drawn and all expecting a massive battle. The ranger took a deep breath before pulling her hood over her head, going invisible as she did so. She continued ahead, the group on edge but following a safe distance behind her.

A rush of magic collided with Amelia, Warren, Chuck and Azura. Each shook violently before collapsing. "I can't move my legs or arms," Azura whispered.

"Me either," Warren responded.

Amelia's eyes looked around trying to gauge where the attack had come from. "Invisible attackers?" she muttered as she saw the room appeared empty. "Camilla, wherever you are, be careful," she whispered.

Camilla had heard the attack hit the others but failed to see where it had come from. She looked around, trying to find the source. Her heart was racing as she readied for whatever fight was to come. Rushing from one side of the room were a half orc-half human barbarian, a feral wolf and a human fist fighter. "Thrall, Flannel and Van," Camilla said under her breath as she moved to engage them in a fight. She parried their attacks as she kept her eyes open for more attackers. On cue a massive fireball was sent in her direction. Camilla barely had a chance to roll to the side. "Kanna and Leila," she noted, seeing the human necromancer and the colossal scorpion.

The ranger bobbed and weaved between the onslaught of attacks as she tried to land any attacks she could. Warren glanced at Azura. "Azura, can you still cast magic?" he asked as he formed a plan.

"Yeah, but my spells are limited without the hand gestures to accompany them," the sorceress responded.

"That's fine, I'm sure any spells you can manage will be helpful," Warren noted as he looked ahead. He smirked as he watched the fight. "If you can cast even one fireball, I can add to it and we can give Camilla some support," he added. Azura followed Warren's gaze as they studied the ongoing fight. "I'm going to use slippery floor, see if I can get that scorpion off balance. Add your fireball, and we might be able to keep the caster distracted enough that Camilla can deal with the three melee fighters," he whispered.

"Got it," Azura replied as she focused where Warren was looking. She saw the floor under the scorpion suddenly become slick as the massive vermin struggled to keep its footing. She quickly followed up with her fireball, setting fire to the floor around the scorpion.

The scorpion hissed as it struggled to move on the slick, fire engulfed floor. Its unpredictable movements made it difficult for the caster on its back to use their magic. Camilla smirked, pressing the small advantage her allies had given her. With a rapid flurry of strikes, the barbarian, fist fighter and wolf dropped. Before she could rush the scorpion, a lightning blast shot at the ranger. "Dragom," she muttered as she spotted the undead wizard. Dragom was an undead half elf-half human wizard. He wore black robes with hints of green accents. In his hand was a wooden quarterstaff.

Then a rapier slash caught her attention as she was forced to block the strike with her shortsword. "Gemma," she snarled upon seeing the demonic looking humanoid. Gemma looked human, but the horns protruding from her head and the thin tail from her backside would cause anyone to do a double take. Her skin was also a dull red in color, clad in black and dark blue attire, she was equipped to stealth. A moonbeam shot forward, striking the ranger and knocking her back a few feet. "Lun," she growled as she got her feet under her. Lun had purple skin and long flowing silver hair. She wore thick silver full plate armor, a bastard sword in her hands and a massive shield with a lion's face at the center floated next to her. Camilla dropped her shortsword while sheathing her longsword and drew her longbow. The ranger quickly nocked three arrows and fired at the dark elf.

The first arrow broke through part of the dark elf's armor, leaving the caster's chest exposed. The second and third arrows hit their marks, both exploding once they were in the dark elf's flesh. There was a horrid shriek as the dark elf's lifeless body slumped to the ground. Camilla turned and shot at the necromancer before tumbling away from the demonic humanoid. Kanna, the scorpion, raised her pincers, blocking the arrows from striking the necromancer. Leila, the necromancer, began casting, her spell aimed at the dark elf's lifeless form.

Azura noticed and muttered a spell under her breath. A massive storm cloud appeared over the dark elf's corpse and rained down fire, lightning, acid, ice and soundwaves. When it cleared, the body had been fully destroyed with nothing that could be resurrected. The rapier wielding rogue snarled as she moved toward the sorceress. Warren called out his next spell, creating a barrier around the immobile group of four. It was resilient but he knew even such would break if it took too much damage.

Camilla pressed her attacks on the necromancer, her arrows firing in rapid succession from the bowstring. "I just need one to land," she muttered as she kept firing arrow after arrow. She grimaced as a lightning blast from the undead wizard hit her and sent her tumbling.

"Dammit all. There has to be a way we can help." Amelia cursed as she tried to move again. Chuck growled in rage as he tried to move but both he and the paladin were completely helpless.

Azura glanced at Warren. "I've got one more hell storm and two fireballs left before I'm out of spells I can cast without hand gestures."

"That's ok, target the scorpion with hell storm. I'm using all my magic to keep this barrier active. We need to bring down that scorpion and necromancer. If she gets one spell off, then one of the ones Camilla's already killed will be up and moving again," Warren noted as he watched the rogue attack the barrier.

Azura looked toward the scorpion. She took a deep breath and began casting her hell storm spell, aiming it at the scorpion and necromancer. She heard the undead wizard unleash another spell, keeping Camilla tripped up.

"Even invisible and all their attacks are landing on Camilla. What magic are they using to do such?" Amelia snarled as she tried to will herself to move again.

Warren looked around. "Their cleric or wizard probably has a spell that allows them to see the unseen. Only explanation I have."

Camilla rolled under the next lightning spell before shooting three arrows at the undead wizard. Each hit their mark and made him fully dead. She turned her attention to the scorpion and necromancer. The hell storm rained down, causing the scorpion to wail in agony as it tried to move. The necromancer staggered, leaving herself open to attack. Camilla shot two arrows, ending the necromancer. She shouldered her longbow and drew her longsword again. The blade began to glow a faint red as she rushed forward, plunging the blade into the rogue's back. "Leave my friends alone," the ranger snarled as she pulled the demonic human away from the barrier.

"Funny, that word coming from you. Friends. You wouldn't know what those are even if you had such." The rogue laughed as she thrusted her rapier forward.

Camilla pulled her longsword back, blocking the strike before slashing out and splitting the rogue in two. She turned her attention to the scorpion that was struggling to move. No words were said as she sprinted across the room and plunged the blade through the scorpion's skull, ending it.

Once the scorpion had been slain, the others found they could move again. "Camilla!" Amelia called as she rushed the ranger's side. Camilla swayed before being steadied by the paladin. "Don't worry, we've got ya," she said as she supported the ranger. The paladin moved in a way that the ranger's free arm was across her shoulder, her own right arm was wrapped around the ranger, keeping her stand.

Warren picked up the shortsword that had been dropped and slid it into the sheath on the ranger's belt. "Who were they?" he asked as he looked around the room.

"My old group, the ones I told you about," Camilla said, her voice reflecting her fatigue. She shook her head as she looked around. "There's one missing though. And he's probably the most dangerous of them."

As if summoned by the words, the group heard someone giving a slow rhythmic clap as they approached. Standing before them was a half reptilian half human, clad in gold armor. He had an impressive looking longsword hanging from his belt and an equally impressive steel shield on his right arm. Around his shoulders was a red cape. Despite his mostly reptilian appearance, he had noticeable fiery red hair and piercing blue eyes. "Impressive display, Camilla. I never thought you'd ever stop being the bow slinging coward," he stated as he came to a stop.

"Been a long time, Roy," Camilla responded as she pulled free from Amelia. The ranger's yellow eyes sized up the gold armored figure. "You really want to fight, five on one?"

"No, that would prove nothing. One on one, you and me." Roy's voice was husky, feral sounding even. He drew his blade in his left hand, ready for battle.

Camilla nodded as she drew her shortsword with her left hand, while tightening the grip her right hand held on her longsword. "I agree to those terms," she responded. Amelia, Azura, Warren and Chuck disagreed with such, but they moved to the side.

Roy took a step forward before charging the ranger. Camilla met his charge with one of her own. She had fought Roy many times in Kardax, each was a sparring match, and every time he would easily defeat her by using his sheer power to force her into submission. She was determined to make this fight end differently. There was too much riding on this fight for her to lose.

The half reptilian blocked her attacks with his shield then slashed out with his longsword. The blade sent a freezing sensation through the ranger as ice quickly coated parts of her body. He pressed his advantage and continued to attack with a ferocity that the group had never seen before. "Whatever history they have, there's a lot of hatred within such," Warren noted as he watched how the two fought.

"How do you mean?" Azura asked.

"That Roy fellow, his attacks are pure aggression, there's no thought or sense in them. Pure animalistic savagery. And Camilla's fighting more recklessly than I've seen. Something about this Roy riles up Camilla's emotions and she's letting those cloud her judgment," the lich explained as they watched the fight.

Camilla took a step back, her eyes never leaving Roy. "What's wrong? Realizing you can't beat me? You never could," Roy snarled as he rushed forward again.

Camilla sprinted forward, meeting the reptilian head on. She saw him move his shield to block her assault and smirked. Her shortsword pressed into the bottom of the shield as she slid low. "What!" Roy growled as he felt his shield getting pushed upward.

The ranger thrusted her longsword forward, tearing a hole in the gold armor. She rolled backwards, narrowly avoiding a slash from the longsword her opponent held. Roy snarled, his blue eyes turning a deep crimson as he lunged forward. His growls echoed as spittle flew from his fanged maw. "I've killed stronger foes. I'll devour you as I did them!" His voice was more gnarled and feral sounding than before.

Camilla had never fought this side of the reptilian before, this was an entirely new side to him. She ducked back and rolled under his attacks as she looked for any opening. Despite the sudden feral behavior, Roy was still possessing enough intellect to use his shield and longsword as a skilled fighter. The ranger managed to close the distance. She shifted the grip on her blades, managing to rip the shield away from the reptilian's grip. His blade ignited with fire as he struck her with four hits in rapid succession.

The ranger winced seeing the burns she had received from the attack. She needed to end this now. Rushing forward, Camilla used her shortsword to block the reptilian's attack and disarm him. Her longsword began glowing a deep blue as yellow lightning began dancing along the blade. She slashed out with a fierce five strikes, completely destroying the reptilian's armor.

Roy roared, causing the other four to cover their ears from the horrific sound. The ring on his left ring finger began glowing as he doubled over in pain. "So be it. If I have to unleash the beast, then so be it!" he roared as his body spasmed. His size multiplied; his impressive seven-foot figure had grown to a horrifying seventy-foot monster. His reptile features were more pronounced, what little human he had in appearance was completely gone. His crimson eyes focused on the ranger as he let out a blood curdling roar.

Camilla backflipped, avoiding the jaws of the monstrous reptilian being. She took a deep breath as she tried to find a weak point. She had never seen Roy do this before. The sight alone frightened her, but she had to stay focused. He slashed out with his massive claws, trying to rip the ranger apart. She rolled and tumbled avoiding each attack but knew at some point she was going to need to fight back. Her longsword was still glowing a deep blue and had lightning magic covering it. Camilla nodded as she rushed forward, her blade leaving deep gashes in the monstrous reptile's legs.

He howled in pain as he tried stomping her but as with before she easily avoided the attacks. The ranger leapt backwards getting some distance as she figured out her next course of action. "Dio ev ack nercan. Evon lu nersian," she muttered as she casted two spells on herself. Roy reared back, flames igniting within his jaws. He lurched forward, flames spewing forth in a massive cone of flames. Camilla tumbled to the side then sprinted at the massive reptile, she saw him starting to recover from his own attack. The ranger leapt up, getting above the monster's head and came down with a slash, her blade glowing even brighter as she struck his head.

Camilla landed nimbly on her feet and flicked her longsword, sending blood to the side. Behind her, she heard the bloodied gurgles of the monster as he collapsed. All was quiet as the monstrous reptile dissolved. Camilla breathed a sigh of relief before turning to look at the others. "Well, that's all of them," she said softly as she walked over to them.

"How deep was the hatred between you and him?" Warren asked as he indicated where the monstrous reptile had collapsed.

"It doesn't matter," Camilla replied as she walked to the far side of the chamber. She pushed open the door and walked through. The rest of the group followed behind.

In the center of the much smaller room was a stone pedestal where a weapon had once been. Chuck growled as he looked around. "Chuck want know where weapon! Why not here?" the barbarian roared.

"We came all this way for nothing?" Azura questioned as she looked around.

Warren shook his head. "That can't be the case. Maybe there's an illusion in effect," he reasoned.

"I am Echoes, fated longsword forged by Ashe Valence," a voice stated. Everyone looked around again, trying to find the source.

Amelia looked at the longsword in Camilla's hand and pointed. "Camilla, your longsword. It's still aglow with that blue light."

Camilla raised her blade and looked it over. "I am the last of the legendary weapons you seek. However, I shall not grant you my power," the voice came from the longsword.

"Why not! We cleared your trail, didn't we?" Azura questioned looking at the blade.

"Yes, you may have defeated the memory tomb, but in your current state, you cannot wield my power," the longsword spoke as Camilla looked it over. "You, reborn under the ashen moon, you are the one I have deemed worthy of me and yet you are not able to use me to the fullest. Recover the lost ties, then I will grant you my power," the blade stated before the glow stopped.

"Lost ties?" Warren questioned as he looked around. "What does it mean, recover the lost ties?"

"My memories. My soul. I need to recover those before Echoes will grant me it's power," Camilla stated as she sheathed the blade on her belt. She turned to the side, seeing the ghostly figure of Ashe appear. "Think you can guide me one more time, Ashe?" she asked.

"Your soul and by extension, your memories, are kept by the god of the underworld, Null. In order to recover them, you'll need to travel to the World Beneath. I can create a path to the World Beneath, but after doing such, I will cease to exist," Ashe stated as he hovered to the pedestal.

"There must be another way," Camilla noted as she felt tears in her eyes.

Ashe smiled seeing such. "You never cried before. I'm honored that your first tears would be for me. Thank you, Celica, for everything," he said before touching the pedestal. A portal opened up, revealing a staircase leading down. "This will take you to the World Beneath. What you face there will make the horrors you've seen here look like pleasant dreams. I wish you five the best of luck," he added, his body slowly fading.

"Ashe…" Camilla began as she watched the ghostly figure fading.

The silver haired paladin smiled at the ranger, his blue eyes reflecting his own sorrows. "May we meet again, Celica. Know this, my final thoughts… both here and back in Kardax, were of you. Good-bye, my friend." His words were barely a whisper as he completely faded away, leaving the five adventurers.

Camilla looked over her shoulder at the others. "I'm not asking you four to join me. But I have to go down there. I have to remember; it's the only way Echoes will grant me its power." She paused seeing the uncertain looks on some of their faces. "I'll go alone if I must."

"You're not alone." Amelia stepped forward. "No matter what's to come, or who you were, I'm with you. I swore I'd help you, so let's get to it."

Chuck let out a war cry as he stepped forward. "Chuck want fight! If there fight, Chuck join!" the barbarian cheered.

Warren shook his head as he stepped forward. "You saved my life more than once. I'm still in your debt. Guess you can string me along again," he jested as he looked at the ranger.

Azura was still on edge but nodded as she stepped forward. "Guess we're all in this together. Besides, we need Echoes if we're to have all five legendary weapons," she spoke up.

"Then it's settled, to the World Beneath," Amelia stated as she began down the stairs. Camilla gave a soft smile as she followed the paladin. Chuck and Warren were next and Azura brought up the rear.

Chapter 23 - The World Beneath

They reached the bottom of the stairs Ashe had created to guide them. Before them was a massive wall of flames with a small area not covered in flames. Camilla hesitated; she swallowed them lump in her throat as her nervousness became clear. She felt someone put a hand on her left shoulder and turned to see Amelia standing beside her. "It's alright, Camilla, we're all here to see this through," she stated giving the ranger a warm smile.

"What if we learn the truth? And what if I am a blue dragon? What if I'm no better than the monsters you four have fought and defeated?" Camilla responded as she rubbed her right arm awkwardly. She removed the glove she wore on her right hand, revealing a mark on hand. It was a blue compass like branding with a yellow star at the center. Despite her hands being covered in blue scales, the compass pattern was visible. "I wondered why I was born with this marking. And now, well, I guess now I'll know the truth. But what if this truth is worse than not knowing?"

"Camilla," The ranger looked up, meeting the paladin's gaze. "No matter what we learn, no matter who you were in your past, you are still you. You are Camilla Windstride, nothing less," Amelia responded as she held her gaze on the ranger.

The ranger nodded before looking at the flames and putting her glove back on. "Right. Thanks, Amelia," she said before stepping up to the flames.

A massive three headed lion stood, looking down upon the adventurers. "Who dares demand entrance to the World Beneath!" his central head roared.

"My name is Cami—Celica and I seek an audience with your master Null," the ranger stated as she watched the lion.

He arched an eyebrow, looking her over before turning his gaze to the remainder of the adventurers. "Only those who lack souls may enter. There are three who may enter the realm of the dead. Amelia Lucia, heir of Highever and soulless vampiric abomination, you may pass. Warren Couseland, king of Frothcrest and undead abomination kept in existence by magic, you may enter. Celica the thunderstriker, watchful guard of the desert wastelands and dragon without memories, you may pass. The other two must wait here." The lion's left mounted head snarled as the beast sat upon his haunches.

Warren turned to Azura and Chuck. "We'll be back, don't worry," he said before stepping up to where the ranger and Amelia waited.

"Pass through the sea of flames and emerge in the World Beneath, the realm of the dead," the lion's right head growled as he eyed the trio.

The ranger nodded as she stepped forward, passing through the flames with no adverse effects. Amelia and Warren exchanged glances before they walked through the flames. Once they emerged on the other side, the trio saw horrors that they could only dream of seeing. There was a long-charred path that led to a massive castle. It felt cold, even for the two who could not normally feel the cold. Their breath was visible as they studied the land. To the right of the path were several beings, from all species, being tormented by various demonic-like creatures. To the left of the path were several beings from all walks being dropped into the realm and being assigned their tortures.

Warren tried to ignore the cries they heard as they continued. Amelia covered her ears at the continued wails and screams let out by those being tortured. The ranger was either unfazed or did a better job concealing her emotions as they traversed the path. As they continued, several ghouls, ghost-like beings and demonic creatures sprung up from the ground and attacked the group. The ranger drew her longsword and shortsword, slashing her way through the forces that tried to stop them. Amelia's bastard sword cleaved through the enemies as she stayed close to the ranger. Warren drew Ironvice and bludgeoned his way to the ranger's other side.

"Camilla, we're going to be overrun at this rate!" Warren called as he fought through the numerous ghouls and ghost-like beings. He glanced over and saw the paladin slashing her way through several demonic creatures, many were spewing fire breath as they lunged and bit at her thick armor. "Amelia..."

"Keep fighting, Warren, we'll break through and win the day," Amelia responded as she managed to clear a path. "Camilla, go! Warren and I will cover you. You're the one who has to find Null. The one who has to reclaim what was lost," she called to the ranger.

The ranger nodded and took off in a sprint. "Don't either of you go dying while I'm gone! I'll be back soon!" she yelled over her shoulder to the pair that was still in combat.

Warren smirked, shaking his head as he continued fighting with the endless waves of ghouls. "Yeah, ok, just beat Null then get your dragon ass back here!" he shouted back, a slight laugh in his voice.

The ranger slashed through a handful of enemies that got in her way. Her senses had heightened greatly since they arrived. She felt something burning within her chest, something that wanted to be unleashed. Her feet came to a stop when she reached the castle. The doors opened, allowing her entrance into the inner keep. She walked deeper and deeper, looking around constantly trying to figure out what to expect.

"So good of you to return to me, Celica," a large creature stated as he stood from his throne. He had goat legs, a man's torso and arms, but his hands were claws. On his back were a pair of massive bat wings. His head was that of a wolf with two horns jutting out his forehead.

"You must be Null," the ranger said as she lowered her weapons. He stood around twelve feet in height, towering over the ranger.

"As your master, I command you to take your true form. Drive out the intruders," Null ordered as he waved his hand. The ranger winced as she felt a sudden pain in her head. She heard roars echoing in her head, her heartbeat quickened as she tried to focus. Null laughed as he gazed down at the ranger. "Stop trying to fight it. You are mine. Always have been. Now awaken to what you really are and purge the intruders."

The ranger snarled as she dropped both her weapons and clutched her head. She struggled to resist; it was taking everything she had left in her to maintain control. "I'm not your puppet," she growled as her yellow eyes shimmered. Her eyes twitched; her pupils became slit just as they had when fought Uldritch's beast form.

"You dare try to resist me? Pathetic wyrm, I own you!" Null roared as he snapped his fingers. The ranger screamed in pain as she felt something within her starting to be unleashed. She felt as though she was being ripped apart as her body spasmed. The ranger fell to the ground, convulsing in pain as she whimpered. Her skin shredded away being replaced by blue scales. Her bones broke in many spots as they grew and rearranged. Within moments, where the ranger had been laying in pain was now a massive blue dragon. A deafening roar escaped the dragon as it stood on all fours. Its eyes were a deep red, no pupil was visible. Null laughed as he assumed control over the creature. "Go, kill the intruders," he commanded.

Amelia and Warren fought their way to the castle, both feeling the fatigue as they forced the doors open. Warren shoved the doors closed and held them closed as Amelia pushed anything she could against the doors. Both sighed heavily as the ghouls on the other side smashed into the doors, but the large structures did not budge. "Now we find Camilla and help her with Null," Amelia stated as she picked up her bastard sword and tower shield from where she had dropped them.

Warren nodded as he looked around. "Alright, let's get to—"

Before the lich could finish, they heard a loud roar from deeper within the castle. They exchanged glances before heading toward the sound. As they entered the massive throne room, they saw Null sitting on his throne and a massive blue dragon glaring at them. The beast was much larger than the undead blue dragon they had faced in Azura's memory tomb. "What manner of beast is that!" Warren gulped seeing the lightning spark that radiated from the dragon.

Amelia noticed the longsword and shortsword on the ground then looked at the dragon. "Null must've done something to her mind. That's Camilla, I have no doubt of such," she stated as she sheathed her bastard sword and left her tower shield to float.

"Amelia, what're you doing?" Warren called as he saw the paladin approach the dragon.

The paladin showed no fear as she walked. Lightning shot forth as the blue dragon rained down its lightning breath. Amelia winced as she took the attack in its fullest. "Camilla! Return to us! I know you can hear me!" the paladin yelled, trying to reach the ranger's mind.

Null laughed from his throne. "Oh, this is priceless. Reminds me of that worm all those years ago. Yet another paladin. Allow me to answer the question, will she remember you? Celica, kill them!" he commanded.

The blue dragon unleashed another rush of lightning breath aimed for the paladin. Amelia winced, taking the strike once more. She dropped to a knee, the attacks and fatigue catching up to her. "Camilla! Stop! It's me! I know you can hear me!" Amelia yelled. As though responding to the paladin's words, the dragon hesitated and took a step back. "You recognize me! Come on, control yourself!" she called out loudly.

"A… Ame… Amelia…" the dragon managed as it fought Null's control.

"What is this?" Null snarled as he stood and waved his hand, forcing more of his control on the dragon.

There was a roar from the blue dragon before it forced itself back to human form. The ranger breathed heavily as she managed to glare at the god. "I'm still me," she snarled as she stood, her legs shaking a bit. Amelia smiled seeing the ranger regain control over herself.

Null shook his head. "Then as with before, I must put an end to these beings that you seem to have formed ties with," he snarled as he unleashed a spell of pure dark energy.

Warren sprinted forward, bringing up his tower shield to block the attack. "Here, you might need these," he said while handing the ranger her blades.

"Thanks for these," the ranger replied as she took the blades. "I don't have much of a plan. I'm… I'm counting on the two of you to keep me in line," she added before flinching slightly.

Amelia drew her bastard sword before calling her tower shield to herself. "We got this. I know we do," she responded in total confidence. Warren nodded as he held his morningstar at the ready. The three rushed forward, each using their own technique to fight Null.

Null laughed as he blocked their attacks and countered with magic. Each was sent back, and he was already casting before they could recover. Amelia felt her breastplate shatter as the second spell hit. Warren was in a similar situation with most of his armor showing cracks. The ranger looked to her teammates, her temper flaring. Without meaning to, she transformed into the blue dragon again. "Camilla!" Amelia and Warren both called out.

"I'm still me," the dragon responded as she lunged forward, unleashing lightning breath upon Null. He shook off the attack but was met with a fierce series of claw and wing attacks.

"Impressive, you're managing to maintain your present mind," Null mused as he evaded the claw strikes.

The dragon snarled as she spewed her lightning breath. Amelia looked to Warren. "I have an idea. Think you can slow him down? That's our biggest problem is his speed," she asked.

Warren nodded. "Keep him busy for about thirty seconds and I can slow him," the lich answered as he shouldered his morningstar and began casting.

Amelia nodded then rushed forward again. She slashed out with her bastard sword, keeping the deity's attention split between her and the dragon. Null was still evading every attack they threw at him; it was as though they were moving in slow motion. "Warren!" Amelia called, getting impatient with the one-sided battle.

"Almost," Warren muttered. He smirked as he fired off the spell a split second later. Null growled in pain as he was hit by the spell from the lich. The deity attempted to move but found the action was suddenly impossible. "Amelia, Camilla, now!" Warren called as he drew his morningstar.

Amelia's bastard sword flashed a bright violet aura as she unleashed her attack. The dragon shifted back to human form and her longsword erupted with a deep blue glow as she landed her flurry of attacks. Null sneered as he was forced to take the repeated onslaught of attacks. He glowered at the ranger. His might taking hold of her again.

The ranger took a step back, clutching her head. "Not again," she snarled as she tried fighting Null's control.

"Fight back, Camilla! Remember, we're here at your side. We're not leaving you!" Amelia yelled as she slashed out at Null again and again.

"We said we'd help you see this through, but you need to fight and show us, show Echoes your resolve!" Warren added as his morningstar smashed into Null's side.

"Camilla! Hang on! We're coming!"

A loud explosion was heard as part of the wall was destroyed. Warren and Amelia rushed forward, both with their tower shields in hand. Chuck sprinted past them and swung his greataxe knocking Uldritch back a few feet. Azura was the last one into the room and sprinted to the boy. Camilla smiled at the others. "Get Eoden out of here. That's the mission."

"We're not leaving you behind," Amelia responded as she took a defensive position to protect the ranger. She looked at Warren then focused on the attacker. "Warren, get her wounds patched up."

"Already doing such," Warren responded as he healed the wounds that covered the ranger.

Amelia just pulled the ranger into a hug. "Know this, if you ever start having doubts, if you ever need to talk, I'm here for you. No matter what happens." The paladin felt the ranger bury her face against the metal armor before chuckling slightly. "What? Wait, I got you to chuckle. Feeling better?"

"It's funny, really it is," Camilla whispered before looking up to meet Amelia's gaze. "I could've sworn we've had this talk. But our roles were reversed. And now here we are, exactly how we were."

"You are Camilla Windstride, nothing less."

The ranger shook her head, the memories helping her to regain her focus. "I'm. Still. Me!" she snarled as she rushed forward and unleashed a twelve-hit combo with Echoes. The blade was shining brightly; its overpowering blue aura left deep wounds in Null's flesh.

As the ranger turned to attack again, she paused, seeing Null holding up a hand to stop. "I see your resolve is far stronger than it was in the past," Null spoke before smirking at the ranger. "I yield, this time," he added as he managed to drag himself to his throne and sat. With a wave of his right hand, he summoned forth a dark blue wisp. "This is what you came all this way for. Take it, Celica the thunderstriker," he added as the wisp floated to the ranger.

She sheathed her blades then glanced over her shoulder at the two who had travelled with her. Her expression was one of concern. "Don't be worried about the past. Even if you were once an evil dragon, you've more than made up for such in the present," Amelia encouraged.

Warren nodded as he gave the ranger a thumbs up. "Come on, Camilla, reclaim what was lost," he added.

The ranger nodded, closing her eyes as she approached the wisp. The blue wisp flew into the ranger, briefly shrouding her in a blue glow. She saw visions, no, memories of the past she had long since forgotten. Her time with Ashe, her time in the desert living alone. Everything. Slowly she opened her yellow eyes, her pupils were still slit in shape, but she was in her right mind. She drew forth Echoes from her belt, the blade still shrouded in a blue aura. "Yes! Yes! That's it. Now you're worthy of the power I grant you. I am Echoes, the last of the legendary weapons. You have proven your resolve and passed my trials; I shall grant you my power as you continue on your quest," the longsword stated.

"We should head back to Azura and Chuck. Still have a Time Eater to defeat," Warren stated. The three nodded and turned to leave but they barely got a few steps.

"Ranger," Null began. She paused and looked over her shoulder at him. "What is your name?" he asked.

"I am Celica Windstride, ranger of Kardax and guardian of the desert realm," Celica responded as she sheathed Echoes on her belt.

Null nodded. "Safe travels, Celica, Warren and Amelia," he stated. Before snapping his fingers.

The journey back to the flame gate was uneventful. None of the ghouls or other creatures attacked them. Soon they arrived at the flame gate and crossed through as they had before. To Warren and Amelia's surprise the ranger was able to cross through with no issue. "Welcome back!" Azura cheered seeing the trio. She sprinted up and threw her arms around the lich, giving him a hug. Chuck grunted and nodded his head towards them.

Amelia looked to the ranger, a slight look of concern. "So, you want us to call you Celica now?" She asked, trying to gauge how she should be speaking to the dragon.

Celica nodded as she met the paladin's gaze. "Yes, it was my birth name and I think it is only right that I take my true name up once more," she answered with a smile. She chuckled slightly as she looked over her fellow adventurers. "I cannot thank each of you enough for everything. But thank you for all you've taught me and shown me," she added.

"Enough! We still haven't saved the world; we still have a Time Eater to defeat." Warren laughed as he looked to the stairs. "Come on, let's return topside and get back to Arcanist."

Upon returning to the top of the stairs, the group found a bag sitting, waiting for them. Azura tugged at the small tag, reading the text scrawled on it. "For Celica Windstride, may this provide you with some connection to your past," she read aloud.

Celica tilted her head as she opened the bag. Sitting inside was an armor piece that looked like a simple shirt, it looked like they had been forged from the scales of a blue dragon. It looked identical to the armor they had seen Ashe wearing when they crossed paths with him. She took a deep breath, the ghost of a smile on her face as removed her longcoat and shirt, putting the dragon scale shirt on then put her longcoat back on. "Bluemail armor, I remember making this for Ashe many years ago. It does not hinder movement but gives the wearer armor equivalent to wearing metal armor," she explained as the armor adjusted itself to fit her form. "Come on, let's get back to Arcanist," she added before indicating the ripple showing them the outside desert area.

Chapter 24 - Lady Beth

It had been a short two-day journey back to Arcanist's tower, where the group had decided to take a moment to determine their next course of action. "Five legendary weapons and six of the virtue stones. You've done well, heroes," Arcanist stated as he thumbed through his books.

"We had a question for you. You obviously know more than you've let on to us. So, tell us the truth, who or rather what is Time Eater?" Warren questioned as he looked across from the grand table.

Arcanist hesitated slightly but saw the looks the five heroes were giving him. He took a deep breath and nodded. "Alright, you've more than earned the right to know," he murmured as he set the books down. Standing before the adventurers, Arcanist snapped his fingers, magic smoke forming around him. "In a long time, pass, Time Eater was like the five of you. A hero of the Outrealms. They possessed a cunning, trickster even, intellect. They were skill with multiple weapons and had a virtuous heart. Time Eater, along with two other heroes of the Outrealms, fought against the first ruthless ruler of Alibi and prevailed. The other two remained in Alibi while Time Eater returned to their world to save it from darkness." He paused, the magic smoke enacting the tale the brass reptile told.

Warren, Chuck, Azura, Amelia and Celica shared glances at one another before signaling for Arcanist to continue. "The year was 1599 and Time Eater returned to Alibi, but their heart, their soul, had become corrupted. The hero was nothing more than a savage killer who sought more power. Time Eater proceeded to kill the other two heroes then used my summoning tome to call forth alternate versions of their past self and consumed them. In 1601, they attacked the four temples and killed the guardian beasts who protected Alibi. Ace the astral dragon, Brazen the sky phoenix, Rowan the light manticore and Raven the blight griffon were slaughtered as a demonstration of power. That was nearly thirteen hundred years ago. You see, time passes faster here in Alibi than it does in the Outrealms. It was then, I realized, Time Eater was pushing the boundaries of mortal bodies and becoming an evil god." He paused again, the smoke showing the events. After a moment, Arcanist continued. "If my recollection is correct, there were only four version of Time Eater that hadn't been consumed. Amillca the savage, hailing from Frothcrest, Millaca the ruthless, hailing from Cress, Licea the fanged one, born in Highever and finally Acile the cunning, from Kardax."

"The various blue dragons we fought in our pasts," Amelia noted as she heard the names.

Arcanist nodded. "Yes, Time Eater could not consume power from them as they had been slain. I had summoned numerous heroes from the Outrealms, each group failing to get past Uldritch, and the few that did were slain by Time Eater's generals. I knew my options were limited, I had to summon heroes who had prevailed against the variants of Time Eater. What I did not expect was to get Celica Windstride. You've never faced an evil such as Time Eater, and yet my summoning tome brought you here. At first it puzzled me, but you were the only hero I've ever summoned who could match Uldritch in combat, alone, and square off against multiple generals. There was clearly something special about you. I researched that brand on your hand, yes I had seen it when I tended to your wounds many moons ago."

"What did you find?" Celica asked as she watched the brass reptile.

"While you've never fought Time Eater, you are somehow connected to that monster's past. I theorize a sibling or former servant. That I cannot be certain," Arcanist clarified before returning his attention to the group. "Without the remaining two virtue stones, you will not be able to defeat Time Eater," he added.

Celica chuckled as she reached under into one of the chest pockets of her longcoat. "You mean without the last virtue stone," she responded as she withdrew an amethyst.

"Where and when did you get that?" Amelia asked, knowing the ranger always had an answer to her *sticky finger* behavior.

"It was in the bag that contained my bluemail armor. Figured I should hang onto it in case it was the virtue stone we needed." Celica chuckled as she placed the amethyst on the table. She looked across at Arcanist, giving the brass reptile a slight smirk. "So, one virtue stone remains. You going to tell us where it is? Sooner we find it, sooner we can go after Time Eater."

Arcanist gazed back at the ranger, he was uneasy and yet he did not know why. He shook his head. "My sincerest apologies, but I know not where it hides. The last of the virtue stones, the planes pearl, likes to warp between realms and does not stay in one place for too long," he stated as he scratched his chin.

"Didn't you say it was safe?" Warren questioned as he leaned forward slightly.

"Yes, by warping itself, it remains constantly on the move and cannot be taken. That's how it's remained sa—" Arcanist came to an abrupt stop when one of the adventurers slammed their fists down on the table, splintering the wood.

"Chuck, please refrain from such violent acts," Azura said not even looking at the barbarian.

"Not Chuck," the half orc responded as he looked around.

Amelia looked over at where the sound had come from. "Celica…?" she said slowly, seeing the look in the ranger's eyes.

"Let me get this straight! We're this close to everything to defeat Time Eater and because of some misinformation, we're going to fall short? And by falling short, we doom all of Alibi! Am I understanding this correctly!" the ranger snarled as she glowered at the brass reptile.

"Now see here, Celica, I've given you all the inf—"

"No! You've constantly hidden information from us! We've made it this far by relying on each other and taking what little information you've given us and asking the people of Alibi! And by constantly having to ask the people of Alibi, we've put them in danger time and time again!" Celica growled as she stood.

"Celica?" Amelia asked as the ranger began walking towards the door.

"I… I need some air," the ranger responded as she left the tower.

Amelia turned her attention to Warren and the others. "Give her some space, Amelia. She just recovered her soul and memories. Probably still dealing with a lot between such," the lich said as he unrolled the map he had. He looked it over as he withdrew his quill and inkwell. "Right now, we need to focus on trying to pin down where Time Eater's lair is," he stated as he indicated the map.

"Right," Amelia murmured softly as she looked at the map. She pointed to the plains where she had first joined the group. "We know it's not in this location, otherwise we'd have seen it when I joined your group."

"And we know it's not Forlorn Keep, it's a fortress but not the lair," Azura added as she pointed to the province where Forlorn Keep sat.

"Not in Faraway Lake," Chuck grunted as he indicated the lake.

Warren nodded, drawing X symbols where they had ruled out. "And we can cross off Waray and the desert area. And the forest too. As well as Spiral Mountain," he noted as he added a few more X symbols.

"That doesn't leave us much of the map," Azura noted as she watched Warren cross off a few more locations, including Darktowne and Loft Ridge.

Amelia tapped a spot on the map. "What about this place?" she asked.

"That's where we first encountered Uldritch. While it's his castle, it didn't have anything indicating Time Eater," Azura replied with a shudder. She did not want to remember that night. Just seeing the location on the map sent a chill down her spine.

Warren looked over the map again. He was at his wits end trying to figure things out. Chuck tapped a spot on the map to the far west. "We not explore," he noted as he tilted his head.

"You're right, we haven't been there. Arcanist, what can you tell us about this area?" Warren asked, looking at the brass reptile.

Arcanist looked at the map and thought for a moment. "There was once a village there. I believe it was called Time Town. But it hasn't been in existence since the days of the guardian beasts."

"Sounds like somewhere to investigate when Celica returns," Azura said as she looked out a nearby window. She smiled slightly before looking down. "I'm still not used to calling her Celica."

"I doubt any of us are," Amelia chimed in as she leaned back in her chair.

Celica walked through the forest to the side of Arcanist's tower. She was frustrated with the situation. They were close; she knew they could defeat Time Eater if they found the planes pearl. Sighing the ranger sat upon a stump she found and looked down at the longsword on her belt. "We've all the legendary weapons. And we've collected seven of eight virtue stones. I won't let this be the end. We will save Alibi," she murmured to herself as she rested her right hand on the pommel of Echoes.

A magic bolt struck near the stump, causing Celica to dive to the side. She rolled a few feet before coming up in a crouch. A disgusted smirk formed on her face when she saw the attacker. "How many times do I have to kill you?" she snarled as she drew Echoes from the sheath on her belt.

Uldritch touched the ground, reshaping the forest floor into an aggressive vine strike. "Fancy finding you out here, and alone nonetheless." The warlock sneered as he continued his assault.

Celica leapt between the strikes before diving behind a large tree. She took a deep breath, pulling her hood over her head. In an instant, the ranger was now invisible. She heard Uldritch's attack stop and knew he was waiting for her to make a move. Carefully she made her way from the current tree she hid behind to the next one. Her movements were muffled thanks to the magic of her coat. "Where are you, damned ranger!" Uldritch snarled as he looked around, trying to locate her.

She drew Echoes in her right hand, while drawing a shortsword in her left hand. It only took a few brief seconds for her to close the distance on Uldritch. Her attacks were savage as she struck him with ten swift sword slashes, five from each blade. The warlock took a step back but was met with another fierce rush of sword attacks. For the first time in their numerous encounters, Uldritch felt a hint of fear. His ice blue eyes scanned the area trying to find any traces of the ranger. "You've gotten faster. Stronger even. Just like her. Perhaps your time to join her is coming after all." The warlock muttered as he used his magic to flee the scene.

"Coward," Celica muttered as she removed her hood and looked around. She saw a nearby stagecoach with two black horses tied to it. Arching an eyebrow, she moved to investigate. The horses were completely at ease with the ranger's approach, neither nickering nor trying to run. Celica paused as she looked toward the side of the stagecoach. She walked over, both blades still in hand. Throwing open the side door. Celica found herself at a loss for words but smiled.

"Celica!" Amelia called as she walked the outskirts of Arcanist's tower. Night had fallen and there was no sign of the ranger anywhere. The paladin let out an exasperated sigh before returning to the area in front of the tower. She saw the lich, sorceress and barbarian had already returned from their searches.

"She's not near the eastern hills," Warren reported as he looked up from where he was sitting.

"I didn't find any traces of her to the north," Azura added before looking back toward the north.

"Chuck not find thing. It like scary lady vanish," the barbarian grunted.

Amelia shook her head. "This isn't good," she muttered.

The sound of horses approaching quickly caught the group's attention, causing them to look up. Two massive black horses came running from the forest; behind them, they pulled a hickory wood stagecoach. The outside was stained a dark brown, but the wood was easy to see. "What in the—" Warren began as he squinted. The two horses began slowing down before stopping. "Celica!" he called, seeing the ranger, pull at the reins for the horses to stop.

"The heck happened? Where did you get this stagecoach!" Azura questioned as she leapt to her feet.

Celica merely let out a low breath as she climbed down from the driving seat. "You know that warlock Uldritch?" she asked; she knew they were very familiar with the warlock.

"What in Alibi did you do!" Warren questioned as the pieces started to fit together.

"Well, I may have encountered him in the forest. And he attacked me." She paused, her tone reflecting her frustration. "So, I'll admit, I attacked him back," she added as she walked toward the side door.

"Celica!" Amelia snapped angrily. All eyes went to the paladin as she stood. "Did you kill him?" she asked slightly more calmed in her tone.

"No, the dastard fled," Celica growled as she gripped the door handle before pulling it open. "I did however," she paused as she reached into the stagecoach, "kidnap his wife!" she said proudly as she removed a woman from the stagecoach. "Well sort of kidnapped her," the ranger added slightly quieter.

The woman was tied at her hands and ankles. Her mouth was gagged. She wore a crimson-colored dress, her black hair was hanging freely. Upon her head was a gold tiara with a pearl resting in the centerpiece. She had emerald eyes, yet they did not look fearful despite the situation she was in.

"Oh no! No no no no no!" Azura, Warren and Amelia began as they assessed the situation.

"Chuck like idea," the barbarian said as smiled and nodded his head in approval.

Celica walked to the front door of Arcanist's tower, kicking it open as she carried the woman. "I swear she was tied and gagged when I found her. I assumed based on the wedding ring on her finger, she's married to Uldritch," the ranger stated as she gently set the woman down on a chair at the table where the map had been sprawled out.

"What's all the commotion?" Arcanist asked as he came out from his study. He looked around, seeing the woman tied and gagged at the table, Celica sitting a few feet from the woman, and the other adventurers coming inside.

"Celica kidnapped Uldritch's wife," Warren said, trying to stay calm.

The ranger rolled her eyes before undoing the gag from the woman's mouth. "Sorry about all this. Tell me about yourself." Her voice was an uneasy calm.

The woman nodded slowly as the ranger undid the ropes that kept her wrists and ankles bound. "My name is Bethany Von Varley, formerly Bethany Foxwell," she began, her voice had a fairly thick sounding guttural accent, sounding as though it came from Loft Ridge.

"Bethany Foxwell? As in soon to be Queen Beth Foxwell?" Arcanist questioned, taken back by the news.

"Wait, you know her?" Amelia asked, looking at Arcanist.

"Yes, that was once my title. When I was engaged to the prince of Alibi. Before Uldritch cursed him and took me from my love," Beth explained as she looked at Arcanist.

"Hang on a moment, you said Uldritch took you and cursed the prince. Can you explain?" Azura responded upon hearing the news.

Beth nodded as she rubbed her wrists. Warren shook his head as he stepped forward. "We apologize for what Celica did. She's still a bit wild and—"

"No. No apologizing. She wasn't the one who tied and gagged me. That was Uldritch. Celica rescued me, even though she claims it was a kidnapping," Beth interrupted. She paused before returning to the topic she was going to explain. "I was to marry Prince Darios Umbercane but before we could be wed, Uldritch attacked the castle. My sweet prince was badly wounded and Uldritch said he would kill the prince right then and there, unless I went with him. I had no choice. But the warlock cursed my sweet prince, turning him disfigured and damaging his memories. He believed himself to be nothing more than one of Uldritch's servants."

"By chance was Prince Umbercane's castle, where I'm assuming all this happened, was it in the far south of Alibi?" Celica asked as she looked at the map. Beth hesitated but gave a nod. The ranger pointed on the map. "Abyssal Castle, where we first encountered Uldritch Von Varley. The servant that tried to persuade me to leave you guys behind and continue on my own."

"Just because you called him Darios doesn't mean that's his name," Warren chimed in as he shook his head again.

"He was a disfigured man, a massive hump on his back, and walked with a limp. One of his arms was significantly longer than the other and was covered with warts and his skin was peeling in some spots. He always kept his head down; there were several lumps upon such. His ears were elongated and twisted, the right ear looking like part of it had been cut off. His clothing was little more than rag, a green piece of cloth covered his torso and brown pants covered his legs," Celica described as she thought back. She looked at Beth. "And he had hazel eyes and stringy blonde hair.

"That's Prince Umbercane, at least what he looked like once Uldritch was done with him," Beth murmured. She shook her head as she stood. "I ask you travelers take me to this castle. Please, I must break the curse that has taken hold."

"Chuck wonder, if you royal, how well you pay," the barbarian said as he looked over his greataxe.

Beth removed her tiara. "The gemstone that's within this, you can have it. Maybe it'll be of use to you," she stated, desperate for the adventurers to hear her out.

Celica nodded. "At the very least, I'll take you," the ranger responded as she checked over her gear.

Amelia shook her head. "I'm going with you. You'll need someone with thick armor to take hits for you in case things go bad," she noted before laughing slightly. "The dangers you lead me into, Celica. Perhaps one of these days, you'll lead me somewhere a bit more normal darlin'."

Celica went outside and got the horses situated for a long journey. "I ask that you ride in the stagecoach, Beth. And anyone else coming, as well. I'll handle the horses," she stated as she got everything ready for the travel. Beth, Amelia, Warren, Azura and Chuck all climbed into the stagecoach, catching the ranger off guard that everyone was coming along.

It was a couple of days before they arrived at Abyssal Castle. Everything was still, eerily quiet as they dismounted from the stagecoach and looked at the entrance. As they entered the castle, Celica took the lead, Amelia to her left. Chuck was in the middle, guarding Beth, while Warren and Azura took the rear positions. Most everything within the castle's entry was destroyed and there was a vile stench that hung in the air. As they proceeded deeper, they noticed distinct tracks upon the ground. "Some sort of reptile, about five feet and some inches in height," Celica noted as she inspected the tracks. She looked where the tracks lead and looked up to meet Amelia's gaze. "These are fresh, less than an hour. Whatever made them is still here," she whispered.

"We should proceed with caution," Amelia replied as she looked around. Celica nodded as she looked for more tracks. She pointed to a set of tracks that were more human-like. Amelia studied the tracks as best she could. "What do you think?" she asked, looking at the ranger.

"I'd wager these belong to the prince we're looking for," the ranger murmured as she pointed down a hallway.

Everyone proceeded down the hallway in question, each keeping their eyes and ears open for any movement, anything in general. Celica paused as she noticed the same reptile-like tracks in the ground. She signaled for everyone to stop and looked around trying to figure out the direction the creature went in. A hiss was heard down the hall, followed by a rush of lightning. Amelia held up Soulfade, blocking the worst of the attack. Celica drew Echoes in her right hand and her shortsword in the other. "Go, I'll keep whatever this thing is busy. You guys protect Beth and find Darios," she commanded before running down the hall to meet whatever shot the lightning.

"Celica, be careful!" Amelia shouted before turning to leave.

Warren and Azura were now leading as they rushed back to the main foyer, Chuck and Beth right behind them and Amelia in the back. They took a moment to catch their breath. "What in Alibi was that?" Azura questioned as she looked back toward the hallway.

"I don't know, and right now, I don't think I want to know," Warren answered as he looked around. He remembered going up a flight of stairs then there was the massive dining hall. There was also the hall with all the bedrooms. There was the spiral staircase that led them into the basement where they each fought a shadow copy. "There's no way of knowing which way will lead us to Darios. And we are not splitting up," he added as he looked around, frantically.

"Chuck think we start at dining hall," the barbarian suggested as he pointed up the stairs.

"Alright, sounds like a plan," Amelia said while catching her breath. The group sprinted up the stairs and made their way to the massive dining hall. On one side of the room was the flipped over table, various dishes lay shattered upon the ground.

"Darios!" Azura called out as they walked through the dining hall. They spotted faint tracks that resembled the human-like ones that were found earlier. Warren took lead position as they made their way from the dining hall toward the hallway with the various bedrooms. "Darios!" Azura called again, hoping they would eventually get an answer.

The glint of steel striking steel and sparks of lightning as they two fought lit up the hall. Celica struck out with her signature flurry of rapid strikes. To her surprise, each was blocked effortlessly, as though her foe could read her movements. "Flurry strike, ah that move was so useful in the fall of Alibi," the creature spoke, its voice filled with heavy growls.

"Who are you!" Celica demanded as she narrowly dodged the swing from the creature's claymore. This foe was strong, much stronger than anyone Celica had fought. She had a hard time keeping up with the savage attacks. And anytime she tried to launch an attack of her own, they read her movements perfectly.

"I go by many names, but the one I prefer most is Time Eater!" the blue reptilian being roared, as it rushed the ranger with a speed she had never seen.

Celica dove under the attack, barely avoiding the sudden attack. This was the monster they had been preparing to face the entire time. It was fast. It was strong. And it was smart. Celica got to her feet and used what little magic she had learned, peppering Time Eater with lightning magic.

Time Eater held up its left claw, blocking each lightning attack. "I must admit, I forgot how droll I once was," it spoke before unleashing a lightning blast shrouded in a black aura.

Celica was launched several feet back from the single attack. As she stood, she saw Time Eater calmly approaching. She sheathed her blades and drew her longbow. Three arrows left the bowstring in rapid succession, each splitting into fifteen arrows. Time Eater merely smirked before twirling its claymore, easily cutting down the arrows. "Next you'll shoulder your bow and rush me with Echoes. I'll easily knock you back, then you'll try to go invisible but I can hear your heartbeat and sense your movements. When that fails, you'll try to fight me head on. Tell me about how much of that sounds accurate?" Time Eater taunted as it twirled its claymore.

The blue reptilian being blocked the attack from Echoes, forcing the ranger back further into the hallway. Celica threw her hood up, going invisible as predicted. She sprinted full speed for Time Eater and lashed out with a single attack from Echoes. Again, Time Eater blocked the attack before grabbing the ranger by her throat and smashing her into a wall. As Celica's hood fell back, she glowered at Time Eater. "I don't intend to kill you. No, I intend to absorb you," Time Eater hissed as it smirked at the ranger.

"Celica!" Amelia called as she threw her dagger at Time Eater. There was a shriek in frustration as the dagger pierced the blue scales. Time Eater was forced to drop the ranger from the sudden pain. The paladin rushed to the ranger's side and dragged her up to her feet. "The others found Darios and are running. Warren and Azura set up a series of spells that will detonate any moment. We need to leave," the paladin stated as she supported the ranger as they fled.

Time Eater hissed before lunging for the pair. Its claymore easily shattered Amelia's armor. "Ah, yes, Amelia Lucia, is it? Heir to Highever?" the reptilian being spoke as it pinned Amelia to a wall. Its yellow eyes glared down at the ranger as the fanged smirk formed. "Choose. Your life, or hers?" Time Eater snarled as it watched the ranger.

"Celica, just run!" Amelia called as she struggled against Time Eater's grip.

Celica slowly stood; Echoes gripped tightly in her right hand. She lunged forward, slashing a deep wound into Time Eater's wrist. The hiss indicated the attack was a direct hit. While the reptilian being was recovering, Celica grabbed Amelia and sprinted down the hall away from Time Eater. The ranger and paladin had narrowly escaped Abyssal Castle before the place collapsed, burying anyone unfortunate enough to still be inside.

"You two cut that a little too close!" Azura called as she saw the pair still sprinting.

"No talk, just run!" Celica ordered as she continued to drag Amelia. Warren looked over his shoulder at the castle. To everyone's horror, the rubble shook and a massive blue dragon emerged. Its roar was deafening, shaking the environment.

The lich grabbed the communication stone he carried. "Arcanist, we need an out! And we need it now!" he yelled in a panic.

"Hold tight, I've got just the thing," Arcanist responded. Time Eater's yellow eyes locked onto the group, lightning crackling from its gaping maw. Before the attack could be launched, a white light enveloped the adventurers, along with Beth and Darios. When it cleared, they were gone, leaving Time Eater alone.

"What was that thing!" Warren questioned in a panic as they emerged in Arcanist's tower.

"It called itself Time Eater," Celica said as she helped Amelia to a chair.

"You mean, the creature we were summoned to defeat? That Time Eater?" Azura asked, worry in her voice. Celica hesitated but gave a nod. It was clear everyone was shaken up from the encounter. Azura slowly turned to Beth and Darios. "Ok, we found the prince, now about breaking the curse."

"Chuck want payment," the barbarian chimed in as he pointed to the tiara.

Beth nodded as she removed her tiara and handed it to the lich. "Your payment," she said before walking over to the disfigured man. Her emerald eyes looked him over before she began chanting a spell.

Warren and Azura watched as the disfigured appearance slowly melted away. Where the disfigured man once stood, now stood a handsome man. His hair was a lush blonde in color, his hazel eyes were deep with emotion. "I thank you Outrealm adventurers for everything you've done for myself, for Beth and the rest of Alibi," Darios began as he dusted himself off. "I am Prince Darios Umbercane, the rightful heir to Alibi. However, Time Eater has made certain to prevent such," he added as he bowed to the adventurers.

"How do we stop Time Eater?" Azura asked as she looked from Darios and Beth to Arcanist.

The brass reptilian stepped forward, taking the tiara from Warren. He looked it over before removing the pearl at the center. "With the virtue stones, combined with the legendary weapons," Arcanist stated as he looked the pearl over. He looked at the group. "I can create an amulet with all eight virtue stones on it. When you encounter Time eater again, it will be your only chance at weakening her enough to fight," he added as he laid out the other seven virtue stones upon the table.

"Arcanist, once you've finished the amulet, could you perhaps help me make new armor?" Amelia asked, the only piece of her old armor was a shoulder plate that was cracked.

"I can help with such," Darios spoke up as he walked over to the paladin. "That way Arcanist can spend all his focus on the amulet," he added.

Celica listened to everyone talking about and their plans about resupplying. She thought back to her fight with Time Eater. It bothered her. The way Time Eater was able to predict every move she made. Every attack was blocked as though Time Eater could see into the future. She shook her head as she tried to hide her worry from the others. She removed Echoes from its sheath on her belt and began sharpening it.

"We still don't know where Time Eater's lair is though," Warren mused as he looked at the map.

Beth tapped a small out of the way section of the desert. "Distortion Tower is located in this spot. And from what I recall Uldritch saying, his master, Time Eater, resides in Distortion Tower," she explained as she marked it on the map.

"Alright, everyone, this is it. Make any final preparations you need. Once we head out for Distortion Tower, we won't be returning until Time Eater is vanquished," Warren said, his confidence shining through to raise morale of the group.

Chapter 25 - Distortion Tower

Arcanist let out a heavy sigh as he placed the amulet upon the table. The pendant at the center housed the eight gems, each looking like it was specifically placed in its spot. "There you have it, the virtue amulet. When you go to fight Time Eater, this should give you the power you need to weaken her so that your attacks might be able to damage her. Remember, you're dealing with a being who can make gods shudder," he stated as he looked at the group. Warren sat in silence, eating the flash from a human thigh. Chuck grunted in response as he looked at the amulet.

Azura nodded slightly. "So, who's going to use it?" she asked the question that plagued everyone's mind.

"All eight virtue stones contain powers that exceed what a mortal can handle. Whoever uses it will likely die to give the rest of you a chance," Arcanist explained. He paused and turned to look at Warren and Amelia. "In the case of the undead, it will destroy you to the point of there being nothing I can resurrect."

"So, five of us are going into hell, but only four of us are coming back? Is there no other way?" Warren muttered, he hated the idea of losing someone he had gone on this long and mad journey with.

Celica looked up from the corner she sat in, eyeing the amulet. "Since this is going to be our final adventure as a team. We should have a drink. Something to not only steel our nerves, but also honor the dead one walking in our group," she said as she stood.

Darios shook his head. "I can't ask any of you to do this for Alibi. The duty falls to me. I must be the one who uses the amulet and—"

"And die for your country? I've seen plenty of rulers attempt to be selfless. If you die, Darios, who then will rule Alibi?" Amelia interrupted as she adjusted her new armor. She shook her head at the prince. "Your role in this tale is to welcome back those who return, be crowned king and build a brighter future for Alibi," she added as she walked over to the table where the amulet sat. "I'll do it, when the time comes. I've nothing to return to in my home kingdom. I've the least to lose," she said calmly.

"I'm the leader, the duty falls to me," Warren argued as he looked at the paladin.

Azura shook her head. "I'll do it. I haven't been of much help to anyone, constantly needing protection. Let me do this to be of some use."

"Chuck have most wrongs. Chuck need make right. Chuck do it," the barbarian growled softly as he finished sharpening his greataxe.

Celica shook her head. "We can decide who uses the amulet when we get there. Besides, we've still a week of travelling to do before we reach our destination," she reminded the rest of the group. She opened her bag and withdrew some strong mead she had purchased while they were in a town month prior. "Now then, will you each have a drink with me?" she asked as she reached into her bag and pulled out eight mugs each looking like it could hold a pint. Silently she poured the mead and handed them out to her friends, Arcanist as well as the two royals.

The eight drank and shared stories of everything that had happened. It was a lively final night in Arcanist's tower, one that all of them would remember for years to come. When the sun began peeking up on the horizon, the Outrealm adventurers began their week-long journey to Distortion Tower. The amulet in question was in a belt pouch on Celica's belt as she did not want anyone doing anything reckless before they reached their destination.

The entire way was constant combat, fighting through lizard people. Fighting goblins, fighting horrific monsters. As they reached the final stretch of desert, they fought a monster much like the one Celica and Azura had fought very early in the adventure. Finally, after a week of harsh travels and fighting, they reached a massive tower. "Heroes of the Outrealms, if you can hear me, I've some final important news for you." Arcanist's voice came from the communication stone.

Warren removed the stone from his pocket and held it out between everyone. "We're listening, Arcanist," he stated as all eyes focused on the stone.

"It's about Time Eater. According to some text that Darios has finished translating, Time Eater can only be slain by her own accord. All other attempts will only seal her away for a few hundred years. Good luck, heroes, you're Alibi's only hope," Arcanist said before the communication stone went silent.

"Only be slain by her own accord? What does that mean?" Azura asked as she looked up at Warren.

"Means Time Eater can only be killed by her own self or her own power," Celica murmured as she glanced from the group to the entrance to Distortion Tower. The ranger took a deep breath before letting it out slowly. "Well, no time like the present. Let's get to it and save Alibi from this brute."

"I couldn't agree more, darlin'," Amelia added as she drew her bastard sword and Soulfade.

Celica threw her hood over her head and drew Echoes and her shortsword. Chuck hefted his Crusher, as Warren drew Ironvice and his tower shield. Azura nodded as she steeled herself for what was ahead. As they entered the tower, they were instantly pulled into combat. Several short lizard people with orange skin rushed them, wielding spears. Before Amelia, Warren, Chuck or Azura could react, they felt a rush of wind and the small lizard people were sprawled out, dead.

A set of stairs appeared, and they rushed up the stairs to the next floor. Much like the first floor, the enemies, ashen-skinned reptilians, were dealt with quickly. More stairs appeared, and they continued to run to the next floor. The third floor had them fighting creatures created from living fire. Chuck shook his head; his weapon would not be useful in this situation. Warren took a step forward, Ironvice easily pummeling through two of the five fire beings. Amelia was already dealing with two others, her bastard sword making short work of them. The fifth was struck by the invisible attacker, ice freezing it in place before it was shattered.

They made their way up to the fourth floor, this time fighting a large wolf monster. The beast easily towered over them and howled loudly as it charged. Chuck roared as he charged forward, Crusher taking the wolf's head off in one clean swing. As they entered the fifth floor, they found themselves surrounded on all sides by ghouls. Azura unleashed a cone of flame while Chuck swung

Crusher. Between the two of them they made short work of the undead beings. Floor six and seven had the same layout and same monsters, both had stone golems. Warren's Ironvice effortlessly crushed through the golems, and they pushed forward. Floor eight and floor nine also had identical monsters, large living ice monsters. Amelia and Chuck unleashed wave after wave of attack, clearing them out.

It was the tenth floor that posed the first real challenge. A massive green dragon was the only creature in the room. Its noxious gas breath caused Chuck to feel nauseated as he tried to fight. Amelia and Warren kept the beast's focus on them as she made small attacks, forcing the dragon's attention upon them. "I can't cast any spells that cause a spark. Otherwise, we'll all be engulfed in flames," Azura muttered as she thought over her spells. She began casting slippery floor, turning the ground beneath the dragon into a slick mess.

Celica rushed forward, her blades cutting through the dragon's scales and making it vulnerable. Chuck shook off the nauseous feeling and rushed forward with his greataxe. The attack connected, taking the dragon's right wing off. Warren's Ironvice crashed into the dragon's ribs, splintering a few of them. While Amelia's bastard sword cut into the green dragon's stomach, causing its organs to begin spilling. The beast roared as it slashed out wildly with claws, trying to rip apart the adventurers. A bloody gurgle came from it as a blade pierced its heart. Celica removed Echoes and flicked the blood off the blade.

They advanced to the eleventh floor where they were met with three twenty-foot-tall ogres, each clad in only loincloths and wielding spiked mauls. Warren and Amelia got in front of the rest of the group, using their shield to block the attack. Chuck rushed out from behind the shields and lashed out with a fierce swing from Crusher, taking an arm off one of the ogres. The group saw the rushing blur and knew the invisible Celica was making her move. One of the ogres completely dropped to the ground. Azura threw a fireball at the one Chuck had already wounded, causing that one to collapse. Amelia took the moment to slash out and ended the last ogre.

"Feels like the defenses of the tower get stronger the higher up we go," Amelia noted as they made their way to the stairs.

"It makes sense seeing as this is Time Eater's fortress," Azura noted as she stayed in the back of the group.

Floor twelve was filled with a thick fog, obscuring their view. All around the room were large webs. "Form up and keep Azura at the center," Warren instructed as he took a step forward. Amelia was to Azura's right and Chuck was to the sorceress's left. They had no way of knowing where the ranger was but accepted that she would be fine.

Several thirty-foot sized spiders rushed forward, spewing webbing trying to catch the group in a trap. Warren's arms were pinned to his sides from the webbing. He smirked as he began casting a spell. Within a few seconds, the webs were engulfed in flames, freeing him in the process. Amelia slashed through a spider that came from the right. And Chuck cleaved through three from the left. Azura took the moment to focus her spell and added her own fire magic to Warren's. The room was ablaze, and spiders were everywhere. Some huge, some small and several were about the size of medium dogs. Warren anchored his shield and drew his ball and chain. He spun it around a few times before throwing the ball and crushing several of the dog sized spiders, as he tugged it back the ball crushed many of the small spiders. They saw the webs move in the distance followed by the shrieks of the spiders before being frozen and shattered.

As with previous floors, a series of stairs appeared, granting them access to the next floor. Floors thirteen through nineteen consisted of combat against assorted monsters, varying from ghouls, to demons, to wild beasts and a manticore. The adventurers took a moment to catch their breath before they went up the stairs to face floor twenty. "Everyone ready?" Amelia asked as she looked over the group.

Everyone nodded before getting back into formation. Amelia and Warren had taken the lead, Chuck in the center and Azura in the back. They did not know where the ranger was but knew she needed to remain invisible to be most effective against their foes. As they climbed the stairs to floor twenty, they saw three elves each brandishing impressive swords, a dwarf with an intimidating greataxe, a human with a spell book, a second human with a quarterstaff, the third human held a double-sword and finally a heavily armored elf with a tower shield and morningstar materialized.

"You have got to be sodding kidding me," Warren groaned seeing his old team. He shook his head as he turned to the others and shrugged. "We beat them once, let's do it again," he stated before rushing the armored elf, the king.

Azura kept her distance using magic to support her allies. Chuck charged forward, trampling the three elves. Amelia engaged the caster and the one with a quarterstaff. The human with the double-sword seemed to be confused as he was barraged with attacks, but no enemy was present. Chuck's Crusher tore through and killed two of the three he fought. Amelia's bastard sword had made short work of the caster and splintered the quarterstaff. The one with the double-sword collapsed, the wounds he had received from the invisible attacker having taken a toll on him.

Warren's Ironvice matched the king's morningstar blow for blow as they fought. The lich however had a sized advantage, using such to keep a reasonable distance while still being able to attack the armored elf. Behind him, Warren heard his allies finish their fights; all that remained was the king. The lich felt his mind becoming hazy and knew what it meant. He used Ironvice to crush the king's armor before grabbing the man and devouring him. He needed to feed, whatever they came across in the tower would have to suffice.

Upon seeing the lich consume the king's flesh, the realization dawned upon the others. They hung back, knowing getting too close would likely cause him to attack them. The stairs to the next floor appeared and everyone hesitated. Warren looked at the others before he shambled toward the stairs. "Give me a head start. I don't want to harm any of you," he growled as he moved up the stairs.

Floor twenty-one consisted of several reptilian enemies. There were five with ashen gray skin, seven with orange skin and twelve very small blue skinned ones. Warren groaned knowing none of these would taste very good, but he had little choice. With a loud ghastly roar, he rushed forward, using Ironvice to disarm the orange ones before snatching them off the ground and devouring them. Out the corner of his eye he saw the gray ones being disarmed but saw no attacker. They were left wounded, but alive. Then there were the blue ones, tiny as they were, their constant bombardment of electric attacks was becoming more than an annoyance.

Warren wiped the blood from his mouth as he advanced on the gray reptiles. They quivered in terror having witnessed what the lich had done to their orange skinned comrades. One by one, the lich grabbed the gray ones and ate the five gray reptilian enemies. He turned his attention to the blue ones; they showed no fear despite their tiny sizes. He still hungered, how long had it been since he last fed? Every time he tried to grab the tiny blue reptilian folk they easily sprinted away before attacking with lightning breath. He saw twelve arrows from seemingly nowhere emerge and pin the small reptilian folk by their tails.

It prevented them from running, making his prey easier to catch. The lich stepped forward, snatching two of the blue ones and popping them into his maw like they were little more than small snack items. The hunger finally faded, and his mind came back to being his own. He looked at the remaining ten tiny blue ones and crushed them with Ironvice. Warren let out a deep sigh before calling down the stairs to the others that it was safe to regroup.

"Are you alright?" Azura asked with concern in her voice.

Warren nodded slowly. "Yes, now I am," he replied as they watched the next set of stairs appear. "Floor twenty-two, here we go," the lich added as the group proceeded up the stairs. Floors twenty-two through twenty-nine were mostly reptilian enemies with the occasional demonic-like entity thrown in to make things more challenging. As the adventurers reached floor thirty, they found themselves face to face with a pair of colossal red dragons. Chuck roared in delight at getting to fight two large creatures. He sprinted forward, his greataxe dealing four quick attacks to one of the dragon's flesh. Amelia went after the second dragon, keeping the attention of the two dragons divided. Warren rushed to aid the barbarian, knowing the invisible ranger would likely be moving to help the paladin.

Azura unleashed a blizzard spell, weakening the fire power of the two dragons. The one Warren and Chuck fought struggled to move as the blizzard also slowed its movements. Amelia endured a rush of flames as she advanced on the second dragon. The dragon roared loudly as several deep gashes formed on its sides. The paladin smirked as she rushed forward and drove her blade through the monster's skull. Warren blocked a claw attack as Chuck slashed through the remaining dragon's claws before taking the head off.

Everyone took a deep breath as they saw the stairs appear. They nodded to one another before heading up the stairs. Floor thirty-one was foggy; it was difficult to see anything. Chuck took a step forward, trying to find their next challenge. There was a loud splash as he took his step, the barbarian looked down, realizing that one step caused him to step into water that was waist deep.

The group saw a light rod ignite, lighting up the room. There was a single platform at the center of the room, surrounded completely by water. Chuck tried moving again, getting deeper in the water. He immediately shifted his stance to swimming toward the platform.

Warren looked around, trying to discern what to do. He paused as he heard a splash from part of the room. In a split-second decision, the lich grabbed the sorceress and threw her as hard as he could, but she landed on the platform. Amelia heard another splash from another part of the room then turned to Warren. "What do you think it is?" she asked.

"I don't know, we need to get to that platform with Chuck and Azura. I don't know where Celica is, but she'll be fine," the lich responded. He looked toward the water and the platform at the center.

Amelia nodded as she drew her crossbow and loaded it with a cartridge ready to fight. "Go, I'll cover you," she instructed. The lich nodded before rushing into the water and swimming toward the platform. He heard something to his left but kept swimming. Several bolts flew from the paladin's crossbow, delaying the creature.

Warren reached the platform and pulled himself up, he was drenched and looked back to the paladin. "Amelia, hurry!" he called as he drew his ball and chain.

Azura readied her spells as she looked around. The paladin removed her armor, storing it in her bag before she dove into the water and swam as fast as she could toward the platform. She heard a massive splash to her right and feared the worst. She saw an ice spell strike something to the side but continued to swim. Upon reaching the platform, the paladin felt the barbarian pulling her up onto the platform. "There's three of them," Azura murmured as she looked around. Amelia was quick about reequipping her armor and preparing for the fight.

Everyone looked around trying to figure out where they would be attacked from but there was no movement in the water. They had no idea where Celica was either; the ranger had been invisible the entire time. They each heard something big crashing through the water before seeing the massive piranha-like monster leap out of the water. They were distracted by the giant piranha; they did not see the massive eel that ensnared the barbarian and began dragging him toward the water. "Chuck!" Warren called as he tried to get to the barbarian.

Several arrows struck the eel, forcing it to let go of the barbarian. They saw more arrows hit the piranha, slowing the beast down. Blood stained the water as both eel and piranha bleed out from the small but numerous arrow wounds they had received. Then there was the massive dorsal fin that broke the water's surface. "A shark as well?" Azura questioned as fear gripped her.

The platform shook as something struck it hard. They saw the piranha launched into the air before being consumed by the jaws of a behemoth of a shark. Celica threw back her hood, revealing she had been on the stairs the entire time as she nocked three arrows. "Azura, Warren, electric magic the water!" she called from across the stretch of water. She fired an arrow volley into the water, each one sparking with lightning magic.

Azura nodded as she began casting her voltage blast spell. The spell struck the water, joining the lightning arrows in turning the water into a pool of electrified water. The eel withered in pain before going motionless. All that remained was the shark. Celica staggered as the behemoth rammed the stairs, sending her into the electrified water.

"Celica!" Amelia called seeing the ranger go under the water.

Warren unleashed a wave of darkness, canceling a small amount of the electricity. "Celica, swim!" he yelled.

The ranger broke the surface and began swimming toward the platform, staying within the boundaries of Warren's dark wave. She heard the shark moving around and feared when it would emerge to attack again. Before she reached the platform, the ranger was dragged under the water. "Celica!" everyone called out as they looked around trying to spot the ranger or the shark.

Celica stabbed her shortsword into a bit of soft flesh between the shark's teeth, anchoring herself. She always feared the water, this was one of the reasons. Echoes lit up from its sheath on her belt. "Celica, I can grant you a brief transformation. Stab me into your chest," the blade's voice mirrored that of Ashe. The ranger hesitated but knew getting out of this situation was going to take some crazy and unusual problem solving. She drew Echoes with her free hand and impaled the blade through her chest.

From the platform, the others saw a massive rush of lighting magic followed by the thrashing of the shark. Even with the water muffling the sounds, they heard a sickening snap as the shark swam deeper. Amelia drew her bastard sword in both hands before leaping into the water. She knew it was a long shot, but the ranger needed help. She saw the colossal blue dragon from before, grasping the shark in its front right claw. The look of bloodlust in its yellow eyes. Lightning shot from the dragon's mouth, killing the shark from the electrical burns. The dragon nodded at its handiwork before consuming the shark.

Amelia realized the error in judgment and began to sink from the weight of her armor. She struggled trying to swim to the surface. Her scarlet eyes saw the blue dragon swim at her, its speed was impressive to say the least. She felt the dragon's jaws grab her; the bite was secure but otherwise was not causing any further harm. "Damnit, what do we do!" Warren growled as he looked at the mostly still water. He saw out of the corner of his left eye, stairs to the next floor appeared. Before the three adventurers on the platform could react, they saw the massive blue dragon lunge out of the water and land on the platform with them. It lowered its jaws before releasing the hold it had on the paladin.

A crackle of lightning overtook the dragon before it shifted back to the human ranger. Celica staggered, Echoes in her right hand and the shortsword in her left. She breathed a faint sigh of relief before sheathing her blades and rushing to Amelia's side. "Are you alright? I didn't harm you, did I?" she asked, her voice having a hint of panic in it.

The paladin shook her head. "May have scuffed up the armor a little but I'm fine," she reassured.

No one said anything further as they made their way up to the next floor. Floors thirty-two to thirty-nine had the five adventurers fighting various aquatic based humanoid creatures, ranging from mermaids to shark people, and even frog people. When the stairs for floor forty appeared, the adventurers did a tally on what their equipment situation was. Azura had used several of her best offense spells already but still had plenty of healing spells. Amelia was out of crossbow bolts. Rendering her arm mounted repeating crossbow useless. Celica counted her arrows and nodded; she still had plenty. Warren and Chuck were mostly melee fighters, both still able to fight though a small amount of fatigue was starting to set in.

"How much more to this tower do you think?" Azura asked as she looked from Warren to Amelia then Chuck and finally to Celica.

"I don't know. But we might need to find a floor where we can rest a bit. I'm starting to feel the fatigue," Warren commented as he looked to the stairs.

"Chuck too. Chuck want rest," the barbarian chimed in as he shouldered his greataxe.

Celica looked from the stairs to the tiring group. "Let's take a few additional minutes here," she said before crouching near the stairs. Everyone nodded in agreement. As they took some time to catch their breath and ready themselves for the next leg of the floors, they each wondered how much more they had. Celica felt her head hurting again, same as it did when she saw visions of her past. Though what she saw was vastly different.

"This kingdom will be yours. You needn't bend to anyone's will," Uldritch stated as he led the ranger to the massive tower. "This is Distortion Tower, built in the days of the ancestors. It harbors great power if you can reach the top."

"And you would let me keep that power? I find that hard to believe," the ranger said as she drew her longbow.

"I already have all the power I need to be the king of Alibi. But I wish you to be my queen, ruling at my side," the warlock explained before revealing his true form, a crimson dragon, to the ranger. He gave her a warm, welcoming smile. "I shall accompany you as you make the climb. But when the time comes to claim the power, it will be entirely yours to claim," he added as they entered the tower. He sensed something in the ranger's heart. Loneliness. Hatred. Betrayal. He pitied her and the emotions. It was something that if he could, he would take them all away. "It was poor of them to abandon you. You have my sincerest apologies for what those in Kardax did. And what those in Alibi did to you."

"Tell me, Uldritch, will you leave me as well when the time comes that I no longer benefit you?" the ranger asked as she held the longbow.

"Never, Camilla. I will never leave your side. Come what may, I will be with you. Always," he promised as they continued.

Celica rubbed her forehead slightly as she looked down at Echoes. She glanced up noting the others were mostly in a light sleep. She rested her hand on Echoes before finding the words. "Tell me, Echoes, have I… we been here before?" she asked softly.

Echoes burned a deep blue before its voice rang in her head. "Yes. This was where another version of us met. Uldritch brought you here and I was laying here, waiting for the hand destined to wield me. You see them too, the waking dreams. The waking dreams of another life that truly isn't your own."

"Show me more. I want to know without any doubts," she whispered.

"Very well, Celica Windstride. I shall share with you the waking dreams," Echoes spoke before the blue aura faded away.

Chapter 26 - Time Eater

The ranger made her way through the horrors of the Distortion Tower, aiding her was the crimson dragon who disguised himself as a warlock. They were a small team but effective in their attacks. They reached floor fifty and while there was no combat, there was a pedestal with a longsword plunged within it. The ranger approached, grasping the blade, she heard a voice in her head.

"I am Echoes, legendary blade meant to save Alibi. If you take me in hand, and not slain by my power, then you are worthy of me. Draw me from the pedestal. Let us save Alibi," the longsword's voice echoed in the ranger's head.

She steeled herself before removing the blade from the pedestal. It felt weightless in her right hand; this was the weapon she knew could change her future. The longbow she held clattered to the ground, splintering as it did so. She looked to Uldritch as another series of stairs appeared. Together they made their way up to the one hundredth floor. Upon defeating the beast that guarded the floor, a crystal orb appeared.

"Thee who seeks power… Take hold of what you see before you. And you will have what you desire," the crystal orb spoke.

The ranger stepped forward, taking the orb in her left hand. She felt an overwhelming power as she saw visions of a past life. She smiled; it was cruel, ruthless even. Uldritch remained in his dragon form and watched as the woman before him transformed into a massive blue dragon. "Uldritch, let us save Alibi and bring forth the new age," she stated.

Towns were burned, people slaughtered. The four guardian beasts that protected Alibi had been sealed away by a being referring to themself as Time Eater. Uldritch aided in her every order as they built a new world. He had counted over three hundred versions of herself that she consumed, adding their power to her own. He watched as countless Outrealm warriors fought and died trying to stop her. He even kept a few and experimented on their corpses turning them into hideous monsters that would guard the outer realm. Some were saved for guarding the inner sanctums of Alibi.

Time Eater's claymore clashed against the silver armor, splintering it and sending the knight to the ground. He coughed as he reached for his greatsword only to feel the claymore pierce his back. She wore the cruel smirk as she ended the knight's life. "How well will you die? I've slain your sorceress, the barbarian and your knight. All that remains is you." She laughed as she looked at the queen. Hiding behind the queen was a child, barely even five years of age. Time Eater's smirk grew. "Shall I end the babe first?"

The queen drew her longsword and rapier, lunging for the monstrous humanoid blue dragon. "You will not lay a finger on her!" she growled as she engaged Time Eater in combat.

The two exchanged strikes, the queen keeping pace with the monster, despite the size difference. Time Eater finally landed a decisive blow, sending the wounded queen to the ground. "Celica Anthiese, was it? I must admit, you put up quite the fight but in the end I prevail. Worry not, I shall take care of your child," Time Eater growled as she gripped the queen by her throat and lifted her to be eye level.

"You'll never win, Time Eater. I may have failed, but another will stop you," Anthiese barely managed the words, her wounds taking a toll on her.

Time Eater only smirked before devouring the queen. Once finished with her meal the humanoid blue dragon turned to leave. "What of the child?" Uldritch asked as he looked at the quivering girl.

"What of her?" Time Eater remarked before leaving. Uldritch looked the child over once more before scooping the girl up in his arms and taking his leave.

Uldritch was in his human form as he walked along the stone floor. His mission was simple: find Prince Darios and remove him from the board. "Lord Uldritch," a voice caught his attention as the young man behind him carried Echoes on his belt. "Lord Uldritch, are we going to kill Darios?" he asked. He had fiery orange hair like his father, but his eyes were yellow like his mother's.

The warlock smiled at the young man. "Wintersong, remember the mission. Remove Darios from the board. Once the prince is dealt with, we shall report such to Time Eater. Soon the fall of the broken and corrupted Alibi will come to pass and a new age will be ushered in," he stated as they entered Abyssal Castle. It had been reported to be Darios's stronghold and where he was amassing an army to fight back against Time Eater.

Many soldiers rushed forward, engaging Uldritch and Wintersong in combat. The warlock smirked as he touched the ground, reshaping it into spikes and impaling the soldiers. He heard Wintersong move around the room, blurring as he did so and killing any who avoided the spikes. Soon only Darios and Beth remained.

"It is done, Time Eater. Darios has been slain," Uldritch reported as he held the prince's head before the blue dragon-human. She looked humanoid in size and some features but had blue scales, yellow eyes, a snout with a horn upon it. Large wings remained folded against her back and her tail flicked back and forth.

Time Eater inspected the head. One of her claws ran along the cheek, peeling some of the flesh before she brought it up to her fanged maw. "Excellent work, Uldritch. There is still one pawn left on the board to remove."

"Arcanist," Uldritch growled the name. The brass reptile had been the one to summon Outrealm warriors to fight them. Each being led to their demise. It was also Arcanist who stripped Uldritch of his dragon form. His fury and vengeance for the brass reptile knew no bounds.

"Being an Outrealm warrior, I am unable to kill him. It must be done by an Alibi native," Time Eater stated as she looked over the land. She had assumed power soon after acquiring Echoes. And that power allowed her to become absolute. Every time Arcanist summoned his beloved Outrealm warriors, there was always one that could stop her. But she would consume them ensuring they would not be able to fell her by her own hand. It was the only way she could be killed with the powers she held.

"I shall dispatch Wintersong," Uldritch stated.

"You will go to Abyssal Castle. Our dear Arcanist has summoned more Outrealm warriors. There will be five of them. And one of them is the final past self I require," Time Eater instructed.

"Kill them but bring your past self to be consumed, I understand, my queen," Uldritch responded before taking his leave.

Time Eater sat back upon her throne as she looked towards the outer sanctum of Alibi. "Soon they will be here. Soon they will try as all the others who failed," she muttered before standing. A smirk lit up her face as she rubbed her forehead. "And the one who walks with them, the one that is a past of myself, I will enjoy her flesh as I have all the others," Time Eater growled as she walked a way down her throne room.

"No, Uldritch has yet to be slain. The amulet I gave him will keep him living so long as he wears it," Time Eater retorted after hearing her general's report. She looked at the green armor-clad general and smiled. "General Hugo, take this, use the power from it and bring my past self to me. Kill the others," she ordered as she handed Hugo an emerald.

"Must I do everything myself!" Time Eater roared as she drew her claymore. She took a deep breath and closed her eyes, focusing on the presence of her past self. "Abyssal Castle, is it? I will deal with them there," she snarled as she snapped her fingers warping herself to the massive castle.

Time Eater walked around, as she looked around the castle. "Ah, how long has it been?" she questioned as she made her way down a hall, waiting for the Outrealm warriors.

Her claymore clashed with the longsword and shortsword. "Tell me, do you want to know how they die? How Roy, Van, Kanna, Flannel, and the rest of them die," she snarled as the claymore overwhelmed the twin blades.

"How do you know them? What are you!" the ranger yelled in rage.

"Still haven't figured it out? I must admit I often forget how droll I once was." Time Eater laughed.

Celica sat in silence after seeing the waking dreams. She took a deep breath then exhaled slowly as she continued to rest her hand on the pommel of Echoes. She felt like her entire world had come crashing down. All pieces to the puzzle made sense now. She was not related to Time Eater. She was Time Eater. From a different point in time, yes, but she was still the shadow lightning.

"You and she are not the same. Remember that," Echoes stated. There was a brief silence before the blade decided to speak again. "I know not the choice that you each made that changed the direction of your lives. But I know it was a single choice that changed fate."

The ranger nodded numbly before wiping a single tear from her eye. She was the mortal enemy of the group she travelled with. The reason they had been fighting so hard. The reason Alibi was in the condition it was in. She looked at her clawed hands and let out a deep sigh before standing. "We should keep moving," she said to the others, doing her best to compose herself and not let on how disturbed she was.

"Alright, let's get a move on, darlin's," Amelia replied as she stood.

Chapter 27 - Temporal Spiral

As they reached floor forty, the adventurers were faced with an orc wielding a greataxe, an elf with two scimitars, an orc with gauntlets, a human with quarterstaff, a lizard person with longsword, the estranged caster and an armored being with a warhammer. Chuck growled upon seeing the group that was once his. He charged ahead, Crusher meeting the greataxe of the orc he engaged in battle. Amelia and Celica both rushed in next, the paladin taking on the longsword wielding lizard person as well as the orc with gauntlets. Celica forced her combat against the elf with the scimitars and the warhammer wielding one. Azura began casting basic support spells, covering her companions. Warren moved between the last two and the sorceress. His morningstar easily dealing with the estranged caster.

Amelia and Celica made quick work of their foes, neither holding anything back. Chuck's Crusher cleaved through the greataxe wielding orc, splitting her in two. Without missing a beat, the barbarian closed in on the human and dispatched her just as easily as he had with the orc.

They saw the stairs and shared glances before rushing up to floor forty-one. At first it appeared there was nothing. No fog to obscure their view. No enemies rushing them. It was empty. "I don't understand, what exactly are we supposed to do?" Warren questioned as he looked around.

Azura waved her hand trying to detect any sort of magic. "There's no magical presence hiding anything," she murmured.

Amelia looked around, her senses on high alert but the vampire-werewolf hybrid did not feel or sense anything out of place. Chuck looked up before letting out a deep war cry. Clinging to the ceiling were five abyssal guardians. Their gray disfigured bodies shambling forward, trying to claw the adventurers and their advances. Warren quickly drew his ball-and-chain and began swinging it to build up some momentum. Azura ducked back, lightning spells flying from her hands. Amelia held her tower shield up, blocking the coming claw attacks. Chuck growled as he tried to swing his greataxe at the monsters, but they remained out of his reach. Celica sheathed her blades and drew her longbow, firing several arrows in rapid succession.

The abyssal guardians continued to move, seemingly unaffected by the magic, ball-and-chain, nor the arrows. The five warriors all winced when they heard the ghastly howls of the creatures. It was unsettling and made Chuck nauseated. "It's no good, our attacks don't even faze them," Warren snarled as he moved his shield to block an attack aimed at Azura.

Celica took a deep breath before plunging Echoes into her chest. She felt the electricity coursing through her as she took on the form of the blue dragon again. The five abyssal guardians all turned their attention to the dragon as they shambled toward the blue behemoth. Celica roared, lightning breath rushing forward and striking the abyssal guardians.

Chuck took the opportunity and rushed forward, his greataxe cleaving through two of the unsightly creatures. "Chuck want fight!" the barbarian roared as he finished off the two he had started with. The blue dragon pinned an abyssal guardian under her left claw, then grabbed another with her right claw. The third shambled after the barbarian, his greataxe splitting it in two. He charged forward as the dragon flung the fourth creature to him. The barbarian swung Crusher around, easily splitting the creature across the midsection.

Only one remained. Celica glared down at the one under her left claw. It struggled, trying to free itself from the dragon's clutch. There was no emotion in the dragon's eyes as she pressed down with her claw, the added weight crushing the abyssal guardian. As the stairs to the next floor appeared, the dragon returned to its human form. Celica was silent as she wiped her hand off on the stone of the floor. "Let's go," Celica said, as she stepped toward the stairs.

Floors forty-two through forty-nine were more undead like enemies. The group effortlessly fought their way through ghouls, ghosts, undead humanoids and more. As they reached floor fifty, they found themselves facing off against a purple dragon. It roared at them as it attacked with fire and lightning breath attacks. Amelia and Warren ducked behind their tower shields, as the attacks struck. Chuck and Celica rushed forward, both attacking in quick flurries keeping the dragon tripped up and uncertain who to focus on. Warren held Ironvice in his hand as he lunged forward, the morningstar crushing the dragon's front left claw. Amelia took advantage of the dragon's distracted state and brought her bastard sword around, cutting the dragon's head off.

Floor fifty-one through fifty-eight were battles against various elemental beings. Fire elementals who could only be damaged by water attacks. Ice elementals that could only be damaged by fire attacks. Water elementals that could only be damaged by electric attacks. And wind elementals that blew the group around. Those ones could only be damaged by ice attacks. After clearing floor fifty-eight, which had two of each of the elementals, the adventurers were breathing heavily. The difficulty had spiked significantly since they started the tower. It was becoming a worry as to what would be lying ahead of them.

Upon reaching floor fifty-nine, they felt the ground shake as something massive moved about the room. After a few quakes they looked up and saw it. A massive golem made of flesh; it towered an impressive thirty feet in height. Celica shuddered slightly at the sight of the monster, memories of the prison of undead surfaced. Amelia and Chuck rushed forward, each striking with their primary weapons but horrified when they saw the attacks seemingly bouncing off the monster's body. Warren focused his magic and began casting a fire-based spell. "Amelia, Chuck, I need you two to stall for about a minute," he called as he continued to focus on his spell.

"Understood!" Amelia responded as she kept the flesh golem's focus on her.

Chuck growled, nodding as he attacked again and again with his greataxe. Azura looked at Warren; she recognized the spell. She pointed at the two melee fighters and cast her support spell. Both the paladin and barbarian felt the spell's effect almost instantly. They were weightless and able to move faster between the golem's attacks. They saw three arrows embedded into the flesh golem's body before exploding. Chunks of flesh flew from the golem's body, landing around the area. Amelia leapt back, bringing Soulfade up, blocking a punch from the golem. Chuck stumbled backwards trying to avoid the flesh chunks raining down.

"Chuck, Amelia, Celica, move!" Warren yelled as he flung his spell at the flesh golem.

The ranger rolled to the side, getting out of harm's way. Chuck was staggering trying to avoid the flesh chunks. Amelia sprinted to Chuck, tackling him out of the main blast zone. She brought Soulfade up, using it to shield both herself and the barbarian. The roar of an inferno was heard as the flames creased and licked the flesh golem. A low rumble came from the creature as it was incinerated by the inferno.

Once the flames cleared, there was nothing remaining of the flesh golem. Warren sprinted to the paladin and barbarian. "Amelia, Chuck! Answer me!" he called, fear grasping his voice.

Chuck grunted as he gently rolled Amelia off of him. The barbarian was not hurt in the slightest, but the paladin had some scorch marks on her. She stood shakily, using her bastard sword to steady herself. "I'm alright," Amelia said as she brushed herself off. The stairs to the next floor emerged as the group collected themselves. "Come on, loves, we best head to the next challenge," Amelia added as she walked towards the stairs.

As they entered floor sixty, they were met with the all too familiar sight. The room was laid out the same as the rooftop from House Vaughan's estate. And just as the fight they had in the memory tomb, there were the human warlock, human knight, human paladin, human rogue and human ranger. Azura wasted no time as she flung her storm spell at the enemies. Warren got between the sorceress and the enemies, his tower shield in hand. Chuck, Amelia and Celica rushed forward, meeting the foes head on in melee combat. Chuck was fighting with the rogue, opting to take out the stealth attacker. Amelia's bastard sword clashed against the opposing paladin's longsword. Celica spun her shortsword in a circle, deflecting the arrows that the enemy ranger was firing. From her right she saw the knight charging her. Warren blocked every attack the warlock threw at him, while Azura threw spells at the caster.

Chuck was the first to defeat his opponent, the rogue exploding into a puff of mist as they met their end. He blocked the enemy paladin's longsword with his greataxe, giving Amelia an opening. The vampire-werewolf hybrid nodded her thanks as she plunged her blade through her foe's armor and killed him. As with the rogue, the opposing paladin exploded into mist. Both advanced on the knight, giving Celica an even fight with the opposing ranger.

Warren glanced over his shoulder at the sorceress. Azura smirked and nodded to the lich, knowing full well what the plan was. He returned his focus to the warlock and charged forward, the sorceress right behind him. His morningstar crushed the warlock's chest as the sorceress flung spectral daggers into the warlock's throat. He let out a bloodied gurgle before collapsing. He shook violently before exploding into mist as the others had.

A loud clatter was heard as the knight disarmed the vampire-werewolf hybrid and barbarian. Amelia wasted no time and began punching the knight, ignoring the fact that he was heavily armored. Chuck rushed in from behind, grappling the knight and suplexing him. Before the knight could recover, Amelia had grappled him and held him still. Chuck put his massive hands on either side of the knight's head and squeezed, crushing the knight's skull. Both breathed heavily as they collected their weapons.

Celica pinned the opposing ranger and ran her shortsword through the foe's heart. There was a sickening laugh from the dark copy. "You'll fall to her. Just as I did. It's unavoidable." The evil ranger laughed before exploding into a mist.

"What was she talking about?" Azura asked as everyone regrouped.

The stairs to the next floor appeared, Celica was silent as she walked towards the stairs. "Celica!" Warren yelled. The ranger stopped and glanced over her shoulder at the lich. "What was the doppelganger talking about?"

The ranger hesitated but knew eventually they would learn the truth. She shook her head. "It's not important. Come on, we still have a way to go," she said before beginning the climb up the stairs.

"Dammit, Celica, answer the question!" Warren growled, as everyone made their way to the stairs and began the trek up to floor sixty-one.

"We're a little over halfway through this tower," Celica commented as they climbed the stairs.

"How can you be certain?" Amelia asked.

"Because..." The ranger paused. What was she going to say? That she had been here before? That Echoes had told her? That she was the monster they were to fight? "Because I've been here before. One of my waking dreams, I saw this place. It's one hundred floors. But the creatures have changed since the last time I was here," she noted as she continued walking.

"Celica, what aren't you telling us?" Amelia whispered to the ranger. Celica came to a stop; her heart was hammering in her chest. "Darlin', you can tell me. Whatever it is, please," the paladin stated as she put a hand on the ranger's shoulder.

The ranger shook her head. "We should stay focused on the remaining floors. I believe it's only going to get harder from here," she added as she began walking again.

As they entered floor sixty-one, they were instantly under attack from all sides. Arrows and magic rained down, forcing those with shields to bring such up to defend themselves and the others. Celica pulled her hood over her head, going invisible. Azura and Warren were ducked under his tower shield. Amelia and Chuck had ducked under Soulfade. As they recovered and had a brief chance to survey the room, they saw they were surrounded on all sides by beast-like humanoids. Some looked like coyotes mixed with humans, others were closer to bears mixed with humans. But the more disturbing ones were the two that began approaching the group. They were tall, sixteen feet in height, and they looked like their gray skin was stretched over their figure, antlers were sticking out from their heads and they had elongated limbs. Blood-stained claws, and each was wielding thick chains with hooks at the end.

Warren blocked the first hook but the pull from the creature was strong as it ripped his shield from his grasp. The second hook came forward, grappling Amelia and quickly tying her up. Chuck rushed the two tall beings, his greataxe swinging wildly as he tried to force them back. Azura began casting a chain element spell, flames and poison shot from her hands. The various creatures that hung back and were attacking with arrows and magic, found themselves at the mercy of the sorceress's spell. Warren sprinted to grab his shield but was knocked back as the one that ensnared the paladin used her to beat the lich down. Another chain and hook were flung forward, grappling the lich and ensnaring him.

The creatures howled in delight at having two of the three melee outrealm warriors ensnared. Chuck was struck repeatedly by both the ensnared Amelia and ensnared Warren. He staggered and dropped to his knees exhausted from the onslaught of attacks. "Chuck!" Azura called, seeing the barbarian struggling. She was nearly out of magic but knew she needed to do something to save the barbarian. The sorceress reached into her belt pouch withdrawing a few stones she had collected from various town merchants. She flung the stones as hard as she could at the creatures. The first of the four stones exploded into a blinding light. The second let out a deafening bang. The third and fourth created a slick ground, causing the creatures to lose their footing.

Chuck used the opportunity to get to his feet and bring Crusher down on the chains, freeing the others. He breathed heavily as he struggled to stay standing. Warren pressed a hand against Chuck, healing the barbarian's wounds. Amelia rushed forward and attacked with her bastard sword, trying to take out both the creatures quickly. Once he was stable, Chuck and Warren joined the paladin in the fight. In another part of the room, they heard the clashing of two swords against something large and fleshy. "Sounds like Celica's got something she's dealing with," Warren muttered as he brought Ironvice down, splitting one of the creature's skulls open. He saw Amelia overwhelm the other one with a series of sword strikes before she resorted to punching its face repeatedly.

The three rushed to Azura's position as the sorceress had pulled another handful of stones from her belt pouch. She pointed to the darkest corner of the room. "Celica went that way as she went invisible," she said as she watched the darkness.

They heard something land hard on the ground in front of them. Assuming it was the injured ranger, they prepared for anything. Shambling out from the corner was a sickly-looking creature. It was gray in color but covered in blood splotches. As they looked around the room, they noticed long arms with clawed hands poking up from the ground. The creature let out a screech, causing everyone to cover their ears. Once they were immobilized by the screech, the creature began its approach. It went for the sorceress first. Its gaping maw biting down on Azura's shoulder as it dragged her away from the others.

"AZURA!" Warren screamed as he tried to move but could not. He was forced to watch in horror as the creature began to consume the sorceress.

Celica heard the sorceress cry out in pain, as her yellow eyes burst open. The ranger stood, her eyes glowing in the darkness as she dropped her shortsword and Echoes. She lunged for the creature, grabbing its throat with her claws. The ranger ripped the creature away from Azura, before she began her merciless assault. Azura was on the ground, her right hand pressed against her torn open left shoulder as she kept pressure on the wound. She shuffled backwards as best she could while still keeping her eyes on the scene unfolding in front of her. The ranger was savagely ripping the creature apart. It was unlike the ranger to go into this sort of feral state, and yet the sight calmed the sorceress. Another horrible screech came from the creature as it struggled to free itself from the ranger's onslaught. Celica growled lowly as she shook her head, seemingly unfazed by the screech. With one final claw attack, she ripped the creature's head off and threw it to the side.

The various arms around the room withered before sinking back into the ground. Everyone staggered briefly as they found themselves able to move again, Warren rushing to the sorceress's side and began tending to her shoulder wound. The lich cursed under his breath as he noted the huge chunk that had been taken out. "You're lucky your shoulder is still attached," he commented as he healed the injury.

Azura just nodded as she looked over at the ranger who was collecting her shortsword and Echoes. Everyone looked up when they heard the stairs to the next floor appear. Floors sixty-two through sixty-nine were mostly nightmarish creatures. Things that the group had only seen in the World Beneath. They made the ghouls and ghost seem like friendly spirits. Another of the gray skinned beings covered in blood splotches made an attempt on the group as they fought through floor sixty-nine. Once the stairs emerged, the group rushed up to the next floor.

Floor seventy was quiet at first as they entered. As they walked, they noticed two corpses of gold scaled dragons lying upon the stone. "Undead gold dragons?" Warren noted as he stayed between the bodies and the sorceress.

On cue the two dragons rose up, the injuries they already bore made it easy to see they were kept going by malice and evil magic. Chuck growled as he rushed forward, quickly taking out one of the two dragons. Amelia and Celica had engaged the second dragon, the paladin keeping its focus entirely on her while the ranger unleashed wave after wave of arrows. It was not long before the undead beast dropped leaving the adventurers with hardly more than a minor bit of fatigue.

"That's seventy," Amelia noted as she looked to Celica. The ranger was quietly collecting her arrows and putting them back in her quiver. "You sure there's one hundred floors?"

"As sure as I am that my heart still beats," Celica responded as she held her longbow in hand, making her way to the stairs. There were faint nods from everyone as they followed the ranger to the next floor.

Floors seventy-one through seventy-nine were hardly more than just fighting various *were*-animals, werewolves, werebears, wereboars and even a handful of wererats. It was straightforward with no traps or anything unusual. As they steeled themselves for floor eighty, the thought finally hit them. "Then we're likely to fight Balthazar and his covenant again, are we not?" Warren noted as he looked from the stairs to the paladin.

Amelia nodded as she stepped to the front of the group. "Very likely seeing as we've faced off against Chuck's clan and Azura's old group," she replied.

"And Warren's travelling companions," Azura added, recalling that the half vampire was not present when they initially fought Warren's memory tomb.

"Then floor one hundred will likely be the self-proclaimed Guardians of Kardax," Celica snarled as she twirled an arrow between her fingers. She smirked slightly then turned to look at the others. "Then let's get to it. Tower isn't going to be taken down itself," she murmured as she readied her longbow and pulled her hood over her head.

Amelia shook her head as she and the others began their advance to floor eighty. As with the previous floors that were intervals of twenty, they saw what they had fought in a memory tomb emerge. Balthazar and Amelia were instantly engaged in battle. Azura rained down her last storm spell upon the bewitching beauty vampire. Warren rushed forward, engaging the Balthazar look alike in battle. Chuck was fighting with the one that was somewhere between feral and normal. The feral vampire looked around, sensing the ranger but not certain where she was. Arrows rained down, quickly dispatching the feral vampire.

Chuck snarled as he cleaved his foe's head off. Warren made short work of the Balthazar look alike with a series of swings from Ironvice, crushing the skull of his enemy. All eyes went to Amelia as she fought Balthazar. The paladin approached the fight differently from last time; she threw her entire weight into a charge. Balthazar staggered before collapsing. He gasped as he felt the paladin's weight upon him, crushing him. Amelia drew the shortsword she had been holding onto, the blade struck the vampire's throat before being run through his head going from chin through the brain.

As with the previous iterations, the memory tomb foes exploded into a black mist. Once the mist cleared, the five rushed up the stairs. They were close, so very close to being down with everything. They made their way up to floor eighty-one and fought their way through wave after wave of goblins and other underground dwelling creatures. Floor eighty-two was various large vermin creatures, scorpions, rats, spiders and cockroaches. As they came to floor eighty-three, the adventurers fought a handful of satyrs and a minotaur. Floors eighty-four through eighty-nine were in a similar fashion of having mostly satyrs and centaurs for the creatures to be fought.

Floor ninety was next; they were feeling fatigued but pushed through as they climbed the stairs. Azura bit back a gasp as she saw two creatures she had wished to never encounter again. Lit with only dull green flames, two large blob-like monsters moved about the room, they had large gaping jaws, serrated teeth as far as the eye could see lining their jaws. Tentacles stretched from their bodies as they moved toward the five adventurers. Celica cursed under her breath as she fired explosive arrows into the flesh of the creatures. As the pops from the explosions were heard, Warren began casting various spells he had in his arsenal. Chuck and Amelia went to engage the beasts in melee combat but paused when they heard something charging the group from the shadows.

The third creature reminded them of the creature general Todo had become when they fought him near Faraway Lake. Its tentacles shot out, attempting to grab them. Chuck wasted no time as he dropped Crusher and grappled the tentacles. Amelia sprinted at the Todo monster and began slashing it repeatedly with her bastard sword. Warren glanced from the two blob-like monsters and the Todo creature; he weighed heavily what he should do. On one hand he knew how dangerous the Todo one was and wanted to ensure neither Chuck nor Amelia were met with the fate he had. On the other hand, there were two blob things that both Celica and Azura were not taking lightly.

"Help Amelia and Chuck! I'll handle those things!" Celica's voice yelled from somewhere in the room. The lich nodded as he sprinted to lend his support to the other melee fighters.

Azura took a step back as she dug through her belt pouches looking for anything she could use. She paused as she glanced at the quarterstaff she had strapped to her back and nodded slightly before drawing it from the belt along her back. The yellow gem at the top of the staff began glowing with an amber light. Azura felt all her magic abilities be restored as she looked toward the blob creatures. With haste she began casting her storm spell, hoping it would have some effect on them. As the spell left the gem, she felt a tentacle ensnare her and began dragging her. She screamed out as she was dangled above the gaping jaws of one of the blob monsters.

Celica had managed to rain down enough arrows on the first blob beast to pin it to the ground by its tentacles. She heard the sorceress' screams and knew Azura needed help. The others were handling the Todo creature and were unable to help. The ranger snarled as she impaled herself on Echoes, drawing out her dragon form. A loud roar escaped the blue dragon as she clawed at the blob beast that held the sorceress. There were howls of pain from the creature as it began thrashing wildly. Two of its tentacles grappled the dragon but that only provoked the dragon further. She unleashed her lightning breath, trying to make short work of the creature. The sorceress screamed in pain as the electric attack also harmed her. Celica snarled knowing she had to do this entirely with her claws and fangs if she wanted to avoid harming Azura.

Across the room, Warren, Amelia and Chuck were fighting the Todo beast, each doing their best to end the fight and protect one another. Chuck anchored himself into the ground, his grip on the tentacle-whips never faltering. Warren and Amelia were attacking repeatedly with their weapons, trying to defeat the creature. A loud wail flung both the paladin and lich back while also staggering the barbarian. Todo whipped its tentacles around, flinging the barbarian to the side. As it tried to ensnare another victim in the tentacle-whips, Todo hissed in pain as Warren used his shield to pin one of the tentacles. He threw his weight onto the shield, praying the weight of his armor would make him heavy enough to not be moved. Amelia grabbed Soulfade and did the exact action, pinning the other tentacle. "Chuck, go for it!" Warren yelled as he and Amelia used their body weight and weight from their armor to keep Todo's tentacles pinned. Chuck grabbed his greataxe and charged, two powerful swings, took the legs off. The third swing managed to take the monster's head off the body. One foe was dead, two remained.

Warren sprinted toward the creature that Celica and Azura had been fighting, his fear for the sorceress rising upon seeing the quarterstaff lying on the ground. "Azura!" he called, seeing the position she was in. He heard the second blob beast rip itself free from the arrows that had kept it pinned, blood spilling from the wounds left behind.

Chuck and Amelia had already begun fighting the second one. "Help Azura and Celica!" Amelia called as she and Chuck weaved around the tentacles.

Warren rushed over seeing the blue dragon's claws and tail were restrained by the numerous tentacles the blob creature had. He drew Ironvice and flung it as hard as he could at the tentacle that held Azura. There was a horrid wail of pain as the creature finally released its hold on the sorceress, sending her into a freefall toward its massive jaws. "NO!" the lich screamed as he realized the error in his action.

Celica snapped her fangs forward, managing to grab the sorceress. She winced as she felt a tentacle wrapping around her throat, starting to choke her. With a quick motion, she turned her jaws as she flung Azura to Warren before unleashing her lightning breath. Warren barely managed to catch the sorceress, both hitting the ground hard from the impact. Azura rolled off the lich, grabbing her quarterstaff as she did so. "Light magic..." she reminded herself as she calmed herself enough to focus. Three orbs of light magic shot from the gem on the quarterstaff, striking the blob beast and causing it to loosen its grip on the blue dragon. Celica smirked at the opening Azura had created. The dragon grabbed the blob beast's jaws, keeping them open before spewing her lightning breath down its throat.

With the collapse of the monster, only one foe remained. Azura began casting, her light magic causing serious harm to the creature's gelatinous flesh. Amelia was forced to take a step back, the light magic also affecting her. Chuck however continued his assault and cleaved the tentacles off before striking the main body. He saw the blue dragon lunge forward, her claws ripping deep into the creature, exposing a core within it. Azura channeled another light spell, striking the core and ending the nightmarish creature.

Everyone was breathing heavily as they slumped to the ground, exhausted from the ordeal. Celica shifted back to her human form before collapsing next to the sorceress. Both shared concerned glances before breaking into a laugh.

"I'd say that went better than the last time." Azura laughed as she leaned against the ranger.

"You almost got eaten," the ranger responded as she laid still.

"Yeah, but I didn't. Though seeing your fangs was more intimidating than that thing's jaws." The sorceress paused as she looked at the ranger. Celica was still, the dragon transformation drained much of her stamina. "Ten more floors to go, yeah?" she asked.

Celica nodded slowly as she remained on the ground. "Chuck think we rest bit," the barbarian stated from where he and the paladin had collapsed.

"Second that," Amelia chimed.

"I agree." Celica coughed as she rubbed the spot on her chest where she had impaled herself.

Warren silently nodded as he sat alone. He nearly got Azura killed, sure Celica had been there with the save. But he nearly ended the sorceress's adventure with his carelessness. "I'm fine, Warren," Azura called to the lich, knowing exactly what he was thinking. As he looked up to see her, she was giving him a thumb up.

The five sat in silence after those words, each one trying to get some rest while they could. Celica reached into her bag, withdrawing the potion box; she removed a handful of stamina potions and distributed them to the group, as well as handing Azura and Warren magic restoring potions. "How many potions we have left?" Azura asked as she looked over the potions she had been given.

Celica counted the remaining vials of potions, her head shaking slightly as she looked at Azura. "About three health, two stamina restoring, one magic restoring and one explosive potion," she said before returning the potion box to her bag. Everyone drank their potions, restoring their stamina and magic, readying them for the fights to come.

"Ten floors to go and we still haven't addressed the issue of the amulet," Warren finally said after a few additional moments of quiet. He saw everyone's demeanor shift when it was brought up. It was on everyone's mind still but none of them wanted to talk about it. "It should be me, I'm the one who's been—"

"Don't start with that leader nonsense," Celica interrupted as she looked everyone over. She knew everyone had a reason for living, just as much as they had a reason for their willingness to sacrifice themselves. The ranger stood, twirling an arrow between her fingers as she did so. "We've still a way to go. We'll decide once we've finished the rebattle of my memory tomb."

Amelia nodded. "Right then, dears, shall we continue with the remaining fights that await us?" she asked as she stood and readied herself to continue.

"Chuck ready! Chuck fight!" the barbarian roared as he hefted his greataxe high above his head.

Azura took a deep breath, letting it out slowly as she stood and looked to the stairs. "Ten more floors, let's do this," she stated as she collected her quarterstaff.

Warren climbed to his feet before brushing himself off; he glanced over and saw the ranger was already on her feet and at the base of the stairs. "Alright, let's proceed," he responded as he held his morningstar and tower shield.

Celica pulled her hood over her head as she continued ahead, the others following a little way behind. Floors ninety-one through ninety-nine put the adventures against monsters similar to the blob-like creatures and ones resembling Todo's monster form. Floor ninety-nine saw them fighting what could only be described as Uldritch's beast form. Its beam breath attack rained down upon the group. Amelia brought Soulfade up, blocking the worst of the attack. Chuck and Celica rushed forward, using their attacks in tandem with each other to ensure the monster was constantly tripped up and uncertain who to pursue. Azura studied the layout of the room, trying to find anything they could use for an advantage. She began casting and flung four fireballs in rapid succession at the Uldritch like monster, drawing its attention.

Chuck rushed forward, seeing an opening to get off a critical hit. As he brought Crusher down, he heard the beast roar in pain as he split the spine in two. Celica quickly followed up her arrows raining down on the monster. Amelia was next to launch a devastating hit, her bastard sword leaving deep gashes in the monster, and taking one of the wings off. Warren rushed forward while it was recovering from the attack and brought Ironvice down, crushing the monster's skull, ending the fight.

The stairs to floor one hundred appeared and the group looked one another over. It had only been nine floors, but they were exhausted again. Celica felt her head throbbing as she removed her hood. Another waking dream was taking hold.

The town was mostly people who were either sick, elderly or children. What few soldiers they had were barely able to be called such. "We'll train those of you that are willing to fight. The army that comes, together we'll drive them back," a dragon rider stated as he raised his lance high. His proud silver dragon roared in agreement.

"Eric, this is a bad idea. We should continue ahead and stay out of this," the rogue stated as he twirled a dagger in his left hand.

"Argent's right. This isn't our fight," a wizard commented as he sat to the side, only now looking up from his spell book.

"I understand your concerns, Argent, Danny, but we can't save the realm if we don't save one town. These people, they need us," Eric, the dragon rider, responded as he looked to the rest of the group. "What say the rest of you?"

"Chuck want fight! Chuck defend!" the barbarian roared as he hefted his greataxe high.

"I'm not much for combat, but I'll help however I can," the meek sorceress responded as she gripped her quarterstaff.

"I'll train those that can learn in healing magic. We'll need a lot of healers if we're to survive this," the voluptuous cleric stated as she stepped forward.

Eric nodded before turning to face the ranger who had been silent. "And you, Camilla? Where do you stand?" he asked. Camilla was quiet, she was inspecting her longbow, seemingly not listening to the word ongoing. She said nothing as she stood and walked toward the door of the town hall. "Camilla! Camilla, if you walk away from this group one more time, don't bother returning!" the dragon rider yelled as he watched her put a hand on the doorknob.

The ranger flashed him a wave before departing. The sorceress leapt from her seat and followed after the ranger. "Azura, wait!" Danny, the wizard, called seeing the sorceress's sudden action.

"Leave them. We have to fortify this town and their few defenses," Eric growled.

"What's the plan?" Azura asked as she followed the ranger.

Camilla flashed Azura a smirk. "We're going to keep that army from ever reaching the town. They're taking the most direct path; means they'll have to cross through the open plains where there's no cover. I have a bow, you have magic. And there's a hilltop just before they reach the town."

"I see, so we're going to set up on the hilltop and use ranged combat to thin them out," Azura noted as they came to the hilltop. She saw the ranger nod before opening her backpack and setting up a very small campsite. Once the camp was set, Azura watched as Camilla headed out across the field. "Camilla?"

"Don't worry, I'll be back. Just setting some traps along the way," she replied as she made her way down the hilltop.

Camilla held her spyglass up and watched as the army made their way across the field. Azura stood beside her, watching, waiting. There was a bright flash as several small explosive traps went off, trapping some of the enemies within pitfalls. Following that were several flames igniting, scorching any enemies that found themselves hitting the next line of traps. Camilla smirked as she began counting. She drew her longbow and nocked three arrows on it and waited, still silently counting. Azura glanced from the ranger to the field and waited, trusting the ranger's judgment.

The longbow was drawn and angled upward, but there was no sign of the attack being launched yet. "As soon as I release these arrows, you add your storm spell to the arrows," Camilla said as she glanced at the sorceress.

Azura nodded and readied her storm spell. "Ready when you are," she stated as she watched the ranger.

Camilla nodded. "Three... two... one... NOW!" She fired the arrows and Azura cast her storm spell onto the arrows.

Both watched as the arrows began splitting into more and more arrows. The initial three became fifteen, then those fifteen became six hundred, each carrying a storm spell with it. Camilla and Azura watched as the arrows rained down upon the enemies that marched. The hundreds of reptilian creatures were bombarded with arrows and spells. Those that survived the first wave watched as the arrows went through multiple targets before exploding when they came to a stop. Camilla nodded as she nocked three more arrows; she saw Azura cast storm spell on the arrows again and fired. Again, three became fifteen, which became six hundred.

Arrows rained down, taking out the reptilian army in a few brief minutes. Camilla let out a low sigh as she saw the several small explosions from her arrows, what remained was little more than a crater. She turned to the sorceress, a blank expression on her face. "Shall we return to the others?" she asked calmly. Azura nodded as she helped pack their gear.

Celica took a deep breath letting it out slowly as she looked over the group. "You four get some rest. I'll handle the memory tomb rebattle and let you know when it's clear," she instructed as she started up the stairs. She pulled her hood overhead and continued not even giving the others a chance to argue with her.

Floor one hundred was dimly lit with purple flames. Celica saw the nine figures in the room, waiting. They had not noticed her; she had the stealth advantage. She closed her eyes, recalling what she had seen in the waking dream and calmed her heartbeat. Raising her longbow, the ranger nocked three arrows and took a slow steady breath before firing into the crowd. As the arrows left the string, three became fifteen, and those fifteen became nine hundred. She watched as the arrows hit their targets overwhelming them with the sheer volume of attacks. Of the initial nine, only one remained standing. Roy. The reptilian man clad in gold armor struggled to his feet; blood stained his armor as he stood. He looked around, his nerves in panic as he tried to locate the attacker.

Celica wasted no time as she sprinted across the room and swung out with Echoes, taking the reptilian man's head off. She watched it hit the ground with a wet *thunk*. The stairs to the next floor appeared as the rebattled memory tomb vanished. She hesitated, tears in her eyes as she knew what was coming. The fight against Time Eater was next. The fight against another version of her. She quietly sheathed Echoes, then opened her belt pouch. She withdrew the virtue amulet and looked it over. If anyone was going to use it, it would be her. She had nothing to lose, and it was another version, no it was her, who had caused the mess they were fighting. Calmly she put the amulet on, tucking it under her shirt to avoid the others seeing it.

Arcanist's words played out in her head. *"Time Eater can only be slain by her own accord."*

"I have to be the one to end this. When the time comes, I have to kill her," Celica said to herself as she looked down at Echoes. She shook her head before calling down the previous stairs. "All clear, just one more floor," she called out to her allies.

Warren, Amelia, Chuck and Azura came sprinting up the stairs and looked to the final series of stairs. Celica withdrew the potion box and distributed any remaining potions that would be of use. "This is it, our final battle. Everyone ready?" Warren asked as he looked over the group of five.

"Let's see it through to the end," Azura stated, eager to face the final battle.

"Chuck fight! Chuck kill monster," the barbarian cheered.

"Well, loves, it's been a pleasure and an honor fighting alongside of y'all. Let's see it done," Amelia added. Celica just gave a silent nod as they began their march up the final set of stairs.

Chapter 28 - A Fight To Finish

Upon reaching the top, the Outrealm warriors found themselves at the tower's summit. Standing with their back to them was none other than Time Eater. The humanoid blue dragon held her claymore in her right hand, a somber smirk upon her face. "Do you know how horrible Alibi was before I took over?" She paused as she turned to look at them.

"Don't bother trying to monologue about how you're trying to make Alibi better!" Warren yelled as he charged with Ironvice in hand.

Time Eater narrowed her gaze before using a barrier spell to send the lich to the ground. She shook her head as she watched him struggle to his feet. "Alibi was starving; the king ruled with an iron fist. Any who dared question or oppose him were silenced. Uldritch saw the wrongs and knew Alibi needed a new ruler, one not tied to the royal house. One who had endured a life of exile." She continued as she looked at the group. "That was why he summoned me to this realm. Someone who had been banished from the noble house they served. Someone who had lived in the wilds, surviving off scraps. Someone who was exiled from the only group they knew."

Amelia glanced from the monster before them to the ranger, noticing the ranger's unease. "Celica, what's wrong?" she asked, keeping her voice low.

"When I arrived in this realm, Alibi was on the brink of collapse. The only way to save it was to destroy it and rebuild. Then Arcanist summoned more and more Outrealm heroes. Uldritch and the others ensured they did not interfere. Then came your group. Starting as four, you not only bested the cardinal dungeons, you survived Uldritch's Abyssal Castle. And that was when I knew, I walked with your group."

"The hell are you talking about?" Warren snarled as he got to his feet.

Time Eater turned her focus entirely to the ranger. "Celica Windstride is it? Or was it Camilla Windstride? Perhaps Celica the thunderstriker? Tell me, which name does my past self choose to use?"

Warren, Chuck, Azura and Amelia all turned their attention to the ranger. "You… You're Time Eater?" the lich barely managed the words.

"Celica, tell us it isn't true," Azura begged.

"Chuck need answer!" the barbarian huffed.

"Darlin', it doesn't matter if—" Amelia was cut off by the ranger taking a step forward.

"Yeah, you and I might have been the same once. But we each made a choice. And that choice made us different," Celica snarled as she pulled the amulet from beneath her shirt. She took a steady breath as she activated the amulet.

Time Eater took a step back, her magic feeling like it had been sapped from her. Celica rushed forward, drawing her shortsword in her left hand as she gripped Echoes in her right. Amelia and Chuck sprinted to close the distance and aid in the coming fight. Azura shook her head, focusing on the fight as she began casting. Warren hesitated; everything came crashing down. Celica was Time Eater; Time Eater was Celica. It all made sense finally, why she knew so much about Alibi. But then why had she not told them anything?

"Warren!" Azura yelled, breaking the lich from his thoughts. He looked at her and saw the fierceness in her eyes. "We need you! We'll sort everything out later, but right now we need to focus on defeating Time Eater!" she called.

The lich nodded as he began casting various support spells to help Celica, Chuck and Amelia. He wanted answers but Azura was right, such would have to wait. He saw Time Eater's claymore easily parrying the attacks that both Chuck and Amelia unleashed. He watched as even Celica was struggling to keep up. "Azura, you'll have to handle spell support. They need help up there," he said before sprinting forward with Ironvice in hand.

Time Eater easily blocked and parried each attack that was thrown at her. She smirked cruelly when the cleric rushed into the fight. Two quick swings of her claymore sent him back and broke most of his armor like it was nothing. Chuck swung out with Crusher, trying to put some form of damage on Time Eater. The blue dragon humanoid blocked the attack and shattered the legendary greataxe using her claymore. As she swung out to kill the barbarian, a longsword redirected her attack. "Ah, care about the team, do you?" Time Eater laughed as she leapt backwards, avoiding the attack from the shortsword.

"What choice did you make! What caused Camilla Windstride to become you!" Celica growled as she felt her head throbbing again. She shook her head, trying to ignore the waking dream that was trying to push through.

"Oh, that one little choice. The best choice I ever could've made!" Time Eater laughed as she parried Amelia's bastard and sent the paladin staggering. She laughed again as she gave the ranger a fanged smirk. "Instead of running from the guards that night, instead of going through the distortion tear like you did, I stayed and fought. I killed them all. I awoke to my power," she taunted.

Celica's longsword and shortsword struck the claymore, she and Time Eater were both trying to overpower the other. "So, you killed people? So what? I've done that two!" Celica responded as she was forced to dodge to the side avoiding a claw strike aimed for her throat.

"That may be so, but you didn't start killing until you were in Alibi. I killed those guards. Then I rejoined the self-proclaimed guardians of Kardax. When they learned what I had done, I was abandoned. Then Uldritch summoned me. With Echoes in hand, I realized my true power. Our true power!" Time Eater laughed as she flung Celica to the side with a lightning strike.

Amelia tackled Time Eater, throwing her full weight into the attack. "Don't you touch her!" she growled as she pinned Time Eater.

The blue dragon humanoid only cackled before easily throwing Amelia off. "Pathetic. Even with the virtue stones, you're still nothing more than mere insects to be crushed." She laughed as she watched the five regroup. The paladin and cleric both had breaks in their armor; another hit and their defenses were destroyed. The barbarian's primary weapon was shattered. The sorceress was already fatigued, and her magic had little to no effect on the blue dragon humanoid. The only one who was holding up decently was the ranger. Time Eater smirked, her fangs visible. "Tell you what, Celica, I'll give you a choice. Join me, become a part of me as the other versions have, and I will spare your friends. Refuse and I'll rend the flesh from their bones, making you watch before I consume you anyway. One life to save four, seems like a fair trade."

"Don't," Amelia said as the ranger had begun glancing about. "We don't trade lives. And we don't surrender," the paladin added as she readied for another round of combat.

"That's something we can agree on," Warren responded as he glanced from the paladin to the ranger. "We didn't come all this way, just to lose everything now."

"Besides, there's no way Time Eater would simply keep her word," Azura added as she drew her quarterstaff.

Chuck roared as he stomped the ground and prepared to charge. Celica nodded, knowing they were right. "I'm going to use the virtue amulet again. A second use will hopefully weaken her enough that we can finish this," Celica whispered.

Everyone nodded as they steeled themselves for another round. Amelia and Chuck rushed forward first. Azura launched a smokescreen spell, concealing their movements and blinding Time Eater. Warren anchored his shield in front of him as he launched three spells into the fight. The first made the floor slippery and difficult to stand. The second was a fireball to distract Time Eater. And the third made contact with the ranger, increasing her stamina. Time Eater gave two mighty flaps with her wings blowing away the smokescreen. She was stunned to see the barbarian was on her right and the paladin on her left. The two managed to grapple and restrain her arms, while the ranger sprinted in from the front.

Echoes struck five times, leaving five deep wounds on Time Eater's torso. Celica winced as she was knocked back by Time Eater's tail. The blue dragon humanoid flung both Chuck and Amelia aside as she glared at the ranger. Celica glanced down shakily noticing the same gashes she left on Time Eater's torso were visible on her own. "Everything you do to me; it comes back to you!" Time Eater snarled as she lunged forward, grabbing the ranger by her throat with her claws. Celica struggled trying to break free, she felt Time Eater's tail knock both Echoes and her shortsword aside as she tightened her grip. "This. Ends. NOW!" Time Eater roared as she opened her jaws to an impossible degree.

There was a loud growl in frustration as Time Eater snapped her jaws down. Instead of biting into the ranger, she had bit something metallic. Celica saw the tower shield and drew her dagger from her belt, slashing wildly to break free. Time Eater flung Celica aside as she struggled to remove the shield from her jaws. Warren breathed a sigh of relief seeing his shield held up. "You alright, Celica?" he asked as the ranger rolled to the side and grabbed Echoes.

"Yeah, thanks for the save," she responded as she looked over her shoulder to the others. Chuck was limited to barehanded combat. Amelia's armor was completely destroyed. Warren's armor was also destroyed. And from what could be gauged, Azura was hitting spell fatigue. Celica looked at Echoes, knowing the only way to win. "Time Eater must be slain by her own accord. I have to do this," she said as she deepened her stance.

"Celica no!" Amelia cried as she watched the ranger seemingly warp to Time Eater's position and run the longsword through the monster's heart. "CELICA!" Amelia called out in horror, seeing the blue dragon humanoid rip the tower shield out of her jaws and throw it aside.

Time Eater breathed heavily as she slashed wildly with her claws. Celica was flung back, the claws sending her twelve feet. She glanced back when she saw the others sprinting to her position. With a saddened smile, she threw a lightning barrier blocking them from reaching her and the monster they had been fighting.

Both the blue dragon humanoid and Celica were exhausted and unable to keep at this fight much longer. Celica forced herself to stand as she closed the twelve feet between her and the monster. "You may share my past." She smirked slightly as the words left her. "But I refuse to be one with your fate," she added as she gripped Echoes tightly. "Goodbye, Camilla Windstride," she said as she took Time Eater's head off with a final swing from Echoes. Time Eater's body shook violently as it dissipated into a purple mist.

She was tired, everything felt heavy as she collapsed. Celica felt her grip on Echoes falter and the blade fell to the ground, clattering softly as it did so. Her senses started to fail her as she collapsed. Someone had scooped her up in their arms, holding her close. She recognized the grip anywhere. A faint somber smile formed on her face as she tried to look up at the figure.

"Celica! Celica, can you hear me!" Amelia screamed as she held the ranger's limp body.

“Amelia? I can’t hear you, Amelia,” Celica said slowly. She could see the paladin’s lips moving, see the paladin’s tears. But her hearing failed her. Blood continued to run down Celica’s face from a few of the wounds she had received. She leaned against the paladin’s body, her eyes starting to close. “Amelia, thank you. You and the others.”

“No! No no no no no! Don’t you talk like that!” Amelia cried as she looked to Azura and Warren who were rushing over. “We’re going to get you healed up! And then… And then we’re going to have a big celebration. We’ll drink, and party, and feast,” she said through tears.

“I’m sorry that I caused so much misfortune to everyone. I wish only the best for you, Azura, Warren and Chuck. Tell the others.” The ranger paused as she inhaled sharply.

Warren and Azura were crouched beside the pair, using any healing magic they had left to try to mend Celica’s wounds. Chuck managed to drag himself over, his body ached and he had a hard time even standing. “Stay with us, Celica. You’re going to be ok,” Warren pleaded as he continued to put everything he had left into his healing magic.

Celica smiled still as she felt the presence of her four closest friends. “My final thoughts are of you four,” she said before wincing sharply. Amelia held the ranger closer, tears running down both their faces. “Ammi, live… for me… ” She took a shallow breath. “In the new world…” Her body began to fade away in a purple mist, just as Time Eater had.

Amelia’s eyes widened as she watched the mist fade away. “CELICA! You promised! You swore you wouldn’t go dying on me! Celica!” the paladin broke down into sobs.

Warren hung his head as he sat in silence. Azura wiped tears from her eyes as she rested her hands on her lap. Chuck looked to the sky before letting out a somber cry of pain. Amelia looked at each of her remaining friends; the pain they shared was something different for each of them. But they were all hurting from the loss. Slowly she stood, trying to compose herself. “We need to return to Arcanist’s tower and inform him of what’s happened,” she finally said. Her words were strong, but her heart was destroyed.

A few months had passed since the battle at Distortion Tower. Villages had been hard at work rebuilding after everything. There was still a manhunt ongoing to find and bring in Uldritch Von Varley, along with the remaining generals loyal to Time Eater. It was the day of Darios's coronation and the Outrealm heroes along with Arcanist were present for such. The crown was regal and gave off the aura of a true leader as Darios stood before the people of Alibi. Everyone knelt to the king as he walked through the crowd.

Amelia, Chuck, Warren and Azura each took a knee when he reached them. "Rise, my friends. For you should not be the ones bowing nor kneeling," King Darios stated. Once they stood, he gave them a saddened smile. "Thank you for everything you have done for my kingdom. Without you, Alibi would still be in turmoil and likely on the verge of collapse. I cannot thank you enough for what you've done for my kingdom. And I fear I can never repay you enough for everything you lost," he added as he walked them through the courtyard and back to the interior of the castle.

"King Darios, we've lost something. Please don't take it too hard. The one who truly made this possible, unfortunately, is not able to join in the celebration," Warren said as he stood in front of the other three. While it had been months, none of them had fully moved one from losing Celica. Warren glanced over his shoulder at the others, before returning his gaze to Darios. "It will take time, but we would like to help in the rebuilding of Alibi. I think that's what Celica would have wanted," he said.

King Darios nodded as they entered the large study of the castle. "Take as much time as you need, heroes. My castle is yours. Stay and rest as much as you'd like," he said before giving a faint smile. "Now then, I must take my leave. There's much to do as a leader, and time waits for no one," he added before leaving.

Warren looked at the others within the group. "That's what we agreed on, yes? Staying and helping or were we going to return to our Outrealms?"

"I'm staying to help. I think that's the best action right now. Besides, Alibi needs help with restoration," Azura stated as she stretched.

"Chuck stay and Chuck help," the barbarian said.

Amelia just nodded quietly as she looked outside. Her left hand rubbing the ring she wore on her right ring finger. She turned, leaving the group. They called out her name, though she ignored them.

Epilogue

It was the night of the anniversary of Time Eater's defeat. Many celebrated throughout Alibi, but a single person walked the fields near Distortion Tower. Hidden from prying eyes was a small fenced off area. Amelia sighed somberly as she made her way to the fence. She walked through the small break in the fence as she made her way to the small plot of land. A simple headstone was at the center, no weeds growing around such. The paladin smiled slightly as she pulled out a bottle of ale and two tankards. "Sorry I haven't come to visit in a while. King Darios and the others have kept me busy with restorations of Alibi," she said as she adjusted the torn black cloak she wore.

Quietly she poured the ale into the tankards before sitting back. She placed one tankard in front of the headstone before taking a sip from hers. "You really were the hero in this adventure. No matter the situation, you always saved everyone else. You always were putting others ahead of yourself," she said before taking a drink. It was a cool, moonless night but such never bothered Amelia. She picked up the other tankard and poured some on the headstone. "Can't let me drink alone, right, darlin'?" she mused before setting both to the side.

"You have no idea how much you're missed. Eoden was asking about you when we paid him a visit. Gave me the remains of your cloak that he kept. Hope you don't mind me wearing it. Let's see what else is new. Oh, Warren's living again. Eoden was able to restore him back to being an elf. He and Azura are rather smitten with each other, before long they'll be having a baby, I'm sure. And Chuck's been training Darios's guards on how to fight. We haven't seen Arcanist since Darios's coronation. The remaining generals have all been rounded up, most actually gave themselves up quietly without a fight." Amelia paused as she looked at the starry sky. "Though Uldritch still hasn't been found," she added.

Amelia was silent for a bit before taking another drink from her tankard. She sat in silence a bit longer before breaking down into sobs. "I really can't believe you left me alone in all this. Dammit, Celica, you promised you wouldn't go dying on me," the paladin wept as she wiped the tears from her eyes. She looked at the starry sky again, seeing a single star twinkle slightly brighter. She smiled slightly. "Telling me, you're still watching over us, huh? Well, that's fine, I guess," she said before finished her ale. She turned, taking the second tankard and pouring it over the headstone until it was empty.

The paladin turned to her bag and withdrew a paper lantern. She lit the small wick inside before casting a spell on it and letting it float away. "Maybe this light will guide you home. Whether that's here in Alibi or back to Kardax. Thank you for everything, Celica," she said softly as she watched the lantern float away.

Always, Amelia.

The paladin looked around; she knew what she heard. But there was no one else around. She withdrew a single flower and placed it on the ground in front of the headstone. "I'll see you later, Celica Windstride," she said before preparing to leave. She took one last look at the headstone.

Celica Windstride

Hero of Alibi, died a noble death

Amelia looked back toward the path before finally walking off into the moonless night.

Afterword

To my readers, thank you for picking up *Tales from the Stellar Realms*, Book 01. It means a great deal to me as you help me along the journey with our heroes. My name is Victoria Warfield, and it is an honor to have you as a reader.

I first started this series in 2018, as a novelization of a tabletop rpg some friends and I were playing. Though work got busy and I put the novel on hold until we finished the campaign. When we first started our adventure in the Stellar Realms, we only knew about distortions and were mucking along as our characters tried to save the world. We started as a merry band of ten, but life events happened and we dropped to four. Overtime we picked up two more into our adventuring group.

I want to take a moment to thank Silver, Dani, David, Chuck and Ammi for the memories and adventures we went on together. You might know them as Uldritch, Azura, Warren, Chuck and Amelia, which leaves me as Camilla/Celica. It is thanks to these friends that the *Tales from the Stellar Realms* kicked off. We have plenty more adventures in the works and hope to share them with all of you as we work towards bringing those books to a close.

I also want to thank Nikki Morris for the cover art for 01 Time. And hope to work with her again for the next adventures.

There is also the friends and family who supported *Tales from the Stellar Realms* as started and have continued their support. Thank you to my family, and friends, and the numerous coworkers who listened to the tales as they developed.

And of course, all of you. My dear readers, you have my thanks again for inviting the Outrealm Heroes into your imagination and reading our adventures. I hope you will continue to follow the heroes in their next adventures across Alibi and the rest of the Stellar Realms.

I truly cannot thank you enough and wish all of you well. We hope our next adventure calls to you the same as this one did. I'll see you there.

Victoria Warfield